From the Choices We Made

From the Choices We Made

Brandy Blackmon

From the Choices We Made
Book 2 of the *Choices* series

Book one available on Amazon and other outlets.
My Choice

You never realize how those crazy 'what ifs' can be true until you actually experience them. Like, "What if I got picked to be homecoming queen?" or "What if I won the lottery?" or even, "What if the son of a multibillion-dollar company wants to be with you, but has to compete with his half-brother?"

A few months ago, I never would have thought any of those 'what ifs' could possibly happen. But after Ken Masidone showed up and showed me how that last one was true, I really think anything is possible. Especially after I made it my mission to be with said half-brother, but instead, proclaimed my interest in Ken to both his parents one sunny Saturday morning after being cornered by them and everything kind of just happened.

It was no secret they were thinking things were going to turn out differently. But, even after I told them that I liked Ken, things turned out pretty well. I mean, I didn't get shipped overseas, and Jenny didn't come and try to put me in an early grave.

I told Mr. Masidone what he wanted to know, and he and Mrs. Baker passed a couple looks to each other, and then said okay to my choice in choosing Ken. Ken had finally decided to come out of his room, and he accepted, of course. Jayson got excited for us, Jenny and Jenifer took the walk of shame back home, my parents are extremely happy that everything went according to their plan, and everything is just all honky dory now between everyone. All the tension was gone, and I was actually feeling good about the whole thing while on a romantic getaway to the islands.

However, that was just how last night's dream went. The other night, Katie appeared in it as one of the maids, and took out Jenny and Jennifer with a serving tray.

What really happened at the Masidone mansion after the morning started off downhill only stayed there. It wasn't anything like how my brain keeps trying to make it seem…

After what felt like the longest, most awkward, silence that followed my deceleration of interests, we heard a door down the hall being opened.

"What are you all doing?" Mr. Masidone, Mrs. Baker, Jayson, and I turned to see Ken holding on to his crutch under his right arm, walking toward us.

"Well good morning, Kenneth. It looks like that leg of yours is healing quite well." Mrs. Baker took her attention over to him, meaning it was finally away from me. But it was something about the way Ken was looking at us that was telling me he wasn't exactly happy right now, and I don't think it has to do with the traces of bedhead I've never actually seen him have.

"The two of you couldn't even wait until a reasonable hour to go harassing Misa. It's eight in the morning and the first thing you do is this? Forcing her to talk and make decisions that takes time to consider? Bringing all this pressure and tension is a bit excessive even for the both of you."

"That wasn't my intention for stopping by. I came in late last night, and I heard she was here." Mr. Masidone explained himself, "I didn't want to bother her then, so I just wanted to see how everything was going with her before I began my work again this morning." He almost sounds as if he felt bad. But something was telling me he wasn't really regretting his choice to talk to me so suddenly this early in the morning.

"Misa and I have talked about everything already. You don't need to bring up situations that have nothing to do with you." Ken didn't get too close to us when he spoke, but I could feel the anger he had from here.

"My, my, such an active morning. Why don't we all just relax and enjoy this lovely day? Mama Baker has returned, so why not have that special welcome back breakfast." Jayson spoke up again still trying to make the mood less—bad, uncomfortable, and slightly suffocating.

"Well, Miss Macky, my apologies if you felt a bit threatened by my presence." Mr. Masidone turned back to me.

"Mine as well." Mrs. Baker added.

I could tell the sun was still rising. I felt the room I stood in front of growing brighter. The hall we stood in shined as the sunlight was coming in from the window in the front entrance hitting the glass of the chandelier. The stormy weather last night was loud even in the walls of this beautiful mansion. But the storm only really felt to have started now knowing Jenny caught me here, Mrs. Baker and Mr. Masidone showed up, and knowing how Ken had to have heard what I said for him to come out to stop us. There was no expression of happiness or joy on his face. Only tension and annoyance.

"Misa, would you mind helping me with something?" Ken called out to me.

"U-uh, sure." His question was sudden. But questioning it wouldn't be a great idea either. I didn't look at Mr. Masidone as I slipped past them and went toward Ken's room. The short walk seemed endless knowing his parents were watching me go into his room, leaving the two of us in his closed space. Just as we went in, I saw Jayson directing the other two downstairs, so it was just us left up here. Ken walked over and sat on his bed putting his leg up.

"So, what is it you need help with?" I asked, taking a hand through my hair trying to straighten it out. Regardless of the situation, talking to someone with messy bed hair will make it really hard to take them seriously.

"Really, what I'd like help with is reversing time." He answered taking a hand through his own head, but I don't think his intention was to straighten out his ruffled hair.

"Uh, no matter how rich you are, I don't think doing that is possible yet. Unless you've discovered something that you haven't told others about." I looked around his room in search of a secret door to a hidden time machine I hadn't noticed before.

"I don't have a time machine. What I meant was…" He paused trying to figure out what he was trying to say. The trouble in his face was growing, making the worry I felt do the same.

"I kind of wish you didn't tell them what you said."

"You what?" I wasn't sure I heard him correctly.

"I would rather you hadn't said that to them just now." He said again. I stared at him making sure this was Ken I was talking to.

"I-isn't that what you wanted me to say this whole time?" I was confused and not sure why he was upset. The whole point of this was to tell his parents whether I liked him or not. I came out and finally told them that I did, but instead of him being happy, he's upset.

"Do you think I forced myself to tell them? You think I'd tell your father something like that, just because?"

"No, that's not what I meant either."

"So, then what? You heard it yourself, right? You heard me say that I like you. What more do you want?"

"I want you to really mean it." His eyes were steady, and his voice was low.

"So, you do think I forced myself to say it."

"I don't think you said it because my father showed up. But part of me does have the feeling you told him with halfhearted feelings." There was a bit of silence as he looked away from me. "From the time we first met until now, I feel your opinion of me has changed. However, for you to openly say that to my father, I don't think it's there yet."

"You don't think it's there? How close does it have to be? Do I have to be wearing a wedding ring and gown to please you?"

"No, you don't. But I would like to ask, what made you change your mind about me?"

"What?"

"You wanted nothing to do with me at first, you originally like Sano, and other than making your surprise visit here, you never really seemed to have shown a lot of interest. Are you sure about your sudden change of heart?"

It is true that I only recently realized it myself, and I wasn't really open about everything to him. To him, it seemed like I didn't really care, but I really was thinking about everything. I even chose him over Sano who told me that he actually liked me the whole time. But Ken doesn't know that. I guess I should understand how he feels since I didn't expect to hear Sano say it either.

"Well?" He asked, waiting for a reply.

"It's not a sudden change of heart. It's just a change."

"A change you say. So, you've been considering it for a while then?"

"Uh, well, I guess you can say that." Trying to explain why I liked him wasn't exactly what I wanted to do. Seeing how he's acting this way almost makes me want to reconsider. What will his father do now that I told him? Will he even be okay with it? Is he going to make us get married tomorrow or something? And what will the other two do now? Are Jenny and Jennifer going to leave or cause an uproar about the whole thing?

Just as if on cue, heavy knocking followed at his door. It sounded like they were going to come through by the intensity of the banging.

"Kenny! You two! I know you're in here and you better open up now!" The anger in Jenny's voice was obvious. Ken got up to open the door, showing two girls on the other side. One of them had their arms folded, and the other almost had flames coming out of her eyes.

"Can I help you?" he asked.

"No, it's not you that I want right now." Jenny said. She looked passed him and extended her arm, pointing to me.

"Why are you up here with him? Why are you even here while I'm not? And who said you could tell Mr. Masidone that you like him? After all you've done, you have no right to say those words. I'm the one who actually cares about him! You would just ruin him if you were with him! Don't make Kenny suffer through your little mind games and your fake feelings."

"How would you know anything? You're not around me to know." I said to her.

"I don't need to be around to know your kind. I can tell just by looking at you. And plus, the things I've heard about you makes it all the truer."

"You guys aren't perfect. Don't think I haven't heard about you either and what you're planning," I said.

"What are you talking about?"

"She's clearly trying to cover up for something by making things up." Jennifer said with an unnecessary hair flip. I wanted to say more, but I wasn't exactly sure what to say, or exactly what I could say while we were at his house. I never know if anyone would hear or listen. I glanced at Ken, and he had a look that said don't.

"Alright, if you two don't have anything important to say, then you can leave." Ken was growing annoyed again.

"If she's here, then why can't I be here too?"

"She's a guest and you live here, and you as you are now will just cause more problems. Now go on. We'll be down soon for breakfast."

"Fine. But I'll be back if you don't show up soon." Jenny said her parting words and they both left. Ken shut the door afterwards leaving it just us again.

"Misa, I know they're going to be a lot to handle for the time being, but I don't want you mentioning anything about the whole parent thing until I find out more about it myself."

"You mean the parents they killed off?"

"Yes, that. I don't want to bring it up until I find out about it myself. Thinking about it now, I've actually never met their parents before, so I wouldn't really know who they were unless they show me."

"So, you've known them this whole time and never met their parents?"

"They were just some girls that started coming around. It's not exactly the first thing on my list of things to do to meet the parents of everyone I come in contact with. My father was the one who introduced us, so I thought they were just more people he wanted me to be associated with. Not to mention I was told they passed. I just don't recall when that supposedly happened."

"How do you plan to find out about them?"

"Haven't thought about it yet, but I'll find a way." He said sure of himself. I guess I shouldn't worry since he always seems to know everything.

There was this sudden silence that filled the air. To pick up where we left off would only seem appropriate, but I wasn't sure how to bring it up.

"We should probably go and join everyone before more people come. And by now, I'm sure they have some kind of response for you, so be ready for that." he stated. A response from Mr. Masidone and Mrs. Baker. Hearing whether or not they'll approve of me wanting to be with Ken.

A response to something even Ken doesn't seem too thrilled about. After coming to terms with that feeling I've been so unsure about all this time turning out like this. I turned to the door, reaching for the knob wanting to just leave when Ken put his hand over mine stopping me from opening the door.

"I don't want you to get the wrong idea," he said from behind me, "I got a little worked up when I heard everyone coming up earlier, so I might not have given you the impression that it actually made me really happy to hear you say that you liked me. I was really surprised. At first, I was kind of skeptical because of how it all just happened, but now I'm thinking better of that". I turned to look at him. I finally saw a smile on his face. The look in his dark eyes was one I don't think I've seen before. "I guess even through everything, you still don't mind it all."

"Well, seeing how everything is, I guess it isn't all that bad. You have so much more than I do. I still don't see why you want to be with me." I looked away from him.

"That's because you're more interesting than all this here. Just because we have a lot of money and hired help, it doesn't mean it's all better than living without it. Plus, being around you and your environment has been quite the experience. I really enjoy being around you." He was finally showing his regular expressions. Suddenly, I felt a tug in my chest. I didn't know he saw it that way. I guess what Jayson said was true. He really doesn't mind my average lifestyle.

"Are you sure you're supposed to go downstairs? I could go get your plate." The mood suddenly changed, and I needed some new air.

"Are you sure you want to go by yourself?" he asked.

"I think I'm old enough to get a plate of food on my own."

"Alright. Just remember that both my father and that woman should be down there. Don't let them get under your skin."

"Yes, yes, I promise not to talk to strangers and look both ways when going down the stairs." Ken knows how his parents make me feel, so of course, he would be worried about leaving me alone with them; especially right now. I said that I would be okay. Really, I was hoping that they were all gone and I could slip in and out without talking to any of them. Who knows what could go on down there.

I took my solo trip downstairs and peeked in the dining room. Everyone was there. Talking and sipping something from their cups. Getting a good look at them now, they all looked so dolled up for it to be so early. Mr. Masidone had his black work suit on, with his jacket sitting on the back of his chair. Mrs. Baker had on a fitted burgundy dress with flared arms. The annoying duo had this reverse twin look. Jenny had on a grey shimmering shirt and black leggings. Jennifer had on a black shirt and grey sparkling leggings. I don't know who they were trying to fool with this girly girl thing, but I wasn't the one to be fooled by them.

I didn't want to go in there. I just wanted to go into the kitchen and grab something. But before I could attempt that, Jayson spotted me.

"Oh Misaky, you came down to join us for breakfast?"

"Uh, well, I came to get Ken's plate to take up to him." I had to walk in now.

"Everything isn't ready yet, so why don't you take a seat and wait until it's all finished." Jocelyn gestured to a chair having all the attention drawn back to me. I took a seat at the end of the table. Sitting with all of them was the last thing I wanted to do.

"Misaky, when breakfast is done, I can take you back home if that's fine with you." Jayson spoke.

"Yeah, that's fine."

"Miss Macky, we were just having a discussion about you." The businessman wasted no time joining in.

"I guess Ken wasn't feeling up to coming downstairs yet?" Mrs. Baker asked.

"Uhm, I said I'd bring it up to him since it's a lot of stairs and I didn't want him to overwork himself again going up and down."

"That's certainly nice of you. You've been so caring of him in his time of need. I can see that you stand by your decision then?" She jumped right to asking about it. There really is no avoiding this.

"Y-yeah."

"That's good. Guess our little Kenneth has finally managed to woo you. Something like that seems to run well in the family." She said with a smile to Mr. Masidone.

"Except I didn't have to do much to get you to come around." He gave her a kiss on the check.

"Now, now you two. It may be the weekend, but it's breakfast time, save that for later." Jayson said. But strangely enough, it wasn't that, that was making me feel uneasy. It was the evil aura around Jenny and Jennifer that was making the air heavy. They've been silent. For them to be quiet like this only means danger.

And a lot of it.

"I'm going to go check and see how the food is doing." Jayson said as he went into the kitchen.

"Miss Macky, I guess now is as good of a time as any since both you and the lovely Jenny are here." Everything around her did a complete turnaround when Mr. Masidone mentioned her name.

"So then, you seem to have discovered your feelings for my son. However, Jenny here has been suppressing her feelings for some time now. But as we all know, Ken was waiting for you to come around," He took a sip of what looked like coffee, "I'm going to have a talk with him later about it, and if there are no other issues then, Jenny, it seems Ken's choice will also be confirmed." He looked to her.

I glanced in her direction. I could see her perfectly made-up face on the edge of tears or an explosion or possibly both. But she held it in and simply said, as if admitting defeat, "I understand."

Does that mean Mr. Masidone will accept me being with Ken and not Jenny? He didn't say anything else. Nothing like I had to jump through hoops or show I was qualified by naming all the brands they were wearing or anything.

"Well, this all seems like a nice, quick little wrap up, however, I still think there's something to consider." Mr. Masidone didn't have anything else to say, but Mrs. Baker did. "Misa is a nice, sweet young girl, but it does interest me how you were able to move on so quickly. You seemed so unsure when we had our drive that day. And now you're so sure about everything dealing with what you were debating. Did something happen between you and that other young man you had an interest in?"

I didn't think she'd bring that up. I didn't exactly know how to answer that. It's not like I hate Sano. I still kind of like him. But that's definitely not the way to answer her question.

"Have you already begun to rethink this?" She had a stern look in her eye. She was calm, but I could tell she wasn't as fine as Mr. Masidone seemed to be.

"N-no, nothing happened between us. I… just had a change of heart."

"A change of heart? I suppose emotions can change. It happens all the time. Even when you don't think they would. And you are still young and a growing woman, so who's to say they wouldn't change again?"

"T-that can happen with anybody, right?" I asked her. She didn't seem like she was expecting that response.

"You're certainly right about that. I guess we'll just see how this plays out then." She took a sip of her coffee without breaking eye contact with me.

There was an awkward silence that filled the air as we all sat quietly around the long, glass table when Jayson came back in.

"Alright everyone, our wonderful breakfast is ready to dine on. Misaky, I was just assuming, but you were going to take your breakfast upstairs with Kenny-kens as well, right?"

"Uh, yeah." I honestly wasn't considering where I was going. Going out the door would be the preferred option. The aura in this room was heavy. All of them had the same kind of blank expression, and I know each of them had different feelings at the moment. All relating to me. But looking at them now, you could hardly tell who was feeling what. I just never know what these people are thinking. I thought Ken was hard to figure out, but these guys are the real experts.

Jayson handed me our plates on a tray. I left out as quickly as I could while trying to balance everything. I was headed upstairs, passing the maids that were cleaning the already perfectly cleaned house. I got to his room and knocked on his door.

"It's me," I said.

"You know, I've seen a show where they had morning visits also." Ken spoke from the other side.

"If your morning visit involves anything other than breakfast, then you'll be disappointed."

"Morning visits can involve anything, but breakfast is fine." He answered. I open this pervert's door and saw he was back in his bed. He had his laptop again. But there was something different this time. He was wearing glasses. This is the first time I've ever seen him wearing glasses.

"Something wrong?" He looked at me.

"Uh, no. I've just never seen you wear glasses before."

"Really? I rarely wear them since I usually put in my contacts."

"So, you can't see well?"

"My eyes are kind of different. I'm far sighted in my right eye and near sighted in my left eye. I can sometimes get away without wearing either, but the strain occasionally gives me a headache. I just grabbed what was closest to me." He put his hand to the side of his glasses. They were square shaped with a silver frame. I didn't know a person could be both near and far sighted. And more so that it was Ken who had a sight issue. Every day, it seems I learn something new about him.

"Do my glasses interest you?"

"It was just a surprise, that's all. Here." I placed the tray on his desk and handed him his plate while I sat on the chair.

"Are you going to accompany me again this morning?"

"Jayson assumed that's what I was doing so I have no choice."

"You could always go back and join the others downstairs," he said. That was an option I completely took out of the choice box.

"I didn't say that I hated this idea."

"Did they say something to you?" he asked. Although I thought that was pretty obvious since it's his parents we're talking about.

"It was nothing. They just continued where we left off earlier. Your father said he was going to talk to you about it later."

"He did, did he. That's good to know." I heard a bit of sarcasm in his tone. I never knew confessing how I felt about someone would be like this afterwards.

"So, do you regret anything?" He sounded as if he didn't want to ask. He looked at me while I glanced at him. He seems really worried that I might change my mind.

"I guess not." I told him as I picked at my scrambled eggs. Now that I've come this far, I knew I needed to prepare for another possible new chapter with Ken Masidone. But looking at that gentle smiling face that was next to me, I can tell it's going to be a long one. A long one that I was considering.

Breakfast finished and I got ready to leave. Jayson was waiting by the door when I came down.

"You all set?"

"Yeah." I told him. We left out and got into the car park right out front. He didn't say much as we drove. He seemed to be thinking about something himself. Looking back as we pulled out the driveway watching the mansion get smaller the further we got makes me feel like I'm leaving another world. But that world is a world I just accepted being a part of.

"Misaky," Jayson finally spoke, "I know how this must feel like a lot. There's not much to say right now, but you know, if you have any questions or worries about anything, you can always talk to me." His comfort was refreshing. I know he just wants what's best for Ken and everyone. It's good to know that someone in that house is on my side.

Just after that, I felt my phone vibrate. I took a look at it. It was just a notification. Then I remembered I had a message from Sano I never read. I figured it couldn't hurt to look at it now that I'm away from wandering eyes.

When I read the message, Jayson must have seen my blood running cold, and the increasing numbers of knots growing in my stomach because I heard him call my name in confusion. But nothing in the world right now, not even Jayson could help me handle the sight of reading that Sano's not going to be in school for a while.

Because his mother had passed away.

It's been a week since then. A whole week has passed since I got that message. I haven't been able to get a hold of Sano at all. I texted, called, and even went to his house. No one was there, not even the kids. He hasn't come to school like he said either.

Jayson had asked what got me so spooked. I didn't tell him because I knew he would tell Ken. I wasn't sure if Sano would be okay with me telling them. I want to talk to him first. But Sano's pretty much gone missing. I can't ask anything.

On top of this, now that he and Ken are gone, I've become the talk of school once again. Thinking since I got Ken injured, I probably did something to him as well on a secret date. Jennifer isn't exactly on my side of defense as I'm telling people that isn't the case. In fact, I think she seems to be enjoying this situation.

Katie thinks this was all part of her plan. I highly doubt that her plan involved his mother dying. I really just wonder what'll happen to him now and if he's okay…

Another day passes and the worry grows more. These series of events are having me lose focus on school. The end of the semester is just around the corner, and I have to at least try to maintain a steady grade. I can't ask Ken for help since he hasn't come back either. I'm not even sure I want him back. To think I verbally told his whole family that I liked him! And here I am worried about Sano. Can I even do that anymore?

It's been a week, and I haven't heard much from Ken at all since then. Maybe after talking with Mr. Masidone, he started to reconsider. Just being the only one in my house like this again makes everything somehow feel a bit bigger, quieter, and even kind of lonely.

Is this what it really means to like someone? Have I really liked Ken's company that much? I mean, I've liked Sano from afar for a long time, but this like feels different since I've actually gotten to know Ken more.

There's a small emptiness in me when I pass by his room. I've been on this earth for almost seventeen years and this emotion is one I clearly haven't been exposed to yet. And this new feeling is so complicated.

It's the beginning of a new week. Still no sign of anybody. Anyone that was of importance that is. Because Jennifer approaching me wasn't someone I would consider of much importance to me or someone I cared to see first thing in the morning.

"Well, hello there," she greeted me.

"Hi."

"Not a very exciting greeting. Something got you down?"

"Nothing that concerns you."

"Have you been worried about our missing student?"

"What brings that on all of a sudden?"

"Just seems like it's been on your mind. I mean, for someone to go missing so suddenly must be shocking."

"I haven't mention anything about a missing student. Are you worried about the missing student? And by the way, Sano's not missing. He's just not here." I lashed out.

"Ooh seems like it has been on your mind. It doesn't bother me much. I just knew he was one of your favorite guy friends, and seeing how he hasn't been here the past week, you've seemed kind of down."

"What's gotten you so interested in him so suddenly? Are you actually secretly interested in Sano or something? You two talked, right? Is that what your curiosity is about?" I must have caught her off guard with that as she hesitated before she spoke again.

"What are you talking about?"

"That day before you left, I heard you two were in the hallway talking." Her mouth dropped slightly.

"So, you saw that?" She tried to keep her cool.

"You can say that."

"Oh, I see, you think I was stealing your guy? You just want everyone all to yourself, don't you?"

"No, she just knows you're a shady character and wouldn't be talking with someone like him for no reason." I was a little surprised at the sound of my own best friend's voice coming up from behind me.

"Why don't you do us all a favor and go back to wherever it is you came?" Katie walked up to her, "The game is over. You lost, Misa won, it's done. The door is right there." She seemed a bit irritated as she pointed behind her to the exit.

"I wouldn't be so sure about that. Mr. Masidone hasn't given his final word on you two being together. And Jenny and Ken have been spending a lot more time together. He might just change his mind after all the quality time they've had." Jennifer didn't say anymore after that and walked away.

"What's she going on about today?" Katie asked, still irritated.

"I think the better question is, what's gotten you on fire today?"

"Nothing, I just have a really bad headache and seeing her made it worse." No matter how many years I've known her, I still wonder does she ever think about what she says before she speaks.

"So, have you still not talked to Ken?" She changed the subject.

"Not a lot."

"Have you tried messaging him?"

"Uh, w-well, no I haven't."

"Misa, Misa. What are you doing here? You can't declare your love and then back it up by going AWOL. I mean, I did say not to say anything at all, but you did. So now you have to stick with it. Unless you are just trying to play with the emotions of really rich and devious people."

"No, that's not it. I didn't intend to say anything, it just ended up that way. But it wasn't a lie, so I was going to go with it."

"Yeah, you certainly went with it and haven't gone back. You should probably try calling or texting him or something. Let him know Sano's situation at least."

"Should I really bring him of all people up? Wouldn't that make him suspicious or something?"

"Suspicious of what? Do you think that if you told him, he might guess that Sano came all the way to your house and told you that he liked you and you were the only one he told about his mother when it happened? I'm sure he wouldn't wonder that."

"Well gee when you put it that way it sounds like…"

"It sounds like you should have waited just another couple of days before you had your revelation."

"Excuse me for not knowing. I thought he didn't have that kind of interest in me even when I was trying. I did a lot of wrong things and thought that made him not interested. Our first meeting was him catching me creeping outside his house. Who would like someone like that?"

"That just means his standards aren't as high as you may think."

"So, what do you think I should do?"

"Well, you can still be friends with Sano. Just nothing more. Can you handle that commitment?" She asked.

"Commitment? That sounds like a lot."

"Well, since you told Ken's parents you liked him, you're pretty much engaged now. That's a commitment, right?"

Whenever I thought about that, I try not to think it that way. It was something I actually agreed to. Me!

The girl who hasn't even had a boyfriend yet could be near a position of marriage. Just what century have I been taking back too? I didn't even think arranged marriages were a real thing. But dealing with the Masidone family, anything can be real.

"We should get to class now. I can't mess up my on-time record. I've been doing good lately." I tried to turn around wanting to forget this thought and nearly jumped out of my skin when I saw John behind me.

"John? When did you show up?"

"Not too long ago. I guess you didn't know I was coming since I didn't express your name in everlasting love. Not saying that I've completely given up hope, but I want what's best for you Misa. So, I'll support you in your quest for the right partner." It was a little bothersome that he was not only able to get this close to me and me nor Katie knew, but it also seemed like a piece of him died when he finally let go.

"So, what brings you around so suddenly?" I asked.

"Well, remember you were asking to keep a look out on something that may seem odd coming from that Jennifer girl? I was still checking that out, and that lead me here."

"Have you heard anything interesting yet?" Katie, who was originally against this idea, asked him.

"Well, since that day, nothing seemed out of the ordinary. Although, when all the talk about Sano started last week, I heard people were asking her if they weren't asking you about him. I didn't know they knew each other enough for people to ask her about him."

"I didn't know that either." I said.

"Maybe she does have a thing for him." Katie thought.

"Let's not jump to conclusions. She's only here to spy on Ken and get rid of me. Why would she have a thing for someone they all think abandoned them?"

"Sano abandoned someone?" John asked. I forgot that was something that hasn't gotten around school yet.

"Uh, no. That's not it. It's complicated to explain. I have to go now. But thanks for telling me." The last thing that needed to happen was for that to get around causing more of an uproar. People live for new gossip around her.

It is strange that people were asking her about Sano as if she knew him herself. She thinks he's a traitor. And that day they were talking in the hallway, she left with anger in her step.

After I came back from Ken's house, she has been different. I don't know what her deal is, but I want to find out before something happens.

Another day with another massive headache. The only good thing about the two guys in my life out of action was being able to go home and relax a little from the school drama.

Or at least that's what I was going to do before I walked through the door.

"Ah, so your home," was the first thing Ken said.

"You're back? When did you get here?" I was not expecting to see him so suddenly.

"You don't seem too thrilled to see me."

"Well, you haven't been here and didn't tell me you were coming today and now you show up in my house. I'm pretty sure anyone would be shocked."

"Were you counting the time? Did you miss me that much?" He used that usual cheeky smile of his. It's the same old Ken. It's been over a week since I've seen him, but nothing seems different about him. But it all feels so different for me.

"My apologies for not keeping in touch and letting you know that I was coming. That part was meant as a surprise. But I also left school right as we were turning in our big project. This is demonstration week, so I can't miss everything." He explained. I didn't question anything. I'm still processing the fact that he's here. I just looked at him.

"Am I missing something?" He must have noticed my facial expression. But I couldn't figure out why it felt like I was looking at him for the first time. Why suddenly seeing him now, here, in plain view felt different than all the other times I've seen him here in plain view. It's like my voice box forgot how to function correctly.

"Uh, you're not missing anything. I guess since it's reaching the end of the semester, you need to get back to your class work to make sure you don't get below your A+ average. No more lazing around getting taken care of. Just make yourself at home, nothing changed around here really." I don't exactly know how fast I was talking, but I walked passed him trying to act normal.

"I was afraid this might happen." I heard him say.

"W-what are you talking about?" I felt my heartbeat increasing each step I took turning around to face him.

"I saw a sign of it before, but Misa you don't have to worry."

"Worry about what?"

"There's no reason to feel so conscious about this."

"What are you talking about?"

"I know you're going to feel like things between us will be different, but just because you came clean and opened up about what you've been feeling this whole time doesn't mean things will change." He tried assuring me.

"Came clean? You're getting pretty high and mighty about yourself don't you think? And who's acting different? I just had a long day today. I have a bit of a headache and your unannounced come back just surprised me. Besides, why did you come back? Hasn't the reason you've been here been… answered?" There was an awkward silence before he spoke. I tried to prepare myself for whatever he would say.

"Well, I need to finish school, don't I?" He asked. "Since things turned out like this, it was thought to be fine to stay here to at least finish the semester. However, the situation is still at hand and hasn't exactly been accepted yet."

"It hasn't?"

"No… Because I haven't confirmed anything yet," he said.

"You haven't confirmed?" I asked. And the sight of him shaking his head made me more confused.

"So then, you don't feel the same way?"

"That's not it."

"So, what is it? You've been playing all along, haven't you? Was it all just for show? Or has your quality time with Jenny changed your mind? You've been back at home for two weeks, and you've needed some help with your leg. She seemed upset that she wasn't able to be with you those three days she was gone. You guys really have been spending a lot more time together making up for lost time. I'm surprised she didn't come back here with you."

"It is true that she has been around a lot more," he said with no hesitation as he took a step toward me. "And I'll even admit, somehow, she hasn't been as bad lately as she used to be. But that doesn't mean anything regarding you and me."

"So then, what is it?"

"Like I said before, I know you've changed your opinion about me, but I want you to make sure you aren't making a mistake by saying yes to me, and not someone else."

By someone else, he most likely means Sano. He doesn't even know that Sano hasn't been around the past week. He doesn't know his mother passed. And he's worried that I might turn on him, and go with Sano without knowing that.

"So, you see, it's not that I wouldn't want to keep Mimi to myself, I don't want you regretting it," he said. He's still thinking I wouldn't want to be with him. I've never seen him this doubtful.

"You don't think I should pick you? After all this time you've been forcing yourself on me, you think I shouldn't like you. You hiding something about yourself?" I questioned.

"You're always accusing me of hiding something." He took another step toward me.

"Well, you are kind of always keeping something."

"It's not like you stay open like a book to read either. You want every little detail. You know, some things are better off not knowing. Especially since it's dealing with me."

"You make it seem like you're a part of a secret assassination group or something."

"I wouldn't say that. But my family isn't exactly the nicest people to deal with either. If you stay with me, you'll have to deal with that." He said.

"It's not like you're the only one with family problems. It's a common thing. You shouldn't push people away because of that. And you know, having someone else with you can make things easier." I didn't expect myself to say that. I don't think he was either.

We were standing right in front of each other at this point. His crutch was gone, but he still had his brace on. He was standing straight up again, making me have to look higher to him.

"Are you offering your comforting support?"

"I was just saying, if you feel so bad about how you're living, you shouldn't be ashamed and keep it to yourself by pushing people away. I've been around you for a while now, and surprisingly I haven't kicked you out yet. And I've met your family already."

"That is a surprise. I guess I should be more grateful to you. Maybe you are serious about me. It's nice to know that someone I like likes me back and still hasn't been scared off. I don't think I've really said it before, but you are a nice, fun, and a very cute girl that I've come to like a lot. I have to admit, at first it was a little awkward, and you were trying so hard to push me away. But I'm glad you gave me the chance." He didn't break eye contact as he spoke. Or when he took his hand and gently rubbed my head.

I don't know if it was the warm friendly face he had when he said it, or how he said it, or if he suddenly had heat powers. Everything inside me, starting from my head down, burned. My chest felt tight, and I really hope my face isn't giving off some kind of stem right now.

"You always say things like that. You don't have to say it again. And I only gave you the chance because I felt sorry for you. So, there you go." I had to walk away. I couldn't endure that moment anymore. It was something different about him. There was something different about me. Normally his, 'you're cute' comments don't hit me this hard. He might've been right. I can't just see him the same way after last week. How is this going to work going forward?

When Ken and I entered school the next day, the world turned to whispers and glances. He just ignored them as he continued his slight limp to his locker and to class. He still wanted someone to help him hold his books and things, so I was his helper to and from our first class. Jennifer was already in class by the time we came in, and the craziest thing happened. She didn't speak to us.

At all!

I was waiting for some Jenny story or some other smart comment now that Ken is back, but she kept to herself. Although, that didn't stop Katie from coming to me when I took my seat.

"He came back?" she whispered.

"Yeah, he did. It was a surprise to me too when I came home and saw him."

"Did you guys have a lovey-dovey reunion?"

"Geez, you sound like *her*. Nothing like that happened."

"Really? There was something different in the air about you two when I saw you walk in the classroom."

"Nothing happened between us." Telling her about his sort of second confession isn't how I want to start this day off.

"Still getting nothing out of you two. Did you tell him about Sano?" She continued her interrogation.

"Uh, no, I didn't get the chance to bring that up."

"You know things aren't back to normal around here. You think him being back in the picture and Sano still out will bring another round?"

"I don't know. It all started when he left. Maybe now that he's back, it'll stop."

"We never know what to watch out for dealing with this place." Katie sat back in her seat.

I wasn't exactly sure what could happen. It wasn't until the end of last week that people stopped harassing me. It was originally Jennifer who kick started all of this. It's like she was leading the pack, yet she got quiet when Ken came back.

At the end of class, I took Ken to his next period. I've only done this one time before, and that was when things were out of hand because of John. Now this just feels weird being here for other reasons.

"Something bothering you?" Ken asked me.

"Uh, no. I was just wondering how long it takes until the elevator comes."

"Maybe it's not working. Hope we don't get stuck in it when it comes. Although, that could be fun." he thought.

"The stairs are always an option." I told him.

"The doctor still doesn't want me to overwork myself. We can't go against the doctor's wishes."

"Coming from the guy who went against his doctor's wishes from the start and injured his injury." I reminded him.

"And that's why I'm trying not to do that again. Because of that, I seemed to have missed a lot more here than I thought." He said in a way that meant more than just schoolwork. He has no idea how right he was about that.

The day passed in the blink of an eye. I was surprised we made it out alive. The regular flow I was finally about to get back took another turn when someone came to me and asked if I was taking turns with them.

The confusion in this school lets me know Sano really didn't tell anyone other than me that his mother had died. He still hasn't returned any of my messages. It does make me concerned about his whereabouts. I wonder will he even come back.

"Misa." Ken and I just made it back home when he called out to me with a serious tone.

"Now that we are home, I think it's time to ask you."

"Ask me what?"

"Ask you if you have any idea as to why I was told to ask you or Jennifer about Sano's absence."

I knew it wasn't going to take long for him to find out. The fact that he got so serious about it did make my heart sort of flip. The time for the truth seems to be coming.

"I heard Sano has been absent all last week. When I asked what happened, no one knew except for my teacher that we have the project in. She just said that he would be gone until next week. Then I heard little rumors that the last people he talked with were you and Jennifer. I heard other little things, but that's besides my question. So, before I ask Jennifer about it, I'd like to ask you, do you know why he hasn't been here?"

The teacher told him that he was coming back next week, but didn't say why he was gone. If his teacher didn't tell him, then maybe he doesn't want people to know.

"Well?" Ken wanted an answer.

"Why does it matter to you where he is? I thought you guys still weren't that close."

"Well, seeing now, he's the one who has our project that is due, anyone would like to know his whereabouts."

"He never turned it in?"

"No, she didn't want them early since there wasn't space for them." he said.

"How do you know he had the rocket?"

"I guess he tried to turn it in at some point. Our teacher said she will excuse us until he comes back with it. But that's assuming he does. I don't know what's going on, but if he's been gone for over a week, then I wonder if he will. Firsthand experience, I know it's easy for him to disappear without a trace," Ken said. Then it hit me why he was serious about this.

I forgot that he left the mansion before when he found out the truth about his mother. Could he have tried that again? Where would he go? Sano wouldn't just up and leave now that he has kids to look after. But his mother dying might have triggered something. He would go see her all the time, not to mention he didn't know her the first half of his life. It probably hit him really hard.

"You know something, don't you?"

"W-why would I know anything? It's obvious that he didn't tell anyone where he is."

"So, he didn't tell you anything when he came to get the project?"

I almost said, *Well he did tell me that he liked me.* But I don't think this is the time to bring that up.

"He didn't tell me anything when he came to get it. He just got it and left."

"Really? I guess I have to wait and see then," he sighed, "See what Jennifer has to do with this that is. I know she doesn't particularly favor him, so how she came in to play has gotten me curious. She's been awful strange lately." He isn't the only one that's curious about that.

"You must be really concern about him," I said.

"Even though we have our differences, he is still my brother. And it is kind of strange for him to stop showing up without a serious reason."

"Maybe something came up for him."

"Maybe. But now, on to something else I came across so quickly. I heard you have been quite the topic of attention and the target the past couple weeks." He must have set his differences aside with John to be getting all this information so quickly.

"I don't know why the students there get so attached to others so easily. When you came over that time and mentioned something about admirers, I didn't even realize that I had so many of them." He said, really believing that. Not knowing all the girls have been watching him since day one.

"Well, you're more popular than you think."

"I wonder why." He thought out loud.

"What do you mean why? You're—" I stopped when I realized what I was about to say. Was I really going to tell him that he's, well, cute and not bad looking? It's something I didn't try to think about seeing as he's always in my face and acknowledging his looks wouldn't help that situation.

"I'm what?" he asked.

"Nothing. And nothing has happened to me at school while you were gone. It's just the usual gossip. Nothing more. I can handle myself if there was a problem you know."

I almost told him everything. I think he's starting to rub off on me. I don't know how much more I can handle with this guy. The only thing I know best is leaving to avoid getting to this topic. One of these days, that'll catch up with me.

What will also catch up to me is Ken finding out that I know why Sano isn't here if he goes prying for answers. He might get upset that I lied. He was really concerned. He really does care about him…

The day felt like it started earlier since I went to my locker before I helped Ken at his. And approaching it, I'm starting to wish I told him to go ahead without me.

"And this is the usual gossip?" He asked looking at the newly added banner hanging over my locker.

"She'll take anyone." He read it aloud. "Nice color scheme, but it's not used for the right thing. Can I start my investigation now." I couldn't tell if Ken was being really calm, or getting really upset.

"No need to." The voice helped bring him back a little. But turning to see Katie dragging Jennifer over by her arm sleeve wasn't exactly what I wanted to see.

"I told you Misa, if you weren't going to do something about it, then I was." She shoved Jennifer toward my locker.

"So, was this your doing or not?" Every bit of Katie's tone was anger.

"What's going on?" Ken asked.

"Your little friend here has been vandalizing her locker, starting rumors about her, and making Misa into a laughingstock. That's what's going on."

"I told you I don't know what you're talking about! I didn't do this." Jennifer flipped her hair with rising anger.

"Jennifer, have you been starting stuff with Misa?" Ken asked.

"I haven't been doing anything. I don't know why they think I did this."

"So, you're telling me you and your friends haven't been doing all of this stuff to her?" Katie asked.

"That's what I said. I don't know why your brain can't process that." Jennifer said. I saw Katie's last good nerve twitch.

"She didn't do it." I said stopping whatever evil was brewing in her.

"And you said that last time and we found out she was. I really don't see why you're trying to defend her Misa."

"This time I'm sure it wasn't," I said.

"But she is lying about something," Ken added, "You can try to fool others, but I know you. I know when you're lying and trying to get away with something." Jennifer rolled her eyes and looked away. "You specifically might not have done it, but you know who did, don't you?" She hesitated before she spoke.

"I'm not a part of any of this."

"Jennifer." Ken's tone was sharp, and he gave a look that I swear even shook Katie.

Jennifer sighed. "I-I told them not to do it, but they did it anyway. I wasn't around when this happened." She confessed.

"So, you were a part of this," Katie said.

"I. Said. I. Wasn't. I had nothing to do with the planning of this." She pointed to the banner.

"If that's really the case, then you need to get your friends under control." Katie ripped off the banner and shoved it to her.

"Don't let this happen again." There were a few kids watching at this point assuming something was happening. The bell rang and they slowly started to leave. Jennifer tried leaving, but Ken stopped her.

"I want to talk to you after school, so don't leave," he said. She rolled her eyes again and left. I just opened my locker to get what I needed, wanting this to be over. Katie shot me one of her looks. I just shook my head.

"You owe me Misa." She said then walked away.

We were a few minutes late to class. But the teacher allowed it for us. Katie and Jennifer were already there. You could feel this sort of unsettling atmosphere in the room. I subconsciously looked to Sano's seat to see if he was here, but he wasn't. I kind of wish I was gone too. But I knew this day wouldn't be over until I got through it.

"Before you all leave today, I'll hand this out now." Mr. Hallens passed out a paper to us just as we prepared for class to end. It was a paper about summer school sign ups. "Make sure if you plan to take summer classes, you sign up on time for them. If you miss the deadline, you will not be able to enroll. We're doing things a little different this year, so look this over and make sure you get it in on time."

With everything that's happening, I forgot that summer school was in my future. It's almost a month left until school is out. Does that also mean that's when Ken will leave? It would be a joke for someone as smart as him to need to take summer school, so would he just go back home then? He's only here to finish school. But he did say he didn't tell his dad if he really wanted to be with me or not. I wonder when he'll tell him. Or if he will.

"Hey, you ready?" Ken showed up next to me.

"Oh, yeah, let's go." I was caught in thought and forgot that we needed to go. It was already almost time for class to end. I shuffled my stuff together and we walked out.

"You know," he started, "I don't know what you're thinking now, but I'm sure summer school won't be that bad." For once, I don't think he knows exactly what's going through my head.

"What do you mean not that bad, it's getting up to come to school in the summer where I shouldn't be. It's prison. Something someone as smart as you wouldn't understand."

"I'll take that as a compliment, thank you. But it's less people to worry about. So that means you don't have to worry about Jennifer either." He brought her up. "I didn't know she was doing that stuff to you. Why didn't you tell me she's been causing problems for you?"

"Like she hasn't always been causing problems." I had to remind him.

"I mean like this. Trying to get people to turn against you, or get in your head somehow, I really don't know what her aim is anymore."

"Well, she's your friend. You should know what she's thinking, right? You know all about her." I said to him.

"Does that bother you?"

"No. That doesn't bother me. I'm just saying what you said. You know her, so you should know what she's up to."

"No matter what you may think, I'm not a psychic, nor have I studied psychology, or anything related to the mind. As much I'd like to understand what is going through peoples' head, I can only know what I can find out."

"But you knew she was lying, and I know you've asked her before, so shouldn't you have found out a long time ago?" He looked down as we walked on.

"Looks like we're here," I said reaching his classroom. I went in and dropped his things down at his seat.

"Thanks for the help," he said.

"Sure, no problem. I assume you have other plans for after school since you're staying after."

"Yes, I do."

"Well then, see you later." I walked out.

I know Ken was just trying to help, but something came over me taking things down a bad road. I don't know why I got like that.

The day continued on, and the last bell rang. I was almost at my locker before I saw Ken at the other end of the hallway, and Jennifer coming up to him. When he said after school, they really didn't waste any time.

"Misa." I turned and saw John. It's a good thing he said something because I didn't know he was this close again.

"Hey, what's up?"

"Oh, not much, thanks for asking."

"I assume you have something to tell me?"

"Well, you are right as always, but what gives you that assumption?"

"You typically come around when you have some information."

"That is usually the case. And it's for the best now since spending more time with you would probably make you and Ken feel uncomfortable. But I did hear a small rumor that you both are having some kind of fight. Does that have something to do with the situation that happened this morning?"

"There isn't a problem with us. Again, it seems to be some kind of misunderstanding out there."

"I see. People will turn anything into something. But that isn't all I had to say." I felt a cold sweat forming.

"Yesterday, I was out on a run for my mom. It took me pass Sano's house." My heart dropped a little.

"What happened? Did you see him?"

"No, but I saw someone else there standing outside his house. I think she might have been a relative. She was talking on the phone to someone, and I overheard part of what she was saying. I didn't catch all of it, but it sounded like Sano might be moving out of the neighborhood."

"He what?!"

"I heard her say now that his mother is gone, he probably will have to move somewhere else."

Maybe the relative he saw was that aunt that's been helping him out. I never considered that he might move. I wondered what would happen to him and the kids if his mother didn't make it. To think he'll actually move. And to where? Who would take in four people so suddenly like that? Would the kids be sent back to foster care? Sano cares for them too much to let that happen. But then, if he has no choice, then what?

I parted ways with John and took my time going home. By the time I reached my door, I had a thought hit me like a fastball. Although, it was a risky thought. But it was a risk that I had to ask about. They're the only people who could take in four new residents with extra room to spare. But would they accept that?

"Hold the door." I heard Ken's voice behind me as I was walking in. He had Eden with him.

"You got done fast." I didn't even know he was behind me.

"More like, you're getting in a little later than usual," he countered, "Plus, this guy has to get going. Thanks again for helping on short notice." He said to Eden.

"It's nothing. I told Katie I'd be at her house in ten. I don't really know what's going on anymore, but please keep her from committing a murder. I can't let her get expelled and sent to jail at the end of junior year."

"Sorry, that's my fault. I'll try to help keep her under control." I said.

"Thanks. Catch you guys later." He handed me Ken's stuff and left.

"Yeah, about that," Ken started, "Although, she is quite amusing, I think dragging Jennifer this morning to your locker from upstairs on the other side of school was a bit much. Just a bit though." He held his fingers close.

"Well, she wouldn't have done that if there wasn't a problem."

"I talked with Jennifer about that. I talked to her before I came back too which is why she wasn't in on her friends' joke this time."

"Yeah, this time," I repeated, "What about next time?"

"There won't be a next time. She agreed to stop messing around."

"Did she tell you what her means of doing it were for?"

"I didn't get that out of her. But it's probably the same reasons of trying to get under your skin."

"That was done when she first came." I said aloud to myself.

"I know I said I'd try to handle her more, but it's been a bit complicated lately."

You can say that again...

"But that doesn't excuse her behavior toward you just to help Jenny out." For a moment, I almost forgot she was a part of this, but then I remembered she is the real source of this problem. "As long as her terror can be stopped and her friends stop turning everyone against me, that's all that matters." I said still a bit bothered.

"That is still the issue, and I do plan on turning that around as soon as possible."

"It's not like I asked you to anyway. I was going to handle it myself."

"This has been going on for a while, and it hasn't been dealt with. Besides, I am kind of a part of this too. I have a right to step in and say something. And once I do, all your problems are done." He said like the hero who just saved the day. But he doesn't realize that was the least of my worries at this point.

"What else is there? Your worries looked like it grew. Something else eating at you?" The new information about Sano is still flowing freshly in my mind. It doesn't seem to be the time to ask about moving back in either. I watched Ken as he got closer to me.

"Once upon a time, I also said that to make our situation work, we had to be in it together. And somehow along the way, we managed to see eye to eye. But right now, you haven't looked me in the eye once. I'm here to help if it's that big of a problem that you have to show your adorable, worried face to the world like this." He took his finger across my forehead.

"You're going to get worry lines at this rate." His finger on my face was warm against my skin. Trying not to make eye contact was hard. He always manages to corner me somehow. But the feeling isn't right with Sano still on the mind.

"My worry, my business." I pushed his hand back and tried to pass him.

"Does this other worry have to do with Sano?" I froze.

"You don't have to always think the worst just because you haven't heard from him."

"I-I don't have to think the worst, I already know the worst." I said out of frustration.

"You know the worst? So, you know what happened?"

I don't know why Sano didn't want to tell anyone, but if I want to help him, then I have to tell Ken first for my idea of having them live together again to work.

"Well?"

"That day I left your house; he texted me saying he wouldn't be in school for a while."

"And that's because?" Ken waited for me to finish.

"Because… because his mother had died."

I wasn't facing him when I said it. There was a bit of silence after I told him, so I turned to see his face. His shocked expression was almost too much to witness.

"You, not correcting yourself, means that's what really happened?" I never heard this tone of disbelief from Ken. I just nodded. He leaned against the wall as if the assurance pushed him off balance.

"And he told you this when?"

"The day I left your house. So, about a week and half ago," I said.

"So, you knew this whole time and didn't tell anyone?" I've never seen this side of Ken before.

"It seemed like he didn't want anyone to know so I thought I wasn't supposed to tell anyone."

"Well, he told you so obviously that wasn't…" He stopped what he was going to say. I didn't dare ask him to finish that sentence either.

"Have you heard from him since?" He went on.

"No, I haven't."

"No calls, texts?" I shook my head.

"Have you tried going to his house?" I didn't want to admit it, but I shook my head yes.

"It's almost like he's gone missing." I told him.

He sighed, bringing himself back. "I didn't want to think something bad had actually happened. But now it makes sense."

"Didn't he tell you that she wasn't doing too well before?"

"Yeah, he did. But he didn't go into detail about it, so I didn't know her illness was this bad." He went and sat on the back of the couch like he was in deep thought.

"So, it really does matter to you." I said watching him.

"Of course, something like this would matter to me. He left us to go be with her. And if she's gone, what is he going to do? When he found out the truth, he completely flipped. Only after meeting with her twice, he was gone after the first week. Didn't tell anyone anything, not even me. After a while, he even got a new number and phone and shut off all contact with us. He liked everything the way it was after that, and didn't have any plan to come back."

"You think he'd come back now?" He looked at me wondering if I just heard what he said. "I mean, now that he doesn't have any parental guidance, he can't live on his own, right? And he also has children with him. He wouldn't be able to keep taking care of them on his own like that."

"My father is technically the one with legal custody of him, so he would be the person to take charge of him, but that's if he comes back. He doesn't show it, but he's a very sensitive person. I wouldn't be surprised if he was out the city," he said.

"Do you know any of his relatives?" I asked him.

"Not me personally, but maybe I can ask Jay if he knows." The concern was written all over his face as he pulled out his phone.

"Are you upset that I didn't tell you sooner?"

"You thought you shouldn't spread something as personal as this, and you aren't exactly sure of our relationship. So, I do understand why you hesitated to say something. But I do wish I was informed when it first happened so we could have maybe helped or something. Not being able to do anything in this kind of situation just makes me feel..." He ran his figures through his hair out of frustration.

I feel awful about this. Now I wish I had told him from the beginning. Between the two of us, he probably knows how much deeper this is to him than I do. This whole time, he actually cared so much for Sano. I guess Ken was just looking out for him since Sano's the one that has the uncertainty about him.

"I'm going to give Jay a call." He said turning to the stairs going up to his room. I still was sorting through what he said. I never realized that about Sano. He would always seem calm around me. You would never guess that someone like him would be quick to make rash decisions. Just goes to show how much I still didn't know him.

The last time I talked to him was here at my house when he needed the rocket. After that, I was avoiding him because I wasn't sure how to act around him after he told me he liked me.

I feel bad for ignoring him when he needed someone to talk with. This just makes me want to see if he's okay even more. I only went to his house when it first happened. Even though John said he didn't see him, maybe he's back.

Ken probably wouldn't like me going to his house, but this is more important than some love affair. Making a quick visit to see if he's there couldn't hurt anyone since he's busy on the phone anyway. I would tell him that I'm going, but before I knew it, I was headed in the opposite direction out the door.

It didn't take me long before I got to his house. Just from standing outside it, I could tell that there weren't four people in there. The house felt quiet. The little ones would be outside playing by now, but as I went to ring the doorbell, I didn't see the kids or get a response. I tried knocking this time and was met with silence. I guess he really isn't here. Has he really not been at home this whole time?

I was about to walk away when I heard something coming from the backyard. It wasn't my place to go snooping around, but I didn't want to leave without knowing for sure he wasn't here.

I peeked around the gate. "H-hello?" I said seeing if someone was back there.

"Yes? Is somebody there?" There was a voice, but it wasn't Sano's. I heard footsteps coming this way.

"My, how you delivery people are getting younger these days." It was a lady who looked like she was doing yard work.

"Uh, no, my name is Misa, I'm one of Sano's classmates." Her eyes widened.

"Ah, I see. So, you're the Misa I heard so much about." She relaxed her face and smiled. "I'm Sano's Aunt, Fay Seo. It's good to finally meet you." She extended her hand.

"Uh, same here." I said, taking it.

"The kids always talk about you. I was a little upset when Sano never brought his friend that would always help him over to let me meet her."

"I would come only for a little while."

"Well, I'm seeing you now, so I got to meet you after all. I just wish it were under different circumstances." She added. There was no need to ask what she meant by that.

"Is Sano around?" I finally asked.

"No, he isn't." She said, "The kids are with me, and he's at my sister's house. We didn't want them to be around him in the state that he was in." I felt my heart sink further down my body.

"Is he not doing so well?"

"Well, you may or may not know, his mother passed, and it was a lot for him to handle. It was hard to hear the news for all of us even though we knew it was coming. But, since he went through so much, it's not sitting well with him at all."

"If it's alright to ask, what was it that she had?"

"Sasha had cancer. It was a surprise to us when they told us it came back. They never told us about it in her check-ups before she was put in immediate care. But she was already sick when she went in. I'm guessing that didn't help. Once she was admitted to the hospice a couple weeks prior to her passing, we had already began preparing for this." The world felt still. I wasn't sure if time was moving in that moment. His mother had cancer. And it took her.

"I'm so sorry to hear that."

"Thank you, but my sister was a very strong woman. It's just her system wasn't able to keep up with her. We had the funeral over the weekend, and we're making do with our current situation."

"Will Sano be coming back anytime soon?"

"We hope by just resting his mind for a bit, he'll feel up to going to school next week. It pains me more to see him as he is now. But he won't be able to stay here by himself and take care of small children on his own. My place is not suitable for them to live there, nor is my sister's; I wouldn't be able to take ownership of this house, so we're not exactly sure what's going to happen in the long run. As he is now, I just don't feel comfortable with him being by himself either. I can understand his frustration though. He only got to know his mother for about four or five years."

I couldn't even imagine what he must feel like. The state he might be in right now. The pain he must be in.

"The problem now is what are we going to do with them. I'd keep kids if I could, but I don't have the proper living space for them and neither does my sister. I hate to say this, but worst-case scenario, the kids may have to go back."

"You don't have anyone that could take them in?" I asked.

"My sister and I are the only ones in town. We don't have the space or money. I've been doing a little work and check in around here. Sano cannot be responsible for the house, his schooling, the children, bills, and everything else there is as he's only a child himself." She stopped and took a breath.

"Oh, forgive me, what am I telling you this for? I'm so sorry. You just came to see about your friend and here I am dumping our problems on you." The distress his aunt had was no secret. They were all taking everything hard.

"No, it's fine. I was worried about him, so I wanted to know."

"I wonder why he didn't tell you. Although, he hardly ever touches his phone now."

"With how he's feeling, I get that he wouldn't feel up to talking to anyone."

"Yeah well, Sano is a strong boy just like his mother. But some things just can't be bared forever." Her eyes were a little red and tired.

"I shouldn't keep you from your work any longer. I'm sorry for your loss. I hope everything gets better for you all soon."

"Thank you so much for that. I can see you're a sweet girl. I'll tell Sano that you stopped by, all right?" We said goodbye and I took my leave. My walk back home felt a bit quieter. Emptier. And a whole lot longer.

When I managed to get home, I tried to creep in the house hoping Ken wouldn't hear me, but that ship was sailed when I saw him sitting on the couch.

"You're still in recovery, you shouldn't be going up and down the stairs so frequently." I said as he watched me in.

"I assume since your friend is busy, and given the circumstances, you went to his house again?" He jumped right to it.

"I did." I had no energy to lie.

"Was he there?"

"He wasn't."

"Did you go somewhere afterwards then?" He must be wondering why I took so long.

"His Aunt was there, and we talked for a bit."

"I see. You must get along well with his side of the family." He said, turning away from me. Maybe it's because I suddenly left without telling him, but he almost sounded a bit jealous. I guess I should tell him what happened when I got there before he gets a misunderstanding.

I sat and told him everything his aunt told me. It was hard repeating it all and hearing myself say it, but I feel if anyone could help them, it would be him.

"So, that's the current situation." I dropped my hands to my lap letting him know it was nothing else to be said. He just sat there not really looking at anything.

"I see," He said after a long silence, "Well, I called Jay. He only knew of some of his relatives but no direct contact to them. But he'll see what he can find out."

"That's good then. I just hope everything can work out and not have to send the kids back or anything. Even I've grown a little attached to them." I said. They likely aren't taking it well either.

I looked over to Ken who stayed silent.

"What's wrong?" I asked.

"It's nothing." He said. I had a hard time believing that. He's never just stayed quiet before. I could see something was bothering him.

"Are you sure?" I asked again.

"It's not the best time to talk about it."

"What do you mean? Talk about what?" I was confused. He's never seemed so troubled by something. I watched him waiting for a reply when he let out a sigh.

"I know this'll sound kind of wrong saying this now, but, even though this is Sano's wellbeing we're worried about, it still kind of bothers me that you're so wrapped up in him." He turned away from me.

"So… what you're saying is, you're jealous over someone who's grieving a loss?"

"I admitted that it was wrong, didn't I? You didn't have to say it like that. It just that, when you suddenly disappeared, the feeling just kind of hit me." He told me.

"Well, sorry that I'm concerned about him, but you are too you know."

"Yes, I am, but I don't like him the way you do."

"But that's…" I wasn't sure how to end that sentence.

"Do you still like him?" He asked. The one question I've avoided asking myself since Sano confessed to me.

Sano was the first guy I liked. Sure, it was one sided for three years, but it was still something I had longer than Ken being around. When I started paying Ken more attention and understanding him, he started filling my mind more. That's when I realized he wasn't really all that bad. Sano hasn't done anything wrong. But he has a lot going on. It almost makes it hard to even have a crush on him.

"Is your silence your way of saying yes?" Ken asked watching me.

"I didn't say that did I?"

"So then, if not yes, what are you saying?"

"Um, you know, you put a lot of pressure on people." I told him.

"I didn't intend any pressure, it's just a simple question. Do you, or don't you?"

"I really don't think I have to answer that. It's not like I'm doing anything with him. And you and I haven't actually gotten together anyway, so it has nothing to do with you if I do or don't." I stood and walked away from the couch.

"Well then, should we change that?" He asked. I stopped and turned back to him.

"What?"

"We got passed the first part of a mutual feeling, but didn't get passed the next part." His attitude changed yet again.

"We've been around each other for a while now. You haven't chased me out yet, and you've said that you liked me, and I too like you Misa, so would you like to make it official and be my girlfriend?"

He's asked me this before. But before, I really didn't consider it. Now, I don't know if it has to do with the way he said it, or how I've been considering it, but the feeling this time I'm getting from him asking is hitting a lot harder than it did before. Do I really want to be with Ken Masidone? Son of the Masidone family, and half-brother to my long high school crush?

"You can't say it's got nothing to do with me this time." He told me.

"I know that." I replied. How it came down to this from being upset twenty minutes ago, I don't know, but I know I won't be able to get out of this without an answer.

The first time he asked me, I was having a hard time handling him and everything that came with him. But now there's something about him that makes me want to learn what there is to know about him. Even though Ken can joke, and he likes to have fun, there's still a great mystery about him that I want to solve. And the only way to solve that is if we get closer.

"Well, I figured you'd still be against it after—"

"I-I never said that did I?" I cut him off. He raised an eyebrow in suspicion.

"So, then you're saying…"

"Geez, I've never met someone so impatient. I'm saying… I'm saying sure." I finally said. I looked over to him to see his reaction. He seemed both confused and happy. I turned away, not sure how to take either of those reactions.

"You're not pulling my leg here, are you?" he asked.

"And why would I do that?" I sighed.

"I don't know. I was preparing for another rejection, and to hear you agree, well, it's unexpected. But in a good way. Are you really okay with this?" He was really doubtful of my answer. After all I put him through, it's actually no surprise.

"Well, if you want me to change my mind, then that can always be arranged, Mr. Doubtful." I said to him. I can never tell what he's thinking. So, when he got quiet, I didn't know how to react. But when I saw his hand reach out to grab my arm and pull me toward him, I found myself falling into his lap.

"You won't need to arrange anything of the sort. Now that the last trail has passed, this little game is finally over." His eyes locked into mine. I couldn't help but feel like I was being drawn into him. His gaze seemed different. Different enough to make me blush a little.

"D-do you not understand the meaning of you. Are. Injured?" I had to break it down slowly to him, "What if I landed on your bad leg? You still have a fractured bone that needs to heal." I got up and fixed myself. "You can't keep doing that kind of thing while you're still wearing a brace."

"What if I got rid of the brace?" He said ready to rip it off.

"You still can't! You messed yourself up once going overboard, you're not doing it again."

"Alright fine. I can see you're very concerned about me." He slowly got up. "I'll obey Mimi's wishes for me to have a good recovery. You just have to remind me I shouldn't do certain things while still with the leg brace." He slowly walked over to me.

"Sometimes I forget that I have to take it easy. That gets hard when so many exciting things happen." His voice got lower as he got closer to me. We stood face to face only inches apart. "I'll try to remember that while I'm like this, I should hold back on what I do." He patted his leg.

"That's good. When are you going to start?" I asked as I was able to feel the heat of his words on my skin as he spoke.

"Don't worry, I've already started." He took his hand and lifted my chin for our eyes to meet again.

"And by start you meant how?" He didn't reply. I saw that I wasn't going to get an answer either. He just smiled as he closed the remaining space we had between us.

I closed my eyes waiting for what was coming. But all I felt were his whispered words in my ear, "holding back was just my own suggestion, but I can see it's not a recommendation." And then he kissed me.

I really believe I've gotten myself in way over my head.

The rest of the week went by a lot better once Jennifer and her school crew stopped their tormenting, and Ken cleared the air about the other misunderstandings. Now all that was left was to get Sano back. The week was over and now we just hope he comes back Monday. He's been gone for two weeks without a word still. He picked a really bad time to leave with finals coming up.

"Mimi, it's time for me to take my unfortunate leave." I heard Ken call me. I haven't see him this happy for such a long period of time since I said we could go on that date. I just wonder how long his high will last.

"Come on, don't you want to see your *boyfriend* off for the weekend?" He asked lingering on his most recent favorite word.

"It's not like it's your first time leaving. This has become a regular thing." That 'boyfriend' thing is something that's going to take time getting used too though. For me to actually be within that status of 'boyfriend and girlfriend' is crazy in itself. And the craziest part is that new couples aren't usually living together!

"Should I really go?" He asked himself.

"I'm sure you have better things to do than to do nothing around here. Plus, Jayson drove all the way here already. You can't make his trip be for nothing."

"He loves road trips; it wouldn't be for nothing."

"Don't you have things you have to do there or discuss or something? It's always something going on over there. You wouldn't want to miss that."

"Your argument isn't exactly one that screams 'take me now.' But if you want me to go that badly, then I'll go," he pouted.

"It's your home. You should love going there."

"Yeah, 'love' is the right word for it." He said with obvious sarcasm. There was a honk outside stopping me from replying. "Guess that's my signal to go." He only had a small bag with him, so he didn't need any assistance leaving. I watched him out as he got in the passenger seat of Jayson's car. It makes me wonder if he has told him about us yet.

There's a small part of me that sometime wonders if I shouldn't have said anything in the beginning. But then I think, if I really didn't want to, I didn't have to agree to anything. It's not like I was forced to agree. In fact, Mr. Masidone would have loved it if I hadn't. So why this sudden feeling of uncertainty?

I closed the door and went to sit on the couch, feeling more aware of Ken's absence. I needed to distract myself. I took my phone out of my pocket and sat it on the coffee table and picked up the remote when I noticed I got a text. The remote fell out of my hand. My body grew weak when I picked up my suddenly heavy phone to see the message was from Sano.

Sano!

It's been two weeks, and he's finally messaged me. I'm almost afraid to look at it. But the curiosity of knowing what it said made me open it.

He was sorry for not replying and that he's back home. And he's wondering if I'm free to stop by.

Sano is asking me to come over!

He must have recently gotten back, and he wants me to come over already? By what his aunt said, I wouldn't think he'd want to be bothered by anyone so soon. Should I really go over there? Maybe he has something he needs to tell me. Ken just left, so I wonder would he mind if I went over there.

I'd really be in trouble if I tried to hide it from him now that we're officially together. But maybe I can use this chance to ask about the idea of going to stay at Ken's house if he has to move.

Ken didn't say it was a bad idea, it would just be up to him. So, it couldn't hurt to ask. I told him that I could come over and he okayed it, so I cautiously left on my journey to Sano's house. This will be the second time this week. But this time, he'll actually be home.

Approaching his house that I've been to many times, it seemed a little different this time around. There seems to be a different air about his house. Maybe because the guy I knew that was calm and cool and seemed to carry everything so well was supposed to be on the verge of a break down or recovering from one. I should be prepared.

I went to knock on the door and waited for it to open. I know it was a short wait, but it felt like forever before I saw the brown door being pulled back and showing me the guy that's been lost for two weeks.

"Hey," He said upon seeing me.

"Hi." I wasn't sure if my voice cracked or not, but I cleared my throat making sure it wouldn't happen again.

"Sorry for the sudden invite since you haven't heard from me in a while." He stepped aside letting me in.

"It's no problem. I wasn't really doing much anyway." I told him as I walked in. It was kind of quiet aside from something playing in another room. The kids must not have come back yet.

"I had heard you came by the other day." He said. I looked at him after getting inside. Before I said anything, I noticed his hair had gotten a little longer and he might have lost a little weight. Sano was always small, but his already small frame seemed lost in his clothes. He never had Ken's taste in clothing, but his thrown-on track shirt and loose-fitting sweats says he didn't put any effort in what he chose to wear today.

"I uh, just wanted to see if you were doing okay since I hadn't heard anything from you since you sent me that message."

"I'm doing alright now. Things were a little rough at first, but it's getting better."

"That's good to hear. I never got to tell you, but I'm sorry for what happened. I know how much she meant to you."

"Thanks. I know I must have worried you a lot since I never contacted you. Sorry for missing your calls and messages."

"It's fine. You had a lot on your plate. The good thing now is that you're better and feeling up to talking."

"Yeah. Although, I'm not sure what will happen now."

"What do you mean?" I watched him as he searched for an answer.

"Well, I don't have many relatives around, and now that my mom isn't here, my aunts that are close by both think it's not good for me to stay here by myself."

"So, are you moving out then?"

"They're still thinking about what to do."

"What about the kids?" I blurted next. He walked past me and sat on the edge of the couch.

"I'm not sure about them. The thought of needing to raise three more kids isn't sitting too well with them. And since I'm still in high school, they don't want me to take care of them on my own. My mom first adopted them three years ago. They're little brothers and sisters to me, and to them, little nieces and nephews, so we're trying to figure out what we should do before they go to the worst-case scenario." He said looking at the ground. Thinking that they've been here so long already and may have to leave. He definitely doesn't want to consider that an option.

"I was just wondering, but how did you guys end up adopting them?" I asked.

"My mom always loved kids. But, other than me, she couldn't have any more of her own. She wanted to help those that were given up, so she ended up adopting them. She had thought about this long before I had come back, and even after I came, she still wanted to, and I didn't see anything wrong with the idea. It was one of the better things that happened; bringing them here to stay." Sano seemed calm, but I could tell that he was still far away. He was still somewhere getting himself together.

"You all will think of something. I'm sure everything will work out." I tried to stay positive.

"Thanks. I'm glad I asked you over. You always help make things better." He said giving me a little smile.

"You had them already for a long time, taking them back would be an absolute last result right?"

"I wish it weren't even an option. But they weren't the ones that adopted them and don't feel like they'll be able to handle the responsibility of raising them properly."

"If you all are really uncertain of what will happen, have you ever considered…" I slowed down easing into this, "maybe if things don't work out, moving back in with Ken and his family?" I didn't think it would be such a bad idea. However, he clearly never considered the idea since his facial expression went from neutral to distressed.

"It was just a thought I had since you guys are related and have the same dad and all. Maybe if all else fails—"

"I'm grateful and appreciate that you're thinking so much about this, but I don't know if that would work out." He cut me off.

"Your dad seemed to have wanted to patch things up with you, so he probably wouldn't have a problem with you coming back. And there's plenty of room there for you all."

"I'm not saying it wouldn't work out because of a space issue. I know if I wanted to, that would work out, but I don't see myself groveling back to them after I was the one who chose to leave in the first place."

"But your father wouldn't see it that way. He'd be happy to have you back."

"It's more to it than just that Misa," he said in a low voice, "It's not about him being happy about me moving back in. I don't think I'll be comfortable there. And having the kids go to a place like that and grow up in that environment; I don't want anything to happen." He said it like it was a dangerous place to be. I guess Ken was right about him not wanting to go with this idea. Now I kind of wish I didn't say anything.

"It would be a completely different setting for them with Ken, your father, his wife, and everyone else there." I said. He looked off into space again.

"The girl from our class and her sister, they live there too, don't they?" He asked.

"Yeah, they do."

"I guess it's none of my business on why they're there." He still wasn't looking at anything specific.

"I think it's like how Ken is at my house to get to know me." I said.

"You two must be getting along well now. Before I left, I had heard my teacher saying something about you going to take him his work that he was missing when he was absent." I couldn't help the gasp that slipped out.

"You knew about that?"

"The teachers took a strong fascination to him, so they wondered about him and his injury when he left." I guess that's why he was able to joke with them so well.

"I also couldn't help but feel you were avoiding me then." He continued. He knew about that too!

"It's understandable since I said something that put you in an awkward position." I searched for words trying to respond.

"I don't want that to change our friendship though. If you feel uncertain about it, or you're still considering it, don't let that change how we've already gotten along already." Even though he was the one that told me he liked me, he still wants to remain friends no matter what I tell him.

"Well, it took me by surprise, but don't worry, it's not going to change how things are now." I said, hoping it wouldn't.

"That's good. I thought about it after I told you if I should have said anything, but with all that you were going through, I wanted you to know that somebody was on your side."

I was completely lost for words. After going through so much himself, he was thinking of me. Sano really is a good guy, but I can't do anything now that I'm with Ken.

"Everything with me has calmed down a lot so I'm good now. You should worry about yourself more with so many things that need to be worked out." I told him. I need to get him to stop thinking and worrying over me when he has his own problems.

"I'm glad everything is going better for you now. I'll try and focus on myself then."

"It's too bad you can't just stay here, but I wouldn't want you living on your own needing to handle so much yourself either. It's better if you stay with a relative that can help."

"I'm glad you're so concerned about me. It makes me wish that Ken wasn't my competition."

"C-competition?" I repeated. It was only then I realized my phone was vibrating and it wasn't just my heartbeat. And even though he just left, it was Ken calling me. I ignored the call and pushed my phone back in my pocket.

"It's not a problem if you answer it."

"Uh, it's fine. It's probably nothing."

"You didn't tell him you were coming by, did you?" He guessed it right away.

"I, well, he left to go back home for the weekend when you messaged me, so he wasn't around. I was going to tell him though. He was actually kind of worried about you too." I told him. He raised an eyebrow in suspicion.

"When he got back to school, he heard you were gone and wanted to know what happened."

"You told him?"

"Yeah, I did. Sorry if you didn't want me too, but he got really concerned when he found out you had been gone so long." I couldn't tell if he got upset or not. He just keeps getting quiet and staring out into space. I can't figure out what's on his mind at all.

"At first, you weren't so easily in his defense, a lot of things must have change since I've been gone, huh?" He said.

It's true that I wasn't at his defense at first. If I told him that a lot of things changed while he was gone, would that make him upset? He already seems so bothered. I can't really tell him that he already lost the competition.

"Um, why the sudden curiosity?" I asked.

"I guess that may not be any of my business. I guess I just wanted to know where I stood." The way he speaks feels so distant. The fact that he doesn't seem focused on anything really makes me wonder if he's really as okay as he says.

"I can't help but feel there's something bothering you." I needed to change the topic, but I don't think that's what I wanted to say.

"Well, I do have a few things on the mind, but it's nothing you should worry about. I'm not sure what my aunt told you when she met you, but I'm not eternally grieving, or some loose cannon now. There was one incident that may have surprised her, and she's been overly worried about me since." I'd ask him what it was, but that's probably not something he wants to talk about.

The room echoed in silence. I don't think I've ever been around him in his house when it was just the two of us. Normally, there's little munchkins running around interrupting any alone time we had to play with them. My phone rang again, breaking the awkward silence. It was Ken.

"You don't have to keep ignoring it." Sano said. Ken wasn't going to give up either.

"Sorry, I'll make it quick." I walked away from him and answered my phone.

"What do you want?"

"That's not a very cute greeting Mimi," he said.

"Well, you just left. Did you forget something?"

"Not exactly something, more of a someone. I forget to tell you that you were requested to make another trip here with me today."

"He wants to see me!?" I might have been a little louder than I wanted to be.

"Remember how I said Jayson was going to try and find out something for Sano? Well, turns out him finding something somehow got to my father, and he wanted to talk to you about the situation."

"I'm sorry Misaky!" I heard Jayson yell in the background. But that didn't make me feel any better about this news.

"I was trying to avoid this meeting, but I just got a message from my father and thought I should at least ask you about it without completely lying to him about why you didn't show up."

"Uh," I turned slightly wondering if Sano was paying attention. His father probably wants to ask me since, out of the two of us, I know him better then Ken currently. Sano has already said he's not interested in staying there, so telling his father wouldn't be the best thing to do.

"Are you actually considering it?" he asked.

"Uh, well, going there and talking with your father seems kind of sudden."

"Are you doing something now?"

"What, me?" I asked a little guilty.

"You're talking like you're trying not to be heard." He noticed I was trying to keep my voice down.

"That's not it. Going with you now isn't exactly what I hand in mind."

"Well, I thought that's how it would be, but you sure nothing's going on?" He asked again. It's always so hard to get something passed him.

"Yes, nothing is going on. Geez, you ask too many questions."

"It's just that, you sound almost like you're hiding. You're not doing something you shouldn't be, are you?" He said that jokingly, but he was still able to see through me again. Now isn't exactly the time to tell him I'm at Sano's house, but I don't want him to think I'm hiding anything either. How do people normally handle these types of situations!?

"You know, thinking about it, I think I might have a change of heart." I slowly turned and saw Sano looking my way.

"Are you with someone?" Ken asked.

"Uh, well…" I could end that sentence with a lie or the truth, and both sound like bad options.

"But before any decisions are made though, I'd need to see for myself what's going on." I don't know exactly what Sano is thinking, but I have a feeling he was listening to what I've been saying.

"Are you with Sano?" I heard Ken finally ask as I was still trying to figure out what Sano was on about.

"He wants you to go with him to see our father, right? Would it be a problem if I joined you?"

I don't know about a loose cannon, but I do think something came loose in his head while he was gone. Is he seriously asking to go with me and Ken to his house!? Is he trying to get me in trouble?!

"Misa?"

"Uh, well," I hesitated in answering Ken as I continued to look at Sano. He didn't have a look that said he was joking. He was serious. He really saw an opportunity and took it. I mean, I was the one that brought this up. I can't just say no now.

"D-do you have room for two?"

Sano seemed very clear about not wanting to go. For him to just change his mind so quickly, he must have a good reason, right? And who am I to deny him his right to see his father. He should be able to see him. But me being there when it happened isn't what I prefer.

Would I be able to take a rain check for this visit?

Another Saturday morning has come. The skies were clear, the birds were flying, the trees gently shook as a cool light breeze went through the air, and everything else was going completely opposite of how I was expecting today to go.

Waking up today, I only expected Ken to leave for the weekend. Not Sano coming back to existence and asking me over. Or Ken calling while I was at his house to tell me I was asked to talk to his not-so-easy to approach father again.

And certainly not for Sano, who hasn't seen that unapproachable father in years, to so easily ask to go with me to talk to him! But that isn't the crazy part about it.

Ken agreed to it!

He, of all people, should know that this probably isn't the greatest thing to do. Who knows what will happen by taking him there when the annoying duo could be home, and the wife that always questioned about the other person I said I liked.

Let's not forget Mr. Masidone, who only wanted to see me, and not the son that abandoned him. How do I explain him coming along? Would he actually be happy to see him since he's who he wants to talk about?

"You alright Misa?" Sano looked at me like I was going a bit crazy, which only makes me hope I wasn't speaking aloud. With the little pacing I was doing since hanging up the phone, it would only make sense to wonder if I were okay or not.

We've been waiting for twenty minutes so far for our ride. With every waiting second, I worried more and more about it. I should probably just relax. I mean Sano doesn't even look the least bit worried about this. But then again, I couldn't tell if he was planning some sort of assault right now. He never showed a lot of emotions, but now, I really have no idea what's going on in his head.

"Yeah, I'm fine." I couldn't think of anything else to say.

"Do you want something to drink or anything while we wait?" he offered.

"No thanks. They'll probably be here soon anyways. He said they weren't that far away."

The way my stomach was knotting, I don't think anything would get down.

"Are you bothered by my asking to go with you?"

"No, I don't have a problem with you going. But uh, aren't you the least bit anxious knowing you're going to see your father again?"

"I am a bit curious about how this will turn out, but it's nothing that you should be troubled over." Maybe he's right, I'm just over thinking things.

"Are you sure you're able to spare the time out of your day for this?" I asked, still trying to see if this is really what he wants to do.

"I wasn't doing much today. It should be fine. I message my aunt saying I was leaving out, so everything is all right." I heard a honk outside. Then I got a message from Ken saying they were here.

"They're outside."

"Guess it's time to go then." He stood and looked out the window as if making sure they were out there. We walked toward the door before I stopped.

"Something wrong?" he asked.

"No, I thought I dropped something. But I have everything." I lied. It just came to me about how both of us coming out of his house together will look to Ken and Jayson. Ken didn't say anything when he found out that I was here. But I can't help but think back to how he's previously acted toward me about guys, and how he even got upset when I came here earlier this week to check on him.

Sano opened the door and walked out. I kept my head low as I followed behind him. We reached the car, and he got in on the driver's side. I got in behind the passenger's seat. Ken was sitting there.

"Well, it seems the gang is all here! How's everyone doing?" Leave it to Jayson to start a sunshine war.

"I'm good." I told him.

"Same here," Sano added.

"It's so good to see you again. But I heard about what happened, and I'm so, so sorry to hear about the loss." Jayson said with grief.

"I'm sorry too." Ken chimed in.

"Thanks, I should be the one apologizing for my sudden request to come with you all."

"It's no problem at all. It's almost like old times again." Jayson said. No matter how he tries to keep the mood going, the knots in my stomach refused to go away.

Especially after catching a glimpse of Ken's face through the rearview mirror. He did not look too happy. I realized this was going to be a long ride as I felt my chest tighten as he pulled off.

After the long uncomfortable ride back to the Masidone mansion, I surprisingly couldn't be happier to get out of that car for more than one reason. One reason is that I got a cramp in my leg from staying completely still the whole time. I didn't want to make any possible wrong moves.

Walking along the grey paved walkway up to the doors with the scripted 'M' always has me wondering what will be on the other side when they open. I looked at Sano who was kind of looking around like everything was coming back to him. But he had the same poker face Ken had as we all reached the double doors. Jayson put in a passcode on the alarm system to the left of the doors then opened them letting us in.

Nothing spectacular happened.

Other than a couple of the maids who must have been doing some afternoon cleaning greeted us and suddenly froze. That shock was directed toward Sano. They were looking right at him. They must remember who he is.

"Welcome back." They blurted, unfreezing their state and started cleaning again. If they got the things in this house any cleaner, it would all disappear.

"Alright then Misaky, I can take you over to papa Masy's office and let him know you're here." Jayson started and turned to Sano, "Did you want to go with Misaky, or maybe take a look around first?"

"I'll go now. In case it could take a while," Sano answered.

"Okay then. You two can follow me."

"Since you guys are headed that way, I'll make my way upstairs," Ken said. I watched him up the right flight of stairs to his room.

"Alright, you two can follow this lovely leader this way." We took the left down to the mysterious regular door. No matter how extravagant the rest of the house is, he decided to keep his office door plain and normal.

"Papa Masy, I have your lovely visitor here." Jayson knocked on the door when we made it there. He had said 'visitor' as in I'm the only one. He must enjoy giving people surprise attacks like he did when I came to visit Ken.

We waited to hear someone from the other side, but there was no response.

"He must have stepped out. You two wait here, I'll go find him."

"Going on a search for someone?" A voice from back down the hallway asked. It was the same tone that made me think of the person who was standing beside me.

"Oh, there you are," Jayson said to Mr. Masidone.

"I was starting to wonder if you all would come back."

"Of course we would. We just picked up someone who had a sudden urge to come by."

"Is that so?" Mr. Masidone said with a bit of confusion in his tone. I saw Sano shift in stance as we heard him coming closer. When Mr. Masidone finally reached the three of us, he spotted me, but didn't take long before he took his attention to the tall guy next to me that wasn't Jayson. It didn't beat Ken's, but the shocked expression of a multi-billionaire is still a priceless scene. I saw Sano move again as he looked at his father for the first time since he left years ago.

The stare off lasted another minute before Mr. Masidone spoke.

"I take it that this is the someone you picked up?"

"Yes, he is. He was around when I came to grab our precious cargo and wanted to know if he could come along. I hope it wasn't a problem." Jayson said with a questionable smile. No matter how positive Jayson tries to be, anyone would be a bit anxious after seeing a man like Mr. Masidone so struck like this.

"Not at all," he said still looking at Sano, "Always got something up your sleeve don't you Jayson?"

"You know I wouldn't be me without it."

"Well then, won't you two come in?" Mr. Masidone gestured to his office.

"I guess I'll take off now. I'm only a page away if you need anything." Jayson said leaving.

Leaving me with the father and son reunion I really feel should stay between father and son, and not with girl who said she didn't want to be with said son, but the other son to the father's face.

"That Jayson is always full of surprises." I heard Mr. Masidone say aloud to himself after we entered the room.

"Today is just a surprising day, yes?" he asked. But I hope it was one of his rhetorical questions because neither of us said anything as we just sat down at the seats in front of his desk. "I presume Ken didn't tell you until last minute that I wanted to see you, right Miss Macky? He put up a bit of a fight about it when I asked him the other day." He sat in his seat across from us at his large freshly polished desk.

"Y-yeah he did," I said.

"But you counter that fight he put up by bringing me my son that I've had such a hard time getting to bring here," he laughed slightly still observing Sano.

"So, how long has it been?" He asked him. Sano looked as if he was wondering if it were a rhetorical question or not.

"It's been around five years." He finally answered.

"Five years huh? You've grown so much in that time. I hardly recognized you. When did you get so tall and fit?" Mr. Masidone was studying Sano so intensely like he was a rare piece of art.

"When I got to high school and joined the track team, all that sort of happened." He responded like he was at an interview.

"My, you two must be around each other significantly. You're both so formal and uptight. I told you to loosen up some." He told us, which was kind of hard for me to do given the circumstances.

"I wasn't aware that I was being too formal. This is how I always address people." Sano said. Which I couldn't really see as a lie since he's always so nice and considerate.

"I see. You really do take after her so much." Mr. Masidone said not really directing that to him or me.

The last time I was here I wanted to jump out a window because I was in a difficult situation. Now I want to jump out a window because I'm stuck in this extremely awkward situation. This reunion should not include outsiders. When I first met Mr. Masidone in this office, he had the look of someone who wanted me to be banished as he saw me a distraction to his plans. Now, he has the look of a parent who finally got their kid back from war.

I wonder if he intends to talk up five years' worth of conversation. I really should have considered that rain check idea. Ken said that he wanted to talk to me about Sano. Since Sano is here, that means I really didn't need to come.

But if I didn't come, would Sano still have? He only came here after I mentioned something about it. It seemed like he hasn't considered this place since he left five years ago, yet he decided to stop by anyway. For him to not have favored his father this whole time, he seems to be handling him well now.

"Miss Macky?"

"Y-yes! Mr. Masidone." I was startled.

"I can see why you may be drifting off into some other frame of mind. A slight drop in the stocks I can handle, but someone I haven't seen in five years, I hope you understand that I may be taken aback."

"It's no problem. I understand."

"I should actually be thanking you." He added.

"Thank me for what?"

"You don't remember when you first came to visit? If you don't, then I guess you were already on top of things. I asked you to keep an eye on Sano for me. Make sure he's doing okay and try to help him open up. Then maybe he'd try giving me another chance." He reminded me. "Oh, that."

"And now, here we are today. You've accomplished all the things I've asked of you to do."

The things he asked me. The choice he wanted me to make was the other thing. And I still haven't told Sano that yet.

"That's not it exactly," Sano interrupted, "I don't exactly know what you two have been passing back and forth about me, but I came here to ask a favor." He stated.

"And that would be?" Mr. Masidone asked a bit interested.

"I'm sure by now you've heard about what happened to my mother."

"Yes, I have, and it was quite the news to hear."

"With her gone now, there's a bit of an issue I have dealing with my aunts and them not wanting me to live on my own. So, to get to the point, there's a chance I may need to move back here." Sano just came out and said it. He didn't hesitate at all. He went from not wanting to consider this an option, to its being the first thing he talks about.

Mr. Masidone looked like he was taking in what he just said to him. But before he could speak, there was a knock on the door.

"Kenneth, it's me."

There were four voices I've recently come in contact with that I don't prefer to start a conversation with. All of which live in this house.

The two biggest ones belong to the man across from me who said, "You may enter."

And the woman walking in.

"I just wanted to let you know I was on my way out." Mrs. Baker said. She glanced at me as she was approaching him.

"Oh, that was today you wanted Misa over?"

"Yes, I asked her to come with Ken when he came."

"I see. How are you doing today, Misa?"

"I'm doing fine." I told her. Or as fine as I can be being here…

"That's good. And now who might this be?" Her words slightly faded as if she may have remembered.

"I don't think you two have officially met before. Jocelyn, I'd like to introduce you to my son here, Sano Sanders. And Sano, this is my wife, Jocelyn Baker."

"Ah, Sano, that name has shown up a bit around here. Nice to officially meet you." She didn't offer any handshakes with that.

"Nice to meet you too." Sano said studying her.

"So, I've heard of you, but I've never seen you here before. Is today some sort of special occasion?"

"Not really a special occasion, but a situation has come up and we were just discussing it." Mr. Masidone said.

"Oh, it must be serious for you to come all the way here to talk to him about it." Mrs. Baker thought.

"Yes, it's more on the serious side. Serious enough, we may have a new resident. Excuse me, a returning one."

She stared blankly for a second at him. "So, you've come back to stay."
"I haven't decided anything yet." Sano replied without missing a beat.

"We were still going over things." Mr. Masidone told her.

The rising tension in here was almost suffocating. The only window close to me is behind Mr. Masidone, so I don't think I could make a quick escape unnoticed.

"It seems you all are having quite the conversation here. And poor Misa looks like she's stuck in the middle of things. Was little Kenneth not invited to join this family discussion?"

"He went to his room," Sano said.

"Then it sounds to me like this situation could be a private conversation, why don't you go up and wait with little Kenneth until everything is done here." She said to me. I don't know what she's thinking or why she decided to give that suggestion, but surprisingly, she doesn't seem like such a bad guy right now.

"Well, Miss Macky, seeing how things have turned out this way, and I did have a few more questions to ask him. If you want, I know Ken wouldn't mind you going to him. I didn't intend to have you here for show, so if you feel more comfortable doing that, it's not a problem." Mr. Masidone gave me the option to leave.

"I uh, guess doing that isn't a problem."

"Alright then. I'll have Jayson get you if I need you back." Mr. Masidone gave me the okay to go. But now I'm wondering if I should. This could be a trap that was set up by her. I walk out the door now, and I'm transported to the dungeon I know they have somewhere within these walls.

But if she didn't know I was here, maybe that isn't set up today. So, I slowly got up and turned to the door. I took a glimpse at Sano who was watching me out of the corner of his eye. I looked straight ahead and walked out the room.

I wonder what they will say now. Sano had just brought up the living thing before she came in. They'll probably continue where he left off. Will Mr. Masidone actually let him come back here?

This is my third time being at this house, and I'm already left to walk through it alone. I wonder how much of it may have changed since Sano left. Which one of the many rooms did he have? And will Mrs. Baker accept him moving back in? She didn't seem exactly thrilled about it when Mr. Masidone mentioned it.

The only person who seemed calm about the idea was Sano. He's been acting strangely since I saw him. He doesn't normally speak his mind, but he seemed more out of his mind than usual.

I got to Ken's door and stopped my train of thought and switched it back to the possibility of him charging at me because I didn't tell him I was with Sano. I raised my hand to the door and did three light knocks almost afraid to touch it. I guess they weren't light enough because I heard him yell out, "Yes?"

"I-it's me." I said hesitantly.

"It's me? She's here again!?"

And that voice marks the third person I prefer not to have a conversation with.

The door flew open with Jenny standing there. She seemed especially dolled up. Her glitter brown eyeshadow seemed to pop as she squinted her eyes in anger.

"Can I help you?" She didn't hide the irritation in her voice.

"Well, I kind of didn't come here to talk to you." I said to her. The last thing I need is to hear from her.

"Jenny, as I've already told you, you should leave now," Ken said.

"But I just got here. Is it because of her you want me to leave?"

"Haven't I already discussed this with you?" Jenny got quiet. She looked at me with disgust and stormed out. I watched her down the hallway. She gave in so easily. I guess they have been getting closer in the time he was back here. But he shooed her away like they weren't. And she was still so casually up here in his room.

"Are you all done with your talk?" He asked me.

"They're still talking. He said I could leave out if I wanted since I wasn't really needed." I came in and skeptically closed the door.

"I was wondering if that would happen seeing as the topic of conversation was here. But didn't think he'd let you go so easily either."

"It was actually Mrs. Baker who brought it up."

"She did? She was there?"

"She came in while we were talking."

"I thought she was leaving."

"She said she was, but she wanted to know what was going on." I couldn't really look him in the eye as we talked. Somehow, the feeling of guilt was weighing on me.

"They'll probably be talking for a while; he doesn't have to leave until later so, you can make yourself comfortable." Ken said. I made my way to the chair at his desk and sat a little more formally than I wanted.

"Something bothering you?" he asked.

"Why do you ask that?"

"Just seems like you got something on your mind."

"Not really, just thinking how sudden this all was."

"I guess that's my fault for not telling you. I was assuming this could be overlooked, but Jay said my father was waiting so I at least figured I'd mention it."

"Well, it was unexpected, but Sano coming along was unexpected for you too."

"That was very unexpected. I could only imagine my father's expression when he saw him."

"He was surprised. He didn't think he would ever come by." I said. Although we were talking, Ken felt a little distant.

"It seemed about time to change things up." He thought aloud.

"Is that why you agreed to let him come?" I asked. He thought about it for a second.

"My initial thought was that this probably wasn't the best time actually, but what would come of prolonging something that needed to happen?"

"So, you're not upset that he came along too?"

"Having him come along didn't really inconvenience anything, so that didn't upset me." He said. But something else did upset him.

"But I have been trying to figure out why the desperate need to say you weren't doing anything and you were by yourself when you weren't."

I felt my heart sink. I knew he was upset about that.

"I know the circumstances, so if you would've just said what was going on, I wouldn't have gotten angry or anything." He told me.

"He suddenly messaged me right after you left. It's not like I wasn't going to tell you. I just didn't think I'd hear from you first."

"So, your reaction was to lie about what you were doing?" He looked at me.

"I didn't intend to do that. I was just surprised you called, and then to tell me I was needed here, I freaked out. I'm sorry for not telling you. I know how you can get, so I didn't want you to get the wrong idea."

"How I get?" He repeated.

"Don't act like you still don't know you're a jealous person."

"I'm aware of some of my actions." He answered reluctantly.

"Yeah, so because of that, I was going to tell you. I wasn't going to keep it from you this time."

"At least it sounds like you were thinking about me. With him coming back, I got a little worried." He admitted. I can't blame him. I wasn't prepared for Sano to contact me. I'm still worried about him; especially after seeing his behavior. But as soon as I thought about him, Ken popped into my mind. And I didn't actually want to upset him this time.

"Can't have you going on a rampage at home now, can we?" I tried to tease him.

"No. Having any sort of outburst here would most definitely draw attention. *However*," he lingered on the word, "I think I should be rewarded for not doing any of this 'rampaging' you speak of for lying to me."

"What do you mean reward you? I think that's reward enough that you tamed yourself."

"Still so mean," He said. He looked back down at his laptop he had opened. Even though I said I'd be his girlfriend, he still doesn't force anything on me. I'm always trying to avoid furthering things between us. Most people would get bothered by someone like that.

He was still looking down when I decided to get up. He looked over when he saw I was moving awkwardly to his bed where he was.

"Is something the matter?" He wasn't sure what I was doing. I wasn't sure what I was doing. I sat on the bed next to him. That's when he really got confused. I wasn't used to doing things with people, so I did what I thought was appropriate.

I hugged him.

I wrapped my arms around him completely. I could feel all the heat rushing to my face holding on to his broad shoulders. I could see the confusion on Ken's face not expecting this. I let go of him and got back up to sit on the chair.

"You satisfied? There's your reward." I said. I didn't look at him. I think that was the first time I've actually hugged him on my own. I think he was still trying to understand what I did. But he didn't get a chance to give a response when we heard a knock on the door.

"Kenny-kens, it's me." Jayson said.

"It's open." Ken replied.

He opened the door and came in. "Oh, Misaky, I didn't know you were up here. I hope I wasn't interrupting anything." He said that jokingly, but it's good he came in now, and not a minute ago.

"Not entirely, what's up?" Ken asked.

"Well, Misaky, when did you get up here exactly? Were you with papa Masy at all talking to him?"

"Yeah, I was for a bit."

"I was just on my way there to see if you all needed anything, but I saw Mama Baker leaving out from that direction. She didn't seem too happy. And when Mama Baker isn't too happy, things can get a little iffy. I came up here to get an idea on what could have been said down there to get her all fired up."

"When I left out, the last thing that was mentioned was Sano wanting to possibly move back here."

"Did she say or do something?" Ken asked him.

"Well, that's another thing, she got on the phone as she was leaving out, and I heard her ask to speak to Aiden."

"Aiden? Who's that?" he asked.

"If I remember correctly, I believe he's some kind of detective."

"Detective?"

"Is she going to have Sano investigated or something?" I asked.

"I don't know exactly what she's planning. But she might." Jayson said.

I know she didn't seem found of the new idea of Sano staying here, but what is she planning to do if she was trying to contact a detective? Is she going to have people watching after him like they did me? And for what exactly?

8

"Mama Baker is very discreet about the people she talks to. I've only heard the name once or twice, but I'm sure that's who it was." Jayson said.

"Is there something we can do to like, stop her from what she's planning?" I asked.

"We can't stop what we don't know." Ken said.

"If Mama Baker is anything, she's very good at being furtive. We didn't even know her and Papa Masy were that serious when they got married." Jayson said.

"Which is one of the main reasons I don't approve of her. I just know she got in his head making him want to get together." Ken added.

"Now, now, let's not back track here," Jayson looked to Ken. "I'm going to see how everything is going with those two downstairs. Maybe I could see if she said anything before she left." He told us as he walked out.

"He sure does look out for you," I said.

"Yeah, he does. I think it's mostly because he felt bad for me."

"Felt bad for you? Why?" I asked.

"Well, this is just my assumption, but I think it has something to do with how things turned out after my mother and father got their divorce," Ken looked to the door. "I don't think I've told you this, but Jay is my cousin on my mother's side of the family."

"He's you're cousin?" I asked not expecting that.

"Yeah, he is. He's my mother's favorite nephew. And because he liked her so much, he was the one who watched me and Sano when they would leave out or were busy doing something. When they split up, he said he'd stay to work around here and to help me out."

It isn't too hard to believe that Ken and Jayson are related. It's no wonder they seem so close and alike.

"But I could be wrong about my assumption," He started again, "Jay respects my father, but he didn't really like that he picked her just as much as I didn't."

"I still don't know why you dislike her so much." I know she always seems up to something, but he never told me anything that she actually did.

Ken didn't respond right away. If it has anything to do with why Jayson was trying to keep him calm, then maybe I shouldn't have asked.

"If you don't want to say, then I don't have to know."

"It's not really that, I just don't feel this is the time to talk about it," he started, "Actually, I think we should talk more about Sano now." My eyes bulged at the changed in subject.

"If she really is going to do some investigation on him, you can't do anything out of the ordinary. Otherwise, she might suspect something."

"What makes you say I'd do something out of the ordinary?" I asked.

"Well," he started, "it wasn't completely out of the ordinary, but it wasn't expected to have him here right now, now, was it?"

"I told you I didn't know he was even back until right after you left."

"I know I know, but you like to act on impulse. You don't want to tip her off or let him know."

"So, you don't want him to know that he's going to be watched?"

"We don't want to raise suspicion. Plus, you said he was talking about moving back here, so it shouldn't be much of a problem." The way he said that last sentence seemed like he might've been taking it as a problem.

"Are you okay with him moving back here?"

"I'm just curious to know why he would want to."

"Well, you know the situation he's in. Why is it so hard to believe he would consider coming back home when he doesn't really have a home to stay anymore?" I was waiting for an answer when we heard another knock at the door.

"It's me again." Jayson said. No matter how big this place is, there's always somebody around. He opened the door, but this time he had someone with him. I could see Sano standing behind him.

"It seems like this little guy and the big guy have finished their discussion, and he wanted to take a quick memory trip before we head back home. He has something to do, so if you weren't busy at the current moment, did you want to come with us Misaky to keep things moving?"

I looked to Ken, but he didn't do anything. "Sure, I'll go." I said slowly, getting up heading to the door.

"Alrighty then. Kenny-kens, I'll see you later. Oh, papa Masy said he wanted to speak with you, so he'll be stopping by since he still doesn't want you to move around too much."

"It's been three weeks, and I'm still stuck like a sitting duck." Ken sighed.

"You know he only wants you to recover well. We can't have you getting hurt again. Next week you'll be going to the doctor, so maybe they'll give the okay for you to be free of restrictions." He told him. "We'll be going now."

He was about to close the door when Sano said, "nice room you got." Ken looked up to him as we closed the door.

"Thanks." Ken told him.

"Oh, that's right, you haven't seen his new room." Jayson said, "You're probably curious of how your room looks, so why don't we head there first." He closed his door, and we went on my second tour of this house.

"I made sure that nothing got thrown away or taken out, so don't think everything is probably long gone by now." He told Sano.

We went down the stairs and went in the opposite direction of where I was earlier. If I remember correctly, there is a room at the end of the hall that belongs to a certain duo that is incredibly annoying.

"This is so unfair!" There was a loud voice that belonged to one of the said duos.

"Those two seem lively this lovely afternoon," Jayson started, "I don't know if you are aware, but we have a couple more little ones living here with us." He put that mildly. Inside that room might hold a bunch of glitter and colors, but the so-called little ones' in there would be the nightmare of any regular girl.

We reached further down the hallway before we stopped at a closed door, which was right next to Jenny and Jennifer's room. He opened the door, and we walked in.

"And here it is. The housekeepers come in here every so often to sweep and keep the dust bunnies out."

The room was big. Everything was clean and organized. There was only a bed, dresser, and a few boxes that sat in front of a walk-in closet all at the far end of the room.

"We weren't exactly sure what was going to happen after you left, so I packed away some of your things in case you wanted to stop by to grab some stuff." Jayson told him. Even though Sano was the one that left them, Jayson was still thinking of him and didn't see him as a traitor or anything.

"If feels smaller somehow." Sano slowly walked in. I looked at him in confusion to his 'smaller' comment. If he thinks this is small, what does he consider big?

"Well, you have shot up over the years. I'm sure it would seem different." Jayson said. Sano looked around some more, then looked in the large empty area that was closer to us.

"When did Ken move out?" he asked. It was the first I've heard of them living in the same room. That would explain the space big enough for another king bed and dresser.

"He changed rooms around three years ago maybe?" Jayson tried to remember.

Sano made a move toward the boxes and opened one of them. What showed seemed to be his old clothing. He was pulling out really expensive looking shirts and pants with the brand symbols I see on Ken's clothes. Sano usually wears casual clothes and not big-name brands like the ones Ken always wears. But to think he did seems kind of hard to believe. This whole time I thought he was just a regular person like me. But he really was once a part of this world.

He looked at another box and pulled something out of it. "Oh, I remember that." Jayson said, "That came from the day you and Kenny-kens tried to play that one prank on me." Sano was holding a shirt that had holes and what looked like burn marks on it.

"I forgot I put that in there. Misaky, you have to watch out for these silly little mischievous boys. They tried to get cute with some fireworks one day and was going to set them off in my room of all places. But because I taught them what they knew, they never made it there." He smiled as he went down memory lane.

"You hid behind our door and somehow managed to light them when we walked out," Sano said.

"It wasn't my fault I was able to see through you plan. You guys had been trying to get me that whole week. You're lucky Papa Masy never found out about that. He would've had a heart attack seeing you kids like that." Jayson laughed slightly. I even saw a smile on Sano's face. All I could do was look in at them.

Jayson must have noticed my expression. "Misaky, this isn't even the start of the things those two have done. Or tried to do I should say. Although, you almost got away with taking out the screws in my door, closet, and bathroom. That was a fun day. Too bad I wasn't as drunk as you must have thought I was."

Even as kids they were really smart. I would never know how to take apart a door! I knew there were still a lot of things I didn't know, but to think that they were into extreme practical jokes. Maybe I was right, and they really are spies. I used whoopee cushions and small things when I was younger. Not fireworks and door removals to get a laugh!

"Not too much else has changed around here though." Jayson pulled himself back from the past. "Just a bit of redecorating here and there. We could take all day reminiscing, but if you want to get back at a reasonable time, we shouldn't take too long in one place. Weekend traffic can be hectic around this time." Sano shook his head understanding. He put the things back in the box and came back toward us. We left the room and Sano shut the door.

"So, I was hearing voices." We all looked up and saw Jennifer standing in the hallway.

"I hope we didn't disturb you two while we were talking. I can't have our little kittens baring their claws at us." Jayson was kidding, but the way she looked at Sano tells me she didn't get the joke. She looked back to Jayson.

"No disturbance. It's just not often we hear something from that room. Normally it's closed and no one ever goes in it."

"The owner of the room has stopped by and wanted to see it." Jayson said. Jennifer looked back to Sano, and then to me.

"Well, it's good to see you're alive and well. You were gone for so long and had Misa here worried out of her mind." I gasped a little louder than I wanted.

"It's nice to know I was missed so much, but I am okay and back." Sano told her. She debated on whether to respond or not. She just gave him a look and went back into her room.

"Leave it to Saturday to be an active day." I looked away from Sano wondering if active should have been the word for Jayson to use.

We continued on Sano's memory trip throughout the house. It was a lot shorter than the tour I had when I was first here. He only showed him the changes like the new connecting hallway from the living room to the other side of the house by Mr. Masidone's office and the new extension in the kitchen. But this only brings back my wonder of how either of them found an interest in a regular girl like me. I don't have nearly the number of things they have, nor have I done half the things they've done. Sure, I've nearly burnt down the kitchen lab at school, but that was entirely by accident. The things they've done were on purpose.

"Misa, wait." I heard Sano call my name then I felt myself going backwards. There was a door that opened in front of me when Sano pulled me back. We were still by the kitchen.

"My deepest apologies! I didn't hurt you, did I? I just pushed the door not paying attention."

It was one of the maids coming out with a tray in her hand.

"No, I'm fine. I should have paid more attention," I said. I looked at my shoulder where Sano was still holding on to me. He must have seen me looking and let go.

"You're fine Anna, luckily, she was stopped before the door opened all the way." Jayson told her.

"Forgive me, I was in a rush to get this to the president. I'll be sure to be more attentive of my surroundings." She apologized again and walked away.

"You okay Misa?" Sano asked me.

"Yeah, thanks. I guess I spaced out for a second." I said, pulling myself together. My hand brushed passed my pocket, and I reached in there realizing I didn't feel my phone. I checked my other pockets, and it wasn't there either.

"Did you lose something Misaky?" Jayson asked while watching me.

"My phone. I had it in my pocket, but it's not here."

"Oh, maybe it fell out as we were walking." He thought, looking behind him. But come to think of it, I haven't felt my phone in my pocket since I was in Ken's room. It might have fallen out when I gave him that hug.

"I think I might have left it in Ken's room." I told them.

"Well, we were done with our little trip here anyway. You can go up and see if it's there and we'll wait over by the door for you." I agreed to that and headed up the stairs. I was back again knocking on Ken's door.

"I see you've come back." I heard him say without me even saying who it was. When we're at my house, I hardly ever go in his room. But when I'm here, it seems that's all I do.

"I think I left something." I said. He said I could come in, so I opened the door. I didn't see him lying in his bed this time. He was at his closet.

"You're just in time for the show." he said.

"What show?"

"You came as I was about to change into something more comfortable." He smiled and held up some joggers he pulled out his closest.

"You're such a perv. I just came because I thought I left my phone up here." I couldn't help but feel embarrassed just hearing that.

He reached in his pocket and pulled it out. "Saw it laying in my bed just now. I thought you might come back for it."

"I did, so give it back." I extended my hand out with my guard up.

"There won't be any shows today so no need to be so alert. But, if you want this back, you'll have to come get it." He put it back in his pocket. I don't know what happened between the time I left and now, but surprisingly, this seemed more like his normal self. I had no choice but to cautiously make my way over to him.

"I'm not going to run away if you make any sudden movements." He said watching as I inched over.

"Just hand me my phone, and I'll be on my way."

"Seems like someone doesn't trust my word." He took the phone out of his pocket and tossed it on the bed. Somehow, it felt like a test. I still only inched closer toward his bed now. I reached the edge of it and headed for the phone. He was looking into the closet when I got there, so I thought the coast was clear to grab and go. But as soon as I grabbed my phone, he reached over, putting his hand over mine.

"Really now, do you lack that much faith in me?"

"You're all about tricks. I know better than to let my guard down." I told him.

"Sounds to me like you're the one expecting something to happen. Maybe you're the one I have to watch out for." He said with that cheeky smile of his. He picked up both my hand and phone. "I never got to repay you for your cute surprise attack on me earlier. But unfortunately, you're getting ready to leave, so now isn't the time for something like that." He said. He then brought my hand to his face and kissed it. "I'll see you Monday."

I pulled my hand back. He seemed to be enjoying himself as he smiled watching my reaction.

"See you later." I said and left out not saying anything more.

"There you are. Was your phone up there?" Jayson asked when he saw me coming down the stairs.

"Y-yeah it was."

"Did you hurt your hand?" He asked watching me.

"Uh, no I didn't." I hadn't even realized I was still holding my hand.

"Well then, are we all ready?" Sano and I both replied yes and went out the door. I could tell Sano had been looking at me, but I couldn't really look at him right then. I just kept my head lowered as we walked out the double doors into Jayson's car, and back to our regular world.

The only time I really realize that I've crossed back over to my world is when I am brought back to my house. Jayson dropped me off first, so my regular life has once again started.

"Well, Misaky, things had turned out slightly different for you when you got to the house, but you did help papa Masy out a lot." Jayson must have meant bringing Sano there. "By the way, I didn't ask, and I'm so curious to know, are you planning to come back to the house Sano?" He asked him. I looked up in the passenger seat waiting to hear his answer too.

"I think I am."

"Oh, so you told papa Masy that you were coming?"

"I did, but not until school is over. I also have to talk it over with my aunt. This is probably for the best since I don't want to burden them more then they'll have to by taking care of the kids."

"You're going to have your aunt take them in?" I asked without thinking.

"Yeah. I don't want to drag them to the house. I'll have to ask them to take care of them, but I ask my father to help with finances and he agreed to that."

"That sounds like a fabulous plan. I hope this is going to work out for you." Jayson said. It's probably going to be a big change for him to live without the kids around.

"I guess I'll be going now." I told them.

"I'll see you later then Misaky. Take care of yourself."

"I'll see you in school on Monday." Sano said. I got out of the car and waved back. I still didn't look directly to Sano as I turned away.

It wasn't such a bad idea for Sano to go see his father. I was sure something would have happened, but when he came to get me, nothing seemed out of the ordinary with him. And Mr. Masidone said he'd help out, so I guess it's all going to work out. I really do wonder what they said after I left. They seemed to have gotten some kind of understanding between them. I just want things to work out for Sano. He deserved that much.

Just as I had that thought, the back of my hand where Ken kissed it felt warm. I covered it as I slowly opened the door, going in as Jayson drove off.

"And where have you been young lady?" I nearly jumped out of my skin when I heard my mother from the couch.

"M-mom? When did you get here?"

"I've been here for a couple hours. I thought I'd surprise you, but you seem to have gotten an early start today. You didn't answer my text. You're coming back from somewhere?"

"Uh, yeah." I'm not sure if I should tell her I came from Ken's house again.

I looked out the window to see if they were gone, feeling for some reason they were still there. But when I looked to the end of the block, I saw a black car turning the corner. Of course, cars pass by all the time, but something seemed off about that car.

Maybe I do watch a lot of movies, but it wasn't your average black car from around here. The windows were all tinted and they seemed to be moving slowly.

Now I'm starting to wonder if Jayson's assumption about Mrs. Baker was right. They did turn the direction you'd go to Sano's house. Were they trying to follow them? And if so, should I call and tell them? But what if I'm just over thinking it? I've seen some black cars around here before. They didn't look like that one though. That was a far nicer car than the mini vans people around here have. I don't want anything to happen to him. But I don't want to worry him if it's nothing.

"Misa, I know since your father and I are always gone, I can't keep my eye on you, but that doesn't mean you can always go roaming around on your on and not tell me where you are going." My mom stood and looked to me.

"I'm sorry mom, but could the lectures wait a bit?" I needed to figure out if I should say something about that car or not. But Ken did say not to do anything that could raise suspicion.

"Did something happen out there?" She walked to me out of concern.

"Uh, no. I just thought I heard something."

"Did Ken go home again?"

"Yeah, he left. Is there something wrong with you?" Now it seemed like she was the one I should be concerned about.

"Well, I'll get back to you in a minute, but there may be something going on within the company. There have been some issues around the department I'm in and management has been getting really strict lately. They're starting to do background checks on everyone again because they think there's someone leaking information. But that isn't exactly what I'm worried about. The policy has changed a bit since I started working there, and with them checking us, they might cut me or your father for having a relation to one another."

"But didn't they like, know that already?" I asked.

"They recently had a change in VP's. They're booking down on everything. They've already gotten rid of three people and two others were forced to transfer."

"But, couldn't you say you have connections with Mr. Masidone?"

"It's not that simple Misa. There has been some serious issues lately, and if they think I'm causing a problem or violating any regulations or policies, they'll terminate me." She had a look of distress. She seems really worried about this. I know my mom wouldn't do anything wrong at her job. She wouldn't do anything that would hurt her position. If she's really this concerned, I could maybe talk to Ken about it since his father is the head of everything.

But I still have my matter of trying to figure out if I should spook them with what I just saw. If I noticed something like that, then I'm pretty sure Sano or Jayson would have noticed also. So, if it were anything, they'd be able to handle it better than me trying to do it. At least, I hope.

"You're lucky I was busy this weekend, or else I would've been at you're house to see what was going on since you act like you forgot how to work a phone." Katie came to me upset when I got to my locker at school since I hadn't contacted her all weekend.

"I'm sorry. I was also busy over the weekend, and I forgot to text you."

"What had you all tied up?"

"It's a really long story. I'd have to tell you at another time."

"Oh, something juicy has happened, I can tell. I want detail." I could see the glow in her eyes.

"Well, I guess I could start with—"

"Morning Misa." I was interrupted when I heard Sano speaking to me.

"Oh, hey. Did you get back home okay?" I hadn't planned to speak to him first thing in the morning.

"Yeah, I did. The kids came back yesterday, so it seems like everything is getting back to normal."

"That's good. They must be happy to be back home."

"They were. But I haven't broken the news to them yet about the move, so I'm hoping that won't be too bad." He said, then the warning bell went off.

"Guess I'll get going then." He gave me and Katie a little wave as he walked away mixing in with the other kids getting to their classes.

"Alright Misa, we have two options here. We can either walk out the doors now or I pull the fire alarm, either way, I want to know what went down over the weekend asap." Katie pushed some hair back behind her ear. She couldn't have been more serious right now.

"Well, I was going to say that Sano came back from his long break, but I guess you can see that yourself now." I tried lightening the mood, but that didn't work at all.

"Okay, I swear to fill you in on everything, but right now isn't the time. We should be getting to class."

"Hm, class and lecture, or incites about the missing boy and girl who no longer should be getting all close and personal with missing boy. Which seems better?" Katie held out her hands weighing the options.

"You're not making anything better you know. I'll tell you all you want, just not right now." I saw her jaw clinch as she realized she'd have to wait for me to talk.

There's one thing I always forget and that's to never forget to tell her anything. Especially if it's something like this. With how things have been going lately, not telling her something isn't my best idea. But that just shows how much she looks out for me. She's almost like my second mother. Which can be a good thing since I can't tell my real mom everything.

We got to class, and everyone was there. I could see some people whispering and looking in Sano's direction. He doesn't seem to be paying it any mind. He probably expected that there would be some talk of his return. Ken was sitting at his desk looking through his notebook. He came back this morning and refused to use his crutch. So, since he refuses to use it, I refused to carry his bag to class.

"I hope everyone had a good weekend." Mr. Hallens came in the room, "I see you've come back Mr. Sanders. Hope everything is going well for you now."

"Everything is good," Sano said.

"That's good to here. You're one of the good students. Masidone over there had an excuse, but it was unusual to see you gone so long."

"I bet you someone's happy." I heard somebody say.

"I think it's more than one someone." Another girl behind me said to them. Just as everything was dying out, it seems like things might start up again.

"The things you kids occupy yourself with while you're not doing your homework." Mr. Hallens used a tone that suggested he doesn't want to hear about this just as much as I didn't.

Class got started and I wasn't able to stay focused. I tried stealing a few looks toward Sano without seeming obvious about it. He didn't seem bothered by anything as usual. But he's also extremely hard to read.

"Because you all tried so desperately to bring your grades up after midterms, I've decided to go with the final project to only be the trifold poster and not the paper." Mr. Hallens told us. There was a sigh of relief throughout the whole class. I even got happy to hear that.

"There will be five different times and events for you to choose from. I only want three. I'll explain this in more detail tomorrow. For now, just look it over and get an idea on which ones you'll pick." He handed out the paper about the project to us. He's giving us till the end of next week to complete it, but it still wasn't something I was looking forward to. It's not like it'll help me much anyway. I didn't do so well pulling my grade up, and I did horrible on the midterms.

"Hey, you ready?" I looked over and saw Ken. Even though he's not using his crutches, he's still allowed to leave early since he has his brace on. All he's doing is taking advantage of this. Not to mention probably trying to make up for not helping him this morning. It wouldn't look good if I refused him now, so I gathered my things together and got his bag and we left out.

"Is there something bothering you?" Ken asked me when we got into the hallway.

"I'm fine." I replied, but I don't think it was believable. I'm really thinking about how I haven't been focused on schoolwork at all. I told myself I was going to try to bring my grades back up to avoid taking summer school, but that isn't going to happen. School is almost over, and in the fall, I'll be a senior. I can't keep messing up like this.

"Did something else happen while I was gone?" he asked.

"I'm fine, okay? Can't a girl move an eyebrow without it being mistaken for a change in emotion?" I turned, not wanting to look at him. I mean he is part of the reason these past couple months I haven't been able to focus in school. Before he came around, I still wasn't doing well, but I at least managed to avoid summer classes.

Ken got what he needed from his locker, and we headed for the elevator. It didn't take long for it to open before we got on. I pressed the '2' for it to go up. The doors closed and the next thing I know I was hitting the wall, and Ken had his hands stretched out on the sides of me.

"You got a problem?" I asked looking at him. The elevator stalled before going up.

"Do you enjoy it when I get concerned about you? You keep saying you're fine, but you had this blank expression since you walked into class. You know, you don't always have to hold it in." He looked at me like he was genuinely concerned. Ever since I said I'd be his girlfriend, he's been watching me more and more.

"I'm fine, really. It isn't anything." The elevator doors opened, but he didn't exactly move right away. I heard the bell ring freeing everyone from their classes. Bodies and conversations filled the hallway fast. That's when he put his arms down and backed up.

"Don't think this is done." He said. He stepped aside, letting me get off the elevator first. I didn't say anything else as we walked to his class.

"You still got this poor thing taking care of you?" His teacher said when we walked in. "You know, it's fine if you let him do it himself. You'll spoil him if you keep babying him like this." She told me. Then she stepped out of the room.

"Spoiling sounds fun." Ken smiled. I gave him a *'yeah right'* look and dropped his things on his desk.

"I'll see you later." I told him. I turned to leave out, but I stopped when I saw Sano walking in. He looked at me, but he kept going to his seat. Talking to him now while Ken is on my case isn't such a good idea. So, I just kept my eyes on the road and left out.

There was something off throughout the day. The school was a buzz again now that Sano is back. Somehow, word got out about his absence being about his mother's passing, so everyone is feeling sorry for him now. That at least stopped the idea of it involving me, but to talk about something so personal so casually doesn't make it any better.

"Maybe these people will grow up by next school year. Only a couple more weeks left, then you won't have to be the talk of school for one reason or another." Katie was obviously getting tired of the gossip just as much as I was. We were walking to my locker after school when we passed two people taking and heard them one girl say, "No wonder he seems more distant now."

"I think that girl was one of Sano's fans before Ken came." Katie told me.

"I guess I wasn't the only one that had huge crush on him."

"And just like how you've moved on to Ken, they did too. But now the competition isn't as strong. I think Ken has turned down a lot of girls already."

"How do you know that?"

"Since we found out Eden and those two share classes, I've been forcing info out of him. So, he tells me what he hears and what goes on in class."

I remember when I first started taking Ken to his classes, someone said he rejected them. Are people still asking him out? I know Ken is one of the popular guys here, but I would've thought they'd give up by now.

"By the way," Katie started again, "did you look over the project for history?"

"Not exactly. He said he was going to talk about it tomorrow."

"Yeah, but you should at least look it over like he said. You're really at risk of failing. This project is worth a lot. So, if you do well on it, you still have a chance of passing."

"He already said I'd have to go to summer school, maybe I don't have that chance."

"You know he says things to scare us. You won't be walking out of the class with an 'A', but you could at least walk out passing. Do you really want to spend your last summer as a high schooler in summer school?"

"Mimi." I looked up and heard Ken calling to me.

"Why don't you ask him to help you?" Katie said, "he probably already has it done. He's sure to help you do well on this." She gave me a wave and walked away without letting me respond.

"Didn't mean to interrupt your conversation" Ken said approaching me.

"Were you looking for me?"

"I simply couldn't be wanting to see my Mimi?"

"You don't usually come for me after school."

"I was walking by and so happen to see you. I wasn't intentionally looking for you, but I do have something I want to talk to you about."

"If it's about earlier, I told you, I'm-"

"It's not about that. It's about a gathering my father is planning this summer at the villa."

"A gathering?" I repeated.

"Yes. I'll be happy to explain when we get home. Jennifer may or may not be looking for me in regards to it, and I don't have anything else to say to her about it." I don't know what this gathering thing is all of a sudden, but Ken looks as if this has been an issue for a while now.

I was done at my locker and Ken left most of his things in his, so we left to head home together. Ken's leg must be better since he's walking faster. We didn't say much on the way home which made me a little worried about this gathering talk. And it's at the villa. Is this some fancy rich people party he wants to invite me to or something? Why would his father and mother want me to be a part of something like that? I doubt they're reconsidering me.

"So, what is this gathering?" We barely got in before I asked.

"Anxious, are we?" He asked putting his bag down on the couch.

"Well, a gathering at the villa kind of just sprung up out of nowhere."

"It's something we do every summer around mid-July. Although, this year, it will be a little earlier. We usually just go for something like a mini vacation, but my father has mentioned a couple other guest coming too, and wanted to know would you be interested in being one of those additional guests to come with us?"

"Isn't this like a family thing?"

"Yes and no. Yes, because it's typically us going. And no because it has never been limited to just us. There have been years when we've invited friends along. My father recently made a huge contract deal and thought to make this year's gathering a little more special. We're usually out there for a week and have a big barbecue the day before we leave. That's kind of a long time, so you can talk to your parents about it if you say yes before I let my father know."

"Well, won't you all be tight on space? If all of you that live in the house, plus some others, and me, and Sano is supposed to move back in…" I stopped myself. I have a bad habit of always bringing up Sano.

"This isn't something we just started. We've been doing this since before he left. Although, I'm not sure how he'd feel about going. I wouldn't be surprised if he sat out."

"So, you all would just let him stay at the house by himself?"

"I'm sure we'd figured something out if he decided not to attend. He hasn't even told our father when he plans on moving back in."

"Di-did you find out yet if Mrs. Baker was doing something suspicious?" I really didn't want to bring it up, but it was weighing on my mind.

"You really shouldn't worry about that. Jay hasn't mentioned anything, and Sano hasn't gone missing again, so nothing is going on from what I can tell. I don't want to make him more troubled than he already is giving him the idea someone is after him." He seems to be thinking of him a lot too. No matter what has happened, he still seems to take his feelings into consideration.

"I don't think they've ever met before the other day though," Ken started again, "so if anything were to happen, she'd want to personally ask to meet with him at some point to get to know him."

She'll do the same thing with him that she did with me. I wonder how she plans to invite him out. And will he actually want to. Seeing as he'll be living with her, it'll happen at some point.

"So, back to my original question. Would you like to come to the villa with us this summer?" He looked at me with hopeful yet concerned eyes. I wouldn't mind going back to the villa, but a whole week with him, his family, and possibly Sano? I can't even imagine what could go on with all of us in the same space for that amount of time.

"Well, I have to see what happens with school. I'm very close to being in summer school, you know. But, if I did really good on this project, then I might get my grade high enough to be safe from going. But I doubt that'll happen." I said. What are the odds of me finally doing well in this class?

"What's this doubt talk you speak of? Of course, with a little of my help, your worries will be over. We can work on it together and all will be fine." He looked at me with an 'ok' hand gesture. He didn't even think twice before offering to help me. I'm sure he has all kinds of other hard finals he has to prepare for, but he's still willing to work with me to help my grades. I was upset earlier about my academics, and he was concerned about me. All I had to do was tell him and he'd try to help. I shouldn't be so afraid to talk to him about this kind of stuff.

Ken looked as if he had more to say, but before he could, his phone started vibrating. He pulled it out of his pocket and made a face when he looked at it.

"Sorry, we'll get back to this in a second." He told me before answering. He walked away as he started talking. He was calm when he asked, "what do you want," to the person on the phone. But if I saw right, in that moment he put the phone to his ear, the name on it said Jenny. Last time she called, it wasn't programmed, and he isn't usually that calm when he speaks to her. Even when I was at his house, she was with him a lot more than usual. What exactly happened between those two when he was on bed rest for two weeks?

My phone was next to start vibrating as I watched him go into the kitchen. I took it out my pocket and grew stiff as I saw a text from Sano. I looked up to see Ken leaning against the counter not paying any attention to me. Something about him talking so casually with Jenny isn't sitting right with me, so I opened Sano's message to take my attention away from him.

But now this isn't sitting well with me. He's asking if I can come over tomorrow to talk about something. What does he want to talk about? He just got back, and we hardly spoke today. I would have to tell Ken if I went over to avoid what happened last time.

Although, he seemed quick to cut our conversation short to start talking to Jenny. I looked back to Ken and almost thought something happened to my vision seeing him talk with a little smile. Whatever they were talking about, he was enjoying it. To think that was possible.

Without thinking, I responded to Sano. He doesn't look like he'll be another second like he said. If Ken can talk so casually to Jenny knowing what she wants, then I can talk to Sano. He shouldn't care if his time is already occupied with her, so I'll be coming home late tomorrow.

I don't know what's more shocking. The fact that Ken and I haven't said much to each other since that phone call, or the fact that I'm waiting for Sano at school to walk home with him. I am waiting at the side exit where not many people leave to avoid being seen, but I figured it's already too late to sneak and go separately. I messaged Ken saying I was going somewhere after school. I think he replied but I haven't looked to see it. I still want to know what's going on with this sudden change in behavior with Jenny. If he's so crazy about me then maybe it's nothing. But Jenny is crazy about him though. Maybe it's finally getting to his head.

"Misa," I almost thought Ken was calling me, but I turned and saw Sano coming toward me.

"Sorry for the wait. My teacher wanted to talk to me."

"Is everything okay?"

"Yeah. I just wanted to know how's everything and gave me some assignments I missed. Are you ready?"

"Yeah," I answered. He opened the door, and we walked outside. I saw some people walking ahead of us and turned down a street. I don't think they noticed us but somehow, I still felt uneasy.

"Sorry for asking to talk with you so suddenly, but it's been a question on my mind for a little while now." We made it off school grounds when he started talking. "Is Ken alright to go back on his own?"

"Yeah, he's fine. It's been a few weeks since the accident and he's doing better."

"That's good," he said. He didn't say anything else after that. He just kept walking with his head forward.

I was just at his house over the weekend, but each step feels harder and harder to make.

Maybe because it's the first time he's walking with me that it feels different. What's this question he's been wanting to ask and how important is it to have to talk privately about it?

I could see his house coming up ahead as we turned the corner.

"The kids will be surprised to see you," he said.

"You didn't tell them I was coming over?"

"Well, I wasn't sure if you'd change your mind. I didn't want to get their hopes up since it's been a little rough for them."

"I had nothing else planned today, so stopping by isn't a problem. But you've only been back a few days. Are you sure you want company so soon?"

"It's not a problem having you over," he said with a small laugh, "plus, I think I might be bothering you with what I want to ask." My chest tightened hearing that.

"What is it that you want to ask me?"

"Well, it's a couple things actually. So, feel free to tell me you don't want to answer them." We made it to his front door. I could hear a lot of noise on the other side. Part of me was expecting the kids to be too sad to be so energetic like they used to be, but from the sound of it, it sounds like they have the same amount of energy as they always do.

Sano opened the door and to my surprise, the noise I was hearing wasn't from children playing, but children cleaning.

"Look, it's Misa!" Dejavu never felt stronger when I was spotted and the three of them rushed toward me.

"It's been so long since we've seen you!"

"I'm so happy you came by!"

"We missed you!"

"My, my what's going on in here?" A fourth voice I didn't expect to hear came from down the hallway. It wasn't until I saw her, I remembered who it was. "Oh, if I had known you were having company, I would've waited to start moving things around." It was his aunt I met last week.

"You're starting already?" Sano asked. She was holding a large basket with clothes in them.

"You're only going to be here a few more weeks and we have a lot to move around, so I figured it's better to start now than later. Nice to see you again Misa." She said to me with a wink and sat the basket she was holding down.

"Do you want to help us clean?" Cindy asked me, "We're moving to Auntie Fay's house."

"We're not moving today. And I'm sure Misa didn't come here to clean someone else's house. The four of us can handle it."

"I had something to discuss with her." Sano told her.

"We got a bit of a mess in here as you can see. I don't want to interrupt you from us moving around."

"It's okay, we can go to my room."

I think one of the kids noticed my blood stopping when Sano suggested that. I didn't intend to be alone with him in his room!

"That's fine with me. I'll be here and there if you need me." She went back down the hall. The kids followed behind her.

"I hope that's alright with you?" Sano turned to me and asked. It was kind of late to say no, so I said it was fine, and he led us up the stairs. My first time going to his room.

It was almost just like my house, except there were two rooms on the left, a bathroom at the end of the hallway, and a room we stopped at on the right. He opened the closed door and walked in. I trailed behind him feeling like I've walked in this room already. But it wasn't Sano's room, it was Ken's room.

His bed was against the left wall with his desk next to it. His dresser and tv was across from it. Everything was so neat. Like a mirror imagine of Ken's room back at his house. Now that I think of it, when we saw their old bedroom the two of them shared, it looked just like their rooms combined.

"Would you like anything to drink?" He asked me after putting his things on his bed. My throat was a bit dry from the nerves.

"Um, water is fine."

"Alright. Make yourself comfortable. I'll go get some." He left his room as I stood there watching him leave. I looked around his room again. It's not as big as the mansion rooms, but it was still roomy. He didn't have many decorations. His bedding was a solid blue and white. And he only had one picture on the far wall of a runner.

I looked back to his desk and saw a picture against the wall. It was a picture of him and his mom. They were standing on the track field, so it must have been after a competition. His mother was all smiles and looked so happy with him. I've never seen Sano look so happy either as he hugged her. He was taller than her, but she still wrapped her arms around him looking up to his face. No wonder I couldn't tell Ken and Sano were related. He takes after his mother. They both have the same complexion, dark hair, and even smile the same.

I noticed a cup with pens in it next to the photo. One of the pens stood out to me. Without thinking, I reached for it looking at the nice and glossy silver pen with the words, *For My Masidone Men*, on it. I remember Ken having a pen like this. His mother had them made for him. She must have had some made for Sano too. What does it mean for him to keep something like this if he wanted nothing to do with them anymore?

"We can play after you're done helping Aunt Fay." I was startled by the sound of Sano's voice coming down the hallway. I quickly put the pen back and sat at the seat at his desk.

"Got your water." He said coming in.

"Sounds like someone wants to play."

"No matter what goes on, they always fine time to play and have fun." He sat down a glass of water on the desk. "But from the looks of it, it may not be much of that for now since we have a lot of stuff to move."

"Are you going to take all of your things with you to the mansion?" I asked.

"Not right away. A lot of our stuff will be going in storage, so I'll be leaving some stuff there." He sat across from me on his bed. But the mansion is so big, it could hold everything in here and more.

"But that kind of brings me to one of the things I wanted to ask you." My heart rate started going up as he got right to it.

"Like I said, you don't have to answer if you don't want to. From the looks of things when we went to the house over the weekend, everyone seems to know you well. The house is over a hundred miles away in another city. I don't know what they do now, but back when I was there, we hardly got out to go to different places, so how did you and Ken end up meeting?"

"H-how did we meet?" I was preparing for a lot of possible questions, but that wasn't one of them. Do I tell him he just appeared in my house? Or go all the way to how he stalked me before actually knowing me?

"My parents work for the company. Somehow, Ken found out about that and wanted to get to know me for some marriage arrangement thing Mr. Masidone was doing."

"So, without knowing you, he moved into your house?"

"Well, when you put it that way it sounds kind of strange. Apparently, we met once before, and he remember me." I tried to make it seem less strange, but I think that made it worse. Sano sort of looked away then turned back to me.

"This meeting before," he started, "was it at a mall?" My eyes grew wide as I looked at him.

"It was around the time I left, so I didn't really put it together until that one time I saw your bracelet. You were at the mall trying to buy it and Ken helped you pay for it."

"You were there?" I asked. I don't remember seeing him at all...

"Jayson, Ken, and I were out that day. We were passing a store that you were in, and I told him to go in there. He ended up talking to you, but that didn't last long after you ended up running off."

"He told me that before. But I didn't know you were there too. I only remember seeing Ken. You told him to talk to us?"

"We both went in the store and overheard you two talking. I think it was about not having the money to get what you wanted. I told him to go over and talk to you, and he ended up going after hesitating for a while. We were just messing around that day. I didn't think he'd actually do it. And I didn't think he'd remember you from back then either."

"It wasn't that hard to do since he had people following me."

"He told you about that?"

"You knew about that too?" I was surprised, but I guess if he was there, he'd know the rest too.

"After he got slapped by Katie and they found the wrong girl, Ken wanted to keep the information that was gathered. At the time I didn't know why, but now it all makes sense." I didn't know what to say. So that means Sano has known me since then too.

"Were you also watching me?"

"During that same time period is when I left, so I had a lot on my mind. I guess Ken was still looking into things. It wasn't in bad intentions, he just seemed very curious about someone who didn't seem to have grown up the way we did." He sounds as if he's defending Ken and the stalking he did. This just proves they still have a bond. They just haven't realized that yet.

"There was something else I wanted to know." Sano went on to another topic.

"My dad's new wife. Do you know her well?" Another tough question I wasn't prepared to answer.

"I've met Mrs. Baker a few times..." I trailed off not sure what else I could say.

"Do you know anything about her?"

"Not a lot. Well, I just know Ken doesn't like her."

"That's to be expected I would think."

"Jayson doesn't like her that much either."

"Did they say why?"

"He never went into detail about it. Just that she's someone to watch out for." I told him. He got really quiet again as if he's thinking.

"There was something about her," he started, "I didn't want to say anything yet, but she seemed very familiar. I think I remember her from somewhere."

"Do you remember her from when you lived in the mansion before?"

"No, I remembered seeing her after I moved. Before my mother and I moved over here, we lived in a smaller town that was a little closer to the house. We lived by this popular bar that we would often drive by. My mom told me she knew the person who owned it. When we would pass by the place, I saw someone that looked like that woman hanging outside with the owner. I would see her with him almost every time we passed the place, so I'm sure that was her when I saw her the other day. But then, out of the blue, I never saw her there again. Come to find out, the bar owner had died in a bad car accident." The room filled with silence after Sano stopped to take a sip of his water he was holding.

"That's why I was wondering about her. My mom thought they were together, but he never told her they were. Anyway, it's not just that, but my mom would also go to that bar sometime to talk to him, and she said that he had kids that he wanted to arrange a 'play date' with me. I never saw them and that meeting never happened, but I know his last name was Jamison." That name rang a bell. Do I know someone with that name?

"So, what does this mean then? You think she has another family or something?"

"These are just some things I remember. I haven't really figured anything out since the other day was the first time I saw her since back then.

"That must be why she's keeping an eye on you."

"She's keeping an eye on me?" I pressed my lips together as that was not supposed to be said out loud.

"I, well, I don't really know. Something was said and I saw something, but that could've been nothing." I started panicking.

"Well, what did you see?" He asked curiously.

"Um, well, it was the day we when went to the house. When Jayson dropped me off, I saw this unusual car that looked like it might've been following behind you guys. But it could just be my imagination."

"What made you have the thought of someone following us?" Sano's been talking this whole time and the few words that come out my mouth are already getting me in trouble.

"When we were at the house, Jayson told us that after she left the room with you and Mr. Masidone, she called someone that he said was a detective or something. But for you to be found so quickly, it was probably nothing."

"I wouldn't be surprised if she did have someone on a case that soon. If it's one of my dad's people, they move fast," he said.

"There's probably nothing to worry about." I didn't want to add to his worry, but I think I already did.

"If it were just me, I wouldn't be bothered by it. But I have the kids, and my aunt will be around a lot now. I don't want them getting involved in something that they have nothing to do with." He seemed serious as he continued to think on it.

"I have one last thing to ask you."

"W-what's that?"

"If I'm moving back in the house, I don't want there to be any problems, so I want to get some things cleared before I get there. So, would you go back with me one more time? I forgot to ask about some more concerns I had and want to ask about this too. Seeing as you were the one that saw what happened."

Things just took a turn for the worse. Not only is he asking me to go with him to the place that is watching what I do with him, but he is also asking me to talk about the one thing Ken said not to talk about. How will I explain this to him?

"I can see how that might be uncomfortable for you, so you don't have to."

Sano has been through a lot and the last thing I'd want to happen is Mrs. Baker doing something to make his move harder.

"I guess that wouldn't be a problem. But uh, I want to ask Ken first. Between the both of us, he's known them longer, so he'd probably know if it'll be a good idea for you to mention anything about what I just said."

"Were you hesitant on telling me because he said not to?"

"What?"

"You didn't seem like you wanted to tell me. I'm wondering was it because he said not to say anything about this." He clarified.

Is it a Masidone thing that makes these guys able to read me so well?

"I didn't tell him about the car thing because he said not to worry about any of it. But since following people seems like something they like to do, I got worried anyway when I saw that car behind you."

"It may be nothing like you said, but with the idea being there, I would still like to see if I could find out why." I guess that's another way to look at it. She may not be doing anything now, but what if she does it later?

"Oh, I forgot there was something else." he said. I don't think I can handle anymore…

"I'll wait on it though. I've already asked too much. Thanks for answering what I wanted to know. I also need to tell my father this, but as you heard my aunt, we'll only be here a few more weeks. So, I need to let him know to prepare."

"I think have a question for you now." Sano raised his eyebrow a little surprised.

"Ken mentioned something about a summer vacation thing at the villa."

"Oh really? I didn't know they still did that."

"If you're moving back in, are you going to go to that?"

"I completely forgot about the villa trip. I guess he really does enjoy doing that every year. Are you supposed to be going with them?"

"I don't know. I haven't talked to my parents yet."

"Do you want to go?"

"I… Don't know." Going to the villa isn't the problem. Being there for a week with his parents and the annoying duo is the actual problem.

"I don't know either. It feels a bit too soon to go on a family vacation, but I'll decide when it gets closer to time," he said. I finally took a sip of my water to help wash down everything.

"I don't want to keep you longer than you have to be here. Plus, my aunt might get the wrong idea." The water sat heavily in my throat.

"Uh, guess this could be taken as a misunderstanding. Especially since I came by last week too."

"I was still really down when she told me you came to check on me. That kind of helped me feel a little better. I appreciated your concern even though I was distancing myself. I shouldn't be asking you over so much when you have Ken, but I enjoy our friendship and don't want to lose it." I could feel my face turning red. The way he speaks sounds different. I had been waiting so long to get him to like me. But is it really too late?

"Well, that's what friends are for. They check in on each other even if you haven't heard from them." I felt my eyes wondering not able to look at him. I noticed him shifting a bit. I glanced at him, and he was staring right at me. I watched him thinking he was going to say something, but he stayed silent.

"I um, should get going." That sounded as unsure as I felt. I took out my phone and saw it had only been an hour, but it felt like forever in this moment.

There were also the unanswered messages from Ken. I'm sure he knows where I am. He didn't say anything to me earlier, but since he knows I'm here, he wants to talk.

"If you need to get back to him, that fine." Sano said after watching me stare at my phone.

"Well, I don't need to, but I probably should get going." I slowly stood and picked up my book bag. Sano also stood and opened the door for me. He stood unusually close as I moved passed him and headed down the stairs.

"Are you leaving already?" The others were in the living room folding clothes on the couch when we came down.

"That was a short discussion. Do you have to go so soon, Misa? We can take a break, and I can make you all something if you'd like." His aunt seemed almost as sad to see me leave as the kids did, but part of me really wants to get back and see what Ken has to say about me being here.

"Sorry, but I have to get back." I told them as I made my way to the door.

"Will we get to see you again?" Cindy asked me. I didn't know what to say since I wasn't sure if I'd be back over before he leaves here.

"Of course you'll see her again," his aunt said, "Misa is always welcomed to stop by." His Aunt was nice, but I hope she isn't giving out promises I can't keep.

I let everything Sano said to me float around in my mind as I walked home. By the time I made it, I kept coming back to wondering about Mrs. Baker and how he knew of her from back then.

"I didn't think you'd come back so soon." Ken was sitting on the couch with papers laid out on the table when I came in.

"Are you actually doing homework here?"

"You said you needed help with the project in Mr. Hallens' class, so, as I was getting my project together, I thought I would have some ideas out for you to look through." I walked over to the table and saw information on events that happened in the time periods we had to choose from.

"When did you get all this?"

"I got some of it at the library and printed a few more things off here while you were out." He didn't look my way when he spoke. I didn't know what to say. I was expecting him to interrogate me on why I didn't tell him where I was. Not ready to help me with my work after I ignored him.

"I didn't know which periods you wanted to do, so I got something on all of them." He continued to speak without looking at me. I wasn't sure if he was upset or really just trying to help. Everything was so neatly laid out. He was reading one of the papers as I stood in confusion. I slowly started walking around the couch to sit down and left a bit of space between us.

"Do you think I'm going to bite?" he asked.

"I wouldn't be surprised if you did."

"So, it wouldn't be a problem if I bit you?"

"Yes! Yes, it would be a problem!" I told him. I was looking to him, but he still hasn't looked at me once. Was he avoiding eye contact? I don't think I've ever seen this much of his side profile while talking to him. His eye didn't drift over. He has them focused on the table and the papers he had spread across it.

"I'm getting the feeling you're waiting for me to bite you since you keep staring at me."

"That's not why I'm looking at you!" I said a little more flustered than I thought.

"So, why are you staring at me?" He asked, still not looking. Everything he's said has been so calm. He has to be thinking something.

"Well, you haven't exactly looked my way since I got home, so I was wondering if there was something wrong." He stared at his paper for another second then put it down and turned to me.

"Is this what you want?" Ken put his complete focus on me and his dark eyes locked with mine. His gaze was calm, but strong. It was almost too much to handle.

"N-not exactly. I just couldn't tell if you were maybe upset or something."

"What would give you the idea that I was upset about something?"

"I don't know. You're usually questioning me when I come home late."

"Considering I saw Katie leaving with Eden after school, it was pretty obvious where you were. So, there wasn't much need to ask the question I knew the answer to."

"But you told me you always knew where I was, and you kept asking anyway."

"You're right, I did. But somehow, that game seems old now. But let's play one more time, shall we?" He held a finger up.

"You were distancing yourself from me today, you only told me you were going somewhere last minute through a text, and you didn't reply when I messaged you. So, where did you have to suddenly go today?" No matter how steady his voice was, it was no secret that he was upset.

"I wasn't distancing. I just didn't have anything to say."

"What about telling me where you were going?"

"I didn't think it was a requirement to have to report to you where I am throughout the day. But if you really want to know, yes, I was with Sano today. He needed to talk to me about something."

"Must have been some talk to be done in private like that."

"He wanted to know some things before moving back in the mansion." I told him.

"So… he asked you about the place I live?" I guess from his point of view it seemed as bad as he made it sound.

"I didn't tell him a lot since I didn't know a lot. He said he'll be moving in a few weeks, and since he saw everyone kind of knew me, he thought to ask me."

"Not much has really changed since he left. What did he want to know?"

"Well, the place hadn't changed, but apparently some of the people did. He asked me did I know much about Mrs. Baker." Ken seemed to be surprised by that.

"What did you tell him about her?"

"Not much since I still don't really know her. Just what you've told me."

"That you shouldn't get close to her?"

"Something like that. And he wants to go back over there again to talk to her and Mr. Masidone."

"Already?"

"Yeah. I uh, accidentally mentioned that she might be watching him because I saw a car following them."

"A car? You never told me about a car following them."

"That's because I'm not certain. It just looked like it. I told him it might be nothing, but he wants to talk to them anyway." Ken leaned back on the couch with a new look of distress.

"I don't know anything about a car. And going to them first about it is not the right idea."

"I said I'd talk to you about it to see if it was a good idea or not."

"Oh, you were still thinking about me even though you were with him?"

"It's not like that. He just wanted to talk, what's wrong with that? You were giggling and talking to Jenny forever on the phone, so why can't I talk to him?" I finally brought up.

"I guess you've made your point." He said and paused, "but I think it's my turn to talk to Sano now if he's intending on speaking on that matter."

"You're going to talk with him about it?"

"It's only best since we'll be the ones living together again. I think I know the place a bit better. So, me telling him about her and any changes that may have occurred during his time away may give him a bit more insight on what to expect." Ken stared out into space.

"And about Jenny," he started, "she was only asking about the gathering. This will be their first year going and my father had begun the arrangements and planning, so she wants to know what to expect going in to it." He explained. If this is their first time going, then of course she's going to want to hang around Ken the whole time. How is she going to act if I tag along in this trip?

"You still have some time before you decide if you want to go or not. I know those two aren't your favorite people to be around, but it's a pretty sizable place. I already told her you might be going and not to expect to be around me a lot which mean you shouldn't have too many interactions with her there either." He tried assuring me that I wouldn't have to be with those two for an entire week. I didn't get to look at the place when I went the first time, so I don't know what's all there.

"I'll talk to my parents about it."

"That answer sounds more promising than yesterday." I could hear the tone in his voice relax.

If he told her they wouldn't be around each other during the stay, that might help the situation. I guess I can't keep letting Jenny get to me. Even if I don't like her, they're still friends, so she'll be around. Just like with me and Sano. If Sano decided not to go, then going to the gathering wouldn't be as bad, but if he does, things might get complicated.

"I will never get tired of the four of us getting together like this! It really feels like the old days only with Misaky with us now." I couldn't be the only one watching the sun getting darker and Jayson getting brighter absorbing all of its rays. We were about halfway to the mansion, and he was still feeling overjoyed being with Ken, Sano, and I. I could only keep my focus out the window watching the world move at sixty-five miles per hour.

I'm still unsure how I ended up here. Why it seems I'm making as many trips to the mansion as Ken. Ken talked to Sano and managed to get him to stay away from the topic of Mrs. Baker and being spied on, so that should've meant I could have missed this trip back home. But somehow, I'm still here. I have absolutely nothing to do here or anything I need to say to Mr. Masidone.

I'm sure he'll have a lot to say to me. I always feel so uneasy when he comes around. Maybe it's because he's the CEO of a worldwide company. Or maybe because he's Ken's father who only keeps me around because Ken wanted me here. If it wasn't for Ken, I would've been locked up in their dungeon a long time ago.

It was a nice sunny Saturday morning as we got closer to what could be waiting for us at the Masidone mansion. Sano was sitting next to me in the back seat as Ken was in the passenger seat. Jayson tried making conversation, but I did my best to stay hidden. I haven't gotten used to being with the two of them at the same time yet. And I don't think the two of them have gotten back to being how they used to either, so it isn't just awkward for me.

"Misaky, to my understanding, you're not really doing anything with the heads today right?" Jayson spoke to me, pulling me into the conversations.

"Not really."

"Super. So then while these boys handle their business, I was thinking we could have a little fun like we did before and make a special Saturday lunch for everyone."

"Uh, sure. I don't mind." Between the three of them, Jayson really is the easiest to be around. Maybe because I don't have to choose between him and the others. Although, despite his upbeat behavior, I couldn't help but feel like something was off with him. I think Ken has noticed too. I can see his reflection in the rear-view mirror, and it looks like he wants to say something but hasn't.

"Alright, we're pulling in!" I looked out and saw the large shiny grey estate coming closer as it was our destination. As always, it looks as neat and polished as can be. The bushes were trimmed. There wasn't a speck of dirt or loose gravel anywhere on the sidewalk. Even the water fountains look as if they've been washed since last week. Everything looks so new and untouchable like art in a museum.

Jayson parked the car in the driveway, and we all got out. I got a look at Ken who was looking around as if this was his first time being here.

"Uh, Jay, any reason everything got spit shined out here?" He seemed to have noticed too.

"Papa Masy is expecting someone. So of course, you know him. He likes to make everything look as presentable as he can." Jayson answered both our questions.

We made it to the big M, which also seems to sparkle more than usual, and opened the door. The maid show wasn't quite ready to greet this guest that's coming, but they were all here straightening up what isn't already shining.

"Welcome back Mr. Davis and young Masidone." One of them turned to us.

"Anna, could you let Papa Masy know that our lovely little Sano is here to see him now."

"Not a problem." She answered and went toward his office.

"If you're ready, you can follow her." Jayson told him. Sano hasn't said a lot yet. He only nodded and headed to his office.

"Mama Baker should be there too." He yelled after him. I just hope that doesn't give him a reason to try and slip in a certain question he should avoid.

"So, Kenny-kens, it's up to you. You can cook with us, or you can wait and experience what our skills can do."

"As both options sound nice, I don't think my father will be happy about me moving around with this still on my leg." He pointed to the thigh brace.

"Oh right, right. Papa Masy doesn't want you up and running too much just yet. And with his eyes out here, I'll call you down when we're done on walkie." Jayson must have been referring to the room of maids. There's at least five of them. All of them must report everything to Mr. Masidone. "I'll be waiting to taste Mimi's skills." He gave me his little grin before walking off.

"The two of you are just so cute. Shall we get to it then?" Jayson said.

"Yeah sure." Sano is talking with the parents. Ken can't move around much here. And I'm going to cook. The world always changes when I cross over to Masidone Land.

"This will be Sano's first meal here in years, so I want to make something I remember he always enjoyed when I cooked for them." Jayson said when we got to the kitchen.

"What's that?"

"Quesadillas!" He pulled out some tortillas and put them on the counter.

"He used to love these to death. It's simple yet always makes the taste buds sing." He started moving around gathering the things he's going to use. I don't remember Sano ever making them when I would go to his house. But he might've been making what the kids like more than what he would want. Jayson hasn't forgotten anything about Sano. I wonder if Ken remembers he likes these too.

"Misaky?" Jayson called me out of thought.

"Yeah?"

"You don't mind that we make something a little special for Sano, do you? I'm sure you and Ken are always making something spectacular together."

"Um, well, not exactly."

"Oh no. Don't tell me there's something going on between you two again?"

"I'm not sure if it's really something, but I've just been unsure lately."

"What's gotten you so unsure?"

"I--don't know." I can't exactly tell him I've been thinking a lot about Sano since he disappeared. And even more so now that he's back and has been wanting to talk to me a lot more.

Ken hasn't done anything, but with Jenny getting closer to him, it also makes me anxious.

"You know," Jayson started talking, "when I was around your age, I was also dating someone, and I loved them to pieces. But then, this other friend that I used to like suddenly started to like me. And you know what I did?" I looked to Jayson hoping he didn't actually want me to respond.

"I told them I was already in love, and you missed your chance." He walked over to the cabinet proud of what he did and grabbed a pan.

"I later thought about it. I wondered if it was really okay to dismiss them so easily. I was so wrapped up in the relationship I was already in and didn't think to consider their feelings. And you want to know what happened? The one I thought was the love of my life left, and I was so hurt. So very hurt. I didn't talk to anyways for days." He stopped at the island next to me and took a breather. It's so hard to imagine Jayson not bright and sunny…

"A little while after that breakup, somehow, the other person got back in contact with me. We eventually started dating and they were all I thought they would be. But I was so afraid of being hurt again, I broke it off before it got serious." He went back over the refrigerator.

"The moral of what I'm trying to say Misaky, is that it's so hard to know what's right until it might be too late. So, the only thing I can really tell you when it comes to my little men, is do what you really want to do. You'll never know what the right answer may be, so just keep following your heart."

It must have been obvious why I wasn't sure to him. Sano was the one I liked first. Then Ken came along and somehow, I started to like him. Then Sano told me he liked me, and he's been getting closer lately. I'll either need to put some distance between him or put Ken in a really awkward spot.

"I think it's time we put our chef hats on and make our masterpieces!" He's using his happy rays to make me feel better.

I've never made quesadillas, so this will be another meal he's teaching me how to make. This will be the third time I've cooked with him, and each time I learn something new. It's no wonder Ken can do so much; Jayson seems to know a lot about everything.

We were almost done making enough for everyone when Jayson looked at the time on the stove. He stopped and stared at it for a while. I looked to see it was just after noon. We had been at the house for about an hour. The only thing that comes to mind is that Sano has been with Mr. Masidone and Mrs. Baker for a long time.

"Mr. Davis," One of the maids came into the kitchen, "President Masidone's guest has arrived, but he's still meeting with young, um, Sanders. So, she may be waiting around until he's free." I looked to Jayson who was still turned toward the stove.

"That's fine. Thanks for telling me, Julie." He replied without even looking.

"Not a problem." She said as she left. But I felt a big problem coming. Not only did she seem a little concerned, Jayson's tone was calm. A bit too calm. He was still turned toward the stove putting together the last quesadilla. I wanted to ask who this guess could be, but before I could, I heard everyone greeting someone.

"Oh, my stars! It's so great to be back!" I heard a loud energetic voice that reminded me of Jayson. I looked back at him to make sure it wasn't him. He was standing still in the same spot not moving at all.

"What a minute! Do I smell… Jaycee's tacos?" The person headed this way as she was led by her nose. Seconds later, I saw the kitchen door open.

"Jaycee bear! It's so good to see you!" If I didn't know any better, I'd say the happy young woman that just walked in was some kind of actress or model. She had long electric blue ombre hair, with blue eye makeup to match. She had perfect features. Even her simple solid black top and ripped skinny jeans fit her small yet curved figure. Who was she?

"I should've known I'd find you in the kitchen. How's it been?" She asked standing directly behind him. Jayson didn't turn around right away. It almost looked as if he took a large inhale before slowly turning to greet her.

"Amy, so good to see you again." I don't think either of them saw me being taken aback by Jayson's greeting. It wasn't his usual upbeat response. He had a really forced smile and spoke through his teeth.

"Look at you!" Amy didn't seem to notice as she looked him over, throwing her arms up to give him a hug. She wrapped her arms in a tight embrace around him while he lightly patted her back as if she would break if he tried any harder.

"I leave you alone for a few years and you get this killer look. What have you been doing?"

"Oh, you know, the usual. They say beauty comes with age." Jayson said still with a forced smile.

"And it does! I look like old fruit compared to you."

"Old fruit? I'd say the catch of the day. I love the hair."

"You know, I got it done especially for you since I know how you feel about electric colors. Although my roots are a bit too dark." She said pulling on her hair.

"Your roots are as fine as you are. So, Papa Masy invited you here today?" Jayson asked her.

"I had a shoot in this area and thought I'd give him a ringy ding and said he wanted me over. Who would pass the offer of Mr. Masy and seeing my Jaycee." She gave a million-dollar smile as she clung to him while Jayson's looked more like a counterfeit bill.

I wasn't sure what was going on, but the Amy woman seems very fond of Jayson. I'm not sure if I can say the same for him. I may not know him well, but I can say without a doubt he was uncomfortable with her. I noticed he grabbed something in his back pocket. It looked like the walkie he uses. He pressed a button on it several times and pushed it back in his pock.

"Well, Papa Masy is talking with someone right now, so he may be a minute," Jayson said.

"That's totally fine. Gives me more time to chat with you. Oh, but who might this be?" She finally noticed I was in there with them and walked over to me. I was organizing everything on the far end of the island counter.

"Misaky, let me introduce to you, Amy David." Jayson introduced us.

"Misaky. Now is that a cute nickname he gave you or is it really your name. Either way, I love."

"Uh, it's a nickname. My actual name is Misa."

"Misa. I love it. It's unique and fresh." She said with a hand gesture. I didn't think it was possible, nor did I want to believe it, but she seems more dazzling than Jayson.

"I just can't get over how I've gone so long without being here. Reminds me of the old days, doesn't it?" She went back to talking to Jayson.

"Mmhmm it sure does bring back memories." He walked the last plate over to me.

"Alright Misaky, everything is done and looks too good to even eat." He tried sounding like his usual self, but I can tell it was still forced.

"I got tired of waiting, is everything finished?" I was a bit surprised not expecting to hear Ken suddenly come in the kitchen.

"Oh my! Little Kenny!" Amy changed her focus from Jayson to Ken. She ran up to him and gave him a tight hug like she did Jayson, except Ken gave more of an attempt to hug back, but didn't look any more thrilled about the happy woman than Jayson did.

"My goodness have you grown. You guys got secret handsome creams or something? Look at you!" She examined Ken from head to toe.

"Oh, what's this now?" She noticed the brace on his leg.

"I got in a bit of an accident a few weeks ago."

"A few weeks ago, and you're still wrapped up? It must have been awful. But regardless, you still look great. I'm getting waves of nostalgia. We're just missing one more. Little Kenny and…"

"If you're looking for Sano, he's with our father." Ken told her.

"Yes! Is that who he's with? I should be able to go see him then, right?" "I'm pretty sure it wouldn't be a problem." Ken told her.

"Super! I'll be back in a hottie!" She sang as she bounced out the kitchen. I couldn't help but feel confused after the show that just went on. Something about Amy seemed off.

"You alright Jay?" Ken went over to Jayson, "did you know she was coming over?"

"I wasn't completely sure, but I had heard she was in the area. I know how much Papa Masy likes her, so I had a feeling that it might've been her coming."

"You should've told me; I would've stayed around if that was the case."

"No, no. I didn't want to worry you." Jayson said, finally looking a little more relaxed. The more they talked, the more I got confused.

"Ah, um, that was Amy." Ken said looking to me, seeing the confusion on my face.

"Yeah, I got that much." I told him.

"And she's Jay's ex-fiancé."

"Ex fiancé?" I tried to hide my shock, but it was too much to keep in.

"Remember that little story I told you Misaky? Ironically, that's who I was talking about." He pointed to the door Amy just walked out of.

"You told her about Amy?"

"Kind of. I didn't go into detail about what happened."

"Something happened?" I asked. Ken looked to Jayson, who nodded his head.

"Um, well, long story short, she left him a week after he proposed and moved to LA. She waited six months before she contacted him again and pretty much said she forgot about the proposal." Ken explained it short and sweet. Jayson just stood there. I looked between both of them waiting for him to say that it was a joke. Neither of them spoke, so I had to assume that actually happened. I couldn't believe it. Ken looked at Jayson again and back to me.

"She went to Broadway and also does modeling as well." Ken continued. I was right about her being both an actress and a model.

"She still feels strongly for Jay, but as for him..." Ken stopped. He didn't have to say more as the rest was obvious. I didn't know what to say. From the way she acted, she didn't seem like she'd do anything like that.

"This happened some years ago. But till this day I can't comfortably be around her without thinking back to that time. That's why I called Kenny-Kens down." Jayson said.

"It's been a while since you used our 'SOS' code. I thought it was a mistake, but something said check anyway." Ken said. Jayson was doing some secret code when he pulled out his walkie.

"What could he want to see her for?" Ken asked.

"I'm not sure. He's been so hush, hush about things lately, I'm having a hard time keeping up with what he's doing." They must be referring to Mr. Masidone. Why would he want to see Jayson's ex-fiancé that broke his heart like that?

"Well, I don't know what's going on with Papa Masy and her, but I do know we have this amazing lunch that Misaky and I prepared, and I think we should enjoy it while it's still warm and ready to melt in your mouth." Jayson changed the subject.

"You made quesadillas?" Ken came over by me and looked at the plates of food. We made both chicken and steak quesadillas giving each plate some of both.

"Yeah. It was kind of a special thing for our lovely little Sano since he hasn't eaten here since he left."

"I see. Sounds like a nice thing you *both* thought of." Ken said lingering on his words.

"Now Kenny-kens, before you get the wrong idea, this was completely my doing. It was my plan from the beginning since I know it's been hard for him the past few weeks."

"Who said I had misinterpreted your statement? I think that was a nice thing to do."

"Kenny-kens, you can't pull that one on me. I'll have you know, Misaky wanted to make something for you." That caught my attention more than it should have. Did Jayson just lie to Ken?

"Did she now?" Ken looked to me, and I avoided eye contact.

"Come now, don't be shy." Jayson said and gave me a little wink. I don't know what he's up to. Maybe he's going back to how I said I was unsure about Ken. Is this his way of trying to get things moving?

"Here." I said grabbing a plate that was off to the side. Ken just looked at it.

"Did you make this one?" he asked.

"Is that a problem?"

"Not at all." He picked up a piece and bit into it. "Ooh, Mimi's cooking has improved so much."

"Of course it has. She's been cooking with I, the best Jayson in this kitchen. I told you his taste buds would melt like butter having your specially made meal."

"Does this mean I can start expecting more homemade dishes at your place?"

"Uh, I don't know about that yet."

"Don't worry. A few more lessons with me and she'll be chef Misaky. Has such a nice ring to it, doesn't it?" Jayson said.

"Has Sano really been with our father and Jocelyn this whole time?" Ken asked.

"I haven't seen him since he went so, I assume so." Just as Jayson said, we heard someone talking outside.

"I really think it would look good on you if you grew it out. You have such good features." Amy came back into the kitchen talking with Sano.

"Jaycee, don't you think Sano would look great with highlights? Look at him. Sharp jaw line, easy on the eyes, which might I add are hazel! You don't see that too often. If he grew his hair a bit more, I think it would look really amazing on him."

"Thanks for the idea, but I think I'll stick with my dark brown. Plus, I don't intend to grow my hair any longer." Sano told her. She looked upset, but I could tell Sano really wasn't interested.

"Are you all done with Papa Masy?" Jayson asked.

"Yeah. Everything has been settled. I'll be moving back in a week after school ends."

"I can't wait to have you back around. If you need any help moving things around, let me know."

"Thanks, but my aunt has a van and plans to drive me here that day. I'll be staying in my old room, so I did want to go and have a look around to see what I could leave behind."

"Of course you can, but would you like to eat first? Misaky and I made an old favorite."

Jayson handed him a plate. He took it and looked at it. I couldn't tell if he like the meal choice or not.

"Ooh, Jaycee, did you make extra? I would love some too." Amy asked.

"Well, if you can give me a few minutes, I can whip one up for you."

"Oh yay, I want to watch you." I could see Jayson wanting to say something, but he just turned his head.

"I'll make her something really quick, you kids can go ahead and dine." He went back over to the stove as Amy followed him closely. I was left standing between Ken and Sano. It couldn't get any more awkward.

"It's been a while since I last ate here or hand these." Sano said after starting on his food.

"You've been missing out on Jay's meals. But can't give him all the credit this time since Mimi here helped him."

"Well, I'll admit that it's getting easier the more I do it." I said.

"You've improved a lot since the first time you tried helping me." Sano added. I stole a glance at Ken then back down to my plate.

"I think the final test should be for you to make a special kind of meal on your own." Ken took another bite while grinning. How did I go from almost burning down the school kitchen lab to making special meals without a fire department nearby? I thought to protest that idea when Ken suddenly turned to Sano.

"Did you talk a lot with Jocelyn?" He spoke a little low.

"Yeah. She likes to talk, so that wasn't a problem."

"I've been stuck in that a few times. You didn't mention any thing, did you?"

"No, I didn't. But from what she said, I didn't have to."

"What did she say?"

"Not really what she said, just how she said it. It was obvious from the number of questions and input on the conversation she had. She seems like an interesting one to be around." I'm pretty sure that last statement was sarcasm.

"Since you'll be around her a lot more when you move in, it's best to understand that now."

"I'm already starting to understand. But there's still something I haven't put together yet."

"What's that?" Ken asked. I really wanted to know too, but Sano couldn't finish before the kitchen doors opened again.

"Looks like we got a full house today." Mr. Masidone came in along with Mrs. Baker. "Miss Macky, here with us again I see."

"It's always a pleasure to see you Misa dear." Mrs. Baker added.

"With everyone in here like this, it feels like old times." Mr. Masidone said.

"We're just missing the girls, and it could really be a full house. Where are they anyway?" Mrs. Baker asked.

"The little kittens are in their room. Papa Masy, Mama Baker, please help yourself if you're looking for something to cure your lunch cravings." Jayson turned to them.

"Oohh, you're here now!" Amy sang happily. "So, what is it that you have to ask me?"

"Since I was finishing up with my son, I didn't want to mention it in that moment. As we all are aware, Miss Macky, I would assume you are as well, the annual Masidone vacation is coming up next month."

"I remember that! Are you going to ask me to go?" I saw her light blue eyes glowing.

"It's not simply asking you to go, but a journalist for a magazine contacted me and wanted to take shots of the villa and surrounding area. They also mentioned something about using one of their models in it, and I mentioned I knew the perfect model for the job."

"So, you want me to model for this magazine?" Amy asked completely in shock.

"If you're interested, I can have them contact your agent to discuss it further—"

"I'm totally interested!" Amy cut him off.

"That's perfect. I figured a friend of the family would be better to use than someone else. For your convince, you're welcome to stay with us during that time. Unless you have prior engagements to take care of."

"Not at all! After this shoot I have next weekend, I'm free for a month so this will be perfect! Thank you for the chance to work at the one and only Masidone villa! I can't tell you how much I love that place."

"I expect us all to have a nice time this year. Both my boys are here, the lovely Amy will be joining us, and Jennifer and Jenny will be experiencing their first stay there. It will be a nice break I'm sure we all could use." The more Mr. Masidone spoke, the more I wondered if he knew about Amy and Jayson, and also the fact that Sano still isn't back in the 'family' groove. Will this really be a break or the ultimate disaster?

"Miss Macky, since you're appearing more frequently and haven't decided against your decision with Ken, I personally invite you along with us all to our lovely home by the lake." My food almost got stuck in my throat. Did he just ask me to in front of everyone?

"Thank you for inviting me, but I haven't had the chance to talk with my parents about it yet."

"Of course. I wouldn't keep you around that long without their consent first. Please let us know if you will be joining us or not after you've discussed it with them."

"I will." I don't think I'll ever get used to Mr. Masidone.

"I'm sure she'll love to go. After all, she won't be seeing Kenneth as often anymore. Aren't you moving out of her house in a couple weeks?" Mrs. Baker asked. The food is now sitting heavy in my stomach. I could tell it also took Ken also grew still.

I hadn't really thought about what would happen once school ended. He isn't staying at my house forever when he was only there to get to know me since he lives so far. It's only dawning on me now that there's only a couple weeks of school left. So that means only a couple weeks left with Ken.

"Oh, Misa dear, as much as I'm sure you enjoy his company, he can't stay. It was agreed that he would only finish out school. Have you two not discussed this matter?" Mrs. Baker noticed my expression.

"A lot of things came up along with preparing for finals, so the subject hasn't had the chance to surface." Ken told her. I wasn't sure what to say so I'm glad he did.

"Well, Miss Macky, I hope you two can find the time to discuss it. It just hasn't been the same around here without Ken. I am looking forward to his return." Mr. Masidone said. I looked to him then at Ken who was looking to me. I just looked down at my food, losing my appetite.

"Oh, that's right. Sano, you wanted to look around your room before we head back, right?" Jayson suddenly brought up. "If you guys are done, we can go ahead and do that so we can get you back. You probably have a million things to do between now and when you move in. As much as we all enjoy going down memory lane, my job isn't done until everyone is where they're supposed to be."

"Oh Jaycee, you've always been such a parent to them." Amy said admiringly.

"What can I say. I've looked after them for so long it's only habit." He said. Jayson must have sensed the storm that was forming and turned on his Jayson magic to stop it.

"If that was a part of the plan, then please don't let us keep you. I look forward to spending more time with you Sano dear." Mrs. Baker said. Part of me felt like she knew Jayson was trying to change the subject, but she didn't say anything else. I can tell there's a lot of understood unspoken things said around here. My only hope is that they can't also read minds.

This is my second time being in this room that Sano and Ken apparently shared growing up.

Having another look around really confirms that Ken's room upstairs is one side of this room, and Sano's room at his house is the other side. I wonder did they intend to do it like that?

"We really didn't take much out of here aside some of Kenny Kens' things," Jayson said. "The main thing I'd say you'd need to bring would be clothes. Even if you didn't shoot up over the years, I'm sure you wouldn't want those old things."

"But don't throw them out! If there's one thing I've learned, it is that you can do a lot with your old clothes." Amy added. Jayson tried getting her to go with Mr. Masidone to talk about everything, but she wanted to 'play parent' with him and insisted on following us around.

"I probably won't need as much as I thought then. Which will work out since I didn't want to haul a lot over here."

"We have everything you need and more. Don't you ever forget that." Jayson reminded him.

I wasn't sure, but I think I saw Sano smile a little. But it left as soon as it came.

"Am I the only one that can hear something? Is there someone else around here?" Amy suddenly asked.

"Well, the little kittens are in their room next door. I'm surprised they haven't come out by now." Jayson answered. I was surprised too. Usually, Jenny is causing a scene, or Jennifer is trying to start a fight…

"Can I meet them? I want to make sure I know everyone around her."

"Um, well, they sometime like to keep to themselves. So, they might be busy right now." Jayson told her.

"Really? I'll have to meet them another time then. What are their names? I don't remember 'little kittens' coming up from before." Amy asked.

"They're sisters. Jenny and Jennifer."

"Jenny and Jennifer? Hmm. Different. Are they twins? I once knew someone who had twins who named them the same, but different spelling."

"Jennifer is the older sister. Jenny is a year younger," Jayson explained.

"Oh, I see. So, who do they belong to? They couldn't be Mr. Masy's kids, right? I thought it was just the two of them." She pointed to Ken and Sano.

"Oh no. That's kind of tricky to answer as I'm not entirely sure. Papa Masy only said they belong to a friend of the family and we're temporarily watching after them due to some unfortunate circumstances." Jayson said.

"I don't fully understand, but if that's what you say Jaycee, then I'll go with it." She smiled wide. If I hadn't heard about what she did, I would say she had the perfect model look with her smile so big and bright. But if what happened really happened, then Jayson was right to give another forced closed lip half smile in return.

Sano continued looking through the room. He opened the dressers which still had everything in it. His desk even had old papers and notebooks. He must not have taken much when he left before. I kept watching him as he made his way over and sat on his bed.

"If I remember correctly, you two and your silly antics may or may not have caused the headboard to come lose a bit. If you want, we can have something new ordered for you and ready when you get here." Jayson told him. Sano moved around on the bed a bit.

"This should be fine. Don't think I'll notice it much."

"That's good. Then everything has been arranged and is settled for you to come back here?"

"Yeah. We've already started packing things at my house. My aunt knows and I've talked to our father about everything. So, it's all settled."

"And you're sure you're okay with coming back here?" Jayson asked a bit more seriously. Sano must not have been expecting that question since he got a little quiet.

"I feel like the subject is a bit taboo, but I really want to know will you be alright being here? I know you don't have a lot of options right now, but if there's anything I can do, I'm sure we can work something out with Papa Masy."

Jayson has been with them since they were kids. He probably knows more about what happened than they do. He understands the pain Sano felt and went through at the time, so wanting to know if he can come back here and act like everything is alright really will actually be alright.

Sano looked away into the distance, taking his eyes over the boxes of clothes and items. Looking at the TV he used to watch. The dresser he used to go through for clothes. Back over to the desk that holds old notebooks and pens. This is probably a tough question for him. Before he decided to move in, he really seemed like he didn't want to come here. It's been years since he's been in the mansion. He'll have to get used to this lifestyle all over again.

"I'll see what happens." Sano started, "I'm older now, and can kind of grasp a better idea of the situation. I won't make such a rash decision again. If things don't work out, then I'll address the issue before up and taking another leave." He finally spoke after closing the top desk drawer.

"You know we all only want what's best for you. You're going to be eighteen this year, so you can start making some of your own decisions, but once you're back in here, papa Masy won't make it easy for you to leave again. He was at an all-time low back when you left us. I had never seen him like that before and it was just heartbreaking. Kenny-kens knows this too." I took a glance towards Ken who was looking down with his arms folded. The mood is turning serious. Even Amy is staying quiet.

"I appreciate your concern, Jay. A lot has been on the mind so I couldn't tell you anything for certain. As of now, I'll just stick to this being the plan." He didn't say anything more. The room stayed quiet as he turned back to the dresser by his bed. He opened the drawer again and this time a pen rolled out from the back. He stared at the pen lying there. I looked over at it and saw it was the same engraved pen he had in his holder at home. I looked back to Sano as he stayed silent looking into the drawer.

"I think I'm done here for today." He suddenly said and pushed the drawer close again. "I'll have more to move around here then I will at home."

"Would you like us to have anything taken out?" Jayson asked him.

"No. I want to sort through everything myself."

"Alrighty then. We can get ready to head out if we're all done here."

"Do you really have to leave so soon? How long will you be gone?" Amy asked.

"We have a long ride back to take Misaky and Sano home. I'll probably be gone most of the day."

"Oh no, so long? I wanted to spend more time with you. But I have to meet with my agent in a few." She looked down with a sad face, or at least as sad as she could while still looking as if she were posing for a picture.

"Maybe that's for the best." Jayson told her.

"For the best? What do you mean?" Amy asked. Jayson looked away and took a deep inhale.

"You all don't mind I take a few minutes with Amy, do you?" He turned to us and asked.

"Not at all." Both Sano and Ken answered at the same time. They looked at each other and then back at Jayson. He seemed to have finally exhaled with a smile to them. He turned back to Amy and had her walk out with him.

"How many times will this make?" Sano said looking at the door.

"I lost count after the tenth talk." Ken answered.

"I guess not much has changed over the years."

"The only thing that changes is her persistence. Part of me believes it's her trying to make up for what's she's done, but nothing will change the damage that was dealt." Ken said, looking out the door.

"You'd think she'd move on by now. Jay doesn't seem to have a change of heart about her." Sano said.

"Well, since a certain someone is having her come around, it's going to be hard on him for a while." By a certain someone, Ken must mean Mr. Masidone.

"He's trying his hardest to bring us together all of a sudden even though we're not all on the same page." Ken looked over at me.

"With her going along with us to the villa, Jay won't exactly be able to keep her away. And since those two will also be coming along for the first time," he made a gesture to the room next door, "it's going to be pretty interesting this year. But if Mimi decides to go, maybe it won't all be bad." Ken tried to smile to lighten the mood. Even he knows this could be a disaster.

"Speaking of the trip," Ken continued, "Jay already brought up the issue, but just out of curiosity, would you want to sit out on this get together?"

"I really can't answer these long-term questions. There's nothing I can say for certain at this moment. Right now, I'm just focusing on the move, and making sure the kids will be alright. Once everything is arranged and settled, I'll see if I'm interested." He wasn't angry or sounded as if he was bothered by the house and the memories it holds. This whole time, he's just been concerned on the move itself and the kids.

"So, you really are moving back in here I see." We all looked to the door and saw Jennifer standing there. Her coming in wasn't the problem. This afternoon avocado face mask and pink long shirt with black shimmering leggings is the part that's bothering me. Are they really doing facials right now in the afternoon?

"Jens, I said not to go." I heard another voice from the next room coming this way. Jenny made her appearance dressed in the same fashion. The only difference between the two is that Jenny doesn't have the permanent 'I'm up to no good' look. She actually seemed a lot calmer than she normally is.

"Sorry. I guess I'll just have to get used to someone being in this room now. See you around then neighbor." She didn't move her face much with the mask, but it was obvious she wasn't really excited to have a neighbor. She turned around and went back to her room. Jenny was still standing there, and she was looking at me. Then she turned to Ken.

"Before we leave tonight, I want to see you." She said to him and left. Ken seemed confused as he watched her walk away.

"Just to confirm, those two were around before, right?" Sano asked.

"Yeah. Not much though. Although, it was really only Jenny at the time. Jennifer didn't really speak to me or show up until sometime after you left."

"Did she not like you?"

"I don't know if it was that. They both were really quiet back then. Then suddenly I heard from Jenny more and more and eventually Jennifer started coming around. Shortly after that, I was told they were moving in. That's when they really got social. To say the least." Ken told him. The room went silent again as Sano just sat there slightly shaking his head.

"Is there something you're wondering about?"

"Kind of." Sano said. He didn't say anything more than that. I was looking at him when he looked over at me.

"Sorry, you got dragged along with us."

"It's nothing. I don't mind coming here." That took me by surprise.

"I want to say this now before we keep moving forward." Sano got both of our attention. I felt the room getting smaller and the air getting thinner as I waited to hear what he had to say.

"Misa has been a big help and a great friend to me. Since I'll be around more, I don't want you to think I'm coming between you and feel uncomfortable with me around." Me and Ken kind of looked at him. It's like he was admitting defeat and handing me over. Even after calling Ken his competition, he goes ahead and loses?

"You've always been around, so all will be fine." Ken spoke up. I had a feeling Sano wanted me to reply, but such a statement made me unsure of what to say.

"Why don't we go wait by the front for Jay. They'll probably be done talking soon." Ken suggested. We didn't argue the thought, and all walked out of the room and headed back to the entrance. Ken came next to me and walked with me as Sano was on the other side of him.

I guess I'm the only one really unsure of everything that's happening. Maybe that's because I'm the only outsider. Even Jenny and Jennifer are closer in this even if Ken wants nothing to do with them. But if I plan to stay around, I'll need to get comfortable with this Masidone life. And to do that, I'll need to come around more. So, with school ending soon, and Ken moving back home, I'll have to figure out a plan, and fast.

13

"Oh good, you haven't left yet." Mr. Masidone came from his office and saw us by the table in the entrance room. "I want you to give this to your parents when you speak with them about staying with us." He handed me a manila folder.

"It's just information about the property, what's around it, a sample itinerary of what we may do, and some other minor details. In case they wonder about where you'll be." He explained. Leave it to a businessman to be prepared for everything.

"As for you Sano, I just transferred over everything and put in for what we discussed. If Fay has anything else she needs, tell her to give me a call anytime."

"Oh, can I give you a call too?" Amy joked as she appeared with Jayson coming from the living room. Nothing seemed different about her attitude, so I wonder how that talk went.

"Of course, you're free to call anytime. But since you're here Amy, would tomorrow be a good time to arrange your shoot with your agent?" Mr. Masidone asked.

"I'm meeting with her in a little bit. If you're free, we can set this up today. I'm so excited, I want this in my planner now!"

"I don't have anything to do until later tonight, so that'll be fine. I'll go call the publisher. I'll see you both again." He turned to me and Sano before taking off.

"Sorry about the wait. Are we ready to head out?" Jayson asked.

"It was nice meeting you Misaky. I hope to see you again. I'll be going for now." Amy wasn't sad or seemed upset as she walked to open the door while reaching in her bag and put on some sun glasses. She pushed back her hair and walked out. I could have sworn I was watching her walk down a runway.

"Oh Kenny-kens, whatever you do, don't ever get to know someone like Amy." Jayson said almost a plea after she was gone.

"I think I already have." Ken looked back down the hallway.

"Oh no. Those two are nothing like her. Yet at least. I still see a chance with them, but with her, that was gone before it even came. Let's get going you two." Jayson sighed as he walked over to the door.

"I'll see you Monday." Ken stood close to me as he spoke low. I watched him as it looked like he wanted to kiss me, but he didn't.

"See you Monday." I simply told him. And then we finally parted.

The drive home was accompanied by the blue skies, bright mid-afternoon sunlight, a light breeze, and enough awkward tension to almost make me want to jump out the car to be relived of it all. It was clear Jayson still had Amy to think about, and whatever it was Sano and Mr. Masidone talked about. That just leaves my triangle of troubles with him and Ken.

The air was getting lighter as I saw my house coming closer. I got dropped off first. Just as we pulled up to the curb, I noticed a car parking close behind us. I looked and saw it was my mom's car. Then I saw both my parents getting out. I wanted to hide as crawling out of Jayson's car would surely raise suspicion, but they were already looking over at the unusually expensive car parked in front of our house.

"Misa?" I heard my mom ask after seeing me. I heard the driver's door open as both Jayson and I got out of the car.

"Good afternoon, Mama and Papa Macky." Jayson wasted no time in greeting them.

"Good afternoon. And who might we be having the pleasure of speaking with?" My dad asked.

"I think we've met before. Was it Jayson?" My mom said looking at him.

"That's right. So good to see you again. And nice to finally meet you too Papa Macky. I was just bringing your wonderful daughter home from a quick visit to ours. I'm the one that brings Kenny-Kens back and forth here and basically anywhere else he wants to go. I hope it wasn't a problem, but the kids here had something they needed to discuss with the head of the house this morning." I saw my mom and dad glance in the car to see Sano.

"I trust Misa's in good hands," my mom said, "but I thought we talked about this leaving as you want."

"Oh, please don't be upset with her. We really do enjoy her company. In fact, Misaky do you have the papers Papa Masy gave you?" I had the envelope in my hand and slowly handed it over to him.

"When you all get settled in, please have a look at this. It's about our villa out west. Every year, we have a Masidone get away in the summer for a week, and since Misaky is becoming like family, we have invited her to come along with us. We would love for you all to talk it over and consider her stay with us in early July. I know this might seem sudden, so please take your time looking this over and just let us know your decision." He handed over the folder to my mom, which my dad reached out and grabbed in her place.

"A villa you say? My cocoa is really moving up in the world I see. But a week seems like a pretty long time out somewhere we're unfamiliar with."

"That's completely understandable. Everything you need to know about the villa is there in this information packet. You'll feel as if you've already been there after looking through it." My dad looked at Jayson and back to the folder. I can already tell my dad's unspoken decision. My mom on the other hand isn't as easy to read.

"This certainly is sudden, but we'll definitely be looking this over." She said.

"I'm so happy to hear that. I have to take my leave, but if you have any questions or anything, Misaky here knows I'm just a ring away."

"We'll keep that in mind. It was nice meeting you Jayson." My dad said.

"Oh, the pleasure was all mine. Misaky, I'll see you around." We said our goodbyes as I watched him go back to the car. He looked back saying something to Sano before taking off.

"Well MI-SA-KY, why don't we go in and you tell us about this." My dad gestured to the door. I had completely forgotten they were coming home today. My dad isn't as open about this arrangement as my mom, so showing up like this must really have him upset right now. Talking about going away with the Masidones for a week is almost pointless.

We went in and I did my best to explain the situation and about the villa. My mom is the only one open to everything, so telling her is easy. Looking at my dad's expression on the other hand…

"Alright. We did our part. We've listened to it and looked it over. How long before we give them the big N-O.?"

"Mark…" My mom hissed.

"What? You said I could have the say in the next decision we had to make, and with my luck, this so happened to be the next one." My dad slowly explained.

"And I've told you many times already that I'm over this arrangement with Misa and Ken. I think it'll be a nice experience for her. To think they like her enough to take her on their vacation. Do you know how great that is? Our daughter made that big of an impression on one of the most successful and wealthiest family in the country."

"Wealthy or not, she's still out of range for a week with two other guys I still don't know. At least with Ken here, I would be able to watch them if I wanted. I'm not entirely sure where this place is. Is it even real?" My dad picked up the page with the image of the villa.

"Misa just said she's been there before so yes, it's a real place Mark. I can't understand why you're so against this. Ken has been living here for months, and all they're asking for is a week. It is the summertime, so why not let her have a little fun in the sun with them?"

"That's exactly what I'm worried about. My little girl having too much 'fun in the sun' with some rich teenage boy. Who knows what they're capable of doing with all their resources. They're going to work together to do who knows what with my cocoa. Those boys and the one we just met." My dad put his arm around me like I might disappear.

"I think Jayson is a responsible and sweet young man. He's taken care of her so far, why would he put her in harm's way now?" Mom folded her arms waiting for a reply.

It's been a while since I've witnessed my parents' heated debates. Katie said it's because I'm the only child, my dad is so protective of me. But when it comes to my mom and her want for me to stay involved with this family, it's almost impossible to get her to stop pushing us…

"Unless you have a valid reason that should prevent us from letting her go, I say she can go." My mom has given her final say and stared at my dad.

"A week at some house I've never been to. I'm already not okay with her going back and forth to this mansion of theirs. But if you truly feel this is alright, then I have nothing else I can say." My dad let me go and has finally given in.

"However," he continued, "there are no if ands or buts about it, I will be taking her there to see this place for myself and to personally 'thank' that boss of ours for the 'opportunity.' I think it's about time we met on terms outside of work anyway." The idea of my dad and Mr. Masidone meeting like this does not sound good. It's obvious my dad is reaching his quiet limit on this matter and isn't just going to sit on the sidelines anymore.

"Are you really sure you want to be the one to take me?" I asked.

"I have no problem missing some work to take my own daughter to my boss's house." He said sarcastically. "I just want to make sure though cocoa, do you really want to go with them? You haven't said much on actually wanting to go, so there's really no point in this whole debate if you yourself aren't interested."

"Of course she's interested. Isn't that right Misa? Don't you want to go spend some time with Ken and his lovely family?"

"Um…"

"Um? That's it, she's not going." My dad took my hesitation the wrong way.

"No, that's not it!"

"Then why are you hesitating?"

"I do want to go. I just haven't had enough time yet to think on it myself."

"Take all the time you want. You heard him, you don't have to give in right away. Make sure this is something you want to do." My dad is trying his hardest to get me against going. I told myself I wanted to go. I was unsure because of who was going to be there, and mostly being around both Ken and Sano. But with what he said earlier, should I even have to worry?

"Before we continue," my mom started, "I think we need to address another issue related to the summer. Ken will be moving out after school is done, meaning you'll be here quite often on your own again. We let you stay with Katie because you want to stay at your school, but not only do I not want to impose on them again, I was recommended for a new department in another branch."

"What do you mean another branch? Like in another city?"

"Yes. I was suddenly called in and was recommended for another position. Basically, I'm being offered a promotion. But this new branch location is out of state."

"Really? Where is it? Are you going to take it?" I asked.

"I don't know. Your father and I are still figuring out what would be best. He would still be here. I was the only one offered the new position, and I don't want to leave you two here."

"It's a huge opportunity for her, but that will mean we'd all have to move if she accepts." My dad added.

They've been working at this company for two years. My mom is being offered a promotion, and I know she wants to take it. But if she does, we'll have to move. Meaning I'd have to transfer and leave everyone here. I want to be happy for her, but this sudden weight on my chest at the thought of leaving the place I've been all my life isn't sitting well.

"They said I could take my time in responding, but I don't want to wait too long, and they assume I'm not interested." I could see the trouble on my mom's face. "I know you don't want to leave your life here Misa. But chances like this don't come often. I had no idea they were even considering me."

"We also have to consider my transfer. If I can't go, then I'd either have to stay, or quit." My dad's words came out heavy. He may not like what's going on with me and Ken, but he does like where he's at. And he would never want to live without my mom. They're both at odds about this whole thing. I'm just now hearing about it, so I don't know what to really do or say.

"We just thought it would be good to let you know." My mom stood next to my dad, "In the meantime, until we figure this out, we need to know what to do with you." she said to me.

"After your mother went and talked to Mr. Masidone, we arranged for me to have a little time off when school is out for you. That way, someone is here to make sure Ken can leave all right and you won't be here on your own. But that'll be for just about a week. After that. We thought to have you come stay with us. That is, until we figure out what we'll do with this promotion news." My dad explained.

"You want me to move in with you this summer?" I asked. I usually stay with Katie, but now they want me with them.

"We know how close you and Katie are, and her parents always welcome you like their own. But I think it's time we stopped leaving you with them, and just have you come stay with us. It's summer, so you won't have to worry about going to and from school or being left alone." My mother told me.

I hadn't thought much on what was going to happen now that summer is almost here.

Everything seems like it's happening at once now that we're reaching this point. Ken will move out. Sano will move with him. I'm offered the chance to vacation with the Masidones at the villa, and now my mom is telling me that I'm going to stay with her, and possibly move all together.

"Think of it this way," my mom started again, "we'll be a lot closer to Ken's home. It'll be easier for you two to meet." She saw the confusion on my face and tried to comfort me. I hope my mom didn't hear how hard my heart thumped in my chest. Ken was leaving and going home, but if I'm with my parents at the apartment, then that huge distance between us will be gone.

I should have known that things were going to keep changing from the moment I told Mr. Masidone I liked Ken. Ken and I are supposed to be together. I agreed to that. I wasn't forced to. I wanted to. That's why the thought of moving away from him isn't sitting well with me. There were still things I wanted to know about him. Mysterious I still wanted to solve. I won't be able to solve them if I move away. Now that it's come to this, I really will have to just spend as much time as I can with him if I want to keep things moving with us instead of going in circles like everything else seems to be going.

14

"I told you with my help, this project would be no problem." Ken laid down my trifold after looking it over. I've never gotten a project done so early before. Typically, I would just now be looking at it. But with Ken offering his help, it's gotten done a lot sooner than I thought. And surprisingly, I think I did pretty good on it.

"I guess I owe you a thanks for your help." I told him.

"If only I didn't have to stop payments for my services." He said to himself. Even now after all this time, he still wants a reward for his deeds.

"Technically, I have rewarded you for a past request." I brought up.

"Oh? And what's that?"

"That one time you were helping me with math. As payment, you wanted me to agree to go out with you... well, it's a little late, but it's been fulfilled." I ran my hand across the folded poster board not wanting to look at him. I couldn't help but notice the amusement on his face from the corner of my eye.

"I suppose that has been fulfilled now. Didn't think you'd be the one to point that out."

"I couldn't help but think how working together like this reminded me of then." I told him. We were working at the kitchen table where I usually do my homework. Ken sat next to me while I put everything together on the board.

"I really have been around for a little while now. That time was right after we first went on a date together. You were still so cautious of me. And now here we are." He smiled. I couldn't help but wonder how much different it really was between then and now. It's only been a few months.

"Are you going to miss me when I'm gone?" He suddenly asked.

"What?"

"The last day of school is next Thursday. Meaning we have less than two weeks left before I move out." I knew we needed to talk about what was going to happen after school ended. But now that he's actually brought it up, I have this heavy feeling in my throat. I had to try to clear it before I spoke.

"How do you feel now that you're leaving soon?" I asked him instead.

"Hmm, it definitely will be boring not getting to see you every day. A little lonely too not knowing when the next time I would see you will be." The look in his eye tells me he's been thinking about this for a while.

"So, what about you?" He came back to me.

"Um, it'll definitely be boring around here now that I won't have to keep an eye out for a perv."

"Coming from you, I know that's compliment." Ken said.

"Take it as you wish."

"Will you be lonely knowing I'm not always around?" When he goes home over the weekend, I usually don't find it a problem. But knowing the next time he leaves will be for good, I can't shake the feeling that I will be kind of lonely.

"And if I did, what are you going to do about it?"

"So, Mimi will be lonely without me? What to do? I'll have to tell my father I'll be staying forever." He put an arm around me.

"I highly doubt he'll let that happen. From the sounds of it, they're really looking forward to having you back for more than two days a week."

"I get wanting me to go back, but there's really nothing I'm missing over there. The only time we have planned to really come together leaving all work and everything behind will be when we go to the villa. Which reminds me, Jay said he spoke with your parents when he dropped you off the other day. What did they say about you going?"

"My mom was fine with it, my dad on the other hand wasn't as fine. But he said he'll let me go so long as he is the one to take me there."

"Does that mean you'll go?" I could see this sort of hopeful look in his eye.

"I didn't tell them I wanted to yet."

"You don't want to go?"

"That's not it. I was just thinking about what could happen. Being there as the only one, you know, not in the family. And how the rest of the family kind of doesn't exactly seem to like me much."

"Jay and I like you." He reminded me. I looked at him letting him know that's not what I meant.

"Actually, my father has been warming up to you these days. I think since you brought Sano back around, he's changing his views on you."

So, the only reason he's starting to accept me is because I brought him back his son. Sano is only moving back in because he doesn't have any other options. Mr. Masidone wanted me to stay with Sano, but I chose to stay with Ken. Wouldn't that make him still against me since I didn't pick who he wanted me too?

"You shouldn't worry about it too much. We go there so we can relax and leave our worries behind for a little while. You going along won't make anything different." He tried making me feel better about it.

"Whether it's with my father or Jenny or Jennifer, we're all going to have a good time. You will be with me, so you have nothing to worry about." There was something about how he said it that made me wonder if that's really true. He said it himself that his dad had been trying to get them together, but they weren't all seeing eye to eye. He only seems to think this trip will be good if I go.

"If you decide not to go, it's going to be really hard to see you again. Once I go back, my father won't let me leave and go as I please since he really didn't want me to stay here this long to begin with."

"What if I were closer?"

"What do you mean if you were closer?" He was confused. I didn't want to say anything about the whole promotion thing, but she still wants me to move in with them over the summer.

"My parents don't want me here on my own this summer. So, they want me to move with them in the apartment."

"Really? When are you going?"

"Probably right after school is out. My dad will be here starting Thursday so he can make sure you can leave okay. Then once his vacation time is up, I'll be going back with him." Ken shook his head.

"So, we may not be too far from each other after all." He looked relieved.

"You seem to have been thinking about what was going to happen a lot." I said.

"Everyone I know that I keep a steady contact with is pretty close to me, so I was wondering how us being together with the distance was going to work."

"Knowing you, I'm sure you were going to find a way for us to meet." I told him. He was worried about this little distance. I wonder how he'll react to me making this distance even further apart....

"Are you alright Mimi?" he suddenly asked.

"Why are you asking that?"

"You just seem a little different. You're not usually this... passive."

"What, you rather I yelled and go against everything you say?" I asked him.

"It's not so much I rather, it's just that's what I'm used to."

There was a tug in my chest. I know I'm not always straightforward like he is. He openly says what he feels so easily. I on the other hand have such a hard time doing that. He knows that, but still puts up with me and my unclear ways of responding to him. After hearing what my parents told me, I suddenly felt this want to stop these circles I'm taking myself in and do as Jayson said.

Ken has been going for what he wants this whole time, so I should act like I am too.

Ken watched me as I searched for a response. I noticed a new look of curiosity growing on his face as I felt the hand he still had on my shoulder move. He wrapped his arm tighter around me as he brought us closer. I watched him as he brought his face to mine.

The only real surprising thing about Ken suddenly kissing me was the fact that I wasn't surprised, and I didn't try to resist.

"You really have me wondering what's going through that head of yours." He said after pulling away.

"A lot of things," I admitted, "but one thing on my mind is asking for the exact date of the vacation. So, I can tell my dad when to drop me off."

15

"So, this is it huh?" My best friend looked at me with hurt in her tone.

"Katie, you sound as if you're the one that's moving back home."

"You might as well be going with Ken since you're leaving me." Ever since I told her about the summer plans, she's been super down seeing as today is the last day of school, and one of the last days we can see each other since I'm going with my parents.

"We have all the time now until I leave. Then I'll ask to come back to visit. This isn't forever you know."

"Did you forget you accidentally spilled about the promotion, and you might be moving away altogether? It could be forever for all I know."

Katie has Eden, friends, and family, but the thought of me moving away isn't sitting well with her. Since first grade, we've always been together. Not to mention I lived with her too. Me going away this summer will be the longest we'll go without hanging out. And if I actually move away, that'll make it nearly impossible for us to see each other.

"Nothing is confirmed. I told you, my dad may not be able to transfer with her. So, if my dad can't go, she probably won't do it. I don't want to worry about it too much right now since nothing is set in stone." I told her.

"You're right. Let's focus on the now. How are you holding up knowing Ken will be out tomorrow?" She changed the subject.

"Considering he's kept a countdown and has been reminding me every day that, 'our time together is ending,' I can't help but feel it'll be kind of bittersweet." I said, putting it mildly.

"Come on, don't act like you're not sad. I don't know what happened between you two, but you seem closer. Have you finally settled your doubts?"

"Well, I figured with the way things were going, I should keep my focusing on him and try not thinking about…" I trailed off as who I was talking about walked passed at the end of the hallway heading out the main exit.

Strangely enough, I hadn't heard much from Sano since we came back from the mansion.

"I've been wanting to ask him is everything alright since he seems to be distracted these days, but haven't been able to since I've been with Ken more. Plus, even if I asked, I'd just get the usual 'everything is alright' response."

"Just give him time. I'm sure he'll tell you when he's feeling up to it."

"He'll be leaving town in a week. Today is the last day of school. Not many more chances to talk."

"You're still thinking about him?" Katie and I turned from my locker and saw Jennifer walking up.

"Look, it's the last day of the school year. I'm all for going out with a bang if that's what you want." Katie wasted no time approaching her.

"Anyway, what do you want?" I stepped in front of Katie. She's already upset about me leaving. The last thing she wants to deal with is Jennifer.

"I told Ken that I'd leave you two alone. But if you keep giving me reasons to believe you're still not serious about him, I will not continue to stay quiet."

"Don't you think it's a little late for that?" Katie spoke from behind me.

"Please, It's only the beginning. Ken is moving back. Meaning you two won't be with each other as often anymore." She turned her head slightly then back to me.

"Just know this isn't the end. See you at the Villa." The subtle threat turned to a sweet smile as she waved then walked away.

"It's my last chance Misa, just let—"

"She's gone Katie." I grabbed hold of her arm as she tried to go after her.

"Did I miss something?" I heard Ken walking over.

"Nothing at all," Katie's attitude suddenly changed looking at Ken. "You know, since I probably won't be seeing you again, I figure it's about that time I said thanks for sticking with Misa. Who knew after my slapping you all those years ago would lead us to where we are today. I'm going to go ahead and go. See you this weekend Misa." Just like Jennifer, her anger faded as she smiled sweetly and waved, then walked away.

"So, I'm going to ask again… did I miss something?" Ken asked after an awkward silence.

"Don't mind her. She's not too thrilled about me leaving this summer."

"I can imagine," he said. "Speaking of imagining, did I just see Jennifer over here talking to you?"

"Well, she was over here, but she didn't really say much." I told him. He doesn't need to know about the little threat she just made. I mean, with it being the last time I'll see her this much, how much more harm can she do to me?

"I suppose I shouldn't worry since she can't do much to you now that you won't be seeing her as often." He said what I was thinking as we headed home for the last time.

"The school I was attending before I came here was a little smaller and everyone was a lot less open with each other. To say the least." He had to be referring to the amount of gossip and rumors everyone enjoyed spreading.

"Since I've been here the past three years, it's really nothing new." I told him.

"Both Jennifer and I came from the same school. She seemed to fit right in here. But she has changed schools a lot more than I have. So, it was no problem making more friends and going along with the flow for her."

"That makes a lot of sense." I said. That explains how it was so easy for her to get everyone on her side. If she's changed schools a lot before, then that would mean she knows more than the preppy schoolgirl life she probably came from.

"As for me, it was kind of refreshing being in a new setting. Since everyone was more reserved at my school, it was kind of boring at times."

"Didn't you go to a private school?"

"No, it was public. Why did you think that?" He asked.

"Jennifer once said Jenny went to a private school which is why she didn't want to come here. I figured you all were at the same place."

"Jenny wanted to go to a better school, so she tested into the one she's at now on her own."

Another reason Mr. Masidone would prefer her over me. She wanted to get a better education. And here I am just barely passing my classes. And that was after I had Ken do some intense finals studying with me. Even though he was the reason I lost focus in the first place making my grades get so low…

"As much as I'd like to stay here, I'll be going back to my old school in the fall." Ken said. I don't know why hearing that made me feel this sort of anxiousness. Ken was only here for the last semester. Next school year, he'll be going back to his other school.

I can already see the beginning of my senior year. Everyone asking what happened to him and if we're still together. Which makes me wonder if we will be now that he'll be back home and I'll be here… that is, if I'm still here.

I still haven't told him about the possibility of a move. Part of me doesn't want to take that risk of seeing his reaction to me being the one to leave. I kept my head low until I realized we were almost home. I saw my dad's car parked outside the house. He was already here.

"There's something about your dad that kind of reminds me of mine, which is why I sort of understand the feeling you might get when you see him." Ken told me. Was that his way of saying he doesn't feel comfortable around my dad? Because that's exactly how I feel around Mr. Masidone.

When we made it to the front door, I opened it a little slower than normal as if I were trying to sneak in with someone I shouldn't be with. And from my dad's point of view, I was.

I didn't hear anything. I looked back behind me to see if my dad was still in the car, which he wasn't. The house seemed a bit too quiet for someone to be here.

"Dad?" I called out. We were waiting to hear something, but was only met with silence.

"Maybe he's sleep?" Ken thought. I can't imagine he would be asleep already when he had to have just gotten here. But I also wouldn't be surprised if he was. Ken and I looked to each other and must have thought the same thing. We both went upstairs to avoid my dad's possible attack.

Ken went to his room, and I stopped just outside of it. I saw his suitcase on his bed with his clothes neatly folded in it. He still has some stuff to pack away, but the room I once saw covered with clothes and papers were all gone. He sat his book bag down by the dresser and turned to me.

"It's my last night in this room and you're still afraid to come in?" He said with that cheeky smile of his. With my dad somewhere in the area, I was especially cautious of going in. I watched as he turned back to the closest removing the last remaining clothes that were hanging up.

"Sure am going to miss waking up here and catching Mimi in her 'comfortable' state." He said as he began folding the shirt he had in his hand.

"It's the last night you'll be here, and you're still sounding like a pervert." I said as I walked in and grabbed the shirt from his hand and placed it in his suitcase.

"Packing is easier with help." I straighten out the shirt to try and make it look as neat as the rest. I didn't turn to look, but I could tell he was staring at me. I kept my focus on the suitcase wondering if it was Jayson that taught him to pack like this.

"Looks like someone is in a hurry to get me out." He joked.

"I just thought I'd help since you're leaving first thing in the morning. I can always leave if you prefer to do things on your own." I said walking away.

"It's my last night here," he stated again, "and you want to spend the rest the day in your room?" I stopped just before I reached his door.

"If Mimi wants to help, I still have those things on the dresser I need to pack away." I turned to look at his dresser and saw different bottles of hair gels, body sprays, and colognes. It was no wonder he always looked and smelled nice. He had all this stuff he used every day.

"That notebook can just go in my book bag." He said pointing to the thick black notebook at the edge of the dresser. I picked that up first since I wasn't exactly sure where he wanted the other stuff. I bent down to unzip his bag when something fell out of his notebook. It slid over by his bed behind him. Ken had already moved back to the closet not noticing it. I went to grab what fell and slowly picked it up as I realized what it was.

"Something wrong?" His words faded as he turned and saw me looking at the pictures of us when we went to the photo booth at the mall.

"You kept this in your notebook?" I asked.

"What can I say? I wanted to keep it somewhere I knew I wouldn't misplace it." He said. I had almost forgotten we even took pictures that time we went to the mall. I put mine on my dresser somewhere not really thinking about them since I was still upset about Jenny.

I looked at the different frames of us smiling and laughing. I didn't want to take the pictures, but after being forced and tickled against my will, we took these. Looking at them again, they really didn't turn out too bad.

"I think we should have some after shots." He looked at the photos in my hand.

"What do you mean after shots?"

"Well, these were before us being together, right? I think it's only right to have a picture now that we are." I watched him as he pulled out his phone from his pocket.

"You're serious, aren't you?" I asked him. That answer was obvious by the huge grin that grew on his face.

"Come on, I need to have something for a memory of you when I leave."

"You make it sound like you won't see me again."

"I may not until the Villa. That's over a month from now. It's so long, I don't know if I'll make it." He put his hand to his chest as if it'll kill him without seeing me. Although, I didn't think about the time from now until then. This will be the longest I'll go without him being around.

The longest we've gone without seeing each other was a week when he was resting his injury. His leg brace is gone and he's walking around as if he had never gotten hurt. This time, he's not going home for rest. He's going home for good.

"Fine," I gave in.

"Really?" He asked, not believing me. I didn't want to repeat myself, so I put the photo down and stood next to him and fixed my hair a bit.

"If you want a stupid picture, then hurry. You still have a lot of packing to do."

I watched Ken open his front camera and extended his arm out in front of us, showing us on the face of his phone. He was the only one that seemed prepared for this.

"I can always arrange to get you to smile like last time."

"If you tickle me, I swear, I'll leave." I said. I could see him on his phone looking at me. Then I saw my expression change as he kissed me on the check and pressed the camera button.

"You didn't say anything about a kiss." He said as if he found some loophole. I don't know if it was because he was leaving or what, but he seemed to be getting full of himself. Next thing I know, I felt his hand move behind me, and began his assault on my side.

"Ken, I said don't!" I felt dejavu from the first time he did this. The laughs were out, and I couldn't stop them. I could see he was still snapping photos as I continued to lose my composure. I tried to move away from him, but he had a good hold on me.

"Are you still going to leave?" He asked from behind me. I turned to look at him.

"You're getting awfully bold, aren't you?" I said half angry and flustered.

"I could say the same for you," he replied, "Your behavior around me has changed. You don't seem to run away from me and your guard isn't up as much. Not saying I mind, it's just nice to know you aren't resisting as much anymore. I can't help but want to see how much you're willing to do. And to my surprise, you're talking a lot more than I thought."

"Well, that's because…" I looked down searching for the right words. He saw my change in behavior and had been testing it the whole time. Ken still had a hold of me from behind. He couldn't really see my face so he couldn't see my embarrassment.

"If I'm your girlfriend… then I shouldn't be running away so much, right?" There was a bit of silence. I looked around trying to find a way out of this awkward moment when I heard the floor creek. Both of us looked over and saw my dad leaning against the doorway.

"Your mother would be proud of this moment. If only it were her seeing it and not me." He said as he watched his only daughter being back hugged by her boyfriend in his house.

I don't know what happened first. Ken's hands moving from around me, or me stepping away from him as if he shocked me.

"Nice to see you again, Mr. Macky." Ken put on his best face greeting my dad. My dad still stood in the doorway staring at us as if he didn't say anything.

"Looks like we're still packing away everything. Although, I don't think my Cocoa will fit in that little suitcase." My dad said.

"Dad, please." I put my hand over my face hiding the embarrassment that comes with him.

"Don't worry, I have a bigger suitcase that's a lot more padded and safer for her travel." Ken tried to joke with him. I couldn't help but look away. If my mom were here, she probably would have found it a bit funny, but seeing as my dad has yet to even crack a smile, the joke went completely over his head. I think Ken noticed that, but he still managed to keep a straight face.

"I don't think we've had the chance to really sit and talk. The last time I was here, you seemed busy with your schoolwork. Why don't we take a little time before you go? Sounds like my Cocoa and your family have gotten quite acquainted, I think we should as well."

"Dad, he still has to finish his packing. He leaves in the morning." I tried to tell him. Mr. Masidone is a business owner, incredibly wealthy, and very intimidating. My dad isn't a business owner, incredibly wealthy, or as intimidating. However, when he's not happy about something, I think being in the Masidone dungeon might be easier to handle.

"I don't have that much I need to pack away. I'd be happy to sit and talk." Ken said. He told me my dad kind of makes him uncomfortable, but looking at him now as he spoke to him with confidence and no hesitation at all, you would think he actually liked him and didn't have any problems.

"I like your attitude son. Shall we then?" My dad stood straight and gestured back down the hallway. I saw Ken glance in my direction quickly before walking toward the door.

"Cocoa, you can chat with us too. There's nothing I plan to say to him that I wouldn't say to you, so you don't have to hide. I promise, no stories of you when we went to the fair and you started panicking and shouting for me when you thought you were lost, but I was right behind you the whole time."

"Dad, no…" If my dad could do anything well, it was embarrassing me. I kept my hand over my face as I walked out with them. We went downstairs and he sat on the chair while Ken and I took to the couch. Without realizing, I sat just a bit far away leaving this awkward gap.

"This looks a little different than how I saw you just a minute ago. Come on, let me get a good look at you two together." My dad used his hands, motioning us closer. It felt like a set up. But if I wanted this to be over, I have to do as he says so he'll move on. I awkwardly moved a little to my left closer to Ken. He watched as I shuffled over to him.

"I'm not going to bite." Ken said jokingly.

"Yeah Cocoa. No need to be all shy now. I'm sure he wouldn't dare do such a thing." My dad said each word carefully, almost challenging Ken to try. Maybe he senses Ken's true nature, or just a parent thing. Either way, I moved to where there was still an inch or two of space between us as I pressed my back against the couch with hands between my legs, trying not to make any contact with him.

"Much better." my dad said. "Why don't we start from the beginning. How was your day today? Last day of school, so saying goodbye to everyone must have been pretty tough."

"Seeing as I'll be returning to my old school after summer, it was a little hard leaving today." Ken told him.

"I bet it was. But I'm sure you must be egger to go back to your regular life before coming here."

"I wouldn't put it that way, I enjoyed my stay here changing up my regular routine."

"You mean you don't mind the average joe's lifestyle? I've heard Cocoa has been to your mansion. I can't imagine anyone choosing this over the luxury life." My dad said.

"Most people wouldn't be able to. But I wouldn't consider myself most people either." He told my dad. That was probably the understatement of the year. But my dad didn't need to know that. He just shook his head amused.

"You might not be as bad as I thought. You seem different than that other one Cocoa seemed to be interested in."

"Dad!" I sat up straight.

"What? He doesn't know? I figured you all seemed to know each other since everyone was here that time—"

"I am aware." Ken stated. I looked to him. I wasn't sure if my dad caught it, but I heard the slightest bit of jealousy in his tone. I haven't mentioned Sano at all recently, so him coming up like this probably isn't what he wanted to hear.

"I was your age once, so I know the feeling you must have. I had wondered why she kept you around if she was looking elsewhere, but seeing you both today, I see why. The look in my Cocoa's eye is different now." He said with a hint of sadness like he was losing me. I didn't mind being lost in that moment if it meant getting out of this situation. I can't believe he brought up Sano, of all people.

"I guess my little girl has grown up getting all serious with boys. And now that it's come to this, it must be hard for you to want to leave her here."

"Since I've been around Misa for the past few months, it'll be a little hard to leave tomorrow." Ken admitted.

"How about you, Cocoa? He says it'll be hard to go. Will it be hard to watch him leave?" Both my dad and Ken looked to me. He's actually putting me on the spot like this. I didn't face either of them as I answered, "Maybe."

"Maybe? Don't be all shy. You can tell me how you feel. You never did like to say goodbye. Like the time-"

"Yes, okay, it will be hard to see him leave tomorrow." I couldn't handle another flashback story. It wasn't a lie, but I didn't want to have to say it. I couldn't handle the pressure and just looked down, putting my hands back on my legs.

"To be young like you both again. I'll be away from my wife for the next few days, so I know the feeling of separation. You two will see each other again. That stay at your summer home is coming up, right?" My dad asked Ken.

"Yes, in a month. I want to thank you for allowing her to come with us. It'll be a nice get away everyone could use."

"I'm sure it will be. She'll need to enjoy it all she can since we'll be leaving too by the end of the summer."

"What do you mean we'll be leaving?" I sat up straight again.

"Don't tell me you forgot about your mother's promotion. She decided to take it. We'll be packing our bags and moving by the end of next month."

I really tried making a happy ending. I tried to close this chapter with Ken on a good note. I was even starting to come to a point where I thought this could work out. Even if Ken and I were a little far, the long distance wouldn't stop anything. But since my dad told us that this long distance was going to be even longer, it changed everything.

"Misaky, I'm going to miss picking up and dropping Kenny-kens off here." Jayson seemed the saddest that Ken was moving out.

"I will not say goodbye because I know we will see each other more. You know if you're ever bored or just want to get out, you just say the word and I'll be over in a hottie. Our time together will not end here."

The summer wind was gently blowing as I stood by Jayson's car after helping Ken take his things. Jayson was sad, but he still glowed as the wind blew his hair, and the morning sun peaked through some clouds bouncing off his sunglasses, making him shine even more, almost hard to look at him.

"I'll be sure to keep that in mind." I told him.

"This is it." Ken walked over to us. I wasn't around when he first moved in, so I didn't realize how much he actually had. He put his last small bag in the trunk and came to stand with us.

"I'm not sure who's leaving, me or her." Ken said looking at the sad Jayson.

"Kenny-kens, don't act like you're not a little upset leaving here." Jayson seemed almost shocked looking at the straight-faced Ken. Even since my dad said we would be moving, his whole attitude changed. I don't know if it was the fact that I was leaving, the fact that I didn't tell him, or maybe both, but hearing the news didn't make him happy.

"I'll be waiting in the car. You can take your time saying goodbye. Until next time Misaky."

Ken and I watched as Jayson walked to the driver's side of his car and got in.

"I don't know how often my father will let me go, but as Jay said, if you want to come by, you're always welcomed." I wasn't sure if he was trying to make sure Jayson couldn't hear, or my dad, who was in the living room watching us from the window, but he spoke in a low tone.

"I'll keep that in mind." I said again. Something about the way he was acting didn't really feel like the way I expected this goodbye to be.

"If Mimi wants, we can always take you with us." His voice was still low, but I finally saw a smile on his face.

"Yeah, like he'll let that happen." I threw my head toward the house. My dad just passed by the window again looking out to us.

"You have a good father. He really cares for you. I'm sure if the circumstances had been a little different when this all started, he wouldn't be as protective. But either way, your family is a lot different from mine. Don't lose that bond you all have."

Ken came from an entirely different world than I did. His brother left home, his parents divorced, and he doesn't like his stepmom, nor does he have a great relationship with his dad. The only person he seems to be really attached to is Jayson. I might be an only child, and my parents might not always be here, but they still care for me, and we have a lot more good moments than bad. Going back home will probably be tough in more than one way for him.

"Turn this way." Ken grabbed me by the shoulders, putting my back towards the car, and putting himself in front of me with his back to my house. I couldn't see my dad monitoring us from inside, so I was safe to assume he didn't see the soft forehead kiss Ken gave me.

"If not before, I'll see you at the Villa," he whispered. I didn't respond. Or more so, I couldn't respond. I only watched as we parted, and he stepped to grab the passenger door. Jayson waved to me one more time and I waved back. I watched as he pulled off, taking the most mysterious boy I've ever met away.

"You're just growing up too fast for me." My dad said as I walked into the house. I wasn't really in the mood to hear "my baby girl is leaving" talk. I just went and sat on the couch.

"I guess your mother hadn't called and told you the news yet. She told me she was but must not have gotten around to it."

"So, we're really moving?" I finally felt like I could ask now that Ken was gone.

"She spoke with the heads the other day. We thought it foolish to pass up such an opportunity. So, she went ahead and agreed to take the spot."

"But what about you? You said they didn't have any open positions for you to do a transfer."

"They said they would look into it. They really aren't doing any hiring over there at the moment, but they might accept transfers. I know this might be hard for you since your life is here, but think of this as the start of something new for your mother. This can open the door for more opportunities for all of us even."

"Yeah, I know…" I wasn't angry for the chance. I'm happy for my mom. I just never thought the chance for her to advance her career would be now and we have to leave the place where I've been my whole life.

"I know you're going to be a senior in the fall, and your friends are here, but just give it a little thought. All three of us will talk more about it after we go back to the apartment." He patted my shoulder and headed to his room.

I thought summer vacation was going to be a time for rest away from all that came this past semester. A time for me to be able to finally understand just how I got to be here without the extra worries of going to a new life from the slightly new life I just got. This will be my last summer as a high schooler, and possibly my last summer in this house.

The time felt endless. The summer days didn't seem to end. I keep wondering how long it has been since summer started. It felt like weeks, but according to Katie, it had only been a few days.

"Have you heard from Ken today?" She asked me as I grabbed my phone off the coffee table.

"Just got his, 'so boring without Mimi around,' message of the day." I told her. But what I didn't mention was the, "I want to see you," part of it.

He's only been gone a few days and he's already acting like we've been apart for a year.

"With you guys living so far apart now, you have to get used to that. Long distance relationships aren't easy." Katie said,

"He's told me he hasn't left home since getting back. His dad really doesn't want him gone."

"You would think after moving out for a few months, he wouldn't be as strict. Think there's something else behind it?" She thought.

"I'm sure if it were a real reason, he'd tell me."

"Maybe." She answered. "Isn't Sano supposed to be moving back in soon? Maybe his dad probably wants everyone in one place since he's coming home."

"I almost forgot he was going back. He said he was going within a week after school ended. So, he should be moving out any day now." I said.

"You still haven't been talking to him?"

"I just don't know what to say to him anymore." I told her.

"It's a bit surprising he hasn't said anything after all that 'nothing will change' talk you said he did."

"It's really hard for him since his mother is gone. He's been really strange ever since he got back. It might be better this way."

"I really wish I got to see this family of theirs. Must be something over there for him to leave out and then make such a big choice on whether he thought to go back or not." Katie wondered.

"I've been around them enough to know exactly why he wouldn't want to go back there." I've been to the Masidone side of the world enough times already to understand they're on a completely different level than someone like me. Sano really doesn't seem anything like them. And with this change in his behavior, I really wonder how well this will work out.

"Oh, looks like he's breaking his silence." Katie said as she pointed to my phone. The screen lit up showing a message from Sano. I didn't hesitate to open it to see what he said.

Guess it's time for me to go." Katie said hovering over me reading his, "are you doing anything right now," message. Of course that means he wants to ask me to come over. We haven't spoken in over a week, and this is the first thing I get from him?

"Why is he asking this so suddenly?" I was confused.

"I wish I had an answer. This time, I couldn't tell you why. You said he would be leaving soon, right? Maybe one last visit before he goes?" She shrugged. Even if that were the case, it still seems out of nowhere.

"Are you going to respond?" she asked as she saw me staring blankly at my phone.

"I want to. It's just… so sudden."

"Do you think you have to get permission from Ken first?"

"No, I'm not really worried about that. But he probably would feel better knowing that I'm over there," I said.

"You really have changed. The Misa I knew wouldn't be so cautious of what Ken would think. Then again, the Misa I knew wouldn't have agreed to be with a rich heir to a family business."

"The Katie I knew would also understand that people change." I said standing up. "You said it yourself, right? I have somewhere to go, so you should be going."

"Wow, new Misa is kind of scary. I like it. You better tell me what's going on." She said standing up too. "Don't be lowering my status in your life now that you got a couple guys around you. No matter what, I'm the one that'll always have your back."

"You already know that'll never happen." I reminded her. My best friend of ten years. No matter what, I'll never let a guy come between us. But that doesn't mean I can't go see them.

I thought I was done walking these streets. I thought the last time I went to Sano's house was it. He should be moving any day now. So, this really should be the last time. I just wonder what he has to say to ask to talk after a week. I turned on to his block and saw a van I haven't seen before parked outside of his house. I looked at his house and saw the front door was opened. I stopped by the van as I saw Sano walking out.

"Hey Misa." He greeted me like always. He was carrying a bag on his back as he came towards me.

"Are you leaving soon?" I asked.

"Yeah, in about an hour or so. My aunt rented this van since she wasn't sure if her car would make the drive out to the house." He said. That explained the van, but doesn't explain this last-minute visit.

"We had run into another little problem," Sano started, "with the new living arrangement with the kids and what they were planning to do with this house. My other aunt hasn't been contacting us and ignoring our calls the last two weeks, so it's been a little complicated around here."

"Is that why you seemed to be a little out of it the last week of school?" I asked.

"Was it that obvious?" He laughed a little, "Everything was going so well. Then that happened and that set us back. Sorry I hadn't been talking to you. I couldn't leave without clearing my conscious. I feel bad I keep calling you, but since school's out, I wouldn't see you otherwise."

"I'm actually moving soon too. So, I wasn't doing much since I have what I need packed already."

"You're moving?" He asked. I never got the chance to tell him about moving closer to the mansion.

"My parents don't want me here on my own this summer, so they want me with them at their apartment."

"I think that's for the best. Just like me, it wouldn't be good for us to be living on our own like this. When you first told me you often stayed on your own, I was a little worried. Then I remembered how worried you were when you first found out I was taking care of the kids on my own while my mom was in the hospital, so I was able to understand."

"Well, we both had our reasons, so it's not like it was by choice." I told him.

"Do you like the idea of being able to stay with your parents again?" He asked.

"It'll be different being with them in the city. But I do miss having my mom's cooking every day." I said. Then I realized what I said.

"Oh, sorry, I didn't mean-"

"It's okay." He smiled. "Jay and the cooks are a lot more skilled than I am, so I have that to look forward too." He said finding a positive side. I know he's trying to get over it, so I still try not to mention anything about his mom.

"My Aunt has been careful and hasn't said anything about my mom. Especially for the kids' sake. But I think acting like nothing happened isn't really helping anything either."

"Well, if you need to talk about anything, you can talk to me." I told him.

"You're always trying to help me." Sano said with a little laugh. "But since I'm moving back with Ken, I think it might be better if we didn't stay so close."

"What do you mean?" I asked him.

"We will always be friends. Just, things like me always asking to talk to you, I think it might be better if I didn't. I thought one last time wouldn't be so bad since this is my last day here. After today though, I should focus on readjusting to my old lifestyle."

Sano was still holding onto the bag he had, but it felt like I was carrying a new weight in my chest.

"I guess that would be better." I responded.

"Do you not like that idea?"

"That's not it." I told him. I wanted to say more, but I wasn't sure how to.

I had liked Sano for three years without ever being able to tell him. Now that I was able to get a little closer to him, it feels like we will be going back to the start. We might be friends, but somehow, this still feels like a breakup.

"Ken never did like me coming over here all the time, and I don't want to make anything complicated for you going back there, so you focusing on your move is for the best."

Ken hasn't messaged me back from earlier, but he's still coming to mind even though it's just Sano and I.

"If you come by to see him over the summer, we should all hang out." He suggested. He finally put the bag in the trunk of the van. He walked back over and looked to his house.

"I was only here the start of high school. I didn't think I was going to be moving out so soon. That time when we all met at that mall, we had never been there before and was just curious about it. When my mom was still considering places she wanted to move to, I told her about coming out here since it was all I knew outside of home." He looked over to me.

"I never actually expected to run into you again. I didn't realize it right away even though we went to the same school. How Ken managed to figure it out before I did makes me wonder if he really was crazy." He laughed to himself.

It was like he was just reminiscing about the past. Ken told me about how this all came to be. But it seems like I still don't know the whole story. And now that I've come this far, I don't think I want to hear the full story. It seems like they're able to do anything. And as long as I stay with Ken, I'll see just what that anything is.

There wasn't much left to say after that. I stayed long enough to see his aunt, but the kids were already with his other aunt. We said our goodbyes which wrapped up my chapter with Sano.

I was leaving tomorrow, so we're all starting our new chapters in our new worlds. I've only been to my parent's apartment a few times since they decided to get it. The Masidone mansion is on the outskirts of the city. I'll be staying close by the Masidone business building. My only hope at this point is that I don't run into Mr. Masidone on the streets somewhere.

The same road that Jayson usually takes us to go to the mansion is the road I'm taking to go to my new place of residency. Sure, I've visited here, but knowing I'm staying more than a couple nights makes it feel different.

"You doing alright cocoa?" My dad asked from the driver's seat. I didn't say much as we drove. I only stared out the window looking at the cars passing by.

Summer vacation started a week ago. I'm having a hard time feeling the summer vibe. Katie and I would normally be planning things to do. But I can't even plan when I could visit her since my mom and dad have used up all their vacation time.

"If you're still not too thrilled about everything, we can talk about it more when we get to your mother. She should be home by the time we get there."

"Haven't you already decided everything?" I said. My dad is trying to make it seem like I could help decide what they want to do. If they already agreed to do a transfer, there's no use in talking about something that has already been decided.

I've never made any big moves before. I wanted to finish out my high school days with my friends and people I knew. And with Ken being back home, it would make things as they are now harder for us. And Jenny would have the ultimate advantage since I wouldn't be around.

"Let's think about it this way. Next year, you'll be in college. So, you were going to be somewhere new anyway. This could just get you a little practice to a new environment." My dad said.

It never really hit me how soon I would be in college. The years have flown by, and I only ever just pass my classes. I'm sure Ken is going to college for business management or something. Katie wants to do either law or accounting, Eden plans to do engineering, and I haven't decided on anything yet.

"That reminds me," my dad went on again, "your mother knows some people in our apartment complex that has some kids your age, so we arranged to have a dinner so you can get to know someone here."

"You're putting me in another arranged meeting?" I looked at my dad.

"No, no, It's not like that at all." He laughed, "Your mother has a friend who has a daughter named Zoie. We've had them over a couple times before. Her mother said she could use some more friends, and I think the two of you would get along."

I never thought I'd hear the idea of being put in another arrangement to meet someone again. It must be a custom in this city to try to match everyone with someone. I've already gotten to know someone out here using this method, but it seems they want to try again with someone that wouldn't try to take his little girl from him.

There wasn't much else I could say, so I went back to looking out the window and noticed not the world changing into grassy land that would soon show a large mansion coming in the distance, but a regular lawn a guy was using a riding lawnmower to cut. We drove into the apartment complex and went to the red brick building towards the back. There was no winding road to the door or any letters that covered the main entrance.

I grabbed my things, and we headed in. No maid show as we walked through the door, but I could hear someone talking in a room to the right of us. We went up to the third floor to a door that did have a letter on it, but the regular 3C was not as large or fancy as the scripted M at the mansion.

"You're here." I heard my mom say as we walked in, "It's been a while since we were all home like this."

"Everything has been taken care of." My dad walked over to her, "The boy has left us and now we finally have our family the way it should be." He smiled and kissed her on the cheek, but my mom wasn't exactly smiling back.

"I didn't say anything. I did what you told me to do. I was there to make sure he left in one piece and to make sure Cocoa was able to comfortably prepare to come here."

"I'll believe you for now." My mom told him. "Speaking of Ken, are you two still keeping in touch? I know it'll be tough now that he's gone back home."

"We keep in touch." I told her. I didn't want to say more. Especially since my dad doesn't exactly like the Ken subject. I took out my phone and didn't see any notifications from him. He knew I was coming out here today, but I hadn't actually heard from him since his last message yesterday afternoon.

"I always did like Mr. Masidone, and he has really been helping us throughout everything. We really owe it to them." My mom said.

"Yeah, we owe it to him for causing the people at work to be suspicious of us for getting too close to the big boss." My dad said as he went to the kitchen. I watched him not knowing that was a thing.

"Don't mind him, he's just being a big baby about some stuff at work." She said a little loudly for him to hear. Word must have gotten out about them knowing Mr. Masidone. Of course, my mom wouldn't be bothered since everything has been going according to her plans.

"Once you get settled in, you should invite Ken over. You two should see each other as much as you can since you know, we'll be moving shortly after you come back from your vacation with them." I could almost see a pain in my mom's eye as she said that.

"So, you've already told Mr. Masidone about transferring?"

"I've only really been discussing things with management and the VP. Everything is being looked over right now to be finalized. They still want me to do a phone interview with the manager in the new department."

"I thought you didn't have to?" My dad came back into the living room with us.

"They called me back in saying they wanted to talk with me first, but the manager over there will be out of office until next week, so the interview will be when he gets back in."

"Why do they keep calling you in? You sure that guy knows what he's doing?"

"He's just trying to get everything straighten out. I was on the fence at first, so now that I've agreed, it's time to get it moving."

"So, then we are moving." It wasn't a question, but it came out as one.

"Once I get the okay, it seems so." She said. "I've already looked up apartments near the area. The lease on this one is ending soon, which works out. My sister and her husband said if we go through with this, they'll buy our house since they're looking. Everything is falling into place."

The look in her eyes tells me she seems really excited about this. Moving for them doesn't seem to be a problem. It all just seems so sudden for me, but for my mom to advance is what she's been wanting to do.

"Why don't you get set up in your room and I'll make lunch." she suggested. I took my bags to my little room that had already been set up from my other visits here. The walls were eggshell white, and the light brown carpet looked vacuumed. I looked out the window and saw a woman walking her dog along a full tree line trail. You never know who or what you will see when living in an apartment.

Not only is Mr. Masidone over a large company, but he's also the owner of some smaller places like this apartment building. Most of the people here work at his company since it's a short drive from here. This will be another world from my neighborhood back home. Still different from the other world that's not far from her either.

I stayed in my room for a while putting away my clothes when I heard the front door open.

"You're here sooner than planned. I thought we agreed tomorrow." I heard my mom say.

"She was home, and I was home, and I thought why not? Is she here?" I heard someone ask.

"She is in her room. She just got here not too long ago. I was just making lunch."

"Oh, I'm sorry if this is a bad time. I was just so eager to meet your daughter. We can go with tomorrow like we planned."

"It's not really a problem. We didn't have anything planned for the day anyway." My mom said. Whoever was at the door came here because they knew I was coming.

It must be the person my dad was talking about who has the daughter they wanted me to be friends with. I didn't think they'd move so fast with that since I just got here today. But this is my mom we are dealing with. She got a man like Mr. Masidone to agree to let his son live with us. She's capable of anything.

"Uh, hi, sorry, are you Misa?" I turned from my closet and saw a girl with short brown hair and glasses standing at my doorway. She had on shorts and a tank top and probably didn't plan to meet someone today either.

"Yeah, that's me." I answered her.

"Sorry for coming in so randomly. My mom's crazy and thought popping over the neighbor's house was fine. I'm Zoie. We live down the hall in 3A." She extended her hand to me. I took it noticing the fresh red nail polish on her nails.

"I just did my nails. They're not still wet, are they?" She asked.

"No, I was just thinking they look nice. I should probably do mine." I told her. I was never one for keeping up with the papering myself thing and probably should start doing that.

"My friend and I do our nails at least twice a week. We learned how to do it ourselves instead of paying to get them done. I can help you out if you ever want to get yours done." She said.

"That'd be great, thanks." I said putting up my last shirt.

"I feel bad. You just got here, and the adults already got you doing things like meeting random people." She tried to laugh. I didn't want to tell her this wasn't the first time I've been put in that situation. This is Ken's city. Everyone here probably knows him.

"It's okay. I guess my mom just wants me to have a friend out here since I'm new to the area."

"At least it's not school. Being the new kid in school sucks. Not knowing anyone can be hard. I don't know how my mom and your mom got to know each other though. A lot of people in this complex sort of keep to themselves. But your parents seem pretty cool." She told me.

"My mom loves meeting new people, and my dad just loves to embarrass me, so it's not surprising."

"Trust me, my parents are the same way except it's my mom I'm ashamed to be in public with. My dad just sort of became immune to it." She said.

"Is it just you and your parents?"

"No, I have a younger brother, but he and my dad went out somewhere on some father and son bonding thing. You can blame him for us being here today since he left my mom to be free to do what she wants." She said and walked over to my bed.

I didn't expect her to be an only child. The way she's comfortably able to speak to other people shows she's used to being around someone. And she's older, so she has to be the big sister and take charge.

"This is super cute. Where did you get these charms?" I looked and saw she was looking at my friendship bracelet that must have fallen out of my bag that was open on my bed.

"I got it from a store that closed down a long time ago." I walked over and looked at it. Then I picked it up and looked at the newly added panda charm.

"I'm sure I've seen that one at the mall recently. I really like pandas too."

"This one is new. Um, someone got it for me a little while ago."

"Is this someone a boyfriend?" she asked curiously. If this was a month ago, I could have said no. But things really have changed since then.

"Uh, yeah." I said.

"It must be hard being separated from him like this. He lives in your old town, right?"

"Uh, yeah, he does." I lied. I only just met this girl and I'm already lying to her. But this is Ken's city. Everyone probably knows the son of the Masidone company. They probably don't know he's off the market. All the girls in my school would watch him all day. I'm sure it's the same here.

"I was almost in a long-distance relationship before. But I knew I wouldn't have been able to handle it, so we broke it off. I hope it'll work out for you two though." She said. It would have been a long distance if it didn't move out here. Now, it is only a short distance. I looked at Zoie as she reached into her pocket and grabbed her phone.

"Oh no. I told her not to come." She said.

"Something wrong?" I asked her.

"It's my friend. We were supposed to hang out today, but I told her I couldn't since my mom wanted us to come over here today."

"Oh, I don't want to keep you from seeing your friend." I told her.

"It's no big deal. We see each other almost every day anyway. But she's already outside. You can come meet her if you want."

"I guess that's alright. I've got most of my stuff up anyway." I told her. Meeting Zoie was a lot easier than meeting Ken was. Another person shouldn't be so bad. I never thought I'd make friends with someone so quickly, and she doesn't seem to have a problem with it either. We left out and I quickly said hi to her mom as we made our way downstairs to see her friend.

"Lace!" Zoie shouted as she noticed someone getting out of a silver car. I expected her to be as flashy as her car was, but she got out and frantically started wiping something off her skinny jeans. She seemed more panicked than anything.

"Lacey, what's wrong?" Zoie rushed over to her. I followed behind to see what happened.

"I'm in big trouble that's what's wrong! Oh, hi, I'm not usually like this." She said as she noticed me.

"Misa, this is my friend Lacey. Lacey, this is Misa. She just moved in here." Zoie quickly introduced us. "So, what's going on?"

"I was on my way home from the store and got distracted and ran a red light right as the police was going by and they stopped me and gave me a ticket." Lacey flashed a yellow strip of paper.

"That's your second ticket this year. They're going to suspend your license if you keep this us. Not to mention your dad's going to kill you when he finds out."

"I know that's why I came here. I didn't know what to do. I even spilled my drink on me." She said wiping her pants again.

"You've been way too distracted these days. What were you even doing to run the light?"

"I was minding my own business when Chris calls and I wasn't ready to talk to him. I hadn't heard from him in two weeks and now he decides to say he's sorry. He's going to be really sorry now that I got a ticket because of him."

"I told you to block his number anyway. This is your fault you know. This just proves he's not the one. You should've gotten rid of him a year ago." Zoie said. She looked to me and back to Lacey.

"Sorry. You're new here, and here I am spilling my problems." Lacey said to me.

"That's okay. I understand." I said. Somehow, watching them reminds me of me and Katie…

"You really have a hard time letting go. But I don't want you to end up like last time. You have to move on and find someone else. After you tell your dad about that ticket. Otherwise, you won't be able to find someone else. Remember the first ticket and how your keys were taken for two weeks. You might not get them back if you lie again."

"I know. I just needed to calm my nerves before I went home. I'll figure out how to butter him up before I drop the ball on him. If he doesn't ground me and take my keys again, I'll be back, and we can all chill together. So, pretend like you didn't meet me today. You'll meet the real Lacey next time." She said and got back in her car. She waved again as she drove off.

"So that was my friend Lacey." Zoie said once everything calmed down. We watched her as she turned out of the complex.

"She's really cool and easy going. She's just getting out of a yearlong relationship and kind of taking it hard."

"That's too bad it didn't work out." I said.

"Not really. I never liked him anyway. She's way better off. The only thing is, it ended like her other one before him and I didn't want her to have to deal with that a second time."

Zoie seems like she really cares about Lacey. They must be really close. Lacey came and went just like that, but she also didn't seem too bad.

"We should head back in before my mom thinks I snuck out or something." Zoie said.

I was wondering what was going to happen when I got here and didn't know anyone. Since I met them and now sort of have plans to hang out again, my move won't be as boring as I thought.

18

The difference between staying with my parents at the apartment and staying on my own at home is that after spending all day by myself here, they actually come home in the evening. It's day three of my new life. I thought I'd have more to adjust to, but the only real difference is that I can only text Katie and not see her.

After meeting Zoie, we decided to meet up again today. She's coming to get me when Lacey gets here. She managed to avoid severe punishment with her ticket situation and her dad, so she wants us to celebrate by them showing me the mall. We only met the other day, but it feels like we've already known each other for longer. Katie thinks she's being replaced, but until we can arrange a day we can see each other, I need someone else to talk to in the meantime.

If there was someone else in the meantime that I thought would have tried to make plans, it would have been Ken. He still hasn't messaged me since the day before I came here. He's never gone this long without wanting to hear from me. I wonder if something happened for him not to be able to talk to me.

I put my phone down when I heard a knock at my door. I don't know who I expected that to be because my heart started pounding, but after seeing it was Zoie and Lacey, it slowed down, and I let them in.

"Is this a bad time?" Zoie asked seeing my worry.

"No, no, it's nothing. Are we going?"

"Yeah, if you're ready to have some fun." Lacey said. She was a lot calmer than the other day and was a lot more upbeat. They both had on makeup, loose tanks and ripped shorts. I had my hair in a ponytail, a plain shirt, and skinny jeans on. It really felt obvious that I wasn't from the area seeing the difference in how we look.

"You're definitely going to see that shorts are the way to go here in this summer heat." Zoie said.

"Maybe we can get you some today at the mall." Lacey thought.

"Yeah, and my favorite store is having that blowout sale today."

"That's right, I almost forgot about that. We should hurry before all the good stuff sells out." Lacey said, and we all left out.

"Despite what you saw last time, I'm actually a good driver. Especially when I have other people with me."

"Trust me, I wouldn't get in if I thought it wasn't a good idea." Zoie said backing up her word. When Katie and I go places, someone usually takes us since neither of us have a license yet. Lacey just got a ticket, but Zoie said her car was in the shop, so we have to let her drive us.

"I'll take it slow, so you can see the area." We all got in her car and took off. We drove through the city and the first place we passed by was the office. Both my parents were working today. Mr. Masidone could be in there as well. That still left the wonder of where Ken had disappeared to.

"I still don't see what's the big deal about that place." Lacey said.

"You're just saying that. My mom showed me an article she saw online about them and saw herself in the background. I thought that was pretty cool." Zoie said.

"I guess that is cool. But that's the only thing cool about it."

"Did something happen?" I asked. I didn't want to say anything, but Lacey really seemed to not like the Masidone company.

"I won't say anything since I heard your parents also work there too. It seems like everyone at the apartment works there."

"Well, the guy that owns that place also owns that complex. Plus, it's super close to the building so it's known to be the apartment place for the workers. Zoie said.

Zoie seems to know a lot about the business and what Mr. Masidone does.

"Once you live here long enough, you'll start to know everything about that place whether you want to or not." She said. Zoie seemed unfazed about it. But looking at Lacey, she seems like she has something to say.

The rest of the ride was passing more businesses and the occasional mention of the blowout sale until we made it to the mall. It was only after noon, but there were still a lot of cars here for it to be a Wednesday.

"Guess we're here late." Zoie said.

"We'll still find some cute stuff, don't worry." Lacey told her.

"Misa, you have to tell us what you like so we can keep an eye out for it. It'll be a close call. Today is the last day of the sale, so we are a little late." Zoie told me.

We walked in the main entrance and saw people everywhere. Our mall is usually packed, but this place was much bigger and had three levels. It's been a while since I've gone shopping, so part of me wants to buy something new.

"So, what does a Misa like?" Lacey walked to the left of me.

"Or better yet, what does this boyfriend of yours like to see you wear?" Zoie whispered to me from the right.

"Oh, you didn't say you had a BF!" Lacey got excited. "You definitely need to get something now. What's he like? Is he from around here?"

"He doesn't live here. She's going through the 'LDR'." Zoie said.

"Oh, I'm sorry to hear that. It must be hard. How are you holding up?" Lacey asked.

"Uh, it's not so bad." I said. I can't tell them I went from living with him and seeing him every day to living a short distance and not hearing from him. Lacey just got out of a relationship, so talking about another one might be uncomfortable.

"I say get an outfit to wear the next time you see him. Something different that will make him never want you to leave again. Dark and sexy or scandalous, maybe-"

"Or how about just something cute?" Zoie said. "You have to excuse her, she's a hopeless romantic."

"It's been a while since I've gone shopping, so anything new will be different anyway." I said.

Ken saw me almost every day for a semester. I don't have unlimited clothes, so I did repeat outfits.

We continued walking into a store that was packed. There were tables set up all over with 50-75% off signs on them. These girls seem like they really care about fashion. Jenny and Jennifer were also flashy with how they looked. I thought it was just a rich thing, but it seems like everyone here is like that.

Katie likes nice things, but she doesn't go to all the sales like they probably do.

"Okay, these are amazing." Zoie said holding up a pair of pink shorts that were tied in knots on the ends.

"I think this shirt goes with that." Lacey held up a white half shirt that had a paint splash design on it.

"No, I would wear that with something else. You see anything Misa?"

"This isn't so bad." I held up some light blue jean shorts that were ripped with the pockets lined with jewels.

"Those would definitely suit you." She said.

"Maybe this shirt too." Lacey held up a blue loose-fitting shirt with short sleeves that, from the mannequin, would hang off the shoulders.

"Yes, I approve of that." Zoie said. It wasn't a bad shirt, so I got it from her.

"That covers that part. Now let's see what dresses they have."

"Or, what about a skirt?" Zoie held up a purple skirt with a cross-string split on the sides. They really liked the summer colors.

We continued looking around and seeing more clothes. With everything on sale, I could actually get some things. By the time we were done, they had a hand full of clothes that they were planning to buy. I only got a few things since I didn't want to spend all of my allowance in one store.

"We have a habit of buying too much." Lacey looked at her hands as we went to the checkout line.

"I call it a strategy." Zoie said. "I get everything I like, then when I get to the registered, see the total bill, I only get what I really want since I'm really undecided between this shirt and these pants."

"You guys got some nice stuff. I don't buy too many outfits like this, so it'll be a change to wear." I told them.

"That BF should really like your picks then since it'll be a fresh look for you." Lacey said. Ken liked anything I had. If I changed my style like this, I wonder would he even notice.

Just as I had the thought, I felt my pocket vibrate and took out my phone. It was finally something from Ken. It was a simple apology message for not responding. He didn't say why or anything. I wasn't sure what to say in responds. I looked up and saw Lacey looking over at me and I just slipped my phone back in my pocket.

"You don't have to hide. Was that him?" She asked.

"Don't let us stop you. Go ahead and talk to him." Zoie added.

"That's okay. He didn't really say anything." I said. Which wasn't a lie. Usually, he always has something to say, but he didn't explain anything. He waited four days before he messaged me, so he can wait a little longer for my reply.

"Well, this isn't our only stop. There are some other stores on the second floor I want to go to." Lacey said.

"There was a place we passed to get here I wanted to look at." I told them.

"You should've said so. We could have gone there first." Zoie said.

"Yeah, this isn't just our trip. Drag us wherever you want to go since we're doing that to you." Lacey laughed. They were really nice and treated me like a friend they've known forever.

After we finished in that store, we went back to where I wanted to go and on to the next place. I haven't gone to this many stores in a while, but going around with them was actually fun.

By the time we were done, we stopped at the food court for them to rest their arms. They had a bag from every store we went in.

"I think I'm good for the next month or two." Lacey said.

"I think so too." Zoie agreed.

"This will do for me for a little while." I said looking at my things.

"I really like that body spray you got from the fragrance shop." Zoie told me.

"I've already gotten a bunch of new stuff, and this spray seems like a way to finish that off."

"Definitely, I love the smell. Hang on I got a call." Zoie stopped and pulled out her phone.

"What is it, Ken?" She said. My chest caved in a bit. I know this is the same city, but it couldn't be my Ken she's talking to, right? I looked over to Lacey whose expression changed. She had that same look she had in the car.

"I got it. Just go with Anthony and I'll be there soon. Bye *Kendal*." Zoie said emphasizing the name looking at Lacey.

"That was my brother. He locked himself out again. He's going with his friend for now, but I should get back before he gets home. The name slipped again. Sorry Lace."

"You're doing it on purpose. Like earlier too." Lacey said.

"You started that one. And this was just a slip of the tongue. Warning Misa, don't mention anyone with the name K-E-N around her." Zoie spelled. "It's been like two and half years and someone still can't get over their ex they haven't even spoken to since. Although if you ask me, you are way better off."

"You said that same thing about Chris." Lacey said.

"Chris cheated on you twice. Ken had that crazy ex of his after you. Not to mention his dad who was hardly around but always knew when you were. And don't forget that 'subtle' offer to get you to break up with him." Zoie spoke with anger in her tone. And the more she spoke, the more I felt a cold sweat going down my face.

"So, trust me Lacey, it's for the best that you get rid of both of them from your memory."

"Are you talking about the Ken that's the son of the guy's company our parents work at?" I didn't want to hear the answer, but I really needed confirmation.

"You know him?" Zoie asked. "I didn't think you'd know about him since you're not from the area. All the girls around here love him, and she used to date him."

"Long story short, we were classmates and now still only classmates." Lacey interrupted.

"There's that rumor he transferred though. I don't know where he went. Probably went to school with that Jenny." Zoie thought.

It felt like the world was slowing down. They not only knew Ken, but Lacey used to date him. I remember Ken once telling me he had previous girlfriends. But he didn't go into detail about them. But I told him not to. He didn't seem like he wanted to. Could this be why?

"I don't care where he went. As long as I don't have to deal with what I had to go through again." Lacey crossed her arms.

"If that's the case, then why can't I call my brother by his nickname around you? Just admit it, you still like him." Zoie said.

"It's not like that. I told you I'm over it." Lacey looked around. She wasn't really looking at either of us. Something was telling me there was more to the story. She didn't seem like she was over him. She and Ken were together two and a half years ago and Jenny must have done what she's been trying to do to me with her.

"Misa, I think your phone is ringing." Zoie said. I looked to my pocket. I didn't even feel it. I'm still in shock about this. I looked at the name and saw it was Ken himself. He doesn't always call, and I never replied, so why is he calling now?

"You can answer it. I encourage you to keep up with your BF since you're in a LDR." Zoie told me.

"I uh, I'll keep it short." I said. I answered right before it stopped ringing.

"Mimi!" Ken cried into my ear. "Are you mad at me?"

Ken came through the phone loudly. I looked over to Lacey who was looking to me. I got up and walked away from the table we were at.

"Are you there?" He asked.

"Yes, I'm here. What are you calling so suddenly for?" I asked.

"Well, you didn't reply to my message, and I thought you were upset, so I wanted to apologize verbally to you. Or, if you want, I can come see you and do it in person. You made your move, haven't you?"

"You can't, I'm out with some friends." I said a bit too fast.

"You made friends already? And here I thought you were lonely and thinking about me."

I haven't actually spoken to Ken since he left. It's been a while since I heard that cheeky tone of his.

"You're not with other guys, are you?" he asked almost afraid to hear the answer.

"No, it's not like that. Even though I don't know what you've been doing the past few days." I told him. He still didn't explain anything, and after hearing Lacey and Zoie, I don't know what I want to say right now.

"Things got a little complicated after Sano came back. We were sorting it out. I was going to message you, but my father called me to his office, and it slipped my mind that I never actually sent a message. I should have told you what was going on from the beginning, so I wanted to apologize to you."

Something happened with Sano's move. He probably didn't want to tell me since it's about him. Sano likely didn't tell him we already talked about not staying so close…

"Okay, I understand. But I have to go." I told him.

"Before you go. Leave next Friday open." He told me. "I want to go out somewhere. Would you like to?"

I just discovered that my new friend had a previous relationship with him and that it was bad. Now I'm with Ken and have been going through the same thing. I knew there was something about him, but I didn't know it was always like that.

"Sure." I told him.

"That's what I wanted to here! It's been too long since we've seen each other. I can't wait until then. I'll talk to you later Mimi. Don't enjoy yourself too much without me." He said, and we hung up.

"What was that? You guys didn't fight, did you?" Zoie asked when I came back. She seemed really concerned. I looked over to Lacey who looked up to me.

"That was Ken, wasn't it?"

"Wait, what? Ken? Really?" Zoie asked.

A nice day at the mall with new friends just took a turn for the worse. Ken really picked a bad time to try to make up for disappearing the past couple days. I sat back down in my chair and took a deep breath.

"Uh, yeah, it was. I'm sorry. I should have said so." It was getting awkward fast. I couldn't look at either of them directly.

"Why did you lie and say you were in a long-distance relationship? Or did Ken move or something?" Zoie asked.

"No, he still lives in his mansion. I mean, it was long distance before I came here."

"Did you not say who it was because of me?" Lacey asked.

"We just told her about that." Zoie started, "And you told me that the other day before knowing. Are you guys dating in secret or what?"

"It's not really a secret. But since I came out here, I didn't know what to expect since everyone probably knew him." Which seems like the understatement of the year. I figured people did. But to actually come across someone who not only knew him but dated him was not something I prepared to deal with.

"Well, he is popular, but you shouldn't hide your relationship because of that." Zoie told me. "Have you lived here before? He's told me before he didn't really go anywhere around here, so how did you guys meet?"

"No, I haven't live here before," I told her. I can't exactly say, *he stalked me a long time ago and came to live with me for a while.*

"We met before in the past and then we came across each other again earlier this year."

"Earlier this year is when they said he transferred. Did he transfer and go to your school?" Zoie asked.

"Yeah, he did."

"Wow, so that mystery is finally solved. It was like he vanished into thin air. He didn't tell anybody that he was leaving." Zoie was the only one that seemed really curious about Ken. Was she close to him too?

"Well, I didn't expect you to lie about being with him. I sort of understand though. If the wrong person heard about you two, you would have some crazy people after you."

"But wait. Jennifer was that girl's sister, and she also transferred. Do you know her too?" Lacey seemed more confused than curious.

"Yeah, she came a little after Ken did." I unfortunately had to say.

"If you know her, then you would have to know Jenny. Did she also transfer? Did anything happen after they came around?"

"Jenny didn't come to my school, but we have met a few times." I said.

"And she didn't, you know, try to break you two up? Those two came after Lacey every chance they got." Zoie told me.

"I've had some problems with them. Jennifer came to my school to watch Ken and told Jenny about it. It started some trouble, but Ken did his best to stop it."

"Unbelievable. What's with that girl? She's still doing the same thing even now." Zoie was getting angry.

"And even though she tried to break you two up, you still stayed with him?" Lacey asked.

"Lace." Zoie said.

"Never mind. Forget I asked." Lacey tried to act like she wasn't bothered, but it was obvious she was.

"Anyway, you didn't tell us who you were with, and I said that stuff earlier. I didn't mean anything bad about it. I was just angry about how everything happened." Zoie felt bad, but I feel just as bad for Lacey.

If Jenny didn't get between them, would they have still been together now? They were together two and a half years ago. The time we met at that mall was like five years ago. Ken knew about me but still lived his life regularly. Would we have come across each other again if he continued seeing Lacey?

"Look, I don't want this to come between us. You didn't know, and what happened with them was a long time ago. Let's just put what happened in the past and move on. How about that?" Zoie looked at Lacey.

"I told you, I was done anyway. What he does now is none of my business. So, Misa, forget about what we've said and continue seeing him as you were."

"I have to head back anyway to let my brother in. We can finish the day out with a movie or something."

"Sounds good to me." Lacey started gathering her bags.

"Uh, that's fine." I agreed hesitantly.

"Don't feel awkward now. We've all gone shopping together. We are officially friends now. Just don't lie to us again." Zoie said.

"Yeah, don't feel weird. You can even pick the movie we watch." Lacey added. I realized the world was small and it just keeps getting smaller. To think I would be friends with one of Ken's ex's.

We went back to Zoie's apartment and continued our day as we did before the awkward truth came out. Ken continued to message me as he did before. They didn't look bothered, but I can't help but feel like Lacey wants to say something but isn't saying anything. She hasn't spoken to him since they broke up, so of course there would be something to say. But I'm afraid to ask what that is.

"We have to plan something else to do before I go on vacation in two weeks." Lacey said as she was getting ready to go.

"I start my new job next week so we're running out of time." Zoie said.

"You have a job?" I asked her.

"It's just part time. I have to pay my mom back for getting my car fixed, so need to make some money. Especially after today."

"I'll text you guys with some ideas later." Lacey grabbed her bag and left out.

"I guess I should go back to my place too." I told Zoie.

"Before you do," she started, "you got a minute to talk?" I could've said no and that I needed to get back home before my parents did. But I lied to them once already. I couldn't do it again so soon.

"Yeah, what is it?"

"I love Lacey like a sister. I know how she gets and what sets her off, so I couldn't really ask what I wanted earlier about you and you know who."

"What did you want to ask?"

"I didn't really know him personally. Only through what happen with him and Lace and random articles I've seen from events he went to with his dad." She said. I never knew he went to things with his father.

"My mom likes working at that company and people would droll over that guy, so I sort of keep up with them to see what the hype is about. Ken always seemed to keep to himself. I would've never guessed he'd up and transfer for a girlfriend. I know they're rich, but did he really travel back and forth every day?"

"It wasn't like that. He stayed with me."

"Oh, so it was like *that*." she said nodding her head.

"That's not it either." I shook my head. "This all sort of happened suddenly. I wasn't with him the entire time. It was sort of an arrangement."

"Arrangement? Like someone was trying to bring you two together?"

"Yeah, something like that. Ken was all for it, but I wasn't really interested at first."

"I thought everyone instantly fell for him. Was there something up with him?" she asked.

"I wouldn't say that." I trailed off a bit. Zoie is nice, but can I really just tell her everything? She seems to know a lot about him and Mr. Masidone's company. My dad already said there were rumors going around because of us. I wouldn't want anything else to go around. After an entire semester of rumors, the last thing I want is more.

"I know we've only known each other for a few days so you don't have to tell me everything. I've been trying to get Lace to get over him for forever now. I just wanted to know if anything changed with him between then and now."

"Can I ask you something?" I asked.

"What is it?"

"How did it actually end between them?" The question came out before I was sure if I wanted to know the answer. I've never had to deal with anything like this before, but maybe she could tell me something about them I don't know yet.

"It was bad. It was during freshmen year. Big rumors and things like that hardly happened in the open at our school. If something was going on, it stayed low, so it wouldn't spread too far." That sounds like the opposite of my school…

"But suddenly, these two girls transferred to our school, and everything started changing. People were looking at her funny, someone started spreading lies about her, and Jenny herself would go up to her and harass her saying he deserves better than her."

If I didn't know any better, I would've thought she was talking about me. What happened with her is exactly what happened to me. They haven't changed at all.

"She endured it for a few weeks. Then she went to Ken's house once, and after that it was over. She told me his dad gave her the third degree and offered money for her to break up with him. She didn't take the money, but the next day at school she told him she couldn't do it anymore."

"Did Ken know that was happening?" I asked.

"I don't think he knew at first. After the first semester, Jenny transferred out, so he didn't see her threatening Lace. She told him everything, but it was only so much he could do," Zoie shrugged.

"What about with the thing with his dad?"

"She never told him about that. She got worried after finding out he had been watching her, so, she didn't want to say anything."

I was at a loss for words. Ken was always asking if anything happened. He always asked if Jennifer said anything. Whenever I go to his house, he always seemed uneasy. Was it because he was afraid this would all happen again?

"Has that same thing happened to you?" Zoie asked me.

"Well, I was never offered money, but most of that did happen."

"And you were able to take it all? After being harassed you still agreed to be with him?"

"It did take a while. My friend was going crazy because of what Jennifer and Jenny were doing, but Ken tried to get me to see past them. There were times he got super angry with them, and they backed off."

"Wow. I didn't think Ken could get angry. He didn't try that hard back then. I guess he has changed." She thought.

"I sort of feel bad about what happened to Lacey though."

"If it were meant to be it was meant to be. That's how I see it. Both of them have moved on. Whenever she would see him around school, it would just remind her of the past. I've been trying to get her to get over it, but it's taking a lot longer than I thought."

I got another message from Ken, but it didn't seem like the appropriate time to answer it. I really don't know how to feel about all of this.

"My parents will be home soon. I should probably be getting back." I told her.

"You seem like a cool person Misa, so don't let some guy come between a friendship. We can plan to do something again. There's a movie coming out next Friday I wanted to see. We should go see it."

"Oh, next Friday I can't. I told Ken I would go somewhere with him that day."

"Oh, well we'll figure something out then. If there's something you want to do, just let us know. I'll see you later." Zoie smiled. I got my bags and went back down the hall to my place.

I went back to my apartment and looked around. White walls, grey furniture, and a little too big wood crafted table for the dining area. This was not the home I was used to. This is not the city I'm used to. Those girls aren't the friends I'm used to.

I went and sat on the couch as I let it sink in that this is what I'll have to get used to. The house, I can get used to. The city I could get used to. But the friends will take longer to get used to.

Zoey and Lacey are nice and have seemed to accept me, but knowing they have history with Ken really just made it hard to pretend like he's nobody. Especially since it seems like Lacey still likes him.

I wonder how Ken would feel if I told him I knew her. Would he care? Would it bother him if we were friends? And what about the annoying duo? Would they go back to harassing her too?

I took out my phone to see the unanswered message from Ken wondering would it be okay to tell him who I was with. But this is his ex we're talking about. I shouldn't put her back on his mind. I already have Jenny to deal with. The possibility of him worrying about her too is making something grow heavy inside me.

"Why are you sitting with the TV off?" I looked over after noticing my mom coming in.

"I just got home too."

"Oh, you did? How was it with Zoie? Are you two getting along? There was something about her that reminded me of Katie, so I figured you two would get along well."

"It was fine."

"That's good to hear. It was a long day today and I'm feeling a little tired, so your dad is picking up some takeout if that's okay with you." My mom asked.

"That's fine with me." I told her. Although I wasn't really hungry. I can't get the thought of what happened out of my mind.

"I didn't want to say this with your father around since he would love to hear me admit to it, but it does seem like more and more people are standing against us." My mom told me.

"What do you mean?"

"Just some telltale signs. Someone called the supervisor accusing me of switching document forms for a client when all I was doing was updating their information." She walked over and rested on the couch arm.

"I know who did it. She's been on probation for sharing private information. She's been trying to put the blame on someone else, and after those silly rumors started, she's been eyeing me."

"Did you get in trouble?"

"No, they knew I wasn't doing anything wrong. Now she's on a final warning. I don't know why she would risk her job when she's already on probation just because I have a little connection to Mr. Masidone."

"How did it even get around?" I asked.

"I'm not sure. We talked a few times and that was it. Everything was fine in the beginning. Now all of a sudden, Mr. Masidone and I have a secret relationship, and he gave me the new position himself. I haven't even talked to him about that yet."

Even in a work setting, there are still rumors and people you have to watch for. If it's to the point my mom is worrying, it really must be getting out of hand. But if she's transferring, she won't have to worry about it for long.

Just like me. If I'm moving, then I won't have to worry about the rumors at my school anymore. But that still leaves the people I know. If this really is the beginning like Jenifer said, then it won't be as simple for me even if I leave.

"Jamie and Sean asked about having a summer party at their place. You guys in?" Zoie asked. We were sitting on her balcony when she got a text from a friend.

"You know I don't like Jamie." Lacey said, rolling her eyes.

"But you like Sean. And word has it he likes you. This is the perfect opportunity to talk to him and get even with Jamie." Zoie told her.

"Why would you help me get even with Jamie. You like Jamie."

"That doesn't mean I won't help you settle your differences by getting together with her brother and showing you now have the upper hand, and she can no longer say anything to you." I could see an evil smile growing on her face. My mom was right. Zoie is like another Katie.

"I'll think about it. What about you Misa?" Lacey turned to me.

"I don't know. This sounds like a 'friends only' event." I sunk in my chair a little.

"And you are a friend. Just a friend of a friend." Zoie clarified.

"When is it?" Lacey asked.

"End of the summer. That's when they're shooting for. They're asking around to see if everyone is open then."

"Do they have like a big house or something?" I asked.

"Their house is huge with a huge yard and pool. They had a summer party last year and even got a DJ. I don't think it will be that big this year since the neighbors called the cops and Jamie can't stay out of trouble, so her parents are cracking down on her." Zoie explained.

"I was only going to be here for the summer. By then, I may be gone." I told them. Even if I knew who these people were, I might not be here to go. Or at least that was the plan. My mom had her phone interview the other day. She was already worrying about everything going on in the office, but after that interview, she said something didn't seem right and now she's going to talk to her VPs again. I don't know what's going on at this point.

"If you are here, then you should definitely come with us." Zoie gave me a thumbs up with her approval of me going with them.

"Can I go too?" We all turned and saw Zoie's brother, Kendall, peeking out the window from their room. His window had been open, so he must have been listening.

"How about you do something with your own friends? Weren't you supposed to be with them anyway?"

"I'm leaving out soon. But if your friends are going with you somewhere, I want to go to." He looked at us and smiled.

"Go away Ken!" Zoie stood, and he closed his window.

"You two seem close." I said.

"A little too close. He's at that age now, so I have to keep an eye on him."

If he turns out to be like the Ken I know, then she's going to have to keep full surveillance on him. But with Lacey here, it's not the best joke to make.

"So, are we going to the movies tomorrow or not?" Lacey asked.

"Misa can't make it, so I thought to wait until Sunday when I'm off." Zoie said looking at me.

"You got other plans tomorrow?"

"Yeah, I do." I said. I guess Zoie didn't tell Lacey about my date with Ken.

"Oh, I see. We can do it Sunday then." Lacey seems to have caught on. "Are you just meeting with him tomorrow? You've already been here for like two weeks and you haven't met up yet, right? You should spend as much time with him to make up for lost time."

"I actually agree with that. But that's your call." Zoie said. They think it's only been two weeks, but it's been over three weeks since we've last seen each other. He hasn't said where we're going or what we're doing.

"Are you wearing one of your new outfits?" Zoie's eyes were glowing.

"Um maybe. I don't know where we're going."

"He'll like whatever you wear no matter where you go. He doesn't care too much about that even though he always dressed nice." Lacey said.

"Yeah, he likes whatever I wear, so I don't have to worry too much about that."

"I see that part about him hasn't changed." Lacey looked down. She said that to herself, but we were still able to hear.

This past week, the three of us have talked more and hung out, but Lacey always seems like she's holding something back. I still don't know the full history between those two. I remember Ken saying none of his past relationships lasted that long. Looking at Lacey, it seemed like whatever length of time it was, was enough to leave a mark.

Wherever Ken wants to go, he wants us to leave at noon, so I didn't stay much longer with them. Even though it didn't matter, I still wanted to see my clothing options just to be safe. It was good to leave anyway since it only got harder to talk with Lacey since she gets quiet whenever Ken came up.

Part of me wants to ask her about him. Everything is fine until he comes up in conversation. If we can get past this, there won't be any problems. The next time we meet, I think I will ask her. But until then, I have to prepare to see the topic of conversation for the first time in weeks.

21

With each passing hour, I could feel Ken's energy growing. It was almost noon, and I waited for him downstairs. Having him come up to my apartment wasn't bad. Having Zoie come out of her place is what I was worried about. So, I decided to wait outside for him.

The sun was shining through the trees that shook in the light breeze. I had no idea where we were going. As long as Mr. Masidone or the annoying duo stay away, this could actually be a good day.

I looked over to a car I've seen before driving this way. It was the same car Ken had when he drove us to the mall that time. I walked a little closer to the parking lot as he pulled in front of me. I wasn't sure if I was nervous. I just stood there awkwardly waiting for him to get out.

He got out of the car and rubbed his eyes and stared at me. His hair seemed longer with fresh finger waves. He was sporting a new grey and white top with black cargo shorts and grey shoes to match. Not to mention the smile that was slowly growing on his face.

"I see you are growing accustomed to the city life." He said looking me up and down. I wore the shorts with rhinestones on them and blue top. Zoie and Lacey seemed to really like it, so I thought it was okay to wear.

"Is there a problem?" I asked him.

"Not at all. It's a new look for you. Didn't say I hated it. Quite the opposite actually." He grinned. I just continued to look at him as he extended both his arms out. I stood there not sure what he was doing.

"I can't even get a hug? We haven't seen each other in so long." He slowly started lowering his arms in disappointment.

I was certain not even five minutes had passed, and he's already acting like a sad puppy. The look he was giving me matched the tone he had. Looking at him like this feels like nothing has changed. All the time he acted like this flashed through my mind. I let out a sigh that was sort of relieving.

"A sigh is all I get?" He asked. I didn't respond. I just walked up to him and stopped.

"You're not going to hug me?"

"You're the one that wants a hug." I reminded him.

"So, you don't want to hug me?" I heard that sad tone again. I looked up to him and he was looking at me. I exhaled again and looked away when I wrapped my arms around him. I felt pressure on my back when he put his arms around me.

"That's better." I could hear the happiness come back in his words. I was expecting him to do more than just a hug, but he seems excited just to see me.

"Are you nervous?" I heard him ask. "I can feel your heart beating fast."

I pulled back from him not realizing my own increasing heart rate.

"I hope that means you are happy to see me."

"I can say the same for you," I said. Ken looked at me. He didn't think I was going to notice. But with the pressure he applied putting me against his chest, I could feel his too. I just didn't think mine matched his…

"Well, it has been what, almost a month since we've last seen each other? I was afraid we wouldn't get to meet again until the vacation. But now that things have calmed down, I was finally able to get some fresh air and thought to get it with you." He looked at me. I looked at him but looked away.

"Are you still upset about before?"

"You already explained what happened. It's understandable given what's going on." I hadn't really been thinking about that. He was here in front of me. Part of me wanted to see him. The other part won't let me forget all the things I've learned since coming here.

The last thing I want is for another problem after first meeting again in weeks when he left after finding out I was moving. I need to get rid of these thoughts fast.

"You still haven't said where we are going." I reminded him. I folded my arms and stepped towards him.

"Are we getting anxious?" He asked. He smiled again, not actually answering. He walked back towards his car and went to the passenger door.

"Mimi will have to just go with me to see." He opened the door for me to get in. With his hair a bit longer, it moved more as the wind passed and he ran his hand through it. Being back around Jayson all the time, his aura seemed to be rubbing off on him. I walked towards the ray of light it felt like he was emitting and got in. He walked around to the driver's seat.

"Shall we?" He turned the car on. I looked up to the apartments we were pulling away from. I can see Zoie's balcony window was open. She was home. She knows I'm with Ken today. I wonder if she saw us standing outside.

"I suppose I should stop the guessing game," Ken started, "I hope your expectations weren't too high. Despite this being my hometown, there's not a lot of places I could think of to go to." He admitted.

"You've lived here all your life and don't know where to go?"

"I think I told you before. Growing up, I wasn't really allowed to go a lot of places. You might be in the city now, but I still live outside of it. That doesn't mean I have nowhere for us to go though." Ken was worried when he moved back in about not being able to get back out. It's been like that his whole life. Hard to believe he was able to move out and in with someone he didn't know.

"Anywhere will be new to me since I don't know the area. I'm okay with doing whatever you have planned. But I already went to the mall." I ran my hand across the windowsill. I'm still not good at this whole dating thing. We were around each other almost every day, and now being back in his presence is giving me this anxious feeling.

We came to a stop at a red light. I had been watching my hand doing whatever it was doing going over the car material. That's when I felt a hand land on my upper thigh.

"Hey!" I shouted.

"This mall trip you went on. Is that where you got these snazzy shorts? This top too." He moved his hand up to my arm, gently going over my skin as he did. "It's also new."

"Yeah, I got this last week." My hand stopped moving on the windowsill. I looked over to him and he was staring at me.

"There we go." He smiled. The light turned green, and he took off again. He wanted me to look at him.

"It would have been nice to see you shopping. The last time we went to the mall, you wouldn't buy anything. You were too busy stopping me from trying to buy stuff."

"You wanted everything you saw. And I got this on sale, so someone like me on a budget was able to spend a little."

"You just got here last week, and you were there with friends, right? Did you already know someone here?"

"Uh, no. My mom knew someone in our building that had a daughter. So, we just started hanging out."

"Seems like your mother is pretty good with setting you up with people." Ken meant that as a joke, but this set up, just like with him, had more to it than I knew.

Zoie, Lacey, and I are supposed to go to the movies on Sunday. They might ask what happened on my date today. If it were Katie, I would just tell her everything. These two are different. I can't just tell them everything. Not with Lacey still uneasy every time Ken comes up in conversation.

Ken turned on to the highway. The way he turned looks like he's taking me back to the mansion. I looked over to him and he was looking at the road.

"Even though my father isn't home today, going to my place is not the big plan for the day." He said reading my face. Of course he wouldn't just take me there. His father is only one of many I do not want to see right now.

"If we aren't going anywhere in town, then where are we going?" I asked.

"Since you already had your shopping fun, I thought taking it a bit easier would be nice." He got back off the highway. I know nothing beyond his mansion and my apartment, so we could be going anywhere.

We drove down an open road with just trees and nature passing by. The city was behind us. There were houses scattered throughout. To the left of us, the trees were fading out showing a beach in the distance.

"Soon, you're going to be looking at a lake for a week. But I thought getting a little taste of it with just the two of us will help you get used to the scenery. Good thing you wore shorts, right?" Ken said.

"Is this the same lake the villa is by?" I asked.

"Yeah. If it's clear enough, you can see it in the distance once we get up to the water." Ken turned and pulled in a parking area. There were a few other cars around. So far, no signs of any other Masidone family members.

"I hope you're okay with this being our adventure for the day," Ken said taking the keys out.

"You always have something up your sleeve, but this is fine. I was wondering what the lake looked like since I didn't see it when I went by the villa the first time."

"Technically, this area is a public beach. The water by our villa is more private and we have our boats and stuff out there. There's still a few things to do and see here. I came a couple times before." He said as we both got out the car. I could smell the water. The air was a little cooler. There was a trail that went around the lake. Sand was in front of it leading to the water. I saw far out in the water someone was boating.

"Ready?" Ken came over to my side of the car with a black bag on his back. I was ready for whatever he had planned today. I was sort of looking forward to seeing him today. Yet here I am still unable to shake this feeling I have.

22

"I was going to have Jay come and bring one of our small boats to ride, but he wanted us to enjoy the day together. He really wanted to see you though." Ken and I walked up to the trail. I can see Jayson now sad and wishing he were here.

"We can do that with him at the villa. You said you already have boats there, right?"

"Yeah, we do. A houseboat, ski boat, and a jet boat. We do own a yacht, but the engine died and needs to be replaced. My father was thinking about just getting a bigger one and sailing in the ocean one day." He explained.

Of course they have a bunch of boats. Why wouldn't they? They have everything else...

"Have you ever been to a lake or a beach?" Ken asked. We started walking on the trail. It went on forever. There were people walking on the sand by the water. Someone just passed us going the other way jogging.

"I've seen them in passing, but I haven't actually been. My parents and I were supposed to go to the beach one time, but my dad got sick, and we had to cancel it." I told him.

"Your dad is the one that will bring you to the villa, right?"

"Yeah. He wants to drop me off and pick me up."

"Well, maybe he could have a look around before he goes. It should put him at ease about where you will be and get to see what the lake looks like too." He said. Letting my dad look around is one thing. The fact that he's offering is the surprising part.

"I'm sure he would like to. But I don't think he should stay too long. He either won't leave or will find a reason for me to." My dad still does not like the idea of me staying with them.

"Between the two, I hope it is the first one."

"You must really want me there if you'd take my dad there too."

"Well, if you think about it, you'll be there with my father, so I could handle yours too." I hope he could handle me trying to sail away in one of his boats if my dad and his were to be together for a week.

We continued walking down the road. I looked over to the beach and saw some people playing volleyball. Another runner went past us. Ken put his hand on my back and moved me over out of the runner's way.

"Let's go over there." He pointed to a free area on the sand and took us that way. He stopped once we got to it, but I kept going towards the water. I took my shoes off to move better.

The water was so clear up close. The sand was hot, but cooler as I moved closer to the water. Some of it was still wet. I walked up to the waterline and felt the cool splash as it crashed into my feet. There were small rocks mixed in the sand that dug a little into the bottom of them. I tried pushing them over, but there were more underneath.

"Are you having fun?" I turned and saw Ken watching me. He was sitting on a blue blanket he had put down.

"The water is nice. I didn't know it would be like that." I said walking over to him.

"You mean like, getting in a pool that's surrounded by sand?"

"It's not exactly the same." I said a little bothered. I went to sit on the blanket with him.

"You didn't have to stop playing in the water. I was enjoying watching you."

"Why? It's just a big pool. Nothing special about it." I played with the sand stuck to my feet.

"I didn't mean anything bad by it. Some people can find large bodies of water overwhelming. So, if you just think of it as a giant pool, it doesn't seem as intimidating."

"The water wasn't intimidating. But the rocks hurt a bit, so I didn't want to go in."

"The rocks are everywhere." Ken said and looked down. He dug around in the sand until he pulled out a little brown smooth looking rock. "See?"

I reached for the sand and started pushing it around. I saw another rock start to show itself and grabbed it. This one was black and a little shiny.

"That's a nice one. You should keep it." Ken said. It was a nice rock. I never cared for rocks, but something about finding rocks here in the sand makes me want to keep them.

"I guess I could keep this. They aren't so bad when they aren't under my feet."

"You just have to get used to it. I mean, sand itself is just really tiny rock pieces. You'll always be walking on them here."

"You sound like this is normal. How often do you go to the beach?"

"We've gone to our villa every year since we got it when I was five. We also go to beaches on vacation. You should see the red sand in Hawaii."

"You've been to Hawaii?"

"Only once some years ago. My father had to meet someone there and we all went. My mom took Sano and I to the beach while we waited for him to finish his business." Ken looked out to the water. I wasn't expecting him to be the one to bring Sano up.

"Are things going alright between you two now?" I didn't exactly look at him when I asked, but since he brought him up, it made me curious to know if he settled in okay or not. I haven't talked to him since he left.

"He's been going to his aunt's to see those kids at least two or three times a week. He's been keeping to himself though. I expected that. No matter how much Jay or I try to talk to him, he's still keeping his walls up."

I knew he would want to see the kids. But traveling all that way three times a week. He must really miss them. He talked as if he accepted the move, but not talking to Ken or Jayson must mean he isn't as acceptant as I thought.

"He probably just needs a little more adjusting time." I told him. It's not a good idea to ask more about him no matter how much I want to know. I looked beside me to my phone that fell out of my pocket and noticed I had a bunch of unread messages from Lacey, Zoie, and one from Katie.

But I didn't think Zoie and Lacey would have anything to say to me since they know who I'm with.

"I think you might need a little more water time." Ken looked over to me, "Ready to get in?"

"You mean like this? I don't have a swimsuit."

"Of course you do." Ken said as he reached into the black bag he had. He pulled out a dark blue and white two-piece swimsuit, "There's a restroom over there." He gestured to the building behind me. I looked back to the swimsuit in his hand.

"Is it not to your liking?" He looked at the half blue shirt and white bottoms. If anything, I didn't know he had all this prepared.

"I guess I'll go change." I got up and headed to the bathroom. I took my phone to look at my messages. Katie's message was normal, but Zoie's warning to ignore anything Lacey might send me had my nerves all over the place. I changed into the swimsuit wondering if I should even read what Lacey sent. But before I knew it, I was looking at the messages.

-Hey, how's the date going?
-You're with Ken, right?
-He always surprised me when we went places. Did he surprise you? Where did you go?
-Sorry. You don't have to answer that. Just tell us about it tomorrow.

What friend wouldn't ask how the date went? That's normal. When the friend asks how a date with their ex goes like that, it really puts an uneasy feeling in the stomach. I should have listened to Zoie and just ignored it.

I was trying so hard to keep the fact that Lacey and Ken used to date out of my mind. Now its fresh in it and the only thing I can think about. She still likes him. Why else would she send messages like that?

I didn't bother responding to anyone. I grabbed my stuff and headed back out.

"I knew that would look nice on you." Ken said as I was coming back to him. He was already sitting shirtless and in grey swim trunks. "Ready to swim?" He stood up and looked at me as I did the same to him. I think I remember Jayson showing me a workout room on the tour of their mansion. If Ken isn't allowed to leave, he has to be spending some time in there.

"Did something happen in the bathroom?" He asked me. Normally, he'd make one of his perv comments, but he noticed right away I was bothered. I would have preferred one of his comments to asking if something was wrong.

I can't tell him that his ex texted me the third degree. What would he think if he knew I knew Lacey?

"I was just wondering where you got this swimsuit." I sort of lied. The question was technically floating in my mind somewhere.

"I was doing some online shopping, and this was advertised. I thought you would be cute in it. And I was right." He said. He started walking towards the water and I trailed after him. The water was cold trying to get in. I could hardly let the water go past my knees.

"Come on, the water isn't that cold." Ken said, going further out.

"This is a lot colder than normal pool water. I'll get there in a second." I inched in a little further. The next step dipped down more than the last and now the water was halfway up my thigh.

For it to be such a nice day, the sun hasn't heated up this water at all.

"I vaguely remember a situation like this at a skate rink and only one way to get you going."

Ken said coming back over to me.

"What are you doing?" I watched Ken as he walked up to me and quickly pulled me towards him.

"Hey!" I shouted. But he continued walking backwards bringing the water higher up. He finally stopped pulling us further out when the water reached up to my chest.

"Now, is it really that bad?"

"Once again, you just couldn't let me do it on my own." I said with a slight shiver adjusting to the temperature.

"That's because, once again, swim hours would have been over if I waited on you." Ken said jokingly.

I took a quick look around and saw some others in the water further down and some even further out.

"How far out can people go?" I asked looking at the four people barely staying above water in the middle of the lake.

"Do you want to see?" He asked.

"I wasn't asking to go; I was just curious."

"Are you afraid to go out further? You should be adjusted to the water by now. And if memory serves me, you know how to swim."

"How do you know that?" I asked him.

"Let's just say I found out why that John guy was so attached to you."

It wasn't exactly a secret considering John talks to everyone about everything. Still, it wasn't the response I was expecting.

"Why don't we see how far we can go. I think I can count on you to save me if we go too far." Ken smiled at me.

"As if you couldn't swim already. You're here all the time."

"Who's to say that means I can swim? I think I still need some assistance." Ken bent down in the water. "I think I'm losing my balance. I need some help." He started splashing around.

"If I'm still standing where we are, then you should be more than okay." I reminded him of our five-inch height difference.

"So then, why don't we see how far we can go?" Ken launched forward and took off. He really intends to go into deep water.

I watched him as he swam further away. I had no choice but to go after him. He went at least halfway into the lake. We were now out as far as the others I saw.

"Still can't swim?" I asked when I got to him.

"So, I might've learned when I was younger. I mean, we do have a pool. Would be a waste if I could never use it."

"I think I've reached a point where I'm no longer surprised by the things you say."

"I'll take that as a compliment. So, if you feel you can't handle it out here, your lifeguard will save you." He gave me that sly smile of his. That smile has been growing on me. Something I no longer see every day. I started liking it. And I would probably like it more if I weren't feeling uneasy.

"Looks like you're going under. Do you need some saving?" Ken pulled me closer to him.

"You know, neither of us are touching the ground."

"Is it so bad floating with me?" He asked. I can feel his legs moving keeping us afloat. "Isn't it nice to just be able to swim out here away from it all?"

The reflection of the sunlight move in the subtle waves of the water. There wasn't anyone close to us. It was just us where we were.

It was nice being in the lake. It's been a while since I've been swimming. Seeing everyone enjoying themselves as they play volleyball, others swimming in the distance and sun bathing on the sand. Ken didn't want any problems. Just a nice day out with me. He knows that it could be interrupted with everyone being in the same space at the villa.

"I guess it's not so bad being here." I said and moved away from him a bit. "But I'd at least like to touch the ground and enjoy it."

I don't know why there's always something that makes my mind cluttered. I want to just enjoy the day with him. For all I know, this could be our last swim like this together. I cannot let Lacey or anything else get to me. We probably won't get many chances at the villa to be on our own, so I have to do what I can to make it count.

"I was wondering if this really was a good place to go to today or not, but I'm glad this is where we came." Ken told me. We sat on the blanket he laid out. We were done swimming and finished some sandwiches he brought. I looked down and rubbed away some of the drying sand off my legs. Once I put my thoughts and my phone away, I got to see another side of Ken I hadn't seen.

"Too bad our ball got taken away." I said looking at our little beach ball floating far down the other side of the lake. Had he not thrown it just as the wind picked up, we could have grabbed it.

"I can still go out there and get it."

"Remember the last time you went on a rescue mission? I think your leg does. And those people over there using jet skis don't seem like they want company." I told him looking out to his certain demise with the boaters. Sure, Ken could probably make it if he really wanted to get the ball, but it already traveled so far down the lake. It would take him forever to get back.

"If it keeps heading that way, maybe we'll see it at the villa." Ken joked, "But speaking of the villa. Everyone seems ready to get away and relax by the water." Ken brought his knees up and rested his arms on them.

"We haven't gotten much out of him, but Sano did say he was coming with us. I figured I should tell you so you wouldn't be surprised later." We were both kind of looking out into the water watching the little waves bring the water up the sand. Normally, hearing something like that would have sent my nerves on a trip. But I think a part of me has been preparing to hear that be the answer.

"Staying home alone in that big mansion doesn't sound too fun. It's not surprising that he decided to go."

"Are you going to be alright with him there?" Ken asked.

It's not a matter of me being okay with him being there. But knowing that he likes me does make it a little awkward. I know he said he doesn't want anything to change between us and there's nothing to worry about, but his behavior the last couple of times I saw him makes me worry a lot about what's really going on with him now.

"Why wouldn't I be alright? It's a family vacation, and he's a part of the family. It makes sense that he would be there." I told him.

"You've made a valid point; however, I think you know that's not what I meant." Ken looked over to me and waited for me to look back to him. "You're here with me today, but sometimes I still wonder would you prefer to have been here with him."

"I'm here with you because I wanted to be. Until you brought it up, Sano didn't even cross my mind." I said as I faced him.

"I see. That's good to know then. I still feel a bit apologetic for not telling you about us from the beginning. But the shock of knowing he was there the whole time was too much to process." He told me.

"You really didn't know he moved to that area?" I asked.

"I was having a hard time keeping in touch with him to begin with. Then out of the blue, he changed his number and that was it. Jay had taken me by his house, and they were already gone."

"You're worried about me having him at the villa, but I'm wondering if you're going to be okay with him being there." I told him. Ken knows that I liked him, but that's still nothing compared to growing up with him and seeing him leave you without even saying anything. I've been wondering how Sano was doing this whole time moving back in, but hadn't really thought about how Ken felt having his brother back home.

"I've already told him that I don't have an issue with him being there. I also told him that if he wants to do anything together, we can. So, at this point, it's up to him on what he wants to do."

No matter what, Ken always seems to worry about others. He's not only worried about me, but he's also worried about Sano. He just wants things to work out. I can see why Lacey hasn't let go of him.

"Now that I got that out, I'm ready to ask another question." Ken and I were sitting right next to each other, so I wonder if he could feel my heart drop.

"Could you tell me more about this move you're supposed to be making?"

It's been weeks since that moment my dad first mentioned the move to Ken. Not once has he brought it up until now.

"My mom had been called in and was told she had a chance to move up or something, but the offer was for another city. She was unsure of what to do at first. I guess she thought it over and decided to take the offer." I paused for a moment thinking about it all.

"She's been talking with the VPs a lot about everything and even did a phone interview the other day with a manger from the new branch."

"How did that go?" Ken asked.

"Well, I don't know. My mom said the guy didn't seem like he knew too much about this. She wants to talk to the people here again. But my mom can be a bit paranoid at times. It's a big decision, so she's probably overthinking it." I said. I'm starting to realize where I might get it from...

"You said she's been talking to the VPs. Has she talked to my father about this?"

"I don't think so. She said there's been some rumors going around. She's trying not to talk to him if she doesn't need to."

"Rumors?" He repeated.

"You know, because of our situation, people started wondering what was going on for her to be talking to him so much."

"I see. That would make sense. Although, I'm wondering who exactly has she been talking to." Ken extended one of his legs and looked out towards the lake.

"Do you know something?" I asked him.

"I haven't been close to my father these days, so I'm not too sure what's been going on. Just hearing the VPs solely deciding like this doesn't sound like something he'd normally allow without them talking to him about it."

"Well, I don't know everything, but apparently, it's still not finalized, so I can't say for certain what's going to happened at the end of summer."

"I wish the best for your mom. I also wish that you wouldn't have to move for that to happen." Ken put his hand down over mine. He held on to it, adding a little pressure.

"I'm still here. And the move is still in the air. We'll probably find out soon since this is all supposed to happen next month. But until then, we should enjoy the here and now." I turned my hand over to take his.

It was summer vacation. Our last one in our high school life. I didn't want to spend it always worrying. I know I can't put things off forever. Both of us sitting here worrying about what's going to happen won't change anything.

"Moving here really has changed you I see." Ken looked over to me. "Normally, I'm the one calming you down. Now the tables have turned. I think I can live with these changes." He turned his whole body and laid his head on my legs.

"If I'm to enjoy the here and now, I might as well get comfortable." Sitting here with Ken like this really wasn't so bad. I looked over to our ball I could barely see in the distant water actually floating closer towards the villa. A place I'll be at for a week with him and seven other people in his family. I'm almost certain a moment like this will not be happening then.

We only stayed a little while longer before we decided to pack up and head back. Once I got back into my clothes and put my phone into my pocket, I felt another text come through. I didn't dare check to even see who it was from or what it said. I know the moment I look at my messages, all the anxiousness I pushed aside will quickly come back. I'm already wondering if it would be better for Ken to drop me off down the street and I walk back to the apartment by myself.

"I forgot to mention," Ken started when we stopped at a light, "the villa only has four rooms. We never really thought we'd have this many people staying there, so we had to figure out room arrangements." Somehow, the thought of where I would be sleeping and if I had to share a room didn't cross my mind.

"My father and Jocelyn get the main room, Jenny and Jennifer are in a room. Sano, Jay, and I will be in a room, so that means you'll be with Amy." Me and that Amy lady in a room. She seems so nice, yet with her past with Jayson, she's not really wanted there either.

"I know you'd rather stay with me, but it was the best way we could avoid any unwanted problems." Jayson and Amy together would have been a problem, me staying with both Ken and Sano would have definitely been a problem. And making a room of three with the annoying duo would have been a nightmare.

"That should be fine. I mean, we're only sleeping in these rooms."

"Glad you're okay with it. Aside from what the past holds, Amy isn't that bad of a person. I think you two should get along nicely." Ken tried assuring me these room arrangements would be fine. It'll be just like old times for Ken, Jayson and Sano together. Maybe Amy and I can talk about our outsider status.

The drive back home felt shorter than it was to get to the lake. There was a part of me that wanted to take my mom's suggestion and invite him in since he's never been here. But Zoie and probably Lacey will be there. They may come over wanting details since I never responded to the multiple messages they sent.

"Despite this being one of my father's properties, I've never actually been to this place." Ken said once we made it back to the apartment. I couldn't tell if he was just saying that or if he wanted me to ask him in. If I tell him no, I'll have to say why…

"Well, if you don't have to get back just yet, you can come in and see the place." I got it out before I changed my mind. Ken didn't bother hiding his amused expression.

"I was simply making a statement after a little observation of the building, but if you're offering, I'll be happy to take the opportunity." He smiled. I might have read the situation wrong.

"My parents will probably be home soon, but all they'll do is ask you a ton of question as usual."

"I think after that little sit down with your father, I'm ready for anything." Ken seemed up for the challenge. I just hope that's the only challenge he has to take on by going in here.

"Are you nervous?" Ken asked and put his hand over mine.

"We lived together for a whole semester. What's there to be nervous about?" I looked at him. I hadn't really registered we'd be going in my empty apartment alone. I was so worried about Lacey; I didn't think about going into my place alone with Ken. He's used to my house, but I'm barely used to this place myself.

We both got out of the car, and I lead him to the third floor. I hope he didn't notice I was sort of tip toeing up the starts. I looked to room 3A making sure the door was closed and stopped at 3C. I hope he doesn't mind it's not a fancy script like his door has.

"Misa, you're home." My mom said.

"Mom?" My mother was sitting in the living room. She wasn't supposed to be home for at least another hour.

"Why do you sound so—oh, well hello there, Ken." She noticed him behind me.

"Hello. How are you today Mrs. Macky?" He went in to greet her.

"Probably not better than you're doing. How was your outing? And Misa, I've not seen this outfit before. Looks good." My mom looked me up and down.

"I quite enjoyed today, and I believe Misa did as well. Just a day at the lake that's near the Villa." Ken told her.

"I see. A little preview of your vacation? The weather was great today. I only wish I could have gone."

"Maybe when you're next free, we can arrange something." Ken was sweet talking my mom again.

"Aren't you home a bit early today?" I cut in.

"That's a long story I'll save for later. I don't want to bore you two with my work detail."

"I heard about your promotion. Congratulations," Ken told her.

"Thank you, Ken, but after today, I don't know if that's actually going to happen." She told him.

"What? What happened?" I asked.

"Again, long story. I'll tell you about it when your father gets home. Why don't you two get comfortable? Just act like you would back at the house as if I weren't here." My mom got up from the couch and walked to the kitchen. She's never home this early and she seems off. Something happened today. She's probably not talking because Ken is here.

"I'll make myself at home, but first, I'd like to use the restroom." Ken said.

"Down the hall on your right." My mom told him. Ken went to the bathroom, and I went to the kitchen with my mom.

"Did something happen?" I whispered to her.

"Like I said, we'll talk about it when your father gets home. But long story short, that transfer doesn't look like it's happening. And quite frankly, my position here is also in question."

"What?!" I was shocked. We went from moving to another city to not moving at all and losing what we already had. I couldn't get my next question out before we heard a knock on the door.

"Where you planning a wild party today?" My mom joked as she went to the door. I only wish it were that and not what my sinking heart was trying to tell me.

"Oh Zoie, good timing, Misa just got in." I heard my mom say when she opened the door. I went out to see only Zoie standing in the living room.

"Ken said he saw you coming in. You didn't respond to my message, so I had to come over." Zoie said.

"Misa, I'll leave you all. Let me know if you need anything." My mom left us and went to her room.

"Sorry, I didn't know your mom was already home." she whispered, "What happened today? Lace told me she freaked out on you."

"Uh, well..." it was happening, and I didn't know how to respond. My only relief is that Lacey wasn't with her.

I heard the bathroom door open. With each creak of the floor that came closer, my chest caved in more and more and my heart almost stopped when Ken appeared.

"Oh, Ken...dall didn't tell me you had company." Zoie was realizing the situation, "Long time no see, huh Ken?"

"Zoie, right? It's been a while." Ken said as he slowly walked back in.

"Good to see you back in the area since, you know, you kind of disappeared." Zoie said.

"It sort of just happened and I didn't get around to telling everyone." Ken told her.

"Do you want to come in and hang out." I asked Zoie. I'm surprised I even got that out considering how clogged it felt like my throat was getting.

"Actually, I think I need to go kill my brother, so I'll talk to you later Misa." Zoie threw a quick wave as she spun out the door. I had no choice but to close it and take my time turning back around.

"So, you know Zoie." Ken said. He went and sat on the couch. I walked over and sat a bit farther from him than I intended.

"She's the friend my mom wanted me to meet."

"I see. I think I remember something about her mom working at the company so that makes sense." He said to himself. "Is she your only friend here?" That hesitant question was for me.

"She has another friend that she introduced to me, and we've all been hanging out." I didn't realize I had the TV remote in my hand and was squeezing it as my nerve levels were rising. "Zoie and Lacey have been helping me adjust to my new life here."

It came out and I was still rolling the remote around in my hand. I looked over to Ken, and I think for the first time since I've known him, he seemed at a loss for words.

"They told me you and Lacey used to date a couple years ago. And you don't really talk anymore."

"That is true. Does it bother you?" Ken finally said something.

I already knew he dated before me. I accepted that fact when he told me. I didn't expect to run into anyone he's dated and find out the girl still likes him. They only broke up because she was being harassed. Ken didn't drive her away. So that only makes me wonder, would Ken still want to be with her too if she hadn't broken up with him.

"Does it bother you that I know her?" I looked to him. He was already looking in my direction, but not directly at me.

"I'll admit, this was a bit unexpected to find that out, but it can't be helped who you're friends with." Ken looked at me. But what I saw in his face wasn't the happy go lucky expression he usually has. "As long as you guys are friends and get along, that's all that matter, right?" he smiled.

I think I've been around him long enough to recognize the differences in his smiles. The one he was showing me was definitely forced. What am I to think of that? A forced smile after asking about his ex.

"Sorry, just passing through." I turned around and saw my mother appear again. "Did Zoie leave already?"

"Yeah. She had something to do." I told her. I couldn't tell her she basically told Ken what I've been trying to hide by simply showing up.

"Mrs. Macky, if I may, you said a moment ago, that there could be an issue with your promised promotion. If you'd like, I can ask my father about it."

"You're too sweet. I actually talked to Mr. Masidone before I left today. He said he would look into things for me, but I personally believe it's a done deal. It's nothing you have to worry about." My mom still seems bothered but went on like it was nothing. She went into the kitchen to grab something and went back to her room.

"Are you hoping she gets the promotion?" I asked him.

"I was just a bit confused. You said she hadn't spoken with my father about this and something such as a transfer to another city and promotion seems like he'd be the first to know and quite frankly, he'd want to be the one to tell her."

"So, what are you saying?"

"It's likely nothing now. If my father knows, then he'll take it from here." He reached over and laid his hand on my leg. "You know, I haven't gotten to see the whole place you got here."

"It's just an apartment. You can see the whole place from here."

"You've taken a tour of my home. I had a tour of your house. It only makes sense to keep the tradition going." He was serious. He wants me to take him around this one floor space.

"Alright, fine." I stood up. "This is the living room." I motioned my arms around. Ken stood up with me.

"I do like the interior. The furniture is slightly different, but still reminds me of your house." He ran his hand on the arm of the couch. We have a royal blue reclining sofa at home and this is just a regular grey sofa.

"If you take two steps to your right, you'll be in the kitchen," I pointed. I wasn't exactly taking this tour seriously.

"This is pretty nice. You can watch the TV as you cook." He said going in. The kitchen was open with marble countertops. He leaned on the counter and looked at me still standing in the living room.

"I think I like this place better. I can see you from another room."

"Have you never been in an apartment before?" I asked him.

"I have. It's been a while since I have, however, this one has you in it." He smiled. He's starting to seem like he's enjoying himself. He's a lot more upbeat from a moment ago when he heard about Lacey. I can't get the image out my head of the look he had when she came up.

"Since I'm in here, is it alright to grab some water?" He asked.

"It's a little weird to hear you ask for something." I walked to the counter.

"It's my first time here. Can't make myself at home just yet." He went to the refrigerator and grabbed two bottles of water and gave me one. "Shall I give you a cooking lesson while we're at it?"

"I thought you couldn't make yourself at home just yet?" I reminded him.

"There's exceptions to every rule."

"I don't think there's time for that. My dad will be home soon, and my mom had planned to cook."

"I suppose the lesson can wait until next time." He took a sip of his water. "Where to next?"

"You've already seen the bathroom. So that's it."

"I have seen the bathroom. The white and silver color scheme is very fitting. So that would just leave your room."

"You want to see my room?" I asked him.

"Is it not a part of the tour?"

"It's not that clean right now."

"That's the best time to show it. Mimi in her natural habitat." He did a hand motion in the air. I got out of a cooking lesson. I know I won't get out of this one.

My parents' room was at the end of the hallway. My room was on the left. I really didn't have much here. I thought I would just be here for the summer, so I didn't really decorate.

"Not bad." Ken said looking around. My only hope is that he doesn't see my basket of dirty laundry on the floor by my closet. He walked in a little further and glanced at my little dresser.

"What do we have here?" He reached down and grabbed something underneath a small bag I left up there. "These seem to keep coming back." He said holding up the pictures from our first mall trip. After finding his I went back to look for mine. They ended up in my moving bag and I again left them on my dresser and forgot about them.

"There's something different about yours." He held them closer.

"I think I'll be taking those back now." I went up to him and reached for them, but he turned away.

"Me and a pervert. Did you write that on here?" He noticed what I had written on the white boarder. "You marked and dated it?"

"It just happened a while ago. Now give them back!" I reached for them again and he held them up high.

"How long ago is a while?" he asked.

"Does that really matter?" The blood was rushing to my face. I can't believe he saw this!

"Considering that's your favorite thing to call me, it would seem you quite enjoyed these photos."

"I date all my prints. It was out of habit." I told him. Ken lowered his arm, and I grabbed them.

"Do you really?" He said it with disbelief. He was right to. I did date photos, but only special occasion photos. Sure, we weren't dating then, but I still found myself writing on them when I found them again.

"Glad to see you kept them." He seems pretty happy about that. I know it wasn't the best memory, but it was still a memory I kept. I sat the photo strip down and he leaned in to kiss me. He put a hand over mine on the dresser and the other around my back pulling us closer. I found my free hand resting on his arm.

"Just a reminder, my mom is in the other room and my dad is on his way." I had to break away.

"Just had to live up to my name." He smirked. And with that in mind, I didn't need either of my parents knowing what I call him.

"But, if your father is coming back soon, and I think you all have some things to discuss, I should probably head out." He said. My mom is waiting for my dad to come home to talk about her job thing. She can't say what she wants about the Masidone company with a Masidone in the house.

We went back into the living room. I subconsciously looked back to make sure my mom's door was still closed.

"Next time, we'll have that cooking lesson." Ken looked back over to the kitchen. He really does like the layout.

"As long as it's not Kool-Aid again, I guess that's fine." With the lessons I've gotten from Jayson, I think I've leveled up from his fundamental cooking class.

"I'll message you if I can come by again. Otherwise, we have a large kitchen at the villa as well. Being there for a week, we'll have plenty of time for a cooking session." I stood back as Ken opened the door. Something about the way his body seemed to have frozen made me peak out the door. And seeing your ex standing outside the neighbor's door seemed like a good reason to stop moving.

25

"Uhm, hi." I could see Lacey turned to face him from Zoie's door.

"Hey, there." Ken responded. You would think they were complete strangers by that awkward greeting.

"I was just going to see Zo. I didn't know you'd be here. I hope I didn't interrupt anything." She said.

"I was just on my way out."

"Oh, where're you headed?"

"I was headed home. I've been with Misa today." Ken replied. I poked my head from around the door. Lacey noticed me.

"Oh, hey Mi- "

"Will you get in here!" Zoie's apartment door flew open, and Lacey was taken in. I only wonder what took her so long to answer her door.

"I'll text you when I get home." Ken turned around and said to me. I just shook my head watching him down the stairs before I closed the door.

I went back and sat on the couch. Trying to figure out what to call today is going to take some time. From start to finish, it was a rollercoaster of nerves. Had I not invited Ken in, it would've ended with me just wondering about the messages I got. Now it's still that and whatever just happened in the hallway.

No matter how hard I tried to ignore it, the problem kept coming back stronger. And the strongest blow just happened. Lacey and Ken met and being that awkward with each other has to mean something. Obviously, Lacey still likes him. Ken didn't really say if he was okay or not with me knowing her.

I felt my phone buzz in my pocket and was almost too afraid to even see who it's from. I looked at my phone slowly and it was from Zoie asking me to come over. Come over to face the awkward moment that happened. I know I said I wanted to talk to Lacey about Ken, but I didn't expect to do it so soon.

I sat for a bit wondering if I should go. But I'll never get my answer if I don't. I got up, took a large inhale, and walked out to Zoie's apartment door and stopped there. I looked over at my door like Lacey did seeing Ken walking out. Because of that moment, I'm here knocking on her door.

"Uh, hi again." Zoie opened the door, "I wasn't sure if you were actually going to show since you didn't reply."

"Sorry. I thought my showing up was the reply." I said.

"It's fine. You're here and that's all that matters."

"Why, did something happen?" I asked even though I knew everything had happened.

"Well, aside from way earlier, earlier, and a minute ago, I have a frantic Lace over there wanting to apologize but was afraid to leave out even though we saw Ken taking off." I looked over to Zoie's balcony and saw Lacey sitting on the ground.

"After I pulled her in, she said she needed some air and has been sitting out there. I hope we didn't ruin your date. I wouldn't have shown up if I knew he was there. I've already dealt with Kendal. If you hadn't noticed, it's nice and quiet in here." I looked down the hall to their room. The door was shut, and I couldn't hear anything coming from it.

"You two seeing Ken was by chance. Those messages from earlier are a bit different though." I told her.

"We talked about him for a bit after you left yesterday. I wanted to make sure she was okay with this and…" Zoie turned to the balcony. Lacey was still sitting out there. She finally turned around and looked at me.

"I think you got enough air now." Zoie said. Lacey looked like she took a big inhale and stood up slowly. I would've waited for her to come back in, but I walked over to her.

"I'm sorry Misa." She blurted out as soon as she saw me.

"I thought you were okay with me being with Ken."

"I wanted to be." She started. She ran a hand through her hair and took another big breath. "I know it's been a while since we were together, but I've always wondered what would have happened."

"What do you mean?"

"We never got to talk about what actually happened back then. I was upset at everything that was going on, I just ended it so it would stop. Then I started avoiding him too afraid to talk to him again." She looked at me then averted her eyes.

"Knowing he's with someone else and the same thing is happening, but somehow things are still working out... I just wonder, If I had waited it out; or even talked to him afterwards-"

"Lace." Zoie said. She didn't want her to say anymore just as I didn't want to hear anymore.

"If I can't tell it to him, at least let me say it to her." Lacey told her.

"I don't think that's the same."

"I get what you're trying to say." I told them.

"I shouldn't have asked you all those questions while you were out. It just happened before I knew it. Just like me showing up now."

"Lacey!" Zoie said again.

"Zoie told me he was here. So, I rushed over without thinking. I didn't actually think I'd see him so fast if I expected to see him at all."

"What did you plan to do?" I asked.

"I don't know. Again, I came without thinking. It's been really had for me with my last breakup and now he's back around. When I heard he left school, I really thought that was it and I could never have a real talk with him."

"So, is that it? You just want to have a talk with him?" I waited for a reply. "Or did you want to talk to him hoping you'd get back together?"

"Well… it's too late for that now, isn't it?" She almost sounded defeated.

"So, you do have a problem with me dating Ken?" I asked her. That comment alone made it clear. She wanted to talk to him. She wanted to see if they could get back together after telling him what was really going on.

"I- I don't know. Misa, I like you and all and you had no idea about me and him. But I guess I might be, you know, a bit jealous that you're with him now." She admitted.

"You can't blame her Lace. I mean, you moved on just like he did." Zoie said.

"I know."

"So, can we get past this and figure out what time we're going to the movies Sunday?" Zoie didn't want to hear anymore. I didn't want to hear anymore. Mostly because I didn't know what to say. This was my first time experiencing something like this. I always knew of the girl code, but does the girl code still count when you didn't know the girl?

"I'll give you a time later. I need to go." Lacey said.

"Lace!" Zoie called out to her. She already went back in, grabbed a bag she had and walked out the door.

"Misa, I'm so sorry about this." Zoie came back over to me. I looked down to the parking lot watching Lacey get in her car and drive off.

"If you don't want to go to the movies, I understand."

"Maybe it's better if I didn't go." I said.

"Just give her some time. She'll be over it in like… a month." Zoie tried joking. But even if it was a month, that's still too long if we ever come around each other again and have to keep going through this…

"Maybe I shouldn't come over anymore. I don't want to come between you two."

"Hey, I don't care who you date. Have my exes if you want them. Actually no, James and Rodrick were jerks, and Sam's a cheater. I mean, you can have them. Just be aware." Zoie tried to joke again. Her friend just walked out the door. The mood felt like it couldn't get any worse than this.

"Are you going to be okay?" She asked me.

"I figured she still liked him. But not like this."

"I actually didn't know it was to this degree either. I know he was her first boyfriend and all, but she has to get over it."

"Maybe there's a reason she hasn't let go." That wasn't supposed to be said out loud, but the words came out.

"What do you mean by that?"

"Nothing. It was nothing." I said.

"A reason— do you mean Ken? Did he say something about her?"

"No, he didn't say anything." I told her.

Which was the problem. He didn't say anything about her after acting strange the minute she came up. When it comes to Jenny, he talks without a care. He talked to Lacey as if he was nervous. Ken Masidone, the pervert, nervous to talk to a girl.

"I think I should go back home for now." I told her.

"I'll talk to you later?"

"Yeah, talk later." I didn't run out like Lacey did, but I did need to go. I was starting to get a headache from all this.

"Even here, you're leaving without telling me." I walked into my mom back in the kitchen.

"I went to see Zoie."

"I take it Ken left?" She asked me. I just shook my head and went to my room. I sat on my bed and looked to my dresser. I got back up and went over to it and looked at the pictures that sat out since Ken found them.

"Misa, did something happen?" My mom came in after me.

"It's nothing." I told her. The bad part of being back around my parents all the time is having them around when I don't need them to be.

"I don't know what happened, but can it be solved by talking it out?"

"If it were that easy, then would there be problems?" I said.

"It can be. Just be open and honest and lay out the issues. You kids are young; things happen. And whatever happened, I'm sure you'll figure out what to do."

My mom didn't pry into what might've happened. It's like she already knew. But how do I ask if you still like your ex? And where does that leave me and Lacey? She asked about Ken while I was out with him. She raced over here when she found out he was here. I thought I only had to worry about Jenny doing stuff like that. Is it a requirement that once you like him, you have to be able to find him wherever he goes?

"I think the real talk is about to happened." My mom said when we heard the front door open.

"Oh, Claire." I heard my dad call in the living room. We both walked in to see my dad more confused than I've seen him in a while.

"Hi honey, how was your day?" My mom asked.

"Oh, not as good as yours must have been. I mean, what can be a better feeling than quitting your job?"

"You quit?" I turned to her.

"I didn't quit." She said.

"You sure? Then why are they talking about replacing you? Not for the sake of the promotion, but because you walked out on them?"

"I didn't walk out. Mr. Masidone said I could go if I wanted. So, I did."

"Mr. Masidone? Okay, so one, why were you talking to him again? And two, what was discussed that resulted in you quitting?"

"Why are you insisting that I quit?"

"Because the only time you walk out of anything, is when you're done with it. Even when they offered early leave, you turned it down." My dad was on to something. My mom didn't have a quick response.

"Alright, you're right. I tried to quit. But Mr. Masidone told me to sleep on it before I make that my decision." My mom admitted.

"And again, how did we get to these results?"

"Because they wanted to get rid of me anyway. I was only expediting the process." She told us.

"What do you mean by that?"

"There was never a promotion. I talked to Lance again today because something wasn't adding up. He couldn't tell me anything about the job or the manager from the new office. Not to mention they tried to change the location."

"They tried offering you another place?"

"Yes. They weren't accepting anyone at the original transfer office and tried having me go somewhere else."

"I knew something wasn't right from the beginning." My dad said.

"So, you quit?" I asked.

"I don't know what I did to prompt this. I've been nothing but good to these people, and my reward for that is to be sent away like a bad food dish? Why not just fire me if they had such a problem."

"I know what the problem is." My dad said.

"You're saying I had a problem?" She asked.

"Oh, you had a problem all right. I'm partly to blame for it too. It's a problem almost seventeen years in the making." He gave my mom a look.

"Are you saying Mi—in the room." My mom pointed back and walked to their bedroom.

"Sweetie, give us a minute." She said to me and closed the door.

Seventeen years in the making. My birthday is in a couple of weeks. Something I almost forgot about. My dad is saying I was to blame. My mom is in a position to quit her job. This has to be something about Ken. Is he saying they want her to leave because I was with Ken?

I know Mr. Masidone doesn't really like me that much, but to go this far? Why would he invite me to his villa if he's been trying to get rid of us?

I reached into my pocket for my phone to see I had a new message from Ken saying he was home and had a good time. Does he know what his father has been doing? Ken would always fight his dad when it came to him doing something with me so maybe he doesn't know. He did ask about it earlier.

I feel like the roller coaster of nerves is still going in loops. My mom might actually be out of her job. I might have just lost a friend. I don't know what to say or if I should tell Ken. It's not like he could do anything about it. Especially now that we've gotten this far.

"Cocoa," My dad came back out the room, "we've come to a conclusion. You're not allowed to see that boy anymore."

"What?"

"Mark!" My mom shouted.

"Was that not the conclusion we came up with?" He asked.

"Far from it. That was your conclusion along with your conspiracy theories."

"Are you saying I can't go to the villa?" I asked out of the blue.

"Yes, you can go." My mom came in the living room. "This has nothing to do with you kids. Until we figure out the exact cause, this situation stays in my hands, alright?" My mom gave my dad a look. My dad flashed one back to her.

"So, what's going to happen?" I asked.

"I don't want you to worry about it, but it does seem like my days there could be done. I enjoyed working there, but what I don't enjoy is being played with, and finding out that promotion was just a ploy to get rid of me, I don't think I can stay in that position."

I didn't know what to say. I didn't know if there was anything I could say. I know she liked her job and did what she could. I've never seen her make such a quick decision before. She's completely serious about her choice, and I don't think there's anything Mr. Masidone could do to change it.

"I'm going to continue with dinner." My mom went to the kitchen. My dad went in with her. I wasn't sure what to do and went back to my room.

I didn't have an appetite. Trying to swallow all of today is enough. The only thing left I want to do today is lay in bed, and finally reply to Katie. She's in for a treat.

# 26

"You know, for someone going away to a fancy villa tomorrow doesn't seem too happy." Zoie said.

"I guess I'm a little nervous." I told her.

"Nervous about what?" She asked. We sat on her balcony with the sun on us and music playing. We only just started hanging out again a few days ago. Can I really trust telling her anything and she not go back and tell Lacey?

We haven't talked since the day everything happened. Lacey went on vacation with her parents but hasn't messaged me or anything since then. But she's still talking to Zoie. She can't get anything out of her on the subject either when she talks to her. I guess Zoie was right. Either she's not talking to me anymore, or she'll need a month to get over this.

"I stayed the night once at his house before, and that was by accident. Staying an entire week with his family just seems a bit overwhelming." I told her.

"Why is that? Are those other girls going? Jenny and Jennifer? They're really close with the family, right?"

"Yeah, they are."

"That's rough. It's going to be tough being around them for that long in a secluded place. Have you heard anything from either of them?" She asked.

"Not since we've left school. It's been pretty peaceful."

"Hopefully that peace lasts. Remembering how they treated Lacey, I'd be worried they do something being together that long."

"Ken's parents will be there. I doubt they'd try anything with them around." I told her. Although Jennifer likes to press that thought, remembering the times we've run into each other at the mansion.

"Did he ever say anything about seeing Lacey? I know it was for a second, but it has been a while." She said.

"No, he hasn't."

Tomorrow, I'm supposed to be with him for a week, and I'm going there knowing there's new tension for us. Not just the Lacey situation, but the fact I had to turn down a visit from him since my dad didn't want any early visits from the Masidone family since my mom quit her job and he believes he has something to do with it.

Of course, that's just his guess. Mr. Masidone said he didn't know about the promotion until my mother mentioned it to him. I couldn't tell Ken because I didn't want him to think so too. But how do I face him knowing that there's that possibility? Not only that, I had to lie about why he couldn't come back and have that cooking lesson in my open kitchen he loved so much.

"If he didn't say anything then don't say anything either." Zoie started, "You'll be there for a week. Just enjoy all you can. Enjoy that life of luxury to the fullest and just have some fun in the sun. It's supposed to be sunny all week. I hope you bought sunscreen and a new swimsuit."

"Does the one he bought me count?"

"Oh, nice. That's even better. I don't know everything going on between you two, but I hope you'll enjoy yourself. You deserve a little relief after being thrown out here and dealing with Lacey and her emotions."

Zoie has always been nice since I met her. She only wants to help me and be a good friend even though Lacey, her best friend, doesn't seem to want to anymore. I only hope that there won't be any further problems with Lacey.

After that day, everything just felt different, but I needed someone to help me relax before being with the Masidones for a week. Zoie still wants to be my friend, so being with her did help relax me a bit.

I managed to wind down the day and get the last of what I needed packed. I told Ken we'd be there a little after noon. My dad was up bright and early, and my mom wouldn't let us leave until he promised her he wouldn't do anything other than see the house and drop me off. After that and the several hours it took to come to an agreement, we finally headed out on my last high school summer adventure.

"You know, if you get tired, bored, or just ready to come home, just call me and I'll be here before you even press connect." My dad told me as we drove to the villa. I just agreed, not wanting him to go on his newly found interest in going on rants of the Masidone company and its people. My only surprise is that he still works there and hasn't quit either. I just looked out the window remembering the last time I came here with Jayson and Jocelyn on her 'get to know me' trip.

"Well, I guess this place does exist." My dad made the turn into the concrete path that took us in front of the lake and up to the Masidone villa. "Is this what he's doing with the money we make him?"

"Dad, you promised you wouldn't say anything." I reminded him.

"Do you see Mr. Masidone around? I said I wouldn't say anything to him." He said pulling up to the front entrance. He stepped out the car and I went to the trunk to get my bag.

"Misaky!" I looked up and saw Jayson coming out of the house. "It's been too long. You look more and more like a gem every time I see you. And Papa Macky, glad to see you're doing well."

"Forgive me if I can't remember, but it's Jayson, right?"

"The one and only. I want to thank you for allowing Misaky to be here this week with us." Jayson told him.

"Oh, it's not a problem. This is a fine place you got out here. Seems a bit out the way though."

"It was the best location for privacy, and access to the gorgeous Lake front. You have nothing to worry about. We have a top-notch security system. We're here all the time and have never had a problem."

"I'm sure you haven't. Not with those glass walls you got there." My dad said looking over to the house. He's really pushing the 'Mr. Masidone isn't around' card.

"Oh, fun fact, we have a one-way window setup. We can see out, but you can't see in, and we have blackout blinds unit installed we put down after dark. I will bet you my good looks you could never see in there. Especially at night. Why don't I give you a quick tour of the place? We can head to your room first so you can set your things down Misaky."

Jayson was overjoyed to see me. I did miss seeing him. But now isn't the time to catch up. I needed my dad to get going as soon as possible. I got my bags and walked a bit faster up to the door than I intended. I looked and noticed the door had black scripted *M* that was light, yet still stood out against the white rim of the door.

"After you." Jayson opened the door to let us in. I could tell his maids were here. This place seemed almost more spotless than the mansion. Freshly polished floors. The living room area was sunken in with a black rounded leather furniture set facing a pillar with a mounted flat screen over a fireplace.

"This is the 'relax room," come down here and enjoy a cup of coffee next to the fireplace if we're not enjoy a meal over here in the dinning space." He gestured over to the table similar to the one at the mansion. A wooden round tabled with glass down the center of it with black chairs.

"Follow me up the stairs, I'll show you the kitchen after we get these bags down." Jayson said, taking us up the stairs to see a balcony view of the lower level. There was a door at both ends of the hallway and two in the middle.

"The last door on your right is the bathroom. This room here is the one you'll be sharing with Amy." He told me.

"Amy?" My dad asked.

"Amy David. She's— an old friend of the family. She's going to be doing a photoshoot here of the villa. Misa has already met her and said she's fine with rooming with her."

"This just keeps getting better. My cocoa, rooming with what, a model of sorts?" My dad asked.

"Yes, she's been in all the magazines, TV interviews and more." Jayson told him. I hope it wasn't too much for him to talk about her. I went in the room with two queen sized beds. One already had bags on it. There was another smaller flat screen TV mounted on the wall over a large brown dresser. At the other end of the room was a balcony we could go out on. I've never seen a bedroom with a balcony.

"Misaky, make yourself at home. Amy is here somewhere, but I'm pretty sure she claimed the bed she has her belongings on." She left me the bed that was closest to the balcony. I put my stuff down and couldn't help but go over the window to see out of it. It was a clear view of the lake.

"Just leave it, it should be fine." I heard a voice from the balcony. I opened the window and stepped out. I made eye contact with Ken who was leaning against the ledge. It was an open balcony that allowed us to walk through freely.

"Mimi, you're here!" He said full energy. He came over and hugged me.

"I see this is some sort of open balcony design." My dad came over.

"Afternoon Mr. Macky." Ken said as soon as he noticed my dad was still here.

"Yes, this balcony extends across with a chair and table set at both ends if you feel like taking in the breathtaking scenery. I'm showing Papa Macky around so just give me a few minutes I'll be back up." Jayson told Ken.

"Take your time. I hope you find the place to your liking Mr. Macky." Ken said. My dad didn't respond right away. He sort of looked him up and down first.

"So far, it's a very fine place. Are you in the room next door?"

"Yes. Sano, Jay, and I are sharing that room."

"Ah, that's right. He's here too. I remember hearing about this situation before." My dad said. I forgot I had to tell him everything when he questioned why he'd be here too. This just adds fuel to my dad's burning flame he's trying not to let out.

"We decided to let the girls share a room and we'd share one. I hope you don't find that a problem?" Jayson said.

"Not at all. I think these arrangements are fine."

"Well, if you're okay with it, then shall we continue the tour? Misaky, you have to see the kitchen. I can't wait to have a cooking session together." Jayson said.

"Cooking? Since when could you cook?"

"Jayson has shown me a few things before." I told him.

"I showed her, but she delivered. She's a natural." Jayson stretched the truth a bit. But as long as he has my dad distracted, he can say what he wants. I don't know how many more surprises my dad can take before he breaks his promise to my mom, and I have a shorter vacation than I thought.

Jayson managed to get my dad away from Ken and we headed back out. I turned to take another glimpse of Ken who was still watching us. I also noticed at the corner of the balcony Sano was coming over. Ken turned to him and said something, but I was already outside the room before I could hear it. I wonder why he didn't show up sooner. He probably heard my dad's tone and figured he was better off. That might've been best.

We continued on the tour going back down to the kitchen. It had a large hanging glass chandelier over the kitchen island that had bags of groceries they hadn't put away yet. The floors were so polished I thought I might slip if I weren't careful. It had a full open view of their backyard pool we went to see next. It was so clear and refreshing like a glass of water. I almost wanted to jump in.

"You are the professional. I like that idea." More voices, reminding me how many people were here, were heard coming from the side of the house.

"Jaycee, Misaky!" It was Amy. She was walking with Mr. Masidone from what looked like their outdoor garden.

"Mister and Miss Macky, welcome. I hope you found your way here no problem?" Mr. Masidone asked.

"A nice drive to the forest Mr. Masidone." My dad said.

"Oh please, call me Kenneth."

"Oh, I think that's a bit out of my pay grade Mr. Masidone." My dad told him. This is it. My dad has to go. I was hoping to take this tour without Mr. Masidone being a part of it. Who knows what he'll do now…

"Oh Misaky, I'm so glad we get to share a room. I hope you don't mind; I already claimed a bed. We can switch if you want." Amy said.

"No, it's fine." I told her. Amy is just as nice as before. She changed from blue to purple ombre hair with a pink crop top and black leggings on. I wonder what it's like to always look ready to go down a runway.

"I trust my daughter will be in good hands." My dad said. It wasn't a question. But he was definitely expecting an answer.

"I wouldn't have invited Miss Macky here if I didn't think it was secure. I know she and my son have been getting well acquainted. I figured since they are getting along so well, why not bring her along for a Masidone style vacation."

"Thank you for the opportunity. I think I've seen all I need to see and should be headed back home." My dad said.

"You're going?" I asked.

"You want me to stay? Or is it that you don't want to?"

"No, no, that's not it!" I quickly answered. He jumped to conclusions way too fast. I only asked because I thought he'd interrogate Mr. Masidone, and I'd have to drag him out…

"You're welcomed to stay a bit longer if you're interested." Mr. Masidone said.

"Oh, I couldn't impose. Besides, now that my wife is unemployed, she gets a bit bored being home all day. I don't want to leave her there too long." My dad told him. I was sure I heard Jayson gasp behind me. Mr. Masidone kept his poker face.

"It was unfortunate we had to lose such a diligent worker. Please let her know, we'll always hold her position."

"I'll rely the message. Come on cocoa, walk your old man to his car. Thanks for the tour, Jayson." He gave a quick wave back. I took a peak back and saw him wave as well. That last comment actually left him speechless.

"You can tell your mother I didn't do a thing." My dad said when we got to his car.

"Did you have to go and say that? Now you've made things awkward." I told him.

"What did I say wrong? Your mother is unemployed, and she's been doing a lot of odd projects out of boredom, some of which you had to partake in. What exactly did I say wrong?"

"You know what I mean dad. That was uncalled for!"

"You're starting to sound like your mother. You really are growing up." He gave me a hug. "You be good and remember what I told you to do if they try to corner you."

"Kick and punch, call 911. Got it." He gave me a kiss on the forehead and finally got in the car. I watched him drive away before I walked back to the villa.

"Misaky." I looked over to the side of the house where Jayson stood. Amy was behind him.

"What Papa Macky just said. Is that really true?"

"Uhm, yeah." I told him. I didn't really want to talk about it. I'm just glad Ken wasn't around to hear it.

"I'm so sorry to hear that. Why don't we get you back inside so you can get properly situated." He suggested.

"Oh, Jaycee, can I take it from here? I want to get to know my new roomie." Amy looked to me, "Do you mind?"

"No, that's fine." Amy doesn't know anything. She may actually be the safest person to be around.

"Well, alright. I'm headed up to see Kenny-Kens. I'll be next door if you need me." Jayson took off. Amy came over and looped her arm around mine.

"This is a vacation, so let's enjoy ourselves, yeah?" We walked back to the house. I think she noticed I was starting to feel anxious. I looked over the villa again as we went back. To think I'll be staying in a house like this. I thought the mansion was over the top. But this place has a new kind of overwhelming feeling.

"This is my first time here. It's such a beautiful house. Have you been here before?" Amy asked when we got back to our room.

"I came by once. I stayed in the car though, so I didn't really see it."

"I've stayed at some nice places, and this is definitely at the top of the list." She went and sat down on her bed. "So, you know everyone here, right?"

"Yeah, I know everyone." I didn't want to admit it. Although, I haven't seen the annoying duo yet.

"You got the boys room next door. Then there's the other room with the sisters, Jenny and Jennifer. Or as Jaycee calls them, the little kittens. I didn't get the chance to officially meet them. How are they? I want to get to know them too. I think we should have a little fun, just the four of us girls.

"Just the four of us?" I didn't mean to ask that out loud but that's how surprised I was.

"Yeah! You don't think that's a good idea?" She asked. Even her confused expression was photogenic.

"Well, I mean, we don't always get along, but I suppose since we're all here, we could try something." I couldn't just say no when she got so excited. I know Jayson has a bad history with her, but if it's just us girls hanging out, and I'm not left alone with the duo, maybe this won't be a complete disaster.

"That's great! We should set some activities up for tomorrow afternoon. That way, you can still have some time for little Kenny, right? Jaycee told me that you two were dating. I'm so jelly! Little Kenny is so sweet. You two seem like such a cute couple!" She put her hands together just imagining it.

"Once I got to know him, he's not so bad." I told her.

"Right? Everyone is so nice in this family. Once you get to know them, you never want to leave." Amy seemed like she went into her own world as she smiled and played with one of her bag straps. She must still be thinking about Jayson. I wonder if I could ask her about that...

"Oh, I forgot, I still needed to talk to Mr. Masy. I just got so excited when you showed up. We're doing the photoshoot on Wednesday. Maybe you can be in it too."

She jumped up and rushed out of the room. She seems so full of energy. I can see why she's so attached to Jayson. If we put those two together, the sun wouldn't stand a chance.

"Knock, knock." I turned and saw Ken at the door. "I couldn't help but notice Amy running out. Everything alright over here?"

"She had to go talk to Mr. Masidone." I said.

"I thought they spoke earlier."

"I guess they weren't done. She got distracted when she saw me."

"I suppose I wasn't the only one excited to see you here." He said.

"Are you really that happy?"

"What about you?" He countered. "I know being here with my family may not be the most thrilling thing for you, but I hope this week won't be too torturous." Ken was happy I was here, but still concerned about me being here.

"If I didn't think I could enjoy myself, I wouldn't have come." I told him. He doesn't seem like he's bothered by anything. To him, that was my dad's normal behavior. He doesn't know he was the one far from happy about me being here.

"Everyone is still just hanging out. We're planning what we want to do this week. Want to join us?" He asked me.

"You don't have that planned already?"

"It's not really something to pre plan. It's mostly planning it by ear and how the weather will be." He told me. It is a vacation, but it's not like we're at Disney World and need to map out what to do and see. They're here every year. They probably do the same things all the time.

I got up and went with him back to his room. I noticed at the end of the hallway the door was open. That was Jenny and Jennifer's room. They're out and about somewhere. I only hope they see Amy first so she can ask about our girl time. It'll be harder to say no to her bright smile.

"I hope you're settling in well." I went in and saw Jayson sitting on a couch they had in their room. Aside from that, it was arranged like our room.

"Hey Misa." Sano spoke from the bed. He looks like he did the last time I saw him. I don't know if I was expecting him to look or act different. He's been back home for a while. He's probably well-adjusted to his old life by now.

"Do you think you're going to be okay rooming with Amy?" Jayson asked.

"She's very nice. I shouldn't have any issues."

"That's good you two are getting along. I know what it feels like to have a bad roommate. Had one of those in college. That was a long month." Jayson rolled his eyes.

"Just a month?" Sano asked.

"Wait, is that the roommate that got arrested for stealing?" Ken thought.

"Why do you think it was only a month? He wasn't the brightest thief. He would go to the same store every time. He dragged me out once with him, and since I had found out he stole my last fifty dollars, I might've told security that photo on the wall looked a lot like him." Jayson said with sly smile.

"You turned him in for fifty bucks?" Sano asked.

"I was in between jobs at that time. He also had a bad habit of eating my food. You know how I feel about my food."

"Speaking of food," Ken turned to me, "you hungry? We've already been here for a while and missed lunch."

Even though I've been up all morning, I didn't have much of an appetite. Now that I'm here, I feel a little less tense. But it's way too soon to relax.

"Sure, I could eat." I said.

"You guys coming?" Ken asked.

"I would say you two go ahead, but I could eat too." Jayson said and stood up. Sano got off the bed too. We all headed downstairs. I looked around as we went to the kitchen. I could see outside Amy was still talking to Mr. Masidone. I only hope they can keep talking until we're done in her.

"I know we're on vacation, but who forgot to put everything away?" Jayson asked, seeing the bags I saw earlier still on the counter.

"I thought Jenny and Jennifer were doing it." Ken said. We all went and sat around the island counter.

"That's right. They disappeared as soon as they got here. Though, they haven't been baring their claws lately; they seem sort of quiet." Jayson started putting things away.

"I don't know what's been going on with them. Maybe the fresh air here will loosen them up." Ken added.

"Before I put everything away, what should I leave out?"

"Whatever you want to make us." Ken smiled.

"I could have sworn I just said we were on vacation. I am not obligated to cater to anybody. Except Misaky. It'll be my pleasure to get you whatever you desire." Jayson winked at me. Ken leaned over and whispered something in my ear. I looked at him and he put his hands together asking me to go along with him.

"Could I have a steak, medium rare and a baked potato." I said. Ken whispered into my ear again. "With extra bacon." I added.

"Oh, see now that's not a relationship, that's a cahoots I tell you." We all laughed when we heard the back door open.

"Sounds like a party in here." Amy said coming into the kitchen.

"We're just trying to figure out what to have." Ken told her.

"I can see we're having some fun. Did Misa tell you our big fun day tomorrow?"

"You two have plans?" Ken asked.

"Actually, us four. And by four, I mean us two and the two kittens upstairs." She smiled happily.

"Jenny and Jennifer? You managed to get them to do something?"

"Well, I haven't asked them yet. I was just on my way to do so when I heard you all laughing in here."

"Uhm, Amy. I'm sure you have good intentions, but sometimes they can be a bit rough to handle." Jayson told her.

"Oh, come on Jaycee. They seem like they need a little fun. So, what better way to do that than now? Don't worry, you know me. I'll bring them around." She flashed him a model smile and took off again.

"Did you really agree to that?" Ken asked me.

"Well, it didn't take much for her to bring me around. She wants to do something tomorrow with us girls, so I agreed."

"She must be really good." He stated. He also leaned over again and whispered in my ear, "You sure you're okay with this?"

He asked was I really okay with hanging out with the annoying duo. It's not like I could say no in fear of them double teaming me. The last thing I remember from them is Jennifer telling me how this war wasn't over. But for someone who seemed ready to attack sure hasn't shown themselves yet. It could be a part of their plan. But I didn't want to run away on the first day...

"I'm sure it should be fine." Jayson said. "Like I said, they haven't been baring their claws much lately. You probably have nothing to worry about."

"What's there to be fretted by? This is a no worry zone." Mr. Masidone was next to come in. "We're here to get away from any concerning endeavors, right, Miss Macky? Aside from possible rain a little later this week, the weather calls for clear skies. I expect everyone to be out claiming some of that sun."

"Oh, you already know we will. By the way, what day was someone coming out to check the boats?" Jayson asked.

"Unfortunately, I couldn't get anyone to come out until Wednesday. Which may actually workout since we have to set up for Amy's photo session. Everyone will be free to roam the waters after the inspections are completed."

"Sounds like we have our Thursday planned. I hope you don't mind us calling dibs on the first round?" Jayson asked.

"In honor of all of our new and returning visitors," Mr. Masidone patted Sano on the back, "You kids do whatever like." He sort of glanced over all of us and walked out. "Returning to my room for a bit. I'll see you all later."

I wasn't sure if he heard us talking about Jenny and Jennifer. And if he did, he didn't seem bothered by it. He really is in vacation mode. Normally, he'd say something about me and Ken.

"Alright, back to business" Jayson got our attention, "I, the best Jayson in this kitchen, will prepare you all something. However, we are not having steak." He glared at Ken.

"Alright, fine. I'll just take the potato. Extra bacon." Ken tried pressing his luck again.

Ken seemed so relaxed and sort of normal. It's usually just us two, but seeing him interact with Jayson like this is another new side of him. I looked to the other side of him to see Sano. He really hasn't said much. I can't tell if something is bothering him or not. They all seem so comfortable with each other. I thought they had gotten him to open up.

I might have been staring too long because he looked over to me. I turned back to Jayson who started putting something together. It was only now that it was hitting me that I'm really going to be with the Masidone family for a week.

Jayson kept it simple making us hot sandwiches. After we ate, both Sano and Jayson decided to leave, leaving Ken and I at the island counter. Suddenly, it felt a little awkward being a lone with him knowing anyone could show up at any time.

"Doing alright so far?" He asked.

"It's only been a few hours. Hardly any time for something to happen." I said.

"What are you expecting to happen?"

"I don't know. Anything is possible when you're involved."

"Is that a compliment? Because I'll take it." He said and smiled. "We didn't have much planned for today. So, if you want to do anything. Take a walk, watch a movie, find that ball we lost from last time."

The ball that was swept away from the other end of the lake. It's been over a week since then. Since the last time we met. If we had just stayed at the lake, then maybe everything wouldn't have spiraled downhill.

"Do you really think it floated all the way down here?" I asked.

"Are the odds low and it didn't travel much further than it did and someone else picked it up? Likely so. But is the chance still there and the wind did keep it blowing down the lake? Something we'd have to check out and see. I haven't been out there yet, so I'm not sure which probability proves true." Ken said. He seemed like he really wanted to go out there.

Did I really feel like going for another swim? I'd say staying in is fine, but with there being someone everywhere, I feel like I could never relax.

"Well, well, it's been a while Misa." I turned to see one of the reasons I could never relax entering the kitchen. "How are you on this fine afternoon?" Mrs. Baker walked over to us. Normally, she's dressed up in a fancy dress.

With the loose-fitting red blouse and fitted jeans, she almost looked like a different person.

"Everything is fine." I told her.

"That's good to hear. Glad to see you made it. I know little Kenneth would've been heartbroken if you hadn't come." She walked over to the fridge and grabbed a water bottle. "Please continue as you were. I just needed a refreshment." She sounded as if she was going to leave, but she leaned against the counter drinking.

"Looks like you all made yourselves a snack. Don't forget, you're making dinner with your father tonight." She spoke to Ken.

"That might've slipped my mind."

"I don't see how. You do this every year on the first night. Misa dear, I think you're making him a bit soft." She laughed, "I guess that can happen when you get caught up and distracted by something else." She took another sip of her water. It was obvious she meant me being the distraction. I looked to Ken, who didn't seem bothered by her comment.

"Are you all still here- oh Miss Jocelyn, you've joined the party." Amy came back down.

"What's gotten you so full of energy?" She asked her.

"I came back down to tell Misaky we're good to go for tomorrow! Jennifer and Jenny agreed to our girl time."

"Oh, what's that? You all are planning time together?" Mrs. Baker asked.

"That's right. Since it's all of our first time here, I wanted us to have some fun together."

"You're truly a lovely woman Amy. I think that's a wonderful idea. You know what the rest of us did last year? We had a fantastic, yet very exhausting, round of pool volley ball. I don't think I can do that again, but you all should be much more flexible and full of energy to do so." Jocelyn suggested.

"That sounds great! I haven't done pool volleyball since my friend's party a year ago. What do you say?" She looked to me.

"Sounds fun." I told her. I guess that swim will happen. Just not with Ken.

"Perfect! I'll go let them know to pull out their swimsuits." Amy took off once again.

"She picked the right profession. She's always on the go." Mrs. Baker watched her out. "I'll be seeing you all at dinner." She was next to leave.

"For me, it's normal. Being around so many people might take some getting used to for you. We'll have to go look for that ball another day." Ken told me. He must have realized that time together just got cut short. Going from it being just my mom and dad in our house to a house of nine will take some getting used to.

Day one was done. Looking at the closed blinds and the sun peeking through from the side reminded me I was still at the villa. The day ended after Ken and his dad became chiefs for us. Mr. Masidone seemed to be enjoying himself. Ken seemed as if he was just filling a roll. After dinner was done, they decided for us all to watch a movie. Even though not everyone seems to be on the same page being here, they still do things like family dinner and movies.

I finally saw Jenny and Jennifer. Both of them stared at me as if I did something wrong. Even though in their eyes, I am the something wrong. It's been a while since school was out. I haven't seen them since. Jennifer usually fakes a smile and always had something to say when around everyone. She didn't say anything to me. This only makes me wonder what to expect today when I have to spend actual time with them.

I realized it was still early when I looked at my phone and it said 7:30am. Somehow, I was wide awake. I rolled over to see my roommate still sleeping. After the forty-five-minute skincare routine she did last night, she's probably tired. She tried to show me some of it. I never knew or heard of half the products and skin messaging technics she used. It was no wonder she seemed to glow. She does a lot to maintain her looks.

I got up as quietly as I could to leave out the room. I wouldn't want to ruin her sleep, and she ends up with a pimple or something. I headed towards the bathroom when I noticed Ken's room was empty. All three of them were already up and doing something. I peeked downstairs to see if they were in their relaxing room and didn't see anyone. I did hear something in the kitchen. I decided to go down to see if it had been them, but I was sorely mistaken when I saw it was Mr. Masidone in the kitchen making coffee.

"Good morning, Miss Macky. I hope you had a restful night."

"I-I did. I had no problems sleeping last night." I told him. I didn't tell him that waking up at 7:30 was probably the result of nerves since I can hardly wake up on time to get to school.

"That's what I like to hear. Can I offer you a cup?" He asked, grabbing hold of the coffee pot.

"No thank you. I um, I'm not a big coffee drinker."

"You're on vacation Miss Macky. That timid behavior has no place here. Unless there's something bothering you and you would like to discuss it?" Mr. Masidone took a sip of his coffee.

He watched me waiting for a response. To think he would ask if something was wrong when he knows about my mom's situation and how that has affected us and how my dad acted towards him yesterday…

"Well…" I started. That thought was really weighing on me. I didn't want to bring anything up while here to ruin the vacation. I thought I'd talk to Ken about it first at least, but now that Mr. Masidone has asked, the thought really wants to come out.

"What happened with my mom's transfer?" No matter how I tried to figure out the best way to ask, that was the best thing I could get out.

"From my understanding, it turned out her original transfer location had some complications. When that came to light, it was decided to move forward with another location."

"She told me there was never a promotion. I mean, it was kind of unexpected to begin with. Then she said they couldn't tell her about what was going on. She believes it was a set up."

"That seems a little extreme don't you think?" He said with a little laugh, "You have to understand Miss Macky that things happen. Unexpected things. When we first considered your mother, we had everything in order. Unfortunately, something came up. We offered an alternative, and it seems as though that wasn't what your mother was looking for."

"We?" I asked. Something about that didn't sound right. "The promotion was brought up weeks ago. My mom only just talked to you about it recently." Ken also seemed confused that he wasn't aware of this from the beginning. But Mr. Masidone is saying he was.

"What exactly are you implying Miss Macky?" His tone was even, but something about the look in his eye changed. "I know everything that goes on at my company whether it's brought to my attention or not."

"So, why weren't you the one to talk to her about it from the beginning?" I must be sleep talking. I don't know where I got the courage to ask Mr. Masidone this, but what my mom has been telling me, and what he's saying, doesn't fit together. She said he didn't know about it when she talked to him before. My mom wouldn't lie, but he's speaking so surely of knowing it all.

"You seem to be worried about your mother are you not?" He asked. He put down his coffee cup and leaned on the island counter near me. "As I have already stated, she was offered another opportunity that she turned down. She took it into her own account to leave her current position. Now, unless you would have preferred the automatic transfer, there's not much else that could have been done." The look in his eye was even more stern. His voice didn't change, but the look was enough to say he was done with this conversation.

"I'm sure your reason for coming down here wasn't just to talk to me. You were looking for my son, right?" He went back over to his cup on the counter. I didn't want to say anything else and shook my head.

"Ken, Sano, and Jayson are all in the pool house. I noticed them going in just before you came down. I'm sure they wouldn't mind you greeting them this morning." I turned and looked out the Kitchen window to the smaller house passed the pool. I made my way towards the door.

"One last thing," he called out to me, "I'd just like to thank you again for helping me reunite with my long-lost son. Whether you're going out there to speak with him or not, the fact that he's here is all thanks to you." He held up his cup to me and walked off in the other direction to his room. I don't know what to say to what just happened. Maybe I'm still asleep and this is all a weird dream from being surrounded by the Masidones...

Stepping out to the morning sunrise feeling the cool air across my skin made me realize it wasn't a dream, and Mr. Masidone really said all that to me. What was that about Sano? And what do I believe about the real reason for my mom's job? I am worried about her. She wouldn't just up and quit a place she wanted so badly to work in. Getting Mr. Masidone to agree to some arrangement with his son just so she could have a doorway up. She wouldn't leave all that for nothing. Maybe my dad was right, and it is about me.

"Well sunny morning to you Misaky. Did you sleepwalk here?" Jayson came and opened the door I was standing outside of.

"I didn't expect for you to be up so early." Ken said resting on the ledge of a couch. It was like a little apartment but still seemed bigger than mine.

"If we knew you'd be up, we would have invited you on our morning run." Jayson said. The shorts and tanks they were all wearing made sense. They went out together for a morning workout. I never knew either of them did that. But I only saw those two. Sano wasn't here.

"I'm starting to believe the sleepwalking thing. Mimi you there?" Ken waved his hand in my face.

"If I were sleepwalking, do you think that's how you'd wake someone up?" I asked.

"Well, you do sleep like the dead. I've had to go through a lot more than that to get you up."

"I do not sleep that hard." I folded my arms.

"Oh really? I seem to recall many times I had to go to school on my own since, no matter what I did, you wouldn't wake up."

"Exactly what did you do?" I was afraid to hear that answer. I know how much of a heavy sleeper I am. I never had time to think about what he did to try to wake me up since I was always in a hurry. Before Ken could answer, Sano walked in from a room in the back.

"Morning." He said. He still didn't seem like he had as much enthusiasm as the others.

"All refreshed and ready to go?" Jayson asked him. "For a star athlete, blaming the need for a bathroom break was something I'd expect Kenny-kens to use when he's falling behind."

"In my defense, I am recovering from a fairly serious injury." Ken reminded them, patting his leg.

"In my defense, I've sprained my ankle at least twice this year." Sano told them. I remember him spraining his leg once. I was there helping him at his house when he needed to rest. Trying to show him I could be of use to him and not the klutz I was being.

"All I hear are excuses from the both of you. I have ten years on you and countless leg injuries from my theater days and I can outrun you both."

"Are you joining us on our run?" Sano asked me, changing the subject. It was the first real thing he's said to me so far being here.

"Well, I would, but I'm not really dressed for the occasion." I told them. I was in a shirt and shorts not really meant for running. Not to mention I didn't have shoes on.

"You two go ahead. If any bells were to ring, she'd probably outrun us all." Ken smiled. Sure, my running speed has increased this year due to being late, but he didn't have to say it like that.

"We'll catch up with you later. See you Misaky." Jayson and Sano both left out. They took off running into the forest. They must have a trail they use when they come out here.

"So," I heard Ken from behind me. If any part of me was still sleeping, I was wide awake then hearing that two-letter word.

"You want to talk about what's wrong?"

"What do you mean?"

"You can't hide that look from me. Being up this early for you is one thing, but that's not the face of someone with lack of sleep." He said reading right through me.

"How do you know? You said it yourself I'm not one for getting up early."

"Did someone say something to you?" He continued not paying attention to my response. "Unfortunately, all of them are suspects. Which one was it?"

"I have yet to have a problem with Amy." I told him.

"Okay, that's one down. Now it's safe to assume someone did say something. At this time of morning, the only one that would be up and willing to start an unwanted conversation is my father. I was hoping he wouldn't try anything." He guessed it right away. It's his family we're dealing with. Of course he'd know what they would do.

"It could've been avoided, but he asked if something was bothering me. So, I asked him about my mom's job."

"Did that not get sorted out? I kind of figure it worked out in her favor since you know, you're here."

"What does me being here have to do with it?" I asked.

"I don't know. Part of me thought if something went wrong, you wouldn't have come." It was no wonder Ken seemed so excited to see me. I guess Jayson didn't tell him what he heard my dad talking about yesterday.

"She quit." I put it bluntly. Everyone else knew. It wasn't really a secret anymore.

"She quit? Was my father unable to help her?"

"It's not really that." I told him. How do I say she thinks it was a set up without saying she thinks it was a set up? Things still aren't adding up from what everyone has said…

"Is there something else?" He asked reading me.

"He only explained his side of the story. But his side of the story didn't match my mom's story. So, I'm confused on what to believe." I said. I stood by the couch, but didn't exactly face him.

"You mean as to what lead her to quit? Was it because the transfer didn't go through?"

"It's not just that. My mom thinks it was a set up. She said herself that your dad didn't know what was going on, but he just told me he knew everything. Not only that, the transfer kept changing because they didn't have a place for her. Doesn't that sound kind of suspicious?"

The more I talk and think about it, the more my dad's way of thinking was getting in my head. Then the thought of Lacey came to mind. How his dad wanted to get rid of her by buying her off. I know Mr. Masidone doesn't like me that much. But to think he'd go this far. I thought by now, he was okay with everything.

"I'm sorry." Ken said. I don't know why hearing that made my heart sink. I looked at him and his head was low. Seeing him made it fall even farther.

"What are you sorry for?"

"For starters, that your mother had to quit as the result of all of this. And second, I feel like I let this happen."

"How did you let this happen?" I asked him.

"I kept wondering what was going on and trying to figure out who she was talking to. My father is not the one you need to fully direct your suspicion towards. Jocelyn is the one you should worry about."

"Mrs. Baker? How did she get involved?" I wasn't ready to hear about her. I know she doesn't like me. But to the point she'd bring my parents into it?

"Jocelyn is a site supervisor. So, she's in and out all the time. I noticed a while ago she's been meeting and talking with the managers there. I didn't exactly know what she was doing, but then I heard her and my father talking. She said she would handle everything and to be prepared to be down an accountant." He stopped and ran a hand through his hair.

"This was back when I was home because of my injury. Every now and then she would ask me how things are going. Like she was waiting for something. I did ask her once if she was okay with how things turned out and she told me that in the end, everything will work out for everyone."

"So, you're saying my mom lost her job because of your stepmom? And you knew she was planning on getting rid of her?"

"Although the clues were there, I couldn't really just say I knew. Especially since nothing seemed like it was happening. I only found out that your mom even got the promotion when I left your house. There was really no time to ask about it."

"But did you ever actually ask her about what she was doing? Or even after we told you, did you see if that had something to do with what she was doing?"

"I didn't really know how to approach the situation." He said. He had this look like he was still unsure. Like maybe he shouldn't have told me that he knew Mrs. Baker had been up to something. And now, what he heard, actually came true. My mom, the accountant she was trying to get rid of, is gone. But for what? To get rid of me? Why would she go through all of this to do that?

"So, now what? Did she get what she wanted? Or not because I'm still here?" I asked him. I went closer to him. I searched his face for a response, but he wasn't saying anything. "I mean, that was the goal, right? She wanted to get rid of me but I'm still here."

"Misa." He started.

"What? It's not the first time your parents tried to get rid of someone. I mean, your dad has wanted me out the picture from the beginning. And he was the one that got rid of Lacey. What's with them not wanting anyone near you and going through so much to get rid of them? Why did my mom have to pay the price? I would have preferred being bribed."

"Bribed? Who was bribed?" Ken asked.

"Lacey was bribed. Your father offered her money to leave you alone." If I was planning to keep that a secret, it was out now. It was all coming out and I didn't know how to stop it.

"I didn't want to believe it when my dad first said that I was the problem, but I guess he was right." I turned to walk out the door. He called out to me, but I kept going.

I can handle a little torment from Jenny and Jennifer. Jenny just wanted to be with him, but he wasn't interested. They still accepted her in even though she's been turned down. Now that I'm interested, it's a problem. How do I handle being with someone whose whole family wants to torment me? Can I really handle more of this? Do I really want to see what more they can try?

I went back to my room afraid of running into anyone else. Amy was still sleeping. I tiptoed back to my side of the room and went to the balcony curtains and pulled them back a bit. I could see part of the pool house from there. I don't know if Ken was still in there or not, but he hasn't come to find me yet. I didn't see Sano or Jayson running by anywhere. It doesn't matter where they are. I guess I can believe they don't have anything against me and can be free from their torment.

Suddenly what Mr. Masidone said came back to mind. About how Sano is here because of me. He would never have considered coming back if I hadn't talked to him about it. A place he once said he had no intentions of going back to. He also asked me about Mrs. Baker before. He remembered her in his old town. Maybe I should ask him again about her. There's still something off with her. And the fact that she did this. I want to know who she is to be able to do it.

There was a knock on the door. I didn't want all my work to keep Amy asleep to be wasted. I slowly went over and cracked it open, and to my surprise it was Jennifer.

"Is this a bad time?" She asked.

"Not really. Amy is still asleep though."

"Oh, well, we were just wondering when we were supposed to meet up. Jens and I have something to do this morning." I looked at her outfit. She had on a purple hooded half shirt and leggings. If I didn't know any better, I'd say she was going for a morning run too. But the look in her eye doesn't say she's ready for a workout.

"I know she wants to do stuff at the pool later today. She didn't say what time. So, I guess you're free to do whatever you want for now." I told her. Amy only wanted to wait thinking I would be with Ken all day. But after that talk, I don't think that'll be happening.

"Thanks for the heads up. By the way, if you don't want Jens to find out you and Ken are fighting, you might want to cheer up a bit."

"What makes you say that?" Not only was I shocked she figured it out, she didn't throw it in my face like she normally would.

"Just a guess. But that dead tone of yours is an obvious giveaway. If you plan to survive this vacay, you might want to pretend like you want to be here. Otherwise, someone might think you've been all talk and don't actually like who you say you like. And at that point, is it really worth you being here?" Jennifer took off after that. I watched her go down the stairs before I closed the door.

"Good vacay morning." I heard my roommate yawn behind me.

"Sorry, did I wake you?"

"This is my normal wake up time. I try not to get used to sleeping in. It'll destroy my schedule when I'm booked for work." She sat up in bed and stretched. "How are you this morning? I see you're already up and about."

"Uh, Jennifer was just asking about our meetup time. I told her sometime later. She and Jenny are doing something this morning."

"That's why I figured later would be better. I'm sure you and Kenny have some plans, yeah?"

"Uh, well, he's out doing some morning workouts with the guys." I gave her an easy answer.

"I see. Well, if they're out getting the blood flowing, why don't we? Never too early to start our girls day. If we're doing a water sport, maybe some yoga will help loosen us up. I brought an extra mat; we can go out by the lake. It'll be a great way to start the day." She just woke up and was already ready to go. Maybe doing this will help me get over what just happened anyway.

I agreed to do yoga with Amy, and we started getting ready. I opened the curtains all the way now that she's awake. If I saw correctly, the pool house door just closed meaning someone just went in. I wonder how long their morning workout lasts, and did they ask Ken anything when they saw him.

"Are you ready?" I turned and saw Amy by her bed holding a bag. Her hair was in a high ponytail showing her black sports bra and multi colored leggings. Her figure was so defined. I'm starting to remember seeing her modeling for that brand she's wearing on their website. To think I'm going to work out with someone like her. This is what it means to know the Masidones. But, is it worth it?

"Ready to go." I told her. We both headed out. Going downstairs, I looked around more than I did the first time. Surprisingly, we didn't pass anyone when we headed outside. We walked out the front and across the grass towards the lake.

"I saw this nice open area yesterday when we got here. A nice even ground that's perfect for this." She said. We walked through the grass and up to the lake. It looked just like it did when Ken and I went before without the others. Now that I was up close again, I looked around. I guess we didn't need to see if the ball was here. There was nothing but rushing water.

"Is something out there?" She asked looking out with me.

"No. I thought I saw something." I told her. We set up our mats and she put out a speaker playing calming soundtracks.

"Have you ever done yoga?" She asked me.

"Once or twice. I was never really that flexible."

"Oh, you don't have to be super flexible to do it. We can start off with some basic stretches." She said, reaching up. I followed her lead as we started.

Doing this outside next to the lake with this music and the morning sun shining on us felt like I was in an exercise video. It was actually helping me relax. My morning was already so hectic; doing this away from everyone was relieving.

"Are you hanging in there?" She looked over to me as she did a forward lunge reaching to the sky.

"I could keep this up all I day." I told her as I to try to do the same pose. It wasn't my flexibility I needed to work on but balance as I stumbled a bit doing a simple lunge.

"Don't worry. The more you do this, the easier it gets. Don't let yourself be too tense. Deep breaths and ease into the position." She coached me as we went on. My mind was starting to become clearer. Maybe if I did this more often, I'd do better in school…

"I just want us to have a fun easy day. It wasn't my intentions, but I heard a bit of your conversation with Jennifer earlier." We were looking at each other from what's called the downward dog position.

"You don't have to worry. Conversations like that are normal between us." I told her trying not to lose my balance.

"Well, that doesn't sound like it should be normal. I think I know the basic idea of the relationship between you all. There shouldn't be anything stopping you from being friends. Especially if you never got the chance to establish a relationship, right?"

"You're right, but I wasn't the one that instantly hated the other." I told her recalling the first time I met Jennifer when she subtly threatened me. And how Jenny instantly made a scene when she first saw me. At no point did either of them care to try to find out who I was.

"Don't you think it's time to change that? You can't let someone else determine whether you girls be friends or not. We can bring them around. You leave that to me." She smiled. Getting the annoying duo to stop being annoying. That's something I'd like to see. I never wanted to have an enemy. Had things been different and they didn't approach me with hate, maybe I wouldn't have minded being friends.

We got down to the mat when I happened to glance behind me. I saw Jenny and Jennifer going into the house. Wherever they went, they already came back. I wonder what they plan to do now…

"Oh, Jaycee! Good morning!" Amy yelled out behind me. I turned and saw Jayson by himself holding something going towards the pool house. He tried holding his arm up to wave at us and went ahead back in. Amy continued to smile. She didn't notice how that seemed off. Normally Jayson would have been more enthusiastic and might've even come over. Did he not want to come over because of Amy? Or did Ken tell him what happened, and he didn't want to see me?

We continued doing our yoga. I was finally starting to feel relaxed and calm, but worry was starting to creep back into my mind. Amy wants everything to go well. I don't think she realizes I've been wanting that since the moment I was told about coming here.

"I think this should do for today." Amy said as we finished with an open legged stretch. It's been a while since I've stretched this much. I only hope I don't feel sore from it later.

"You don't mind if I peek in and say hi to the guys, do you? I know it's a girls day, but my time around Jaycee is limited."

"Uh, that's fine. But uhm…" I want to ask about her relationship with Jayson. I know his side of the story. But she acts as if there's nothing wrong between them. How do you go on as if nothing had ever happened?

"I am curious. Did Jaycee ever tell you about us?" She asked.

"Well, kind of."

"I thought so. I don't know how he explained it, but whatever he said is probably true. There's really nothing to lie about since the worse pretty much happened. And I guess that's why I can't let go." I watched her as we both sat on the mat. The glow she had seemed to finally dimmer a bit.

"I did something absolutely horrible to him. Something a simple apology could never make right. I shouldn't even show my face around him yet, I can't stay away. Whenever I see him, I just want to make things right and how they used to be. I'm not asking for him to take me back or anything. I just know I made a mistake, and I want to make up for it."

"Have you told him that?" I asked her.

"With work I hardly get to see him anymore. And when we're together, he keeps telling me what we had is gone. He doesn't give me the chance to explain myself. I don't know if talking now will change anything."

"Jayson said he really cared about you. So, he was really hurt after what happened. I don't think he realizes that you know what you did and feel bad about it. I think if you explain that to him, maybe he'll understand." I told her.

"I know. I want to do that. I'm just not good at this type of thing. That's sort of why I left in the first place. I know that's horrible. And doing that only showed me what leaving something undone can do. I know he would've understood if we just talked about it." Amy said. She leaned back on her mat. She closed her eyes and took a large slow inhale.

"Well, if you're with us this week, now seems like a good time to try and talk." I never thought I'd be the one giving someone advice. Amy really seems like a nice person, and Jayson is pretty understanding. He's always helping me out. He should at least hear her out.

"I'll definitely find some time to have a proper chat with him. Glad I could have this girl talk with you." She seemed relieved. Like she never got to say that before. It would be good for them if they were to make up. Now that only leaves Ken. Me having problems with his family hating me is completely different from trying to make up for a mistake.

We finally packed up our stuff and went back to the house. Amy still went to say hi to the boys in the pool house and I went back in. I still didn't know how to face Ken after storming out. I went in and headed to the kitchen to grab a drink.

"It would've been better if we stayed, but you know she wouldn't let us." I walked into the kitchen when I heard Jennifer talking. They were sitting with two plates of omelets.

"Morning." I said as they stared at me.

"I figured you be with Kenny by now." Jenny said.

"Amy and I did yoga. Ken and the other are also working out this morning."

"Aren't we the active bunch today. Maybe we should have joined the fun. But whose fun would have been better? Your or theirs?" Jennifer wondered.

"I'm sure Amy wouldn't have mind you joining us. It is our girls day, isn't it?" I drank some water as I waited for their response. Amy wants us to get along. The only way to do that is to avoid the problem area. I just wonder if that'll work.

"You sure seem excited about it," Jennifer said.

"It'll be a change of pace don't you think? Aren't you ready to have some fun?" Jennifer and Jenny passed a look between them. They seemed more confused than angry with me.

"You're really getting into the vacay spirit, aren't you?" Jenny asked.

"Do we really have to be at war while we're all here together? Wouldn't it just be easier to get along?" I asked them.

"Of course you'd want to take the easy route. Everything just has to be simple for you, right?" Jenny stood and walked out. For a second, I thought that approach was working.

"This is a different attitude from before." Jennifer said. She stayed seated eating her omelet. "I guess you're taking that pretend like you want to be here suggestion?"

"Do you really hate being around me that much?" I asked her. She looked at me for a bit and back to her plate.

"Listen. I can't speak for Jens, but I don't hate you." She admitted.

"So then, why have you been tormenting me since the day you met me?"

"Because Jens wanted me to." She said it like that was the perfect response.

"You just do whatever she wants you to?"

"Not everything. But if I thought it would make her happy, I'd do it."

"You must really care for her if you're willing to bring down someone else just because." I said.

"I have my reasons." She looked at me like I would understand. There was nothing about what she said that would make this an understandable situation.

"Not that it's any of your business, but for us, we're all we have. If I don't help her, who will?" Jennifer ate the last of her omelet and left out. "See you at the pool." I heard her say as she went up the stairs.

That was the first time we've ever really talked. What did she mean by they're all they had? I do remember Ken once saying their parents died. But then Katie overheard Jennifer calling someone mom. So, what does that mean?

"Oh, hey." I looked over and saw Sano coming in from the kitchen door.

"Hey. Done with your run?" I asked.

"Yeah, we finished up a little bit ago. Amy came in and told us you two were doing yoga."

"Yeah. She heard you guys were working out and wanted to do the same."

"You could have come for a run with us." He said.

"Uh, well, you all already started so…" I didn't have time to come up with a lie.

"Sorry, but we know what happened with you and Ken earlier. We found him on the couch pretty down when we came back to the pool house."

"You did?"

"We were pretty shocked too. Jay thought it best for him to sit for a bit if you were looking for him."

"Uh, well, I've been busy." I took a sip of water to try to swallow down this awkward conversation. What exactly did Ken tell them. And what did they say in response?

"I came to grab so more drinks. I should probably get back since Amy is there. Jay was giving us that look."

"Oh she-"

"When we have some more time, I want to talk to you about something. If that would be alright." Sano seemed a little serious.

"Uh, yeah. That's fine. I actually wanted to ask you something too." I told him.

"Cool, I'll talk to you later then." Sano grabbed more drinks out the fridge and headed back out. I wanted to tell him about Amy, but he hit me with that talking thing he wants to do. Whenever he wants to talk, it's not always good. We haven't really even been talking, so what does he have to say?

Since it seemed like Amy was still in the pool house with them, I just went back to the room and changed. I sat on my bed trying to wrap my head around it all. If I had only stayed in bed, none of the series of events that took place the past hour would have happened.

I probably should not have sat in bed. That turned into laying down and falling back asleep. I sat up and noticed a blanket over me. I looked around and didn't see my roommate. Then I noticed it seemed a lot brighter and saw the curtain pulled all the way back. I went out to the balcony and saw Ken resting on the ledge.

"Sleeping in. This seems more like you." He didn't turn to me when he spoke. I grabbed my phone and saw I had been out for a few hours. I also noticed a few messages, but now doesn't seem like the time to respond to them. Even if one was from Lacey.

"I don't know what you said to Amy, but after all these years, her and Jay seem to have finally settled things."

"You mean she actually talked to him?"

"She came into the pool house with us earlier talking to us and suddenly pulled him off to the side to talk to him. Normally he's the one pulling her off. We were all surprised at the change of direction. Jay heard her out and accepted her story and apology."

"That's good that worked out. I thought she would wait before she tried talking to him. She said she didn't know how to handle those kinds of situations, so I'm surprised she did it so quick."

"Better to dive in headfirst before second guessing yourself." He said. He turned his body to face me. "So, it's time to dive in."

Once again, if I was still asleep at all, I was awake then watching him.

"I really don't know what to say. Part of me wants to just apologize again. I don't think I put into perspective well enough all of what you've put up with just to be with me. I even said earlier everyone is a suspect because you've had to deal with something they've all done to you at some point on multiple occasions. And now it's been taken a step further." He let out a heavy sigh. I can tell he had been thinking about this since this morning.

"I wish it didn't have to be like this. For years, I've had to fight my father for space and freedom. I'm still not over the fact he let me stay with you for the semester. But I guess he still feels the need to micromanage my life. And when Jocelyn came into the picture, she slowly started following his footsteps or fed him ideas to pass on to me. I don't know what I have to do to change this. If I didn't have Jay on my side, I never would have met you the first time and I'd be having lessons five days a week in the dining room."

"I would have never thought someone like him would be this overprotective." I told him. It seems like all Mr. Masidone does it work, yet he still tries to control what Ken does.

"It wasn't always this bad. But after the divorce with my mom and Sano leaving, it only got worse."

The air seemed especially still for the afternoon. There's seven other people here in this house and it feels like it's only us two right now. I've only had to endure his family's pressure for a few months. He's had to endure this all his life. I don't think I'd be able to handle it If I were him.

"So then, what now?" I ask. Knowing the problem doesn't fix it. Can anything really be done as long as his parents are in control?

"Well, if this doesn't run you away, I'm willing to keep fighting. I'll battle with the adults to try and win them over and keep you protected." He said as he reached out to grab my hand. I looked down watching him put his fingers through mine. Ken doesn't want me to go. This whole thing with my mom really affected us. I know it's not Ken's fault, but I'd have to prepare for the possibility of something else extreme happening. Is it really something I can deal with if this war continues?

"We'll see." I said as I leaned against the ledge near him. I looked out to the lake taking in the view. I didn't let go of his hand. I could tell he was watching me, but I didn't want to give him the satisfaction of eye contact. I brought our hands up to rest on the balcony, not saying anything else.

"You haven't eaten today, right? Want to get something before you continue your girl's day? I'll be the chief." He asked. I hadn't even had the chance to think about food.

"I guess I could eat." I told him. We both headed back in and down to the kitchen.

"Looks like someone is awake and ready to party again." Jayson was in the kitchen with Amy.

"You should have told me you were still tired. I wouldn't have dragged you out to do yoga this morning." Amy said sounding guilty.

"I didn't intend to fall asleep. I sat on my bed, and it just happened." I told her.

"I ran up there to talk to you and even called your name. It was like you died! I got so worried! But then Kenny said that was normal." She must have wanted to tell me about Jayson. But waking up so early and dealing with everything took a toll on me.

"Sorry, I can be a bit of a heavy sleeper."

"Well, I hope you're feeling refreshed now." Jayson chimed in, "I wish you came down thirty minutes ago. I already made a little lunch."

"That's alright. Jay isn't the only one around here that can play in the kitchen." Ken said walking over by the stove.

"Ooh, Chief Kenny. I don't think I've had your cooking before." Amy said.

"Of course, we all know who he learned from." Jay said fixing himself.

"You two should have a cook-off. To see who's better. I'd definitely love to be the judge of that!"

"I'm up for the challenge." Ken looked to Jayson.

"You name the time and place and I'll be there." Jayson accepted the challenge.

"Just not today. Misaky and I get to have our own competition." Amy said to me. "I guess if you guys have nothing else to do, you can be score keepers."

"We don't want to intrude on your time." Ken said.

"I said if you didn't have anything else to do. We've already scheduled this time together."

"Are Jenny and Jennifer still joining you? I haven't heard much from them today." Ken asked.

"Yeah. I should probably go remind them." Amy got up and headed upstairs.

"Misaky, I guess I owe you a thanks." Jayson started, "Amy told me she had a little chat with you that helped her want to finally explain our situation. I guess I spent long enough living in the past. A weight feels lifted because of it. I told her that I'll try not to push her away anymore and start over."

"I'm glad you were able to work things out. Maybe things could go back to how it was before." I said.

"Oh, let's just start with us having a conversation and my skin doesn't crawl." He rubbed his arm.

Ken went ahead and started cooking for us. Jayson left out leaving us two again. Ken made Jayson's favorite fish and chips making sure I didn't have anything too heavy before swimming. By the time we were done, the strangest thing happened. I looked outside and saw Sano sitting on the chairs by the pool with Jennifer.

The last time I saw them together was at school when she ran away from him. I don't know if what she said about not hating me applies to him since I never thought she liked him either, but she wasn't running away or seemed completely uninterested.

"Misaky." I looked over and saw Amy and Jenny together. "We're going to head out and soak up a little sun. Join us when you're ready to party!" She put her hair in a bun and had on a stripe bikini that tied in the front under a black mesh swim wrap. Jenny had a burgundy top and high waisted swim shorts. They both looked like they were going to a beach party.

"I'll be out there soon." I told them. They went outside and sat next to Sano and Jennifer as if it were completely normal for him to be with them.

"I guess it's time to have some fun in the sun." Ken said looking outside. "Like Jay said yesterday, those two have been quiet lately. I don't think you have much to worry about being with them today."

"Maybe not." I said. Ken raised an eyebrow at that response. Jennifer was willing to talk to me normally today. If I could talk to her again, maybe we could come to an agreement and get Jenny on my side too.

I went upstairs to change. Ken said he would grab Sano and go with Jayson to the game room. As long as I can get through this, I should be able to get through the rest of the vacation.

I put on the swimsuit Ken gave me, grabbed my towel, and went back downstairs. I rounded the corner into the kitchen and saw a problem.

"There you are. I was wondering when you would join." Mrs. Baker said. She was wearing a sun hat and a red one-piece swimsuit. A swimsuit would indicate she was coming outside with us.

"I hope you don't mind me joining girl's day. Don't worry, I don't intend to play. It's a beautiful day; relaxing by the pool sounded very nice. Plus, the little volleyball game was my idea. I want to see it played out since I'm not actually participating."

"That's not a problem." I told her. Ken told me she's the one I should watch out for. She didn't ask me if something was wrong like Mr. Masidone did. I couldn't just jump in and ask her when they were all waiting outside. Even though Mr. Masidone was the big businessman, something about her does make it harder to approach.

I didn't say anything else and headed outside. Mrs. Baker fixed herself an iced tea and came out behind me.

"Miss Jocelyn, welcome!" Amy said as we went over to join.

"Nice to see the women of the house all together. How are we doing today?"

"It's a wonderful day today. I can't express how much I enjoy being here. It's just so relaxing and peaceful." Amy told her.

"It's hotter than I expected today." Jenny said from the other side of Jennifer.

"I hope you're wearing your sunscreen. You know you can't handle too much sun."

Mrs. Baker said.

"I only had a little left. I forgot to buy more."

"Well, it's up to you if you burn. You knew we were coming here. You should've checked your inventory." Mrs. Baker told her. Jenny leaned back in her chair.

"Oh, you should have said you needed sunscreen. I have like five different kinds. You can never be too sure of the sun rays." Amy reached into her bag.

"Prepared and always ready. I like that." Mrs. Baker said to Amy. Jenny looked at her and turned away.

"I guess I could use a little more too." Jennifer said. Amy handed them what she had, and Jennifer took one and put more sunscreen on and passed the bottle to Jenny.

"You need any Misaky?" Amy turned to me.

"I put some on before I came down." I told her. I watched them reapply and couldn't help but look to Mrs. Baker as she sipped her Iced tea. It didn't seem like she cared much for Jenny even though she was the one to bring up the need for it.

"Now that we're all lathered up, why not get things started and cool off in the pool?" Amy stood looking out to the bright blue water and went to turn on some music from the stereo system. The volleyball net was already set up and ready to go with a ball floating in the water.

"Let's pick partners. Misaky, you and I are roomies, I've been talking to Jenny for a bit, so Jennifer, would you want to be on my team?" Amy didn't see the danger in that question.

"Oh, I suppose that's not a problem." Jennifer said. She gave me a look then leaned over and whispered something to Jenny. I don't have a sister, but I could tell they had an entire conversation with just the look Jenny gave her in return.

"This should be a good game. I figured the girls would stay together and you two would team up. A good opportunity for venturing out." Mrs. Baker said. I don't mind not being on Amy's side. I just would have preferred the sister I confirmed doesn't want to send me to the Masidone dungeon.

"Who prefers being on the deeper end?" Amy asked as we all got in the water. I didn't mind either way, but I didn't know if Jenny could swim…

"Can you swim well?" I asked her. She looked at me and over to the deeper end.

"If I couldn't swim, I wouldn't have agreed to a pool event. I can handle the deep end."

Jenny went under the net to the other end. She just volunteered us for that side.

"Good luck." I turned and saw Jennifer next to me. "Just a heads up, Jens' a little competitive." She gave me a thumbs up. I went to the other side of the net.

"Have you ever played volleyball?" To my surprise, Jenny asked me a question. "Not in the water. And only once or twice on land."

"So, I should keep my expectations low. Got it." Jenny didn't hide her judgment.

"If you expect us to win a round, we'll have to work together." I told her.

"Work together you say? You're already a winner in other ways. Do you really need me on your side?"

"Look, this and that are different things. Right now, we're trying to have a good time, and to do that, we'll have to work together in order to get through the game." I tried to explain to her.

"Look who wants to come together and sing around the fire. Maybe in your perfect little world that can happen. But in this world, that's far from likely."

"You lovely ladies ready?" I heard Amy shout from the other side. I gave her a thumbs up. Jenny moved behind me. I guess I'm in the inner court. Amy was back and Jennifer was staring at me from across the net.

"I'll serve." I heard Jenny say. The ball was by her, so she took it. She threw the ball up and hit it over the net. I was wondering if I should rethink my war with Jenny. She hit it so hard, it flew down right between Amy and Jennifer.

"Wow, that was impressive, and from the deep end at that! I can't even be upset." Amy said. I look to Jennifer, and she mouthed, "told you."

"Very nice. Always start off strong." Mrs. Baker said, raising her glass. Jenny crossed her arms. Must not have been enough of a complement for her.

"I'll serve this one." Amy said. She hit the ball, and it headed straight for me. I tried to hit the ball back. I was still figuring out my balance in the water. My hit didn't connect too well making the ball fly out just next to the pool.

"Ooh, out of bounds, but good try!" Amy shouted to me.

"Oh, Misa dear. If you wanted me to join, all you had to do was ask." She laughed as the ball rolled near her.

"Sorry." I went over to the edge to get the ball. Mrs. Baker handed it to me. "I'm sure you can do better than that. Can't let Jenny have all the glory now. Amy, why not try that again?" She went back to her chair.

"Let's try this again Misaky!" Amy threw the ball high and hit it again. It wasn't as close to me as the first time. I swam over to hit it just before it hit the water. It managed to get it just over the net, but Jennifer was quick and got it back to our side. Hitting the ball hard must run in the family. The ball sailed passed me to Jenny. The ball was too low for her to hit it hard again, so she had to hit it up.

"You better get it." She said to me. Jenny was actually relying on me to get the ball. Maybe if we weren't in water, it would be easier to move around, but I moved as fast as I could to get it. Surprisingly, I managed to hit it back over the net. To my even bigger surprise, it went right pass Jennifer and to the water.

"Nice you guys!" Amy cheered.

"Amy dear, you know that was their point?" Mrs. Baker reminded her.

"I know, but that was still great. Love the teamwork!" Amy flashed us a thumbs up. I turned to look at Jenny.

"Don't expect my expectations to change so easily." She folded her arms again. Even though she said that I think that's her way of saying 'good job' to me.

"Why don't we switch out?" Amy suggested. We both switched positions, so now I was in the back. This means I'll have to serve. The net suddenly feels so far away. I didn't expect Jenny to be good or competitive, so I have to at least make the ball reach the net from here.

"You better know how to serve." Jenny said. It might've been that competitive spirit, but I'll take this behavior over how she typically acts towards me. If we can keep acting like a team, this really won't be as bad to get through.

"That was an enjoyable little event." Mrs. Baker sat up on her chair.

"I must say, I wish I was out here from the beginning." Mr. Masidone said from behind her. The game almost ended early along with my time here when he showed up and I served the ball to the back of Jenny's head. If she was warming up to me at all that froze over again.

"Unfortunately, Amy dubbed this their girls day, so the boys weren't invited." Mrs. Baker told him.

"But you're always welcomed to join the fun Mr. Masy!" Amy told him.

"I was in our relaxing room just listening to the music and splashing, I just had to see what I was missing. I was hopping you'd be in there with them." He rubbed Mrs. Baker's shoulders.

"The way they were hopping around the pool, I don't think I would've lasted a round. But I got to see these ladies enjoy themselves. I didn't know these girls were so active."

"When it comes to having fun, you can do anything. I'm so glad we got together. It helped me get to see who I've missed being away. You all are awesome." Amy said. She was still full of energy.

"I'm still a little surprise you got these two in on this." Mrs. Baker said talking about Jenny and Jennifer. "I can't get them to do anything. They needed to get out of their corner."

"Oh, they're great. Jenny, you impressed me with your skills. You should consider playing real volleyball." Amy said.

"I'm a part of the tennis team. I'm unable to do two sports." Jenny said. I guess that explains her hard hits. She's used to swinging a racket around.

"She's just fine with tennis. You all can play as much as you'd like on your own." Mrs. Baker stood, "I think I've also gotten enough sun. You ladies can continue your time. I'm going to get changed."

"Miss Macky, good to see you're doing better. And Miss Amy, don't overdo it. You have a big day tomorrow." Mr. Masidone told us.

"Oh, this is mostly just exercise I'll be fine. Although, I should go and wash this chlorine off. That's a risk I shouldn't take."

"As long as you are aware. Please, continue your afternoon." Mr. Masidone took his leave.

"I don't want to end the day yet, but I do need to get freshened up. You'll stick around if I leave for a bit, right?" Amy wants to leave us by ourselves.

"That's fine with me. I can hang out for a bit." Jennifer said.

"I suppose that's fine." Jenny added.

"Don't want anything to go wrong for tomorrow. You should go change." I told her.

"Super! I won't be too long!" Amy got her stuff and went into the house leaving me with Jenny and Jennifer alone. I just laid back in the chair and grabbed my phone.

"Don't you want to take this time to see the boys? I'm sure they wouldn't mind you interrupting their guy time." Jenny asked.

"Amy won't be gone that long. I can see them later." I told her.

"And who exactly are you seeing?" She quickly got serious. I sat up on the chair to face her.

"I just don't understand why you're so upset with me when Ken was the one that came after me. Why is it so hard to accept us being together?"

"It's not just about liking him or not." She said.

"Jens." Jennifer nudged her shoulder.

"What? Whenever I see her, it just frustrates me."

"Just hold it in a little longer." Jennifer told her.

"I'll hold it in over there." Jenny got up and walked off towards the lake. Jennifer got up and went to follow her.

"Wait, Jennifer." I stopped her, "Can you please explain what's going on? This doesn't feel like it's just about Ken and I, but somehow, I'm still the problem." Jenny has been hinting at something this whole time. Even Jennifer has been acting differently. If Jenny is going to keep exploding like that, we'll never make it through the week…

"There's just some things you don't know or need to know." She told me.

"So, I have to keep taking that every time we meet? She said it's not just about liking Ken. If that's not the problem, then what is?" I really couldn't take this anymore. Jennifer isn't as short fused as Jenny is. If I can get something out of one of them, it has to be her. Jennifer looked off to the direction Jenny left. She closed her eyes and took a big inhale and walked back over to me.

"Okay, look, it's a long story that I don't want to explain. But in short, Jenny didn't want Ken just because she liked him. She had to get him to like her in order to be officially in the family."

"What do you mean by that?"

"Our time here may or may not be limited now. If Jenny couldn't win over Ken, then we get kicked out the house."

"Kicked out? Mr. Masidone plans to kick you out since Ken is with me?"

"Not him. Although, he's not really doing anything either." She rolled her eyes.

"So, you mean it's Mrs. Baker?" I asked her. Jennifer looked away. She looked to the house like she was making sure no one was looking and shook her head.

"Why does she get to kick you out? Wasn't Mr. Masidone the one that brought you in?"

"He allowed us to stay, but he wasn't the one that brought us there. Our… 'mom' did." She air quoted mom. Did she mean Mrs. Baker was her mom?

"She's not our real mom. Our parents passed away and she took us in, but she never adopted us, so she doesn't technically have to keep us around."

"Can she really do that? Just get rid of you?" I said that almost a whisper. I was at a loss for words.

"She told us she'll make it happen." Jennifer took a deep breath. "Jenny is worried she might be serious about it which is why she's so upset with you. I can't chance worrying like her. I have to stay alert and watch out for what could happen, and to keep her from going crazy."

I didn't know what to do or say. This whole time there was a real reason for them acting the way they did. And It's a pretty serious reason.

"I don't want to talk about this anymore. I'm getting Jens." Jennifer got up and walked in the direction Jenny went. I laid back in the chair not really sure what else to do.

What Katie heard was true, and what Ken said was also true. Their parents passed away, and the person Katie heard her say mom to was Mrs. Baker. But everything surrounding that is the part I don't want to believe.

"I was hoping I could catch you presently or post swimming." I noticed Ken walking up to me, but I didn't really move. "Don't tell me things went wrong?"

"Amy went to change and wanted us to wait for her." I told him.

"I understand the waiting part, but the 'us' part is perplexing seeing as it's just you here." He said, looking around. I sat back up on my chair facing him.

"Jenny and Jennifer stepped away for a bit. They should be back." I told him. I looked over toward the lake wondering if they really would come back. Then I noticed bouncing purple ombre hair coming from the kitchen.

"Oh no, I was worried about being gone too long. Did they leave? I thought I was quick." Amy came back fresh and in lounge wear.

"They just wanted to talk. They should be back." I said again. I looked back over to the lake again, and this time, Jenny and Jennifer were walking back over here.

"There they are." Amy perked back up.

"We needed to dry off." Jennifer told her.

"Oh, I guess we all could have gotten changed. But hey, a little chlorine won't really hurt anybody."

"I suppose I'll take my leave. I'll leave you to resume your activities." Ken said.

"Wait a minute. I had a thought a bit ago. But you have to be on board." Amy looked to Ken whose eyebrow went up with suspicion. "You guys aren't particularly busy, are you?"

"Not in so many words." He said still suspicious.

"Well, if you girls, and you guys don't mind, I think we could make this party a little better if we came together… in harmony?" She flashed us all a smile.

"You want to… Karaoke?" Ken asked.

"It would help me unwind for tomorrow and who doesn't love singing along?" Amy was growing more excited at the thought.

Me, Katie, and a couple others have done it before. I don't mind it. But right now, and with this grouping of people doesn't sound like a lot of harmony.

"You're a performer, right? I don't mind seeing that." Jennifer said.

"Oh, I'm nothing special, although if you want, we can do a duet." Amy offered.

"I'm sure the others wouldn't mind if you want to do that." Ken said. When will the surprises stop? Jennifer was first to say she was in, and Ken agreed.

"Alright! We're moving things indoors then!" Amy said.

"We can head to the game room. Good for making noise." Ken said. We collected our things and headed inside. Before we headed in, I felt my shoulder being grabbed by Jennifer.

"You better not say a word to Ken," She whispered in my ear, "He doesn't know, and we've worked hard to keep it that way. Keep your cool." She went on ahead. She's been living with that secret this whole time. I never would have thought it went that deep for them. Why doesn't she want Ken to know?

"Girl's day has come to crash the party!" Amy said when we got into the game room. It really felt like I was in an extravagant hotel going from the pool to a game room. They had a foosball table, pool table, and a large screen TV with a sound system and games.

"No one told me about party crashing." Jayson said from the pool table with Sano.

"You missed our awesome game of volleyball. These girls got talent in the water. Time to see some other talents they have with a little singing."

"I should have seen that coming. You don't go anywhere without singing." Jayson leaned on the cue stick.

"You know me so well. Maybe we can do one of our duets." Amy smiled to Jayson. I know they had their talk, but I don't know if Jayson is completely comfortable with her just yet.

"If you want to start the party off, one of us will follow suit." Jayson said as he made a shot on the pool table. There were three striped balls left on the table, and he shot the eight ball in the side pocket. "Our game just ended, so we got some time." Jayson blew his cue stick and Sano dropped his head.

"Give it up man, this is his sport." Ken said.

"He got lucky in this last move." Sano put up his cue stick.

"It's okay, he can let himself think that while we go over here." Jayson said patting Sano's shoulder.

We went to the couches next to the TV. The couch curves around the TV creating this little floor in the middle. Amy stood in the middle enjoying her little stage as Jayson set up the microphones. Sano sat next to Ken who sat next to me in the middle seats. Jenny and Jennifer sat on the right side of the couch together.

They both looked pretty straight faced as they always look except, now that I know their secret, Jennifer keeps stealing glances at me. I think I made it to her official watch list. Not because she's watching me and Ken but watching what I might say to Ken.

"Since this was my idea, I'll start us off. Although, anyone is welcome to join! Let's start off with a little energy." Amy was looking for a song. Jayson went to get something after he set everything up. Amy got started with a song I didn't recognize. I didn't need to recognize it because I was taken away with her voice. It was like she was performing on stage dancing around the small space pointing to us all. She was giving us a concert without even trying with all of this surround sound.

"So, do we pay you for this?" Ken joked with her when she finished. We all clapped after that performance.

"Ooh you're so sweet Kenny. I'll only accept money for tomorrow. This is on the house." She gave him a wink, "Would you like to take on the next song?" She extended the mic to him. Ken looked at it for a bit.

"Don't be shy, I know you've done this before. I'll sing with you if you like." Amy kept the mic out to him. Ken finally reached out to grab it.

"I might require payment for this." He said when he stood up with her. They picked another song and got started. I'm pretty sure I've never heard Ken sing before. He didn't seem nervous, but he didn't seem like he planned to be singing either. He cleared his throat preparing. As the instrumental started, I noticed Jenny reach out to the front table and grabbed another mic. I didn't expect her to want to participate in this.

"The more the merrier!" Amy said right before the song started. She set the stage again and Ken joined in. I don't know what I was expecting from him, but he had a clear tenor tone and was a little better than I was going to give him credit for.

When Amy started again, I heard another voice. It was Jenny from the couch. She really joined them. It was a lot softer and almost hard to hear her, but I still could hear the higher tone under Amy's voice. I looked back to Amy and saw another smile on her face. She raved about Jenny earlier being good at volleyball. She's probably glad to see she's still joining in. Even after running off earlier, she's still trying to go along with everything.

"Good job guys!" Amy high-fived them. Jenny put the mic back down. Ken eased the mic out of Amy's hand and walked over and handed it to me.

"Next." he said, smiling. I did what he did and sort of looked at the mic. Rejecting was obviously not an option, so I grabbed it and stepped to the main floor with him.

"What shall it be? Happy, sad, slow and steady?" He moved in closer.

"I'll choose." I told him as I searched for a song. I didn't think he'd go again. Thinking back, I do remember him humming songs when he cooked, or when something comes on the radio in the car. He really doesn't have shy bone in his body…

Singing with Ken wasn't on the agenda for today, but it has been a while since I've done karaoke. Even though Ken isn't Katie, who I usually sing with, being up here with him wasn't so bad. I don't sound anything like Amy, but with the loudness of the soundtrack and backup vocals, I almost didn't sound too bad.

"I knew you guys were holding back talent. You guys are great!" Amy continued to be everyone's cheerleader with a standing ovation.

"Alright, I'll go ahead and perform next." Jayson reappeared, claiming the next round. I handed him my mic and sat back down. Amy went and grabbed Ken's mic and stood next to him.

"He went to the minibar, didn't he?" Sano leaned over to Ken. I thought I might've smelled alcohol coming from him…

"Yeah, he disappeared pretty quickly." Ken told him. "If you ever wondered what Jay used to do, you're in for a little show." He said to me.

"What do you mean?"

"I think Jay needed a little 'liquid courage' to help him through this since Amy would try to sing with him no matter what. So, this might turn into a reunion stage of the theater majors." I looked up to Jayson. His face did seem to be a bit more relaxed.

"I'll grab some regular drinks for us." Ken said and got up. Just as he did, Jay started singing. It was a musical song. I thought Amy's performance was a concert, but he was just as good as her.

"By the way, nice singing up there." Sano leaned over to me.

"Thanks, when are you going up?"

"I'm not much of a singer. And now that Jay has a mic, I think I can hide under the radar for a bit." Both Jayson and Amy were in sync as they continued their song. It really was a show they were putting on. Jayson really was a performer. And it was because of Amy, he stopped.

"You have to at least do one song." I told him.

"If you sing again, sure. I'll do backup. But remember, I don't have that gene." He pointed to Jayson who just hit a perfect high note. I looked back to Sano, and he shook his head.

"Just as good as ever." Amy clapped for Jayson.

"Now that I'm up here, I might as well do one more song. There's another mic available, let's make this a real performance." Jayson offered the mic out to someone. His eyes glossed over us, but Jennifer reached over and grabbed it.

"Since this isn't the right paring." She said to us and joined them. She heard us talking. She really is keeping a closer eye on me.

"Did I miss the show?" Ken reappeared with drinks. "I hope you didn't have much else planned tonight. If we don't stop them, they'll keep going." He said handing me a cup.

I wasn't sure if that was a good thing or not. Amy wanted all of us to hang out and get along. This is the most I've seen Jenny and Jennifer interact with anyone but themselves. But the more they interacted with me the more I wish they hadn't. What am I going to do now that Jennifer is watching me even more? Is it so bad that I know what's going on? Wouldn't it be better if someone else knew to try and help? And just how long can they keep this up if they're running out of time?

I already knew I was going to have trouble sleeping again. Not because of the karaoke, or worrying about Jennifer, or any of yesterday's events. It was the messages I waited to read. The Lacey messages I knew would be a problem. But not how I thought it would be.

I was expecting maybe an apology, a reason why she stopped talking to me, or even more questions about what I'm doing here with Ken. Not questions about what I've told him. Asking why was he was bringing back up what happened back when they broke up. I wasn't sure if she was angry I told him, or trying to figure out how it came up in conversation. But I'm mostly confused as to why this is coming up now.

This series of questions can only mean Ken got in touch with her. He wanted to talk to her about everything. Is it because of yesterday and what I said? From the way she worded it, it seems like they already talked. Have they been talking since they saw each other at my apartment? I knew his behavior was different. He didn't say anything about her, but went to contact her after all this time…

"Misaky, happy morning." My roommate was up. It was 8am already. It was her big day, so she had to be up to get ready.

"Just to give you a heads up, the photographer and everyone will be here in a couple hours. Mr. Masy has his lovely staff here fixing things up now, so it'll be a bit crowded until he shows up." she said putting on one of her morning face masks.

"Do you need help with anything?" I asked, not sure what I could actually do.

"Not at the moment. The only thing I'll have to unfortunately ask is that when the photographer moves to the room or area they're shooting in, we'll need everyone somewhere else. Other than the master bedroom, our bedrooms will not be in the shoot and also the pool house. Only the outside I think, so those areas are safe places. If you want to eat, they are making breakfast now, so go help yourself." Even with her mask on, she already seemed to be glowing. I can tell she was excited for today.

I got up and went to the balcony window and went outside. I looked to the other end of the balcony and saw someone sweeping. I looked down and could see someone trying to clean out an already clean pool. These were the people that are usually at the mansion. Except for one guy I couldn't recognize walking towards the pool house garage.

"Wow, the mechanic is here early. We might get to use the boats today." I jumped a bit not expecting to hear Ken behind me. "Did I scare you?"

"I was a bit startled. I didn't hear you coming out." I said collecting myself.

"I happened to see you out here. It's going to be a little busy around here today."

"Amy already told me what to expect. I've never been around a photoshoot before."

"This isn't going to be that big really. Someone just wants some pictures of the villa with someone in a few of them to express the living style."

"Why didn't they just ask you all to do that instead of hiring Amy?" I asked him.

"My father is going to be in a few of them. But no one else really cared to be exposed like that. You can be in them if you want."

To be in a photoshoot for the Masidones. Somewhere, those photos would be exposed to the public and people would see me in it and think I had connections to them. When Amy first said she'd sneak me in a few shots, I didn't have a problem with it. But now I'm not sure.

"Do you really want me in a photoshoot about your family's house?"

"Well, I don't see a problem with it." He said a little confused. "Would that be a problem for you? Being in a photoshoot for my family?"

I only just realized what I said. Of course that'll sound bad from his point of view. But he knows that we all aren't exactly friends here…

"Being in a photoshoot is fine. But your parents might not like me in the family photo."

"I can understand why you think that. But maybe it's not like that. It's just a little article from a journalist. I doubt this would be front page news anywhere." Ken tried to make it like it was nothing. He tries hard to make sure I don't worry about something, but the more he wants me not to worry, the more worry that pours in.

"We'll see if it's even allowed. But Amy said there was breakfast. We probably should get some before they clean it up." I said. I don't want to bring up the Lacey thing yet. I want to see if he'll bring it up or will he not tell me he's talking to his ex. If I didn't think Lacey would tell me this, he definitely wouldn't think she would. When he came to talk to me yesterday, that would've been the time to tell me, but he didn't.

We both went downstairs to the kitchen. I almost crashed into three of the maids on the way there. One was headed to the relax room, another went to the dining area, and one came into the kitchen with us. Each of those rooms, from what I saw, were already sparkling, but I would've been concerned if someone wasn't cleaning a perfectly clean room when it comes to Mr. Masidone wanting to impress someone.

In the kitchen already was Jenny and Jennifer with a plate of strawberry and blueberry covered pancakes.

"Good morning young Masidone, Miss Macky, can I get you something?" The maid asked us.

"I'll do an omelet with French toast." Ken said.

"And for you?" She turned to me. It almost felt like I was in a restaurant about to give my order.

"I'll do an omelet too." Even though it was my idea, I didn't really have much of an appetite. We went by the island to wait near Jenny and Jennifer.

"Morning." Jennifer said.

"Morning." Jenny repeated.

"Good morning. Are your voices, okay? You did a lot more singing yesterday than I thought you would." Ken asked.

"Were you impressed?" Jennifer smiled.

"A little, yes. You should've told us you wanted to join our karaoke nights."

"We'll keep that in mind for next time." Jenny said.

"You too. We could've done it a long time ago." Ken said to me.

"I didn't know you like to sing or could."

"I'll take the compliment. But when you're around Jay enough his influence kind of rubs off on you."

"Did someone mention my influences?" Jayson came into the kitchen next. "I kept my drinking light, so I thought. Nothing happened last night, right?"

"We were talking about the singing." Ken clarified.

"Oh, okay good. I'm glad everyone participated. Especially my little kittens over here. We have to do this more often."

"There's always the rest of the week." Jennifer told him.

"Now you're speaking our language. Can always join our fun." Jayson was beaming even after doing seven songs straights and having whatever drinks he had to make it through seven songs with Amy.

I looked over to Jenny. The more we talked, the lower her head seemed to go. By now, if it were just me, she would have stormed out. But she knows she can't with everyone around. I can't help but feel bad for her now that I know what's going on.

"You seem a little down. I know you wanted that special song with Sano that he asked for last night. Maybe you'll get it next time." Jennifer just reverted back to her usual self. She went on to dig into her pancakes as if she didn't just say that.

"We can all do some duets with each other next time." Jayson said. "Speaking of our lovely little Sano, where did he run off to this morning?"

"I think he did just that." Ken said.

"We did kind of skip out this morning. But this is the one day Papa Masy wanted me on standby. That's no excuse for you though. You know what happens when you're caught slacking. You don't want to be the youngest and the slowest among us." Jayson said to him.

"It got away from me today, I'll admit. But we'll pick things up where we left off tomorrow." Ken told him.

"Here you both are." The maid brought over our food.

"If you're eating, please, have our seats." Jennifer said standing up. She and Jenny handed their plates to the maid and made their quick escape.

"And here I thought they were getting declawed." Jayson said. "But I do need to make my rounds. I have to make sure the air is dusted." Jay was next to go. Ken and I sat at the island. The maid was fast away cleaning the dishes.

"Since we have to make ourselves scarce today, we were going to hang out in the pool house until everything was done. But, if you did want to see about being in the show, you can talk to Amy about what you would need to do to prepare."

"I guess I can ask her. Or see if she needs help with anything." I told him as I picked at my food. I can't tell if he really wants me to do it or wants to see if I would. She didn't mention it when we talked before. Amy is a professional. I know I like taking photos in the photo booth at the mall, but that's the closest I've been to posing for the camera.

"There's always the options to take our own photos." Ken said, "If you can't be in this one, we can do our own photoshoot." He held out his hands like he's holding a camera.

"Have you ever done a photoshoot before?"

"I've participated in a few of my father's company functions. Some of them had people taking photos and we posed for them." Ken said in between bites.

"Does that really count?"

"It can if you let it." He smiled.

"If you say so." I told him. I managed to get down most of my omelet before I went back upstairs to see Amy.

"Hey, you're back. Did you get breakfast?" She asked me.

"Yeah. Ken and I just finished."

"Oh, where is he? Are you all hanging out today while the shoot is happening?"

"Uh, yeah. They're going to the pool house."

"Before you go back down, think you can me help decide which outfit to wear?" She pointed to her bed. She had a red striped button up with dress pants and another outfit with a white shirt and black vest with grey shorts next to it.

"I was thinking something business casual, you know, since this is Mr. Masy, we're dealing with. Or since this is the vacation home, something a little more casual, casual." She held a hanger holding an oversized white shirt with some grey stripes down the sides and light blue skinny jeans.

"How about the casual, casual. It still kind of has a formalness to it and comfortable for a vacation."

"I love the way you think! You definitely have the makings of a stylist." Amy gathered the other clothes and laid that one on her bed. "I had one more I was going to choose from, but I think you could pull it off better than I can. We can take our own photos if we can't put you in the shoot. Wouldn't that be fun?" A second offer to have a separate photoshoot. She had been considering something for me if the plan to stick me in shoot didn't work. If I agree to that, I wouldn't have to worry about turning down the offer to be in pictures that will be on the internet.

"Do you not want to?" Amy asked, looking at me.

"Oh, no, that's not it. I, uhm, like the idea of our own photos."

"We can do that. Are you nervous about being in the actual shoot?"

"It's not that I'm nervous. I just don't know if I should be in something for a family I'm not a part of." I told her.

"What do you mean not a part of? I think they consider you like another daughter of the family. If they invited you here, they have to care about you."

"I'm only here because Ken wanted me here." I said.

"Well, do you want to be here?" Amy asked. "It just seems like you're here because he wants you to be. Are you not enjoying yourself?"

"It's not that I'm not enjoying myself. There's just a lot on my mind."

"Is there something wrong? You can talk to me if you'd like." Amy went to close the doors and sat back on the bed. "Spill it. What's going on?" This is the most serious I've seen Amy. I know from the beginning, she's been trying to make sure I have a good time, but she doesn't really know what's going on between me and everyone here. I can't just tell her everything. She loves this family. Telling her everything I know would change her mind about that…

"Well, I have this friend. And she told me she's been talking to Ken."

"Oh no, Kenny? You don't mean he's cheating do you?"

"No. Or at least I don't think so."

"Okay, so they're talking as friends. Do you have a problem with him talking to other girls?"

"Well, not really, but this friend also happens to be his ex. And he contacted her."

"Oh…" Amy leaned back understanding. "What did your friend tell you?"

"He asked about why they broke up." I told her. I tried to explain it more without exposing what his parents did to lead us here. Maybe he just wanted to confirm what I told him had actually happened. But Lacey said she had already told him what happened. I guess she didn't want to tell him about the bribe. She wasn't going to tell me that they got back in touch. She only said anything because I told him what she didn't.

"I can see why you're worried. It wouldn't be an issue if he told you that he talked to her. You just need to tell him that you know, and it bothers you."

"I know. I was going to wait and see if he tells me first, but he hasn't so far."

"I know this may not be the best time to talk about stuff like this since we are on vacation, but you'll never be able to relax if you're spending all your time worrying about it. It could turn out good or bad but sitting on your thoughts will make you feel worse than getting them out and clearing your conscious. You have no idea how much better I feel after talking to Jaycee, and that was because you told me too." She reminded me. Even Jayson seemed like he was glad they had that talk.

"Are we back to how we used to be? No, not yet, but it's a start. I sat on those feelings for years and I could never feel at ease. But this and that are a little different. You have every right to be upset about an ex coming back in the picture. You need to tell him that so you can know what it really means so you don't worry yourself wondering."

"What if means he wants to get back with her?" I asked. That question made the omelet sit heavy in my stomach. It was what I was most worried about.

"I can see the way Kenny looks at you. I think he really likes you. It may not mean he wants to get back together with this other girl. He could just want a clear understanding of what happened." Amy hesitated before she went on.

"Or, if it did mean he wanted to, you know sooner than later what to do next."

What to do next. What to do next if he said he wants to get back together with Lacey now that he really knows why she broke it off with him. His dad got in the way. If he knew, he would've tried to stop it like he did with me. They didn't have any issues outside of his interference so of course he could still like her too.

"I guess I'll talk to him today." I said. I've been worried about Lacey since I found out she used to date Ken. And now I have to say something about it if I ever hope to sleep in again…

"Good for you. I'll be here for you if you need anything. But before you do," Amy went back to her closet, "we're going to get you ready for a photoshoot." She pulled out the other outfit she had. A light grey bowed sleeved shirt knotted on the side with black shorts.

"Regardless of what happens, we're going to make sure you have something to take home with you. A photo lasts forever and you're going to look great!" Amy was all smiles again. I'm kind of glad I talked to her. I wouldn't have been able to talk to Jayson like I usually do. I thought her being here would have made things awkward, but so far, she seems to be the reason things aren't staying that way.

33

"I cannot believe how good you look!" Amy is still fawning over me as I looked at myself in the mirror. Although I must admit, she did a good job with my hair and makeup.

"I would have never expected to get my hair done so quickly." I said playing with some of the loose curls in my hair.

"If there is one thing I know is hair. Keeping this much color in takes a lot of maintenance." Amy played with her bangs. She was clothed and had her hair in a curly ponytail with bangs. She worked her magic on me giving me a full makeover. Not to mention added blond highlights in my hair. She has everything you could need with her even hair bleach…

"When you have to do side gigs like this and they don't give me a makeup artist, you have to take matters into your own hands. That's when you learn to do everything on your own without help. you like it, right?"

"I love it. I've always wanted highlights, and they look good. I didn't know you could do it so fast." I told her. She did my hair and makeup and hers in less than two hours.

"I once had just an hour to find an outfit, add a color touch up to my hair, and do my nails. I was all over the place, but it worked out and it was one of my favorite shoots." Amy said very proud.

"You really know your stuff. No wonder you always look great."

"Aww, thanks. If you ever wanted to go into modeling, you could definitely pull it off. You have good features and great proportions for your height and age. I could definitely get you into a real shoot or commercial or something."

"That sounds cool. But I don't think my dad would let me do that." I said. He'd probably have a heart attack if I brought more attention to myself…

"Well, if he ever changes his mind on that, just let me know, I could pull some strings." She winked and went back to adjusting her hair. I never would have thought I'd be getting recruited by a model.

"So, the photographer should be here soon. Do you want to stick around and see the process and then take our photos, or do you want to go with the others? Maybe have that talk?"

"Uh, I don't know if I should yet. Maybe after we take our pictures." I told her. I don't know if I'm ready to bring things up to Ken yet…

"That's fine with me. You can stick around. But maybe pop in and say hi to them? Let them see your transformation. Then leave and keep him waiting. That's how you get them!" Amy smirked.

"I guess I could tell him where I'll be."

"That's the spirit! I'll see you in a bit." Amy said. I took one more look at myself before heading downstairs. I've put on a little makeup before, but Ken has never seen a full face or highlights on me or this borrowed outfit.

"Misa?" I saw Sano at the kitchen door when he looked at me. He said my name as if he wasn't sure it was me.

"Amy was preparing for the shoot and did me over too." I told him. He was obviously surprised by how I looked.

"I see. I was just upstairs and heard you both but didn't know that's what you were doing. It looks nice." He said. I had almost forgotten about him. I can tell he wasn't trying to look directly at me.

"Are you headed to the pool house?" I asked him.

"Yeah. We didn't want to chance getting pulled into anything, so we're staying there. I'm guessing you're going to be in it?"

"Not exactly. We plan to take our own photos after she's done. I was just going to wait around until then."

"Oh, Misa dear, is that you?" I turned to see Mrs. Baker appear. "I was doing a final inspection of the place and didn't know they cleaned you up too. Were you supposed to be a part of this photo session? I thought it was just Amy and Kenneth." She stared me down.

"Uh, no. Amy wanted to do our own photos and helped me get ready."

"I see. Are you also a part of that?" She looked to Sano.

"Misa just told me about it. I wasn't aware of it." He answered.

"I'm just so amazed at your transformation. Those curls and that color. That's a big sign that Amy had something to do with it. Don't you think she looks stunning?" She asked him.

"The new look suits her well." Sano told her. Suddenly, this mission to show off has made me more embarrassed than I thought...

"That's certainly a safe way of putting it. Good to see you two are still getting along. I had been wondering if you would after he moved back in. I know little Kenneth went a while without seeing you Misa, and I know you were leaving out for long periods of time." She said to him.

"I was going to see my siblings." He told her.

"Siblings? Oh, right, the foster children. Kenneth did tell me about that. I suppose that mystery is solved. Well, It's just about time for the photographer to show up. You two better get going. If he sees any of you, he will want to ask questions for the article. I know you two especially don't want to be interviewed about the family and our way of living seeing as you only just returned to it and Misa isn't quite in it."

"We were just going." Sano said. He opened the screen door letting me go out first.

"I was going to go back with Amy, but if they're doing interviews, maybe I shouldn't." I told him. No one told me It was a photo session and questions.

"Well, if she's going to be around, it's probably best you didn't stay."

"I actually wanted to ask you about something. About what you said before about her." This wasn't what I planned on talking about. But running into Mrs. Baker like this makes it fitting.

"Oh, sure. You want to go over there?" He pointed by the lake. I guess he figured this didn't involve Ken and we need to stay out of sight of the photographer. We walked over to where the ground dipped a bit. There was a tall full tree behind us, taking us away from the others. We sat on some large rocks giving us a full view of the water. With it just being us two. It almost feels like old times being back at his house.

"It hasn't been just us two in a while." Sano said reading my mind.

"I was thinking the same thing. We're just missing the kids now."

"They're doing alright with the new living arrangements. I do miss having them around. I try to see them when I can." He said.

"Yeah. You did say that when Mrs. Baker asked where you were."

"I was sure she already knew where I was going. But she made it as if she didn't." He looked at the water. I can tell Mrs. Baker bothers him. Now that he's back at the mansion, he's probably learned a lot about her.

"You once mentioned you remembered her from your old town. Were you able to confirm if it was her?" I asked him.

"I was. She was the woman that I saw hanging around the old bar my mom would go to. She was with the bar owner until he passed. Then she got in with my father and has been with him since."

"How did you find out? Did she tell you?"

"No, she would never tell anyone something like that. The kids the owner had that I was supposed to meet with were Jenny and Jennifer."

"Really?" I asked a bit more surprised than I wanted to be.

"Yeah. I asked Jennifer about it before. It took a while to get her to answer me seeing as I wasn't one of her favorite people, but she ended up telling me."

"Is that why you two seem to be getting along now?" I asked. It makes sense seeing them by the pool talking like they were friends.

"I wouldn't exactly say we're friends or anything. But I know her situation."

"Her situation?" I repeated.

"I don't think she wants me to talk about it."

Does it have something to do with Mrs. Baker?" I asked. If it sounds like Sano knows, am I allowed to say something to him since Ken isn't around?

"Have you talked to her?" He asked me.

"We talked a bit yesterday when we were swimming. Jenny had one of her blow ups and I made Jennifer tell me what was going on with her."

"I'm actually surprised. For years, they have kept it to themselves. The only reason she told me was because I kind of knew already. She almost threatened me not to tell anyone. Especially Ken."

"She did the same to me." I told him.

"I sort of feel bad for them. They don't have any relatives they can go to. The bar was in debt, so they had everything taken from them and had no other choice but to go with Jocelyn. They even think she had something to do with the accident their parents were in."

"The car accident? She caused it?" I asked. Jennifer only told me the basics. She didn't tell me all of this.

"She just knows that evening they all went out, and she was the only one that came back."

"Why hasn't anyone done anything?" I asked. I couldn't believe what I was hearing.

"It's their word against hers. Not much two kids can do that didn't have any evidence."

We sat by the lake on this sunny afternoon watching the water move. The weather was nice, but this conversation turned cloudy and gloomy.

"Even though she doesn't want to admit it, Jennifer is probably doing worse than Jenny is. She's been putting on the tough face all these years trying to find someone that could help them. So, I've been checking on them from time to time. Also making sure they weren't planning anything else against you. I know why they did it now, but that doesn't mean they had the right to do what they did to you." Sano told me.

I didn't know what to say. Sano had his own worries and started looking out for them and me. Maybe that's why he's been so quiet. He's been doing his own surveillance.

"Wow, saying that out loud really makes me sounds like a hypocrite." I heard Sano laugh a little to himself.

"What do you mean?" I turned to him. He was holding some rocks he found and played with them. He got really quiet. I felt my chest sinking in with anticipation to his response.

"I mean exactly that." He finally said again. He didn't face me. He just stared at the rocks in his hands. He twirled them, making the rocks scratch. The sound was rough, but not as rough as the look on his face.

"I'm sorry Misa, but this wasn't supposed to happen."

"What wasn't supposed to happen?" I repeated slowly. He's never sounded like this before.

"Me liking you. That wasn't supposed to happen. And you shouldn't have had any interest in me." Sano continued looking at his hands and not to me as he spoke. "I'm really a terrible person."

"Wh-why do you say that?" I asked. With what he's saying and how he's acting, I don't know if he should answer that. But I kept watching him waiting to continue. He looked up briefly and took a large inhale.

"Because— back when you first followed me home, and I let you in and let you help me with the kids… I only did that because… I knew you were with Ken." Sano took one of the rocks he had and threw it to the lake. It skipped a few times before it sank. And that's exactly what my heart was doing. Sinking.

"Once I realized you were the girl from back then, I figured that's why he was there. And if you were with me, that would make him want to leave." He added.

I was at a loss for words…

"But then my mom's condition took a turn, and I wasn't sure what to do. You started getting concerned for me. You genuinely wanted to help me when all I was trying to do was get back at Ken."

"So… you used me?"

"I'm sorry Misa." He said again. He didn't say anything else. He just kept his head low. I've never felt this cold of a feeling in me before. It was like everything in me was freezing up. I pushed my hair behind my ear as the wind picked up a bit.

"Why are you telling me this now?" I asked him. He kept this in all this time. Why would he tell me this?

"My mother's birthday past recently. She's been on my mind a lot. Before she died, she told me I had to tell you the truth. That what I did wasn't fair to you. I wanted to tell you on a few occasions, but I just couldn't get it out." He told me. He threw another rock and that one just sunk in the water. That explained his behavior and why he was acting so strange when we were together. The mystery is solved, but that doesn't mean it makes me happy…

"You know, I find this kind of funny." Sano glanced over to me as I spoke again. "I had a crush on you since freshmen year. And the only reason I tried to talk to you was because Ken came in the picture, and I wanted him gone too." I stood up and dusted my shorts off.

"But I wasn't trying to use you to do so. It was more of a push to do something I had been afraid to do for years. I thought you were out of my league being the track star and all. And when you opened your door to me, I thought I had finally accomplished something. Not to mention I even had the thought of leaving Ken for you. Now you're telling me I never accomplished anything and that you were just stringing me along? Thanks for letting me know that I was a fool for thinking I ever had a chance." I said and walked away. I don't know where I was going, but I needed be to alone.

I don't think I've ever felt this much hurt from Sano. To think he only let me in because he knew I was the reason Ken came to our school. I mean, I should have known. Who in their right mind would let someone in their house after they were followed home? I should have known from the start something was wrong with that whole situation…

I stopped and stared out to the lake from where I was. I wiped my face and picked up a rock and tried to skip it. The rock immediately sank. At least with that rock, I knew right away there was no hope of it making it.

34

"There you are—oh." Ken was walking over to me. After I stared blankly at the water for a while, I decided to head back, but Ken found me first.

"How did you know where I was?" I asked him.

"I got very brief detail and was told you wandered in this direction." Ken approached me looking me up and down. "I see Sano wasn't the only one you've talked to today. You did originally see Amy. I thought you were still with her." He got closer to me and grabbed my hair looking it over.

"Since things turned out like this, I want to ask you about something." I said. I got straight to it. There was no need to wait since my talk with Sano. I had no feelings left to hide. Ken looked at me and let go of my hair. He could see that I was being serious.

I sat by the lake thinking about everything. I let a lot of things go because I didn't know how to handle it. I'm starting to realize I really should have taken things head on…

"Lacey told me you two have been talking. I know you haven't talked since you broke up years ago, so why have you started now?" I asked him. This was probably the last thing he'd think I would ask him. Amy sees the way he looks to me, but she didn't see the way he acted when he saw Lacey again. She still likes him and couldn't handle seeing me because I was with him. There's no telling what she might have actually said to him.

"I did get in contact with her. I should have told you." Ken admitted.

"Why didn't you?"

"I just wanted to ask her what really happened. The pattern was repeating itself so much I wanted to know what to watch out for."

"What pattern?"

"The pattern of everyone sort of attacking you. I was afraid that if it continued, you were going to leave to." He said.

"So, you asked her what made her leave because you thought I would do the same thing?"

"I knew Jenny and Jennifer had something to do with it. I didn't know anything about my father. So, when you said he bribed her, I was really confused. I knew he was controlling, and he talked to me about his disapproval of her, but I didn't know he went behind my back and did that. Now I'm wondering if he was the one I should have been watching all along."

"Your dad never bribed me. But he did sort of threaten me when we first met." I said, remembering back to my first visit to his house. That was also when I found out about him and Sano. There was a lot going on that day which is why it likely never came up…

"Why didn't you tell me that?" He asked.

"There always seems to be something going on. I can't keep up with which threat you didn't know about."

"So, is this why you've been upset all day?" He asked me. He knew something was wrong with me, but he didn't ask.

"I was upset because I was wondering if you were going to tell me about Lacey. I know she still likes you. She only came over that day because she knew you were there. You didn't like the fact that we were friends. And I saw the way you acted when you saw her."

"Do you think I want her?" He asked me.

"I don't know. But with Jenny, you always gave a clear answer. And I feel like there hasn't been a clear answer since she first came up." Part of me felt stupid for saying these things. I had already had these thoughts with Jenny. She tried hard to get his attention, but he always shut her down pretty quickly. I didn't want to have to go through this again.

"Look," Ken took a deep breath, "like you said, we haven't talked since we broke up when we were freshmen. To say I still like and want to be with her would be wrong. But I don't hate her either. I did get in contact with her to know exactly why we broke up. That did not mean I was trying to reconcile the relationship. I thought she moved on. I didn't know she still liked me."

Lacey didn't say anything else about what they've actually talked about, so I don't really know what could have been said outside of him asking about the bribe. The way Ken is speaking sounds like it's true. But after what Sano just told me, it's hard to want to believe anything.

"Do you not believe me?"

"I want to believe you. There's just so much deceit going on around here. I don't know what to do or who to believe anymore." I told him.

"Does your saying that have anything to do with whatever you and Sano talked about?" He didn't sound like he wanted to ask, but he asked anyway. "He only told me he said something to upset you, and you ran off. I don't know the depth of that conversation, but I feel like that was a first for you two."

"It doesn't matter what we talked about. As far as I'm concerned, you're all the same. You use those poker faces of yours to hide your real motives for deception just to get what you want. And here I am just falling for it."

We both just stood there. We've been at the villa just three days, and in three days, I found out more than I ever wanted about everyone. But it took Sano, the one person I never thought I had to worry about telling me he was just using me, to rethink everything that's happened so far.

"So, what do you want to do?" He asked me.

"What do you mean?" I looked at Ken. He turned away, taking a hand through his hair. He looked back at me with a whole new look of frustration in his eyes.

"I didn't ask you here to make you miserable. But everyday so far, it seems like someone else is trying to. And the fact that this is what I have to live with only means it'll just keep happening. You've been putting up with us since we met. Everyone at some point, including me, has hurt you. There's only so much I can do to prevent something from happening, so if you don't want to deal with it anymore, then… you don't have to." He let out a deep breath.

If I didn't know any better, it sounds as if Ken is asking if I want to stay with him or break up with him. Something I didn't think he would do.

"What happened to fighting?" I asked. Just yesterday, he said he'd fight. Now he's saying this.

"I did say I'd fight. And I'll still try. But every time I turn my back, you're getting attacked. I can't fight what I can't see."

"You're right, you can't. So that leaves me to deal with it on my own. And I'm starting to wonder if I can. No matter what, Jenny and Jennifer will always be against me. Your dad would prefer I'm out of the picture. Mrs. Baker tried to ship my mom away, which turned into her quitting. And for all I know, my dad is next."

"It's not too late to talk Jocelyn." He said.

"I doubt anything we say to her will have her change her mind on what she's doing." I told him. Jennifer said she'll make things happen. If she already has it planned, she wouldn't listen to anything we said. Especially if she's still trying to get Jenny to be with him.

"You sound so sure as if she's already made her next move." Ken said.

"Whether she has or hasn't, I'm not sure if I should be around to see." It came out before I realized I said it. I shocked my own self. That was the first thing I blurted out.

"I knew with her around, nothing good would come with her." I wasn't sure if he said that to me or just out loud. "And if I made you stay, I'd just be hurting you more." Ken sounded defeated.

"No." I stopped him. "It's not you that's hurting me. But everyone around you is making it harder to be here. This is more than I've dealt with before. It's always been me, my mom, and my dad. Katie is also like family. And with her around, I hardly had any trouble." I tried to explain it.

I didn't think I'd be standing here having this conversation with Ken while at the villa. I was hoping so much to get through the week without any problems. But only on day three of being here, it makes me wonder if I could make it through the next four days.

"I don't want to break up. I also don't want to know who could do what next. But I think… I need some space to figure out what I should do next."

It was harder than I thought to say it to him. The knots in my stomach were growing. It was just us two with the sound of the water from the lake seeming louder than normal.

"Okay." I heard him say. With that one simple word, it made me look at him.

"I know this was a lot to take on. So, if you need some space, I'll give it to you." Ken looked at me and then took a few steps back. "Is that enough?"

I know he knows that's not what I meant. I know this isn't what he wanted to hear today. Watching him try and soften his expression as he stepped back was a bittersweet thing to see. I was sort of glad to see he didn't get angry or anything. But the weight in my chest knowing I'm doing this to him still felt so heavy. I didn't know what else to do. This was my first time dealing with a sort of breakup, I figured jumping in the lake wasn't the appropriate thing to do, so I just stood there.

"If you want, I'll go ahead and head back." he said as he continued walking backwards. Further away from me. "Oh, and by the way, you look really great." Ken finally turned around and walked forward.

"Wait." I called out to him. He stopped and turned back around. I walked up to him and kissed him.

"I'm going to go see Amy. I'll uh, I'll probably be leaving. So… enjoy the rest of your trip." I told him. I let go of him and went ahead of him this time. It was probably better if I walked away first.

I didn't travel that far down the path by the lake, but this walk back did seem endless.

"So, are you leaving early?" Amy and I sat at the head of her bed together. After telling her about Ken and I taking time apart, she shut us in our room, grabbed some comfort snack and had me talk to her again. There were things I still couldn't say, worried she would tell Ken or even his parents, so I told her what I could. Part of me was still glad I had someone to talk to. The other part of me is still standing outside talking to Sano and Ken. The two people that lead me to where I am now.

"I don't think it would be good if I stayed now that we're at this point." I told her as I grabbed a chip and sort of just stared at it.

"I don't want to see you leave. But if you've made up your mind already, staying here won't help anything. You just need some time to take a deep breath and remember why you were here in the first place. I think Kenny understands and he'll wait." Amy tried to assure me.

"I know I hurt him. Maybe he won't."

"Of course he will. This is Kenny we're talking about. He's crazy about you." Amy held on to my shoulder. She seemed so sure about Ken waiting. I didn't think I'd tell him I wanted space like this. But when Sano told me about what he did to me something just came over me and now we're here...

Each day so far, I've heard from Sano, Mr. Masidone, Mrs. Baker, and the things I found out about her from Jennifer. There were four more days to stay here. I wasn't sure what else I could hear and if it'll be worse than before. That was the thought that made me say what I did. I didn't want to hear or be a part of any more news. I didn't want to chance hearing any other plans Mrs. Baker might have to get rid of me or my parents just like she might do with Jenny and Jennifer...

"Can I ask you for a favor?" I looked to Amy, "I can't call my dad to pick me up. That would make things a whole lot worse. Would you be able to take me back?"

"Of course, I can. Can I ask you a favor first? Can we still take some photos? We're still all nice and done up we should at least have one good memory of our beauty, right?" Amy still wanted to take pictures. I wasn't sure if I was in the mood to or felt like that was an okay thing to do. She really wanted to have a good vacation with me. Now that I'm leaving early, a few pictures with her is the least I could do.

I agreed to take some photos with Amy in our room. She had this colorful brick wall backdrop with her and put it up. It's like she has an endless supply of everything with her she pulls out of nowhere. She set up a small camera she had in front of the backdrop and wanted us to take turns posing. It was a little hard to get fully into it, but I did what I could and stood how she said to. We took some pictures together when I heard a knock on the door. Amy went over to answer it.

"I hope I'm not interrupting anything." It was Jayson.

"We were having a closed shoot. But if our model doesn't mind guests," Amy stopped and looked to me. I nodded my head, and she turned back around, "You're always welcomed Jaycee." Amy opened the door all the way. Maybe she was cautious of letting anyone in because of the situation. If it's just Jayson, its fine. I wouldn't know what to do or say to Ken or Sano.

"Oh, my stars, look at you! You never told me you modeled part time. Can I have your autograph?" He said looking at me.

"Oh, we just wanted to make this a photo day since I had the shoot. You know I keep my hair supplies for just such the occasion." Amy told him.

"If I had a dollar for every time you did a last-minute highlighting session I'd have my own vacation home." Jayson said. He continued to walk over to me. "I just want to get a good look at you. I'm glad you two were able to have some fun."

"We agreed earlier that we would take photos, so now seems to be the best time since I asked her to take me home." I told him. Jayson wouldn't be here if he didn't know what happened, so there's no need to explain.

"I was going to ask you about that. I heard you might be heading out early and wasn't sure if you would want a ride or call Papa Macky."

"I'm already on it. I already told her I'll take her back when she's ready." Amy said.

"I should have known that you would have handled that already. I guess I just wanted to see you again before you left. I'm so sorry things turned out this way Misaky. If there was anything I could do, I'd do it. But I know it's not always that easy. So just know I'm always here for you, okay?"

"Thanks, I know you are." I told him. Then he hugged me. Jayson was sad like when Ken moved out as if he wasn't going to see me again. Now feels like the same, but this time I don't know when or if I will see him again...

Jayson had nothing to do with this, but he knows what's going on. He's been living with this family long enough to know just about everything. If it weren't for Ken, he probably wouldn't be here.

"Aww, you're going to have me ruin my makeup." Amy said, fanning her face.

"A quiet exit may be best. We'll fill in Papa Masy and Mama baker later." Jayson said. I didn't think about them. Those two finding out I'm leaving could be worse than knowing I'm here. After everything I did to show I'd stay with Ken, here I am walking away.

"You don't have to worry about them, after the shoot, they said they were going to rest for a bit." Amy told us.

"I don't know if you intended to say one more bye to the boys, but they both wandered off. I don't know exactly where they went." Jayson added.

"That may be for the best." I said. I glanced over to the balcony. There was no one standing out there, and I couldn't see anyone down below from where I stood.

"Well, if that's all settled, I guess I'll catch you on the fine side Misaky." Jayson smiled and headed out.

"I've never seen Jaycee so down before." I heard Amy say. I was thinking the same thing.

Amy helped me pack my stuff up and went to get the car. Only three days here and I'm already gathering my things to leave.

"What are you doing?" I turned from my bed and saw Jennifer at the door. "A-are you leaving?"

"Uh, yeah, I am." I guess me leaving quietly didn't include them.

"You, leaving a family vacation, can only mean one thing. You two broke up." She almost seemed shocked as she walked in the room.

"We didn't exactly break up. I just need to think about some things." I said.

"Think? You need to think about what? This better not have anything to do with what I told you."

"Look, this is between me and Ken." I didn't want to argue right before leaving.

"If this has anything to do with that, don't think you're doing us any favors. You leaving him won't change anything, so you can go ahead and say you're sorry now." She said.

"It almost sounds as if you don't want us to breakup."

"I don't really care what you do or don't do. But if your choice to leave has to do with us then I do have a problem with that. We can do fine on own on without you removing yourself from the picture."

"Whether I did it myself or not, she was going to find a way to remove me, wasn't she?" I asked. We both knew I was talking about Mrs. Baker. For once, Jennifer didn't have an immediate response.

"If Jenny couldn't win Ken over, then the next best thing to do was to get rid of me, right? Well, she didn't just try to get rid of me, she tried to get rid of my whole family. So maybe I'm doing her a favor by finishing the job." I turned back to my suitcase and finished stuffing the rest of my things in it.

"If your leaving doesn't have anything to do with Jens and I, then it's too bad you have to go so soon. I didn't get to have all the fun I wanted." She said. I turned back to her, but she was already walking out the door. I waited to see if she would turn back around, but she kept going.

I wasn't sure what to make of that. She almost sounded sorry that I was leaving. From the very first day I met her she made me her enemy. And on what could be the last time I see her, she almost seemed concerned as if she cared in her own way.

I went to the car with Amy. I managed to get out without seeing Mr. Masidone or Mrs. Baker. I watched as we drove out of the winding driveway away from the villa. My time here was short. From the first time it was mentioned that everyone was staying here, I figured there would be problems. I was sure I'd last at least last until Friday. Now my vacation has been cut even shorter. I walked away from my friendship with Sano, and I walked away from my first relationship.

36

I thought my surprises were done for the time being. It has been quiet since I came back home. Or at least it was after getting interrogated by my parents on why I was back so soon and if my dad could go back and give his final goodbye. After giving them the short version of the story including the part where my dad was right and it was a setup, even my mom was on board with letting him go. But if I had any want to talk to Ken again, letting him go back to the villa was far from the right thing to do. Now that the week has finally ended, the vacation should be over, so I don't have to worry about my dad sneaking off over there.

I haven't heard from anyone so far. That's to be expected since I was the one that said I needed space. I wonder if he'll really wait for me to come back. We're not staying at this apartment. Once the lease is up, they're getting rid of it and moving back to our house. As I figured, my dad is planning to leave the company once the lease term is up. Ken is back home now. He doesn't have a reason to travel to my school since he doesn't live with me anymore, so how exactly will I get to talk to him again if I don't get to see him?

"Which bag do you want this in? I can put it wherever you want." My best friend, who showed up not even an hour ago, has begun to pack away my stuff here.

"Katie, you do know I still need to use my stuff, right? We still have a week before I go back with you."

"I know, I know, I just want to make sure you'll have everything, so you never have to come back here again."

"You know, it wasn't all that bad here."

"You moved away from me, got new friends, one turned against you, your folks lost their jobs, and you lost both Sano and Ken. Stop me when I get to the 'not all bad' part."

"I uh, got new clothes and hair." I twirled some of my hair with my fingers.

"That's the only thing you got going. And that's you leaving in style." She said.

Had Katie appeared last week, she would have snuck away with my dad so they could both give their last goodbyes. Katie knows everything and knew being in a confined space at the villa with everyone wasn't a good idea. But it's not like I could've told Ken I didn't want to go after he spent so much time staying with me.

"What do you think I should do about the whole space thing?" I asked her.

"Well, I think you were right to leave. Ken is a nice guy and all, but he has way too much baggage."

"It's not his fault his parents are crazy. He wanted to help me fight against them, but I left before he could." I told her.

"What could he do? Don't you think if he had control over them, he would have stopped their interferences with his life a long time ago?"

"I guess you're right." I said. I didn't think about it like that.

"Either this time apart will show them how much you meant to Ken as he wallows in misery, or they don't care as usual, and you did their job for them."

"You know, I really missed these helpful conversations." I told her.

Katie was only here as a surprise from my parents for my birthday. She's staying here with us this week, and I'm staying with her like old times until my parents get back next month right before school starts. The start of my senior year.

I wondered how the start of senior year would go. Would I still be with Ken, or would I have a story to tell everyone? I only have about a month left to get that story together. The only good thing is that Jennifer probably won't be there to stir up any additional commotion.

"No matter what, you know I'm always here for you. Whether you decide to call him up again, or not, I'm here for what happens next."

"What do you mean by that?"

"I mean if you don't decide to go back, I support you. And if you do go back to him, I hope you support my decision to personally handle any outside interferences this time." She said cracking her knuckles.

"What would I do without you?" I looked to my best friend. Leave it to Katie to want to take on the Masidones single handily.

"It's going to work out for you. And if not, you still got all school year to try again. You know you still have John. He's pretty harmless compared to these guys and he's been devoted to you forever." She reminded me.

"As great as that sounds, I don't think I'll be looking for anyone so soon. Let's just enjoy the last of summer before I have to think about what next school year will bring."

"Can I at least meet this Zoie? You know, the girl you tried to replace me with. You two are still cool, right?"

"If you say it like that, you won't get to meet anybody." The last thing I need is for another problem to arise. I didn't tell Zoie what happened, but she knows I've been home, so she can probably guess the details. Lacey stopped messaging me again after she asked about what I told Ken before. If she finds out about Ken and I, who knows what she'll do…

Everyone will be back in their place soon. I'll be home soon. Ken will be home, and back at his old school with Lacey. If she knows we're sort of broken up, that'll give her the chance to make a move on Ken. He said he didn't want to get back together with her. If that's really the case, then I have nothing to worry about. I just wonder would the torment continue if his parents finds another girl after him.

The Masidone family is really something else. If Ken could just get away from them, he wouldn't have any more problems. But with Mr. Masidone and Mrs. Baker in charge, I only hope he's able to live comfortably one day.